A
SHINING LIGHT

Books by
Judith Miller

FROM BETHANY HOUSE PUBLISHERS

The Carousel Painter

DAUGHTERS OF AMANA
Somewhere to Belong • *More Than Words*
A Bond Never Broken

BELLS OF LOWELL*
Daughter of the Loom • *A Fragile Design*
These Tangled Threads

LIGHTS OF LOWELL*
A Tapestry of Hope • *A Love Woven True*
The Pattern of Her Heart

THE BROADMOOR LEGACY*
A Daughter's Inheritance
An Unexpected Love • *A Surrendered Heart*

POSTCARDS FROM PULLMAN
In the Company of Secrets
Whispers Along the Rails • *An Uncertain Dream*

BRIDAL VEIL ISLAND*
To Have and To Hold • *To Love and Cherish*
To Honor and Trust

HOME TO AMANA
A Hidden Truth
A Simple Change
A Shining Light

www.judithmccoymiller.com

*with Tracie Peterson

A
SHINING LIGHT

JUDITH MILLER

BETHANYHOUSE

a division of Baker Publishing Group
Minneapolis, Minnesota

Published by Bethany House Publishers
11400 Hampshire Avenue South
Bloomington, Minnesota 55438
www.bethanyhouse.com

Bethany House Publishers is a division of
Baker Publishing Group, Grand Rapids, Michigan

Printed in the United States of America

Library of Congress Cataloging-in-Publication Data
Miller, Judith
    A shining light / Judith Miller.
        pages cm — (Home to Amana)
    Summary: "After devastating events, widow Andrea Wilson and her young son sought temporary refuge in Iowa's Amana Colonies of the early 1890s. Will the peace she finds there convince her to stay?"—Provided by publisher.
        ISBN 978-0-7642-1002-0 (pbk.)
        1. Amana Society—Fiction. 2. Mothers and sons—Fiction. 3. Widows—Fiction. 4. Iowa—History—19th century—Fiction. I. Title.
    PS3613.C3858S55 2014
    813'.6—dc23   2013039146

Scripture quotations are taken from the King James Version of the Bible.

Cover design by Lookout Design, Inc.
Cover photography by Aimee Christensen

Author is represented by Books & Such Literary Agency.

13 14 15 16 17 18 19   7 6 5 4 3 2 1

To *Mary Greb-Hall*
for her many years
of friendship
and unfailing assistance.

CHAPTER 1

Early March 1890
Baltimore, Maryland
Andrea Neumann Wilson

Unable to grasp the totality of Mr. Brighton's message, I gripped the brass doorknob and attempted to steady myself against the splintered doorjamb. Concern shone in the eyes of the owner of Brighton Shipping Lines, a well-dressed gentleman who looked out of place in this brick tenement with its leaking roof, cracked dormer windows, and wooden cornices that begged repair. My mind told me I should invite him inside, but the words would not come. Instead, my lips tightened into a thin line, and a lump the size of a hedge apple lodged in my throat.

"I hope you're not going to faint on me, Mrs. Wilson." Mr. Brighton nodded toward the interior of the small apartment. "You should sit down."

Still holding my arm, he propelled me toward one of the rickety wooden chairs not far from the entrance. Of course nothing was far from the doorway of the one-room tenement that had become our Baltimore home. Lukas, my seven-year-old son who had been napping on a narrow bed lodged against the wall, rolled over and rubbed his eyes. His gaze settled on Mr. Brighton.

"Who is that, Mama?" The moment he asked, he cast a glance about the room. "Is Papa home?" A hint of fear edged his childish voice.

Pity clouded Mr. Brighton's eyes. He leaned close and kept his voice low. "Do you want me to tell the boy?"

"No. I'll speak with him after you've gone." I crooked my finger to motion Lukas to my side. His bare feet slapped on the wooden floorboards as he crossed the room. "Put on your shoes and go downstairs to Mrs. Adler's rooms. She told me she would have a piece of bread and butter for you when you got up from your nap."

His lips curved in a smile that tugged at my heart. Instead of growing too large for his clothes, his shirt and trousers hung loose on his frame. He was too thin. So was I. So were most of the people who lived in these run-down tenement buildings.

Unlike me in my youth, when I'd never felt the sting of abuse or felt the pinch of hunger, Lukas had experienced the opposite. He'd lived with his father's wrath and gone to bed hungry far too often. While I had experienced the wonders of nature on our Iowa farm, Lukas had been deprived of a carefree childhood. Instead of running through fields and meadows, he lived in an aging tenement building where I did my best to keep him safe. Too soon, fear and worry had caused my son to seem far older than his seven years.

"I'll come back and share it with you," he offered.

I shook my head. "No. You eat every bite yourself. And stay with Mrs. Adler until I come and fetch you. Understand?"

He shoved his right foot into one of the worn brown shoes, then pulled the end of his sock forward and tucked it over a small hole in the toe of his sock before donning the other shoe. Looking up at me, he grinned. "Now my toe won't poke out."

I tucked a wisp of hair behind my ear. "I'll darn that for you when you come back home. Be sure you remind me before bedtime."

"I will, Mama," he called as he flew out the door. His shoes clacked a familiar beat on the narrow wooden steps that provided the only means of passage from our third-floor room.

Our building was situated in a row of tenements near the foul and ruinous sweatshops where many of our neighbors worked for meager wages and hoped for a better life. Others, like me, were wives of sailors who depended upon the earnings their husbands might—or might not—bring home after returning from sea. The area was plagued with poverty and crime, but right now I didn't need to worry about Lukas going outdoors without me. The expectation of an extra piece of bread provided ample assurance that he'd go directly to Louise Adler's apartment. And Louise wouldn't permit him out of her sight without me.

Mr. Brighton remained standing near the doorway, and though he gave no indication, I knew he wanted to be on his way. "I wish I came bearing better news, Mrs. Wilson, but . . ." His voice evaporated like a morning fog drenched with sunlight.

"You truly believe my husband is . . . dead?" My voice trembled, not so much from fear or sorrow, but from utter disbelief. "If the men didn't recover his body, how can you be certain?"

He drew a step closer and touched my shoulder. "There isn't a person on the crew who believes your husband is alive, Mrs. Wilson. Had there been any hope, I would have waited before coming to call on you. I realize it's difficult to comprehend, but when there's a storm at sea—well, I don't want to go into the details. Suffice it to say that your husband was not seen after the storm. The ship's records reveal your husband boarded the ship in Martinique for the return to Baltimore. However, John Calvert, one of the sailors who is said to be a friend of your husband, reported he saw him wash over. In addition, the crew assures me they searched every nook and cranny of the ship, and he wasn't found after the storm."

"So you believe he was washed overboard during a storm and there's no hope his body will be recovered?" My mind reeled as I attempted to digest the news. Could I truly believe Fred would never again enter this room in a drunken stupor and crawl into bed beside me at night? That he would never again shout profanities and strike me? That he would never again hurt Lukas with his odious words and deeds?

"I'm afraid so." He reached into his pocket and withdrew an envelope. "I know this doesn't in any way make up for the loss you've suffered, but we at Brighton Shipping hope this contribution will assist you and your son. Your husband's final pay is included, as well." When I didn't immediately extend my hand to accept the envelope, he leaned around me and placed it on the dilapidated table. "Will you stay here in Baltimore? I'd be willing to help you find some sort of work."

The man appeared befuddled and uncertain what more to offer, yet it was likely he'd been required to perform this unpleasant duty on previous occasions. After all, sailors frequently were lost at sea, and many were injured or died in accidents on the wharves, as well.

Perhaps it was my lack of tearful emotion that baffled him. "I'm not yet sure what I will do, Mr. Brighton, but I doubt I'll remain in Baltimore."

He cleared his throat. "Well, should you change your mind

and desire my help locating work, you need only send word to my office, and I'll do what I can." With a final glance around the room, he took a backward step. "If there's nothing else I can do, I suppose I should get back to my office." When I rested my hand on the table for support and began to rise, he waved me back to my chair. "No need to get up, Mrs. Wilson. You relax and gain your strength."

I wanted to explain that it wasn't the news of Fred's death that had caused my weakness. Truth be told, the news caused more relief than pain, but I would never utter those words aloud—at least not to this stranger. Touching the envelope he'd placed on the table, I realized I hadn't acknowledged his gift. "Thank you, Mr. Brighton. I appreciate your kindness. I am sure your gift will be of great help to us."

"I wish you well, Mrs. Wilson." He gave a brief nod before he hurried out the door and down the steps. He appeared eager to leave now that he had performed his official duty, and I didn't blame him. No one wanted to remain in this section of Fells Point unless he had nowhere else to go.

Through the open window, I heard the children in the street below begging for money, but when Mr. Brighton ignored them, their beseeching pleas soon turned to angry invectives. If he didn't give in to their demands or make a quick escape, they would soon hurl stones at him. Prepared to shout at the children, I stepped to the window, but Mr. Brighton had already disappeared from sight. He'd obviously chosen to quicken his step.

Returning to the table, I picked up the envelope and lifted the flap. Carefully, I counted the sum. Mr. Brighton had spoken the truth. It wasn't much. Still, any amount was better than nothing. Along with the cash, Mr. Brighton had included an accounting of Fred's wages. I scanned the carefully penned figures. The numbers revealed Fred had drawn against his wages before departing on his latest voyage, a practice that had become all too common of late.

True to form, Fred hadn't provided me with any money before he sailed. Instead, he'd expected me to make do with whatever I could earn taking in piecework from one of the sweatshops. Resentment swelled in my chest. I shouldn't have anticipated anything different. Fred's selfish behavior, his gambling, abuse, and drinking had increased throughout our years in Baltimore. Why would he have given any thought to Lukas or me before he'd departed this time?

My husband was dead. On some level, I should be experiencing grief. Yet how did one grieve the loss of a man who'd taken pleasure in causing pain to his wife and child?

The loud clatter of wagon wheels rumbling on the cobblestone street below drifted through the open window and jolted me back to the present. After tucking the money into my pocket, I descended the rickety steps to Louise's rooms while trying to formulate the proper way to tell Lukas the news. I couldn't be certain how he would react. The child feared his father, and rightfully so. There had been no escaping Fred's wrath when he'd been drinking. Yet, on the rare occasions he had remained sober, Fred would take Lukas to the wharf and tell him stories about the ships and his adventures at sea. No doubt the child would miss those infrequent yet exciting escapades.

After a few taps on the door, I heard the sound of footfalls and the door opened. A cheery smile spread across Louise's face and she waved me inside. Looping her arm in mine, she stepped toward the table. "You're just in time for a cup of tea and a slice of bread and butter." The aroma of the fresh-baked bread filled my nostrils, and I moved steadily toward the scent.

Lukas wiped crumbs from his mouth. "It's really good, Mama. This is my second piece."

I opened my mouth to scold him for taking a second slice, but Louise shook her head. "I insisted. He needs some meat on his bones, Andrea." The older woman lifted a crusty slice from the end of the loaf, smeared it with butter, and handed it to me. "You need fattening, too. Sit down while I pour you some tea." She lifted a kettle from the small stove that was used for both heating and cooking in the small apartment.

"Thank you, Louise. You're good to share with us." I was ashamed to take food from our neighbor, for I knew her means didn't exceed my own by much, but my growling stomach won out. I bit into the crusty bread and savored the yeasty flavor.

"Lukas said a man in fancy clothes came to your room. Did Fred go off and leave the rent unpaid?"

I shook my head and gestured to the other side of the room. "Why don't we sit over there, where we'll have a little more space." I patted Lukas on the shoulder. "You stay here at the table so you don't get crumbs on Mrs. Adler's floor."

"Yes, Mama," he said before taking another bite of the treat.

Louise carried the teacups to a small table in the living area, and we sat down on the couch. With the piece of bread resting atop a napkin on my lap, I leaned a little closer. "I don't want Lukas to hear just yet, but Mr. Brighton came to tell me that Fred died at sea."

Louise clapped her palm to her lips and let out a small yelp. Instantly, Lukas twisted around and looked in our direction. "Did you burn your mouth with the tea, Mrs. Adler?"

The older woman shook her head. "I'm fine, Lukas. You go on and eat your bread." Louise grasped my arm in a tight hold. "Did they recover his body?" The moment after she'd uttered the question,

13

she dropped her gaze. "I'm sorry, Andrea. That was a thoughtless question, but I know sometimes they don't find the men."

I explained as much as I'd been told. "Mr. Brighton gave me what little was left of Fred's wages, along with a sum they pay to widows. If I'm careful, I think it will be enough for food and train fare to get us back to Iowa."

Mrs. Adler arched her brows. "You've already made a decision to return home?"

"What else can I do, Louise? I can't provide a proper home for Lukas in Baltimore. Besides, it was Fred who wanted to come here, not me."

"I know. If the mister and me had a farm to go to, I'd be wanting to leave here, too. I'd rather have the smell of clover blowing through my open window than the odor of dead fish that greets me every morning." Louise took a sip of her tea and then settled the cup atop a chipped saucer. "What are you gonna tell the boy?"

I momentarily closed my eyes. "That his father was lost at sea."

The older woman nodded. "I'm sure your father will be a much better example for Lukas and will give you all the help you're gonna need." Louise shook her head. "I never wished Fred any harm, but he was a mean sort." She shivered and rubbed her arms, as if to erase the remembrance of Fred and his cruel behavior.

"I'm sure my father will be pleased to have someone cook and clean for him again, and I know he'll enjoy having Lukas around. He always wanted a boy. Now he'll be able to teach Lukas all the things he'd hoped to teach me if I'd been a son." A note of melancholy overcame me as I recalled my father's lamenting the fact that my mother had never borne him a son to take over the farm. From that day forward, I'd felt somewhat less important in his life. Maybe returning with a grandson would make up for the fact that I was a girl.

"How can I help you? Tell me what needs to be done and I'll get busy." Instead of keeping her voice low, Louise had spoken in her usual boisterous tone.

Lukas jumped to his feet and hurried to my side. "What do you need help with, Mama?" He lifted his arms and attempted to flex his small muscles. "I can help."

Louise grimaced. "Sorry." She touched her fingers to her lips. "Me and my big mouth."

"You're fine, Louise. Don't worry." I took hold of Lukas's hand. "Let's go upstairs. I have something important to tell you."

Preparing for our departure didn't take as long as I'd anticipated. Probably because most of my belongings had remained in the trunks they'd been packed in when we moved to Baltimore. There had never been enough shelves or cupboards to hold all of my clothing or the household goods I'd brought with me. In this small room that we called home, there was little space for more than the three of us. To try to arrange china or knickknacks in the room would have proved disastrous, especially once Lukas had begun walking. Besides, Fred had discouraged unpacking much of anything, promising he'd find a larger place in a better part of town before long. That empty promise he'd made before Lukas was born.

With a sigh, I lowered the lid of the trunk and locked the hasp. "I'm thankful for your help, Mr. Adler."

Louise's husband glanced at me and shook his head. "I been telling you to call me Bob ever since you moved into this place."

I forced my lips into an apologetic smile. "I'm sorry, Bob. It doesn't come naturally to me, but that doesn't mean I haven't appreciated all your kindness through the years."

He grinned. "Wish I could have done more for you and the boy. I'm sorry about Fred, but the Lord knows best. I probably shouldn't say this, but you may be better off without him. He sure had a mean streak running through him when he was into the drink."

With a grunt, Mr. Adler heaved the last of my trunks from the room and headed down the stairs to a waiting wagon that would transport my son and me to the train station. I grasped Lukas by the hand and glanced around the room one final time.

A rush of unexpected emotion gripped me. Not the feeling of anticipation I'd experienced years ago when leaving the farm with Fred, but one of sorrow for the wasted years that could have been filled with happiness and joy. Sadly, my only delight had been the arrival of our son. But like me, Lukas had been unable to please Fred, so even the joy of our son had been tempered by Fred's anger and discontent.

Lukas tugged on my hand. "Come on, Mama. The wagon will leave without us."

His childish voice tugged at my heart, and I squeezed his hand. "The driver will wait, but you're right. We must hurry or we'll miss the train."

Louise stood near the wagon and pulled me into a tight embrace before leaning down to kiss Lukas on the forehead. She motioned to her husband, who was holding a basket in one hand. "I've packed some food for the journey. Don't argue with me—it's the least we can do for you."

Lukas danced from foot to foot. "Is there bread and jam?"

The older woman tousled his light brown hair. "Now, what kind of friend would I be if I didn't pack you some bread and jam? You be a good boy and help your mama. You've got a long way to travel, so you'll need to behave."

"I will." He bobbed his head. "I'm going to a farm and see lots of animals and meet my grandpa."

Mr. Adler hoisted the boy into the wagon and then assisted me. "Take good care and don't eat all that bread and jam before the train pulls out of the station, Lukas."

"I won't, Mr. Adler." The boy grinned and waved as the wagon pulled away from the ramshackle tenement houses.

If my son harbored any grief or sadness, he was keeping it well concealed. I hadn't expected him to grieve the loss of his father, for Fred had never shown the boy any love. Nothing we had done ever pleased him, and though I believed his rants were no more than an excuse to justify his departure for the bars along the wharf, Fred had always blamed everything, from our poverty-stricken existence to his drunken stupors, on everyone but himself.

"Cost ya extra to have me take the trunks into the station, missus. Up to you." Brows arched, the driver looked at me for further direction.

"I'll need you to take them inside."

He helped me down from the wagon but held out his hand for payment before unloading the trunks. I carefully counted out the money and waited to follow him inside, for I didn't trust him any more than he trusted me, and I could ill afford to lose my few worldly possessions.

Lukas's excitement mounted as we walked into the busy train station. "Stay by my side," I instructed while I purchased our tickets.

The man behind the counter pointed the driver to the platform. "You can place her trunks and baggage out there on that loading area to the left of the doors." Turning his attention back to me, he handed me our tickets. "That's your train waiting out there. You and the boy can go ahead and get on board."

"You're certain they'll load my belongings?"

His smile was forced. "We do this every day, ma'am. Your luggage will be with you when you arrive in Iowa." He signaled for the next person in line to step forward.

Marengo, Iowa

Every bone in my body ached when the conductor stepped down the aisle and called out, "Marengo! Next stop, Marengo." The train ride had been long and tiresome, and I would be thankful when the final leg of our trip would come to an end.

I roused Lukas. "Time to wake up. We're pulling into the train station."

Lukas rubbed his eyes. "We have to get on another train?"

I smiled and shook my head. "No more trains, but we'll need to take a wagon ride to the farm."

The answer pleased the boy, and he sat up to peer out the window. "Do you think Grandpa will like me?"

"He will love you very much. You just wait and see. He'll show you how to milk the cows and feed the chickens. You'll learn all sorts of new things. There will be trees to climb and fish in the pond waiting for you to catch."

He bounced on the hard seat. "And you can cook them for our supper."

"Indeed I will, but first we need to take that wagon ride." Still hissing and belching, the train lurched to a stop. I escorted Lukas off the train, took him by the hand, and led him inside the station.

A paunchy old gentleman stood behind the ticket window. "How can I help ya, ma'am?"

I explained my need for a wagon, and he pointed to a lanky

man leaning against a railing outside the station. "That fellow out there is who you need to speak with."

After a quick thank-you, I crossed the short distance to the door and stepped outside. While keeping an arm around Lukas's shoulder, I made arrangements with the driver, and although I had hoped I might see someone I knew, I immediately realized the improbability of such an idea. I'd never known many folks in Marengo. My parents had purchased most of their supplies at the general store in High Amana. If a trip to Marengo was necessary, my father or one of the hired hands had made the journey.

Once the driver loaded our belongings, he helped Lukas and me into the wagon. Then he circled around the horses and gave each one a gentle pat on the rump.

We hadn't gone far when he looked at me. "You said you wanted to go to the Neumann farm. That right?"

I nodded.

"Guess you best give me directions on how to get there."

His statement caught me by surprise. It seemed a man offering wagon services at the train station should know his way around these parts. When I questioned him, he shrugged his broad shoulders and grinned. "Man's gotta make a living, and Clint—he's the ticket agent you met back there—he told me there's always folks needin' a ride somewhere. So far, it's worked out pretty good."

I arched a brow. "But what if one of your passengers didn't know how to direct you? Then what would you do?"

He chuckled and rubbed his jaw. "Then I guess I'd go back to the train station and ask Clint, but so far I haven't had to do that. Jest my good luck that most folks know how to get where they wanna go. And I'm beginning to learn my way around." He slapped the reins and the horses picked up their pace. "So does this farm we're going to belong to you and your husband?"

"No, it belongs to my father."

"I see. Well, to tell ya the truth, when I first saw ya, I thought maybe you was one of them Amana folks, what with your dark clothes and all. I went over to one of them villages looking for work when I first came to town, but they wasn't hiring. Told me to come back during harvest in late summer and they might have work for me. All the women was dressed in dark colors."

Lukas pointed to a herd of cows grazing in a distant pasture. "Are those some of my grandpa's cows?"

"No. We have a ways to go before we'll get to Grandpa's farm. Why don't you rest your head on my shoulder and try to sleep."

"There's too much to see, Mama. I don't want to sleep."

As I looked out over the rolling hills and vast farmlands that spread around us like a patchwork quilt, I tried to imagine seeing this countryside for the first time. Little wonder Lukas found the unfolding scene fascinating. For all of his young life, his view had been restricted to tenement housing and an occasional walk to the wharf, where he'd wave good-bye to his father when his vessel would set sail. A while later, weariness won out and he finally nestled against me and fell asleep.

Leaning forward, I squinted and pointed in the distance. "Turn to the left at the fork in the road. It won't be much farther once we turn."

A mixture of excitement and dread knotted in my stomach. My parents had been opposed to Fred's decision to leave Iowa, and my father had tried his best to convince him we should remain on the farm. He'd likely be quick to point out the folly of Fred's choice. There hadn't been many letters back and forth, but I hoped my appearance with Lukas would heal any scars in our damaged relationship.

We'd traveled for less than an hour when I straightened my

shoulders and peered to the left. "There! That's the farm up ahead." I leaned forward to gain a better view. Confusion took hold and I raised my hand to block the sun from my eyes. Why couldn't I see the house? Had we taken a wrong turn? Surely I hadn't been gone so long that I'd forgotten my way home.

As the wagon drew near, I let out a gasp and clutched a hand to my chest. In the distance, my gaze settled on what had once been my family's home. Now only ashes and a sandstone foundation remained.

 CHAPTER 2

A perplexed look shadowed the driver's face. "You sure this is the right place, ma'am?"

An unexpected tightness squeezed my throat and stifled my response. I could manage no more than a faint nod.

He shifted on the wagon seat and faced me. "You want me to put the baggage in that barn over there? Looks like it might be the best place, since . . ." His voice faded on the breeze. He held tight to the reins with one hand and gestured toward the remnants of the house with the other.

Hoping to rid myself of the lump that had lodged in my throat, I massaged my neck for a moment. "The barn will be fine, thank you." Had that croaking response come from my lips? I needed to regain my composure, or Lukas would become frightened.

The driver slapped the reins against the horses' backsides, and they slowly trod across the rough, overgrown quarter mile that lay between the house and barn. I'd never seen the place in such a state of disrepair and wondered how long it had been since the fire.

Had my father simply given up and moved into town? Surely not. He'd never been a quitter. This farm had always been his life. Yet he was nowhere in sight, and it didn't appear that any of his fields had been plowed for spring planting. Perhaps it had been too cold and he was waiting for the arrival of warmer weather before turning the ground.

I shifted toward the wagon driver. "Have you heard anyone speak of Johann Neumann or a fire? Someone in Marengo must have mentioned something about this. I realize we're out a good distance from Marengo, but I know word travels in these parts."

"I ain't heard nothing that I can recollect, but since I don't know folks around here, the news kind of goes in one ear and out the other." He pointed to one of his oversized ears and grinned.

In one respect, I understood his response. Much of the gossip that had swirled throughout the tenement building hadn't meant anything to me. Other than Louise and her husband, the occupants had been only a blur of faces. When groups of residents would gather in the stairwells to gossip, I would hear smatterings of their conversations, but I couldn't recall any of it—nor did I want to.

Yet a farmhouse burning to the ground was something entirely different, wasn't it? Would I have forgotten such a piece of disastrous news even if I hadn't known the people or the place where it occurred? I closed my eyes and searched for my own answer. Probably so. In truth, I'd likely heard even worse things, although I couldn't bring one to mind.

"Where's Grandpa?" Lukas's eyes were wide with anticipation as the driver brought the horses to a halt near the barn door.

I didn't fail to notice one of the doors stood partially open. "I'm not sure. Maybe he's inside the barn."

Lukas clambered down from the wagon as the driver assisted me to the ground. "I'll go look for him." Without a backward glance, the boy ran pell-mell through the knee-high weeds and disappeared behind the barn door.

The driver strode to the rear of the wagon. "You sure you want to stay here, ma'am? I can take you back to Marengo—no extra charge."

"Thank you, but we'll stay. I'm sure we'll be fine." Although my voice bore a confident tone, I wasn't at all sure we'd be fine. In fact, I wasn't sure what we would do if my father didn't soon make an appearance.

I hurried after Lukas to ensure he hadn't met with any unexpected calamity inside the barn, as well as to locate a proper space for our belongings. My father had always been known to keep his barn and outbuildings in good repair, but since he'd made no effort to rebuild the house, I wondered if by now there might be leaks or other damage to the remaining structures.

After stepping inside the barn, I waited for my eyes to adjust to the semi-darkness. A stream of sunlight flowed through the open door but illuminated only a short distance beyond my feet. "Lukas! Where are you?"

"Over here, Mama. I don't see no animals. Where are they?"

"Maybe out in the pasture. I really don't know." I walked toward the sound of his voice. When I drew near, he turned. "What do you think of this barn, Lukas? Is it as big as you imagined?"

He spread his arms wide and turned in a circle. "It's as big as a ship, isn't it? I wonder what's up there," he said, pointing to the hayloft.

I chuckled at his enthusiasm. "From what I see so far, probably not much of anything. Right now, we need to find a good place for our trunks." Grasping his hand, I strode to the far side of the barn. "Come along and help me."

He skipped beside me, straw flying beneath his feet while dust motes danced in the shafts of sunlight that beamed through every crevice. I located a spot along the west wall, not too far from the door. A place that appeared dry, but since I had no idea how long it had been since the last rain, my assumption might be very wrong. I could only hope for the best.

"You want 'em over there?" The driver's voice and his footfalls echoed in the cavernous barn.

Wheeling around on my heel, I stepped toward him and pointed to the wall. "I think that will be a good spot."

He settled the trunk on the floor before returning for the next one. Lukas trotted along behind him. "I can carry my mama's small cases."

The driver waved him forward. "You sure can, and I'd be pleased for your help."

Lukas's shoulders squared, and his lips curved in a winning smile. I followed behind. Once outside the barn, I tugged the brim of my bonnet forward to block the sun from my eyes and glanced toward the remains of the house.

Had my father gone to High Amana for supplies, or had he left the farm for good? I needed to develop some sort of plan, but I'd wait until tomorrow before making any final decisions.

The thought was enough to remind me of the basket of food I'd continued to replenish since leaving Baltimore. I cupped my hands to my lips. "Be sure you bring the food basket, Lukas!"

When he waved his hat in the air, I knew he'd heard, and I turned to once again to survey the surrounding acreage.

My stomach tightened, yet I fought back the rising fear. This was my family's homestead. Until tomorrow, I would believe my papa would appear. After that, I didn't know what I'd do, but for tonight we'd sleep in the barn and pretend all was well.

"You certain you want to stay?" the driver asked for the third time since he'd begun unloading the trunks. "I'm not sure 'bout leaving you and the boy out here alone."

I thanked him for his help, and after assuring him we would be fine, Lukas and I stood side by side and watched the driver and his wagon disappear out of sight.

"What do we do now, Mama?" I heard the tremble in his voice. The driver's concern had been enough to signal all was not well, and Lukas hadn't missed the warning.

"I think we'll have us a picnic right out here in the sunshine, and then we'll pull some of the quilts from our trunk and make a cozy spot to sleep." I squeezed his shoulders. "We're going to have a grand adventure tonight."

"But what if Grandpa doesn't come home?"

"We'll ask God to direct us, Lukas. Everything will be fine. Just you wait and see."

Morning arrived with no sign of my father throughout the night or this morning. With no indication of him or of any animals on the property, I became certain he'd decided to leave the farm. Maybe for only a short time until he could make plans to rebuild. Perhaps he'd made arrangements with the farmers in West Amana to care for the stock during his absence. He could trust them to treat the animals well. But until his return, I would need to purchase a few provisions, and my funds were meager.

While Lukas slept, I lifted the bar from across the barn doors and stepped outside. "At least the weather is warm," I murmured, thankful we hadn't arrived in the dead of winter.

"*Guten Morgen! Willkommen!*"

I startled and turned in the direction of the shouted greeting. A broad-shouldered man who appeared to be near my father's age strode toward me. He waved his wide-brimmed straw hat overhead and offered a friendly smile as he approached. Along with the fact that he'd spoken in German, his wide suspenders, dark trousers, and jacket gave proof he was a member of the Amana Colonies. I guessed he'd come from West Amana, since a portion of land owned and farmed by the Amana colonists who lived in West abutted my father's acreage.

Using the familiar German I'd learned during my childhood years, I walked toward him and returned his greeting.

"How can I help you?" He glanced toward the farm. "Your horses and wagon are in our barn?"

I frowned at his question. "*Your* barn? This land belongs to my father, Johann Neumannn. I am Andrea Neumannn Wilson, his daughter." I gestured toward the barn. "My son, Lukas, is inside. We have returned home from Baltimore. My father didn't write and tell me about the fire." I let my gaze settle on the sandstone foundation that had once supported our frame house.

"*Ja*, the fire, it was very bad." His voice was as solemn as his dark brown eyes. "I am sorry you must come home to find such sadness."

"*Danke.*" Not wanting to reveal the tears beginning to form in my eyes, I looked away. "My father? I arrived yesterday but haven't seen him. Did he decide to leave the farm? Do you know?"

"First you should let me introduce myself. I am Brother Heinrich Bosch. I live in West Amana. Some of our men were plowing yesterday and said they saw a wagon arrive on our land. I came to see if their imaginations were working too hard." He tapped his finger to the side of his head and smiled before glancing in the direction of the barn. "This is your son?"

I turned and gestured for Lukas to join me. His legs flew like a windmill propelling in a brisk wind. In a few brief moments, he came to a halt beside me, his breath coming in gasps. He narrowed his blue eyes and angled his head to one side. "Are you my grandpa?"

Confusion shone in Brother Bosch's eyes.

"Lukas has never met his grandfather," I explained and then turned to Lukas and shook my head. "No, this is Brother Bosch. He lives in West Amana." I pointed in the direction of the village.

"Does he know Grandpa?"

"I haven't yet had time to ask him. Why don't you go back into the barn and shake out the blankets for me. You can fold them and put them back in the trunk."

Lukas inched closer to me. "But I—"

"Please do as I've asked, Lukas. I'll come in and get you in a few minutes." I touched his shoulder and gently nudged him back in the direction of the barn.

Lukas shuffled off, but not without glancing over his shoulder several times.

"He is a fine boy." Brother Bosch settled his straw hat atop his graying hair. "His *Vater*? He is with you?"

"*Nein*. His father is dead. He died at sea." If the older man was surprised by my emotionless response, he gave no indication. "That's why we returned home." I hesitated and looked into his dark brown eyes. "You said something about this being your barn. What did you mean?"

He motioned to a leafy elm not far from the barn. "Since there is no place to sit, we can at least go over and stand in the shade, ja?"

I nodded and did my best to match his long-legged stride. I was happy to accommodate his wish, but more than shade I wanted answers to my questions. We had almost arrived at the tree when I said, "You know my father?"

He nodded. "I did. He was a hard worker and a *gut* man."

I stopped in my tracks. Brother Bosch had spoken of my father in the past tense. Either he had left the farm or he was . . . dead. Either way, I needed to know. I grasped the older man by his sleeve. "Is he alive?"

He looked down at me and shook his head. "Nein. He died in the fire."

I gasped and clutched one arm around my waist. I thought I might be sick. With a gentle touch, Brother Bosch led me to the shade of the tree, removed his jacket, and spread it beneath the elm.

He pointed to the jacket. "You should sit. I am sorry to be the one to tell you this sad news about your Vater. Is bad enough you did not know about the fire, but . . ."

His voice trailed off while a group of baby birds in a nest chirped overhead. A fat robin circled, settled at the edge of the nest, and dropped food into the gaping beaks of her babies. A stark reminder that I would soon need to find a way to feed my son. We had little food and even less money. Although I'd attempted to devise a plan as I lay awake last night, my efforts had been unsuccessful. I couldn't farm this land by myself, but perhaps I could sell the acreage. The very idea reminded me of Brother Bosch's earlier remark regarding "his" barn.

A surge of guilt attacked. I'd learned only moments ago that my father was dead, but instead of mourning his loss, I was already making plans to sell his land. Yet what was I to do? Just as those baby birds were dependent upon their mother, Lukas depended upon me. My grief would have to wait. Right now, I needed answers.

He'd leaned his lanky frame against the trunk of the tree and silently stared into the distance. I had to know what Lukas and I now faced. "When you first arrived you said this was your barn. What did you mean, Brother Bosch?"

His eyes shone with concern. "There is so much you must learn in just a short time, but if you want to hear, I will tell you."

I nodded. "I have no choice. I can't make any decisions until I know everything that has happened."

I didn't miss the pity that shone in his eyes as he nodded. "About three years ago, your Vater came and spoke to the elders about selling his land to us. He thought we would be the best choice since we own the adjacent land. After many months and much talking, we finally came to an agreement with your Vater." He pulled a pipe from his pants pocket and knocked it against the tree. A few pieces of tobacco drifted on the breeze before fluttering to the ground. "He was a gut businessman—stubborn." He chuckled.

There was real truth to that statement. My father had always worked hard, and our farm had usually made a good enough profit that we lived as well or better than most of the farm families in eastern Iowa.

"So what agreement did he make?" My stomach knotted, for I knew I wasn't going to be pleased with the answer. I was now certain my father had sold the land.

Brother Bosch trained his eyes on the bowl of his pipe while he filled it with fresh tobacco. "He signed a contract to sell us all of this." Cupping the bowl of his pipe in his left hand, he arched his right arm in a wide circle. "The land, the buildings, the house, the animals—everything. But we could not take ownership until his death."

Though the breeze was warm, a chill coursed through me and

I shuddered. Had someone caused my father's death in order to gain possession of the land?

No! Surely not.

The members of Amana Colonies would never do such a thing—they were an honorable people. My father had always said as much. And if they hadn't been willing to wait until Father's death, they wouldn't have signed such a contract. Besides, my father had always maintained a good relationship with the people of West Amana. They would never have harmed him.

"So the animals?" I gestured toward their land and he nodded.

"Ja, we took them right away, but we haven't begun to plow over here yet. We are still busy with the other land, and a decision hasn't been made if we will till and plant this year or wait until next spring." He lit the tobacco and puffed several times. "We had already paid your father. There is paper work in the village you can examine if you would like. I am thinking you might want to see that, ja?"

My mouth turned dry as the gravity of his words took hold. I could barely believe my ears. If they'd already paid my father, where was the money? I turned toward the burned-out remains of what had once been my home and shook my head. If the money had burned in the fire, there was nothing left for Lukas and me. There was no way I could support my child, and no way I could remain on this land. Desperation clawed down my spine. How would we survive?

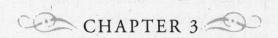

CHAPTER 3

For several minutes, I sat in stunned silence. Finally, Brother Bosch pushed away from the tree. "You and the boy should come back to the village with me."

I shook my head. "My trunks are in the barn. Everything I own."

His lips curved in a gentle smile. Brother Bosch couldn't possibly understand my concern over the baggage stored in the barn, for the people of Amana didn't place a great deal of value on worldly belongings. They lived a communal life and had little need of the items I considered valuable. Long ago Mother told me she'd visited some of the Amana homes, and there had been a few personal belongings displayed in each one. But the farmland, the houses, the vineyards, the crops—all were owned by the Amana Society.

"I will have one of the men bring a wagon."

Bring a wagon, load my belongings, and then what? I didn't know how to respond.

"You can stay in the village until you decide what to do." His voice resonated with a compassion that tugged at my heart.

"I have no money to pay for lodging or food."

"Ach!" He waved his hand in a dismissive motion. "What are two more mouths to feed? You and the boy can eat at the *Küche*, and we will arrange a place for you to stay. Is not difficult. If you stay for more than a few days, you may need to help in the kitchen house or garden, but the work is not so hard, and the sisters will be gut company for you. Will be *gut* for the boy, as well."

The idea seemed outlandish, and yet what else could I do? There seemed no other possibility for Lukas and me—at least for the time being. Once I had more time to think, maybe then I could develop some sort of arrangement for our future.

"Thank you, Brother Bosch. If I weren't so worried about my son, I wouldn't impose on you, but I must find some way to take care of our needs."

His gentle smile returned. "There is a passage in the Bible that says, 'Therefore I say unto you, Take no thought for your life, what ye shall eat, or what ye shall drink; nor yet for your body, what ye shall put on. Is not the life more than meat, and the body than raiment? Behold the fowls of the air: for they sow not, neither do they reap, nor gather into barns; yet your heavenly Father feedeth them. Are ye not much better than they?'" He held out his hand and helped me to my feet. "You have heard this before?"

Walking alongside him toward the barn, I nodded. "Yes, I've read those verses." I didn't go on to say that I'd read those passages and prayed on many occasions when our cupboard was bare and Fred out to sea. Most of the time, my needs had been met by Louise Adler, but there had been a few instances when Lukas and I had ached with unrelenting hunger. When we left Baltimore, I thought we'd left those days behind. All of this seemed a cruel joke, and I now wondered what God must be thinking.

"Then you know God will provide." He smiled. "Right now, He is giving us the opportunity to help you."

I wasn't convinced most people would consider helping us an opportunity, but I was glad to know Brother Bosch didn't think us a burden. "I hope the others in the village will feel the same as you. Don't you need to seek agreement from the others?"

"There will be no problem. We would never turn away a widow and child in need of provision. The other elders will be in accord." He grasped the wooden door handle and pulled back on the heavy door.

So Brother Bosch was an elder. No wonder he'd been so knowledgeable about the sale of my father's land. Maybe he could tell me even more. But I'd wait until Lukas wasn't nearby to ask any further questions.

Lukas scampered toward me, his blue eyes shining with an eagerness that accompanied childhood. "I folded the blankets and put them in the trunk like you told me, Mama."

"Thank you, Lukas." I briefly considered going inside and refolding the quilts, but I didn't want to discourage him from any future efforts to help me. With his short arms, I pictured the quilts stuffed beneath the heavy trunk lids in slapdash bundles, but it truly didn't matter. Right now, there were far more important things to worry me. I tousled my son's hair and rested my arm around his shoulder. "We're going to go with Brother Bosch and visit the village where he lives. Won't that be fun?"

His forehead creased in a frown. "But what about Grandpa?"

I stooped down in front of him and gathered his hands within my own. "Brother Bosch tells me that Grandpa died before we arrived here."

Lukas yanked his hands away from me and shook his head. "That's not true." He glowered at the older man. "My grandpa isn't dead. Only my papa." His voice trembled, and he clutched his small hands into tight fists.

"Lukas! Don't direct your anger at Brother Bosch. He is going to help us, and none of this is his fault." Once again, I grasped his hands and looked into his eyes. "Do you understand me?" My tone had been stern enough that the boy's shoulders relaxed a bit.

"Yes, Mama."

"You should apologize to Brother Bosch."

He scuffed the toe of his shoe in the dirt and gave the man a quick sideways glance. "I'm sorry."

The elder nodded his head and patted Lukas on the shoulder before closing the barn doors. He motioned me toward the village. "We will cut across the fields so it will not be so far to walk."

I held Lukas by the hand as we plodded across the uneven terrain toward the village of West Amana. At least for the next several nights, we would have a roof over our heads and food in our stomachs. After that, our future remained an unsolved mystery.

West Amana Colony, Iowa

Only once could I remember being in one of the villages. The three of us had traveled to High Amana for Mother to purchase some dress fabric. She'd been unhappy with Papa's previous choices and insisted that she go along and choose her own. Papa continued to maintain he liked the dark green material with huge pink flowers, but Mother disagreed and had sewn the fabric into window curtains rather than a dress. After that, Father had been more careful with his choices. The general store and houses I'd seen in

High Amana had been made of sandstone, the same sandstone my papa used to construct the foundation of our own house.

I expected to see similar houses in West Amana but was surprised when I caught sight of a few brick homes and some frame construction as well as the familiar sandstone. When I inquired, Brother Bosch explained that sandstone was much more prevalent in High, so it had been used for all of the houses there. He gestured toward the south. "In South Amana, the houses are of brick because that is where we make our bricks. In Main Amana, many of the houses are of frame construction because there were many trees nearby. We used what was most available for each village. Here in West, we have more of the sandstone, but we have a little of the others, too." He grinned. "We have nice variety, ja?"

"Yes, very nice." With Lukas still holding my hand, I continued to survey my surroundings.

The houses were larger than most family homes, and certainly larger than our farmhouse had been. During my years on the farm, I'd heard a few stories about the communal society, but I hadn't been particularly interested in their way of life, and most of what I'd heard had long since been forgotten. This village exuded a sense of orderly arrangement and tidiness that refreshed my memories of High from years ago.

When Lukas tugged on my hand, I looked down into his bright blue eyes. "Are we going to live here, Mama?"

"Maybe for a little while, Lukas. Do you think you would like that?"

He shook his head. "I want to live on the farm with Grandpa."

I inhaled a deep breath. "That isn't going to be possible, Lukas. We're going to make new plans. Now, come along. Brother Bosch is going to take us to the kitchen house to meet some of the people who live here."

The boy lagged a few steps behind, and I didn't blame him. His uncertainty about this new arrangement likely ran even deeper than my own—if that was possible. I moved a bit closer to Brother Bosch and lowered my voice. "I may have enough money to pay for one night at a hotel. Is there a boardinghouse or hotel in the village?" Some of these houses appeared as large as hotels in the small towns where Fred and I had stayed on our way to Baltimore years ago.

The older man shook his head. "Nein. We have hotels only in the villages where there are trains passing through. No trains in West, so no hotel, but do not worry. For you and the boy, there will be a comfortable place to stay."

His offer was both generous and kind, and I was thankful, yet a tiny part of me worried about this arrangement. Brother Bosch was kind, but what if the other villagers didn't want us there? How would we be treated? Surely they didn't like outsiders. Why else would they segregate themselves in these villages?

When the elder motioned to a nearby house and led us to the rear entrance, unexpected trepidation assailed me. My palms turned damp and I could feel the prickle of perspiration beneath my dark bonnet. He opened the door and gestured for us to enter. Rather than step forward, I longed to turn and run, but I forced a smile and tugged on Lukas's hand.

Brother Bosch removed his straw hat before stepping inside. "Guten Morgen, Sister Erma."

A small cluster of women turned to look at us when we entered. All but one turned back to her work. A rosy-cheeked woman with graying hair and bright blue eyes crossed the kitchen and stopped in front of us. Her full lips curved in a broad smile that she directed at Lukas, and I assumed she was Sister Erma.

"Guten Morgen." Her gaze passed over all three of us before it settled on the elder. "Who do we have here, Brother Bosch? Some visiting relatives, perhaps?"

"Nein, Sister. This is Mrs. Wilson and her son, Lukas. She is the daughter of Johann Neumann, who lived on the adjacent farm that we purchased." He turned toward me. "This is Sister Erma Goetz. She is in charge of this Küche, and everyone who eats here will tell you the best meals are served in the Goetz *Küchehaas*."

The color in Sister Erma's cheeks heightened at the flattery. She waved a dismissive gesture at Brother Bosch. "Is true we serve gut food in this Küche, but the food is gut in all of the village kitchen houses." Waving us into the adjacent room, she gestured to one of many long tables. Backless benches were aligned on both sides of each table. "You sit down, and I will get you some coffee." Before heading back to the kitchen, she pointed at Lukas. "And for you I have some milk." Hesitating for only a moment, she tipped her head to one side. "And maybe some bread and jam, ja?"

Lukas turned to me, uncertain how to answer. He'd doubtless understood very little the woman had said, for during his lifetime he'd heard me speak only smatterings of the German language. Mostly when Louise Adler and I would relax over a strong cup of coffee and talk about things we didn't want others to hear. Although Lukas had picked up a few words of the language, his German vocabulary was far more limited than his English.

I repeated the question, and Lukas bobbed his head with enthusiasm. The older woman laughed. "We will have to teach him to speak German."

Though I nodded my agreement, I didn't expect to be here long enough for Lukas to learn the language. Brother Bosch excused himself and returned to the kitchen. Moments later, I heard the back door close, and I wondered if he'd left Lukas and me in Sister Erma's care. Although the room was void of decorations, it exuded an air of warmth, perhaps due to the pale blue walls, or maybe due to the orderly alignment of everything in the room.

Soon the sister returned with a tray bearing two cups of coffee, a glass of milk, and a plate heaping with thick, crusty slices of wheat bread. Beside the plate were two small white bowls, one containing butter and the other filled with jam.

Lukas straightened to attention at the sight. "Strawberry jam, Mama."

"I think it is rhubarb jam, but you will like it every bit as much," I said.

Without asking, Sister Erma prepared a slice of the bread, cut it in half, and placed it on a small plate in front of Lukas. "First you give thanks; then you eat." She folded her hands together as further explanation.

Lukas smiled his understanding before he bowed his head and repeated the prayer we recited before eating our meals—at least when Fred hadn't been present. While Lukas was eating, Sister Erma explained that Brother Heinrich, the name she used when referring to Brother Bosch, had gone to speak to the other elders about my living arrangements.

"If the elders agree, you and the boy will remain here at the kitchen house with me." She pointed a finger toward the ceiling. "My rooms are upstairs. There is a parlor, my bedroom, and another bedroom that belonged to my daughter before she married and moved to South Amana with her husband. The bedroom is large enough for you and the boy." She angled her shoulders toward the kitchen. "Since my husband's death, I spend a lot of time in the kitchen. It will be nice to have some company."

"That's most kind of you, Sister Erma. I'm thankful for a place to stay until I can make plans for our future."

She lowered her head and patted my hand. "Ja, Brother Heinrich tells me you have had lots of troubles. To have a husband die so young is hard and then this tragedy with your father . . ." She shook her head and poured a dollop of cream into her coffee. "For sure, you have had your share of heartache. If I had not been living in the colonies when my husband died, I don't know what I would have done. To be an old woman on my own would have been very hard for me, but the Lord made provision for me, and now He's doing the same for you."

Sister Erma had tied all the loose ends into a tight little knot of understanding. I, however, hadn't stopped to consider any of this the Lord's doing. But who could say? Perhaps the Lord had decided to send a bit of sunshine in our direction. Of course, I wasn't certain whether living in the colonies would prove to be a total delight, but at least Lukas would have food and a comfortable place to lay his head. And I wouldn't have to worry about being alone at night without protection, a fear I'd wrestled with each time Fred went out to sea.

Pots and pans clattered in the other room while we drank our coffee and Lukas continued to devour his bread and jam. When he picked up another slice, I stilled his hand. "No more. You will make yourself sick." I patted his extended belly. "You can have more after a while."

Before the child could offer an argument, Brother Bosch returned and advised that an agreement had been reached. We would stay at the Küche with Sister Erma. "Since you will be remaining in the colonies with us, it would be gut if you could help Sister Erma in the kitchen. She is short of help, and I am sure she will put your hands to gut use."

I'd never worked in a kitchen with anyone other than my mother, but I quickly agreed to the request. Sister Erma pushed up from the table. "We will go upstairs, and I will show you your room before I get busy with the noonday meal."

"On my way to speak with the elders, I asked one of the men to go for your belongings. He should be here soon." Brother Bosch turned his attention to Sister Erma. "When Brother Dirk arrives with the trunks, you will show him where he should put Sister Andrea's belongings, ja?"

I whirled around, startled by his remark. My dark mourning clothes closely resembled the plain clothing of the Amana women, but exactly when had I become a sister?

 CHAPTER 4

Dirk Knefler

My plain blue shirt pulled tight across my shoulders, and the midmorning sun warmed my back as the wagon rolled at a lumbering pace. I leaned forward and encouraged the two horses to move with a little more spirit. Even though this journey to the Neumann farmstead was going to delay my work in the tinsmith shop, I was glad to be outdoors on such a beautiful day.

Brother Bosch's request had surprised me, for generally one of the farmhands would be asked to perform such chores. However, the large groups of workers had already departed for the fields, and the trunks would be difficult for the older brother to wield on his own.

"The Lord placed you in my path, Brother Dirk," he'd told me when he stepped inside the shop a short time ago.

I had smiled at his comment, for I wondered how I could be in his path when I'd been indoors working, but I refrained from asking such a question. And when he said he had a chore for me to complete, I didn't mention the fact that I had more than enough work to keep me busy for several weeks. When a brother or sister needed help, others were expected to lend a hand. Such was the way of life in the colonies.

Werner Buettner, the fourteen-year-old assigned to apprentice with me, entered the shop before Brother Bosch departed. "Take young Werner along. He has a strong back and can help you lift the trunks into the wagon. With my aching bones, I could never provide as much help as Werner."

Once again I had agreed, though I would have preferred to have Werner remain and complete a small task or two at the shop. Then again, perhaps having him at my side would be a better choice. Although he'd expressed interest in learning to become a tinsmith, the boy hadn't proved to be a particularly capable student. Only after the elders had assigned him to work with me did I learn that he'd already proved a poor fit at the tailor's shop, the bakery, and the cooper's shop. In addition, both the cobbler and the broom maker had declared Werner unable to satisfactorily complete tasks in their workshops.

After failing in one or two of the trades, most young lads were assigned work in the fields. Werner had been no exception. Somewhere between his job at the bakery and the broom-maker's shop, he'd been appointed to work in the fields. Unfortunately, that hadn't been a success, either. Each time he went to the fields his eyes watered and he would develop a terrible cough. As a result, he'd been excused from that work, as well. His previous experiences had left Werner feeling like a failure, and I wanted the boy to succeed at something. Thus far, I doubted it would be tinsmithing.

Werner shifted on the hard wooden seat as the wagon rumbled along the rutted dirt path. "Sometimes I wish I could get on a horse and just keep going."

"Why is that, Werner?" I pushed my hat further back and gained a better view of the boy. "Are you unhappy in the village?"

"Nein. I'm not unhappy, but I'd like to see what's beyond our villages. One day I want to see the ocean and the mountains. I'd like to see something beyond these fields and the few stony hills here in Iowa. How about you, Brother Dirk? You ever want to leave and go see the world?"

I shook my head. "Nein. The world doesn't interest me much. I'm content here, but you wouldn't be the first to want to leave and see what's beyond our boundaries."

"My Vater says those who leave usually come running back when they discover it's hard to make do out there in the world without anyone to help them along the way. He says I should learn to be content where God placed me."

I shrugged my shoulders. "It is gut to be content, don't you think?"

Werner wrinkled his nose. "Maybe, but what if Brother Christian and the elders had decided to stay where they were planted? They were discontented, so they left and came to America. We would still be living in Germany if they had stayed where they were planted, ja?"

"Their reason for leaving was very different, Werner. Our people were being persecuted because of their faith. Brother Christian Metz received a word from the Lord that our people were to come to this new land. You have learned this in meeting, ja?"

Werner bobbed his head. "Ja, from the time I was a little boy, I was taught in meeting and prayer service about the inspired messages Brother Metz received. But that doesn't change what I feel in my heart."

"I don't challenge what you feel, but maybe you should ask the elders or your Vater to help you understand the difference between a worldly desire and God's truth."

The boy's frown deepened. "How do you know the difference, Brother Dirk?"

I inhaled a deep breath. "If what I want doesn't align with what is the truth of God's Word, then I know it is my own desire and not what God wants for me." We were nearing the farmstead, and I slowed the horses. "Does that help?"

"A little, but what if the Bible doesn't say?" His lips curved in a mischievous grin. "I do not think I'll find a verse that says it isn't gut for me to leave the Amana Colonies, do you?"

"Nein, but you will find a verse that says you should honor your *Mutter* and Vater and submit to authority. You are still young, Werner. When you are a full-grown man, you will think differently." I pulled back on the reins, waited until the wagon was at a halt, set the brake, and jumped down. "Come on. Let's get the trunks loaded so we can get back to work."

Werner shuffled behind me. I sensed my answers hadn't pleased him, but I'd done the best I could to give him proper direction. It wasn't my place to tell the boy what he should or shouldn't do, but like any member of the community, I had an obligation to lead him along a righteous path.

"Who owns these trunks, Brother Dirk? Were they pulled out of the fire?"

"Nein. By the time we got over here, the fire was too hot to go into what was left of the house. These trunks belong to the daughter and grandson of Mr. Neumann, the man who owned this land."

Werner hoisted one of the smaller trunks onto his shoulder. Sunlight filtered through the open doors, and shadows danced across the straw-strewn barn floor. "How come their trunks are out here in the barn? Did they die in the fire, too?"

I repeated what Brother Bosch had told me when he'd come

to the shop. Werner shook his head. "I doubt they'll stay with us for long—not after living in a big city. How come they're going to live with us? Why not return to Baltimore?"

If nothing else, Werner was full of questions—questions for which I had no answers. "I told you all I know, Werner."

"You should ask more questions, Brother Dirk."

I grinned at the boy. "And you should not ask so many." I waved him back to the barn, where the two of us hoisted the remaining trunks and carried them out to the wagon. Once we'd loaded them, I motioned toward the barn. "Run back and close the doors."

Arms pumping, Werner raced and closed the doors and then galloped back to the wagon. He was gasping for air when he pulled himself up and onto the wagon seat. "I was thinking maybe I could ask the new lady what it was like where she lived before. You think it would be improper?"

I released the brake and called to the horses to move out. "She has a son. I think it would be better to speak with him rather than the woman. She's an outsider and—"

"And a woman," he said, interrupting me.

"Ja, she is a woman, but I was going to say, she is an outsider, and it might cause her discomfort or pain to be asked questions about her past. Brother Bosch did tell me her husband died at sea."

The boy's eyes grew wide. "Ach! That is terrible. Maybe the ocean is not such a gut idea for me."

I smiled and patted his shoulder. "Maybe you are right, Werner."

As we arrived at the outskirts of the village, I considered taking Werner to the shop before delivering the baggage to Sister Erma's Küche, but when I mentioned the idea, he was disappointed, so I relented.

After stopping in front of the Küche, I grasped his arm. "You should not make a spectacle of yourself, Werner. The sisters will be busy in the kitchen, and we need to be mindful of them. You understand?"

He bobbed his head, and together we lifted the trunks from the wagon. One by one, we carried them to the porch. By the time we had carried the last bags to the doorway, Sister Erma appeared.

"Follow me." Waving us forward, she trundled through the kitchen, into the dining room, and up the stairs that led to her private rooms. We continued along the short hallway and into the back bedroom.

"You can put the trunks in here. Once Sister Andrea has unpacked what she will need, one of you can return and carry them out to one of the storage sheds."

"I'll do it!" Werner's declaration was so loud that Sister Erma took a backward step.

"Never before have I seen such eagerness to work. When I need someone to carry heavy barrels of sauerkraut to the cellar, I'll remember to send for you, Werner." The older woman arched a brow. "You will be just as happy to lift barrels of kraut, ja?"

The boy's smile faded, and when he hurried to go downstairs for another trunk, Sister Erma nudged my arm. "Why is he so eager to help with the baggage?"

"The outsiders have captured Werner's interest. He is no different than I was at his age. He wants to discover what life is like outside the colonies."

Sister Erma shook her head. "You should remind him that he is not to mingle with outsiders—especially with a woman. It is not proper."

Proper or not, I was afraid young Werner would eventually find some way to talk with these new arrivals. And though I wouldn't have admitted as much to Sister Erma, I was interested in the young woman and her son, as well. Not because I wanted to explore the outside world, but because I knew the heartache of losing a loved one and the feeling of desperation that sometimes followed such a loss.

I'd been only seven years old when my own Vater died, and the loss had weighed heavy on me throughout my childhood. Because of my loss, I might be able to help the boy through this difficult time. Perhaps it would be a good thing for both of us, but I would bide my time, pray for the Lord's guidance, and see if an opportunity arose when I could help him.

When we'd carried the last of the items upstairs, Sister Erma shepherded Werner and me back to the kitchen. She hadn't offered us an introduction to the boy or his mother. Although I could see the disappointment in Werner's eyes, I was certain Sister Erma didn't want to do anything to encourage Werner's ideas about the outside world.

When we were out of earshot, he groaned his disappointment. "It wouldn't have hurt her to introduce us." Pointing his thumb over his shoulder, he said, "And after all that work, she didn't even offer us a piece of plum cake."

I chuckled and shook my head. "We are not to help each other with the hope of receiving anything in return, Werner. Besides, you did not have to help. I wanted to take you to the tinsmith shop, but you insisted on going with me, ja?"

The boy ducked his head. "Ja, but I thought—"

"I know what you were thinking, but you should not be angry with Sister Erma. Her thoughts were not the same as yours. She has a meal to prepare. Can you imagine the grumbling she would hear if she announced she couldn't serve dinner on time because she was busy introducing you to the two outsiders who arrived this morning?"

Werner's frown remained. "It does not take so long to make

an introduction. I think she likes to be in charge of everything that happens in the Küche."

I gently slapped his shoulder and grinned. "Perhaps you are right, but just like Sister Erma, we have much work that needs our attention. Visiting is for when our work has been completed."

The boy's frown remained as we walked into the shop. "Our work is never finished." He picked up a broom and began to sweep the floor. "There is always another pail or kettle to make or utensils that need to be patched."

I didn't argue with him, for he was right. There were few days when we lacked work in the shop. With only three tinsmiths to take care of the needs of all seven villages, we remained busy filling orders for colanders, ladles, food baskets, and utensils of every shape and kind for the kitchen houses. In addition, washtubs, pails, and lanterns were needed by residents of the villages. When needed, the tinsmiths were called upon to fashion or repair gutters and downspouts for the houses. And there were the people from the surrounding area who placed orders for new items or brought their damaged utensils and tools for repair, as well.

With the steady flow of work, the elders had realized my need for an apprentice. When they'd assigned Werner, I had hoped he would prove to be a young man with dexterity and an ability to learn the trade.

During his first days in the shop, Werner had shown interest in the heavy equipment. He had been drawn to the bar folder, the grooving and beading machines, as well as the stovepipe formers and gutter beaders. Unfortunately, his enthusiasm far outweighed his attempts to follow my instructions in the proper use of the machinery. Then I tried to teach him how to use the braziers to heat soldering irons so that handles could be attached to the kettles, pails, and ladles. After he nearly set the shop ablaze, I decided working with fire wasn't a good choice for him, either.

My thoughts remained on the lad as I picked up a scratch awl, but before I set to work, I bowed my head and asked God to help me find some way to help Werner. If I was going to meet with success as his teacher, I'd need some divine insight and wisdom. After concluding my brief petition, I lifted my head and set to work striking a pattern into the tin. If Werner could learn to tinsmith, he would be an asset to the villages. On the other hand, if he should decide to leave the colonies, he'd need to have some way of supporting himself. I couldn't give up on him.

I'd worked for only a short time when I realized that the thrushing of the broom had gone silent. Glancing over my shoulder, I spied Werner sitting at the far corner of a worktable with his head bent low. Unable to gain a view of what he was doing, I quietly walked to his side and stared down at the figures he'd sketched on a piece of paper.

"You can draw! Why didn't you tell me?"

He shrugged one shoulder. "Brother Urbinger told me that drawing wasn't important."

I knew the schoolteacher frowned upon the children using their time for anything other than their regular lessons—and art was not included in those lessons. I didn't want to contradict the teacher, but I wanted to affirm Werner's talent. "Maybe it is not as important as your other school lessons, but I am thinking that your ability to draw might be useful here in the shop."

A spark shone in the boy's dark brown eyes. "Ja? You think so? What could I draw for you?"

"Maybe you could draw patterns for a few new cookie cutters."

He bobbed his head. "For sure, I could do that."

Though I knew Werner's ability to sketch wasn't the skill most needed in the shop, an idea flashed into my mind. Perhaps if he could complete the entire process of drawing and making his own creation into a usable cookie cutter, he would pay more heed and put my instructions to good use. If the idea worked, such a project could give him a sense of pride as he developed his skills. I smiled at the thought. There was no way to be certain if the idea was an answer to my earlier prayer, but I believed it was, so before picking up the drawings for further examination, I uttered a quiet thank-you.

CHAPTER 5

Andrea

One morning during our first week in the colonies, Brother Bosch departed after breakfast to go to High Amana to meet with other members of the *Grossebruderrat*. He had agreed to present a list of questions I'd posed regarding my father and his property.

Brother Bosch had explained that each village had a group of elders known as the *Bruderrat* who made decisions for their village. He'd also told me a little about the Grossebruderrat.

From what I understood, the population of each village determined the number of representatives who served on the Grossebruderrat. While the Bruderrat made decisions for their own village, the Grossebruderrat made decisions that affected all of the villages. So as not to show any partiality about where they would gather, the meetings moved from village to village. This month they would meet in High Amana.

"When the Grossebruderrat met in West two months ago, they chose to eat their meals in my Küche." As if remembering the event, a slight smile played at Sister Erma's lips.

The thought of serving meals to fifteen or twenty additional men caused me to cringe. "I'm sorry. I know preparing extra food must have been a burden."

As she shook her head, a wisp of graying hair floated free and danced about her right ear. "Nein! To serve the Grossebruderrat is an honor. Every *Küchebaas* is hopeful her Küche will be chosen as the one to serve the elders."

Taken aback by the stern tenor of her voice, I quickly changed my frown into a smile. "Then I am pleased they chose your Küche. No doubt they were delighted by your preparations."

"They ate as though they had never before had such gut food." A hint of pride colored her comment, so she quickly added, "But I am sure they do the same at each Küchehaas. The elders are quick to show their appreciation." She inhaled a deep breath. "I am sure all of the Küchebaases in High have been waiting with great anticipation for the last week. I will be interested to hear who they chose." She swiped her hands down the front of her apron. "Of course, they must take turns in order to prevent hurt feelings, but they have their favorite Küches in each village."

I arched my brows. "And how do you know this?"

She chuckled. "Brother Bosch has told me. Besides, they choose to eat more than once in the Küches they prefer. They eat in mine every third visit."

The older woman attempted to tamp down the pride in her voice, yet her effort didn't succeed. But I understood. Like everyone else, Sister Erma needed an occasional pat on the back—indicating her efforts were appreciated. While married to Fred, I'd longed for a kind word about my efforts to be a good wife and mother, but those words hadn't ever come.

Instead, I'd received his rancor and criticism for the meager meals I'd provided. Of course, I'd never understood how he thought I could prepare a decent meal when he didn't give me enough money for the necessities. Instead of being thankful for the potatoes and broth I would set before him, he'd heap his drunken criticism upon me. After hearing him repeat the same condemnation throughout our marriage, the words had become seared into my mind, and I carried them like a scar.

"Ja, is gut to have the Grossebruderrat eat in your Küchehaas." Sister Erma's comment pulled me from the disturbing thoughts of Fred, and I looked up to meet her intent gaze.

Before he'd departed, Brother Bosch explained that the Grossebruderrat met only once a month, so I considered myself fortunate they were meeting so soon after my arrival. Sometimes the group would forgo their meetings if the men were needed to help during planting or harvest. But this month, even though plowing had begun, the men decided to hold their council.

After the noontime meal, as I was helping Sister Erma in the kitchen, I asked, "When do you think Brother Bosch will return to West?" I didn't want to sound impatient, but I was eager to learn what answers I would receive.

"Depends upon how much business requires the attention of the elders and how easily they reach their decisions. Sometimes they discuss matters for a long time. Other times, not so long, but I don't expect Brother Heinrich will return until after the evening meal."

I sighed and hoped she was wrong. Then again, if the answers he brought weren't favorable, perhaps it would be better not to know too soon. "Do you think he will come to the Küche and speak with me or wait until tomorrow?"

Sister Erma patted my shoulder and smiled. "Who can say? For sure, not me. I do not know any more about what Brother Heinrich and the others will decide than you. If you remain busy, the time will pass quickly. Weeds are always growing in the kitchen garden. I am sure Sister Verona would appreciate your help. She is preparing the garden for planting vegetables."

"Yes, of course. I'll be glad to help her." I removed a wide-brimmed sunbonnet from one of the pegs near the back door.

Sister Erma had instructed me to use the bonnet whenever I went outdoors. "To protect you from the sun and to present yourself with modesty," she'd said.

I hadn't argued. I was pleased to have the protection. Long ago I'd learned that even when the sun wasn't particularly bright or the temperature overly hot, my fair skin had a tendency to burn. After suffering a few childhood sunburns, I'd learned to protect myself with a sunbonnet and long sleeves when working outdoors.

Sister Verona greeted me with a welcoming smile, though she didn't stop hoeing the weeds when I approached. She tipped her head to one side and peeked from beneath her sunbonnet. "You come to help me, ja?"

"Yes. Where would you like me to begin?" She pointed to a spot not far from the row where she'd been busy pulling weeds. "Carrots?" I asked, noticing the short, fernlike growth above the earth.

She chuckled. "Nein, weeds. We have not yet planted the vegetables. Once the weeds are cleared and the ground is warm enough, then we will plant." She leaned down and grabbed several of the invading culprits and tossed them atop the pile she'd already pulled. "Would be easier if the vegetables grew as fast as the weeds. I have asked the gut Lord why He made the weeds to grow so quickly, but He has not yet given me an answer." She chuckled and glanced heavenward as though she half expected the heavens to open and an answer to burst forth.

"There is another hoe in the shed." She pointed to the open door of the wooden structure. "Just inside the door and to the right."

I followed her instructions and found the hoe. By the time I returned to the garden plot, Sister Verona had completed the length of a row and begun on another. She moved with the speed of a seasoned worker, chopping weeds from the ground with expert ease. Once I set to work, I soon matched her stride. It had been years since I'd worked in a garden, but during my early years, I'd worked alongside my mother, cultivating the large garden on our farmstead. Mother had given excellent care to her vegetable garden, and I sensed Sister Verona possessed that same desire to see things grow.

"You have a very large garden." I leaned on the end of the hoe and surveyed the huge plot.

"Ja, we are most fortunate to have our garden close to the Küche. Some of the Küchehaases do not have a great deal of space around them, so their gardens are planted far away. Most of those are even larger than ours, and they have a *Gartebaas* who raises the young plants and oversees all the garden work."

"So you have no Gartebaas?"

"I am the Gartebaas, but I am also a Küche helper. Sister Marta has a much larger garden, and she grows the seedlings for our garden as well as her own. Gartebaas is her only job, so she has the time and the space to nurture the young plants, while I have neither the time nor the necessary room."

Though I didn't completely understand the assignment of duties or how such matters were determined, I withheld any further questions and continued to chop weeds. I'd been working for nearly an hour when I realized I hadn't seen Lukas lately. He'd asked to play outdoors while I was talking to Sister Erma in the kitchen, but I hadn't seen him since I'd come outside.

My heart thrummed a new beat as I ceased the chopping motion and surveyed the area. "Sister Verona, have you seen Lukas?"

"Ja, he was here a while ago. I saw him over by the pump, but I have not seen him since then. Maybe he went back into the house." Her lips curved in a delicate smile. "Maybe he hoped for another piece of bread and jam. You go and see. I will continue hoeing."

I hurried from the garden, crossed the patch of grass, and climbed the step onto the back porch just as Sister Erma opened the door. She took a quick backward step to avoid a collision. "I'm sorry." I glanced around her shoulder hoping to catch a glimpse of my son. "Is Lukas in the kitchen or maybe up in his room?"

"Nein. I have not seen him since you told him he could play in the yard. Maybe he is out by the chicken coop. Did you look there?"

I had to admit I hadn't, but I'd told him before he shouldn't go there. "No, but he knows he's to play in the backyard."

She shrugged a shoulder. "He is a boy, and they like to wander. If he is not at the chicken coop, I am sure he is nearby."

Though I worried I wouldn't locate him, I did as Sister Erma instructed. After a quick patrol along both the sides and front of the house, I rushed to the chicken coop. My spirits wilted like a flower in need of a drink. Lukas was nowhere in sight. I called his name several times, but to no avail. Fear clutched and gnawed at my insides until I thought I might lose the contents of my stomach. Instead of returning to the kitchen house, I strode to the front of the house and hurried along the wooden sidewalk bordering the dirt road. My shoes clacked on the thick boards as I passed the tailor's shop, the broom-maker's shop, the cooper's, and the furniture-making shop. At each door, I peeked in long enough to see that my son was not inside.

My gaze traveled toward the huge barns that were at least a half mile from where I stood. Surely he hadn't gone that far. I was preparing to turn around and check the shops on the other side of the dirt street when I heard laughter. Was that Lukas? I hurried toward an open door and looked inside.

The man who had delivered our trunks was standing at a workbench with his young helper. And Lukas was standing between them, laughing as though he hadn't a care in the world.

"Lukas Wilson!" I hadn't meant to shout, but my fear and anger outweighed my capacity to remain calm. Like soldiers receiving a command, all three of them swiveled toward me in unison. "What are you doing here, young man? I was worried sick about you. Didn't I tell you to stay in the backyard?"

"No." He wagged his head back and forth in slow motion. "You said I could go outside, but you didn't say I had to stay in the yard."

Fearing I might faint, I leaned against the doorjamb. Until that moment, I'd been unwilling to acknowledge my deepest fears. If something had happened to Lukas, I would never be able to forgive myself.

I inhaled a deep breath and turned a steely gaze on the tinsmith. "We have not met. I am Andrea Wilson, Lukas's mother."

He nodded. "Ja, I know. I am Dirk Knefler, the tinsmith. I am—"

Glowering, I interrupted him. "You, Brother Dirk, are irresponsible. I have been worried sick about my son. I thought he was playing in the yard but then discovered he was gone. Can you imagine the thoughts I had while searching for him?" I didn't wait for an answer but continued to unleash all the fear and anger that welled in my chest.

The three of them stared at me as though they'd been accosted by a lunatic, but I didn't care. They all needed to understand the worry their actions had caused me.

Lukas pointed to the worktable. "Brother Dirk is showing me how he uses these machines to make buckets, and big spoons, and even cookie cutters. I stayed away from the machines like he told me." He held out his hand and splayed his fingers. "See? I'm not hurt at all."

Dirk nodded. "The boy is fine. He wanted to see the machines, and I enjoyed having him here. I was teaching him some German words. Because I must do business with the outsiders, I have learned enough of your language to make myself understood. I thought it would be gut to help him with his German."

"That isn't the issue, Brother Dirk. You should have realized how worried I would be when I discovered my son was missing."

Dirk tapped Lukas on the shoulder and motioned that he should speak to his mother. "You have something to tell your Mutter?"

Lukas looked at the floor and scuffed the toe of his shoe against the wooden floor. "I told him you knew I was here."

"What? You told Brother Dirk a lie? You know better, Lukas. Why would you do such a thing?"

"All the boys my age are in school, and you were busy working. I wanted to talk to someone. When Brother Dirk asked if I had your permission to come to the shop, I told him you knew I was here because I didn't want to leave." His lower lip quivered. "I like it here and Werner and Brother Dirk are nice to me."

I knelt down in front of my son. "I don't doubt they are nice to you, but you should not tell lies. You owe Brother Dirk an apology." I lightly grasped his shoulders and turned him toward the tinsmith.

"I'm sorry I didn't tell you the truth."

Brother Dirk nodded. "I accept your apology, Lukas, but you must also promise that you will never again come here without your Mutter's permission. Do I have your word?" The tinsmith extended his hand to the boy.

Lukas shook Brother Dirk's hand. "I promise."

As I stood up, I met Brother Dirk's gaze. "And I owe you my

apology, as well. Anyone who knows me will tell you that there are very few instances when I raise my voice in anger, but—"

"Your apology is accepted, Sister. If this fine boy were mine, I would worry about him, too." He squeezed Lukas's shoulder. "And he is bright. Already he has learned some German words."

"And I've seen how they solder the buckets, too." Lukas looked at me, his eyes shining with excitement. "Since you know where I am now, can I stay awhile longer?"

Brother Dirk's lips lifted in a half smile. "It is up to you. I am glad to have him here with us. He is not a bother, and until he begins going to school with the other children, he has little else to occupy his time."

I wasn't certain Lukas would be going to school in West, so I didn't respond to Brother Dirk's final comment. Instead, I glanced around the shop. The host of items being created there was truly astonishing. Patterns of every size and shape hung on the walls, and the heavy workbenches were covered with tools and partially completed projects. While I was impressed by the obvious talent of the tinsmith, the machinery and tools could prove dangerous to a child. Still, despite my earlier accusations, Brother Dirk appeared reliable, and it was true that my son had little to occupy his time while I worked in the Küche.

"You can remain until you hear the bell ring for supper. Then you must hurry back to the Küche."

He nodded, and I thought how odd it was that our lives had become controlled by bells. The day we arrived, both Lukas and I had learned that when the bell clanged, it was time for something to happen—time to get up, time to eat meals, time to go to work, time to attend prayer services, or time to go to bed. The bells helped keep everyone in the village on schedule.

I tousled his sandy-brown hair. "If you don't return when you hear the bell, there will be no more visits to Brother Dirk's shop. Do you understand?"

Lukas bobbed his head, but it was Brother Dirk who said, "I will see that he returns on time. Both Werner and I eat our meals at the Goetz Küche, so we will go to supper together."

Lukas clapped his hands and I turned toward the door. Whether out of fear or disbelief, Werner, the young apprentice, had been silent since I'd entered the shop. As I prepared to depart, he stepped forward. "Would you please tell me about the city where you lived? I think I would like to live in a big city some day."

I glanced at Brother Dirk, assuming he would not want me to remain and keep the boy from his duties, but the tinsmith gave a slight nod. "I will tell you a little, but I must return to the Küche in a few minutes, or Sister Erma will begin to worry about my whereabouts."

Using my poor German, I explained that my husband and I had moved to Baltimore, where Fred first worked on the docks and later became a sailor on one of the large vessels.

"The work is hard and the pay is meager, but that is true of most any work, especially for the unskilled. My husband was a farmer before we moved to the East Coast. Those skills didn't help him make a living in a city that relies upon the fishing and shipping industry."

Werner's smile faded. "What other work is in that city of Baltimore? I do not think I want to work with the fishing or on a ship. Maybe I need to go to another city. I want a job that will pay gut money."

While I couldn't be sure, I feared Werner might not be the brightest young man in Amana. I looked at Brother Dirk for confirmation, but he'd gone back to work.

"No matter the place you live, without a skill, you won't earn a high wage." I glanced at Lukas, who was tracing his fingers along the edge of a large kitchen ladle. "The three of us lived in one small room on the third floor of a dilapidated building where we could barely afford to exist. The area near the docks was unsafe, and there was no police protection for us. It was a terribly frightening place to live. Not like this peaceful village. It is hard for me to explain all of the problems you will likely encounter if you leave without a proper plan for your future."

Werner's lips drooped as I related my experience, but I didn't want to give him a false impression of what he would discover in the outside world. "I would not want to return there unless I could afford to live in a much safer part of the city."

"And then you would go back?" Werner's lips lifted a bit.

"I don't know, Werner. I'm not keen on large cities. But if it is your plan to leave, you best have enough money saved to support yourself for at least several months. There's no telling how long it will take you to find work. And if you haven't some trade, any work you find will pay a meager wage."

The boy's shoulders sagged, and I knew he'd been discouraged by my comments. But I couldn't mislead him. Our life had been hard in Baltimore, and I wouldn't let him believe he could walk away from this place and easily support himself in the outside world.

I glanced at Brother Dirk as I started toward the door. His eyes shone with a look of appreciation, but I wasn't sure why. Was it because I'd taken time to speak with Werner, or was it because I'd reinforced the things he'd likely already told the boy? I couldn't be certain, but I liked this man who appeared to have a kind and nurturing heart.

CHAPTER 6

Lukas arrived at the kitchen house with Werner and Brother Dirk, but instead of taking a seat at the table where the outsiders ate their meals, he scooted in between the two men. When I crooked my finger and signaled for him to come and sit at the outsiders' table, he turned away and acted as though he hadn't seen me. For a moment I considered going across to the men's side of the dining hall and escorting him back to the proper bench, but such an act would draw too much attention.

I lifted my gaze and was met by Brother Dirk's kind blue eyes. He placed one hand on Lukas's shoulder and gave a slight nod that seemed to indicate Lukas could remain with him. Though I wasn't happy with the arrangement, I nodded and returned to the kitchen.

"Lukas has returned?" Sister Erma continued to heap boiled potatoes into large bowls as she asked about the boy.

"Yes, but he's sitting on the men's side between Brother Dirk and his apprentice instead of sitting at the outsiders' table."

"Ja, well, the two of you are not exactly outsiders. You are both living in the Küchehaas. Brother Dirk is a gut man. If Lukas needs correction, Brother Dirk will teach him the proper way of doing things."

Her comment was meant to mollify my worries, but it had little effect. Correcting and teaching Lukas was my responsibility, not a task to be assigned to some stranger. I swallowed my rebuttal and followed the other women into the dining hall, where we bowed our heads while one of the elders offered a prayer of thanks for the meal. As soon as he uttered amen, the helpers and I scurried back into the kitchen. We picked up the overflowing bowls of potatoes and green beans and the platters of roast pork to be placed on each of the tables.

The men's door leading into the dining hall opened, and I looked up to see Brother Bosch enter the room and take his regular place at one of the tables. He cast a quick glance across the room, and I wondered if he was looking for his wife. I found this custom of men and women eating at separate tables odd, but I'd soon learned that not only did men and women enter separate doors and eat their meals at separate tables, they did the same when they attended church meetings. One door for the men, another for the women. Hard wooden pews on one side of the meetinghouse were designated for men and those on the other side for women.

When I questioned Sister Erma about the practice, she explained the separation was something that had begun long ago. *"We believe that a man or woman can devote more of themselves to God if they do not have a spouse or children who need their time and will frequently fill their thoughts."*

I had been amazed by her reply, for many of the colonists were married.

Noting my surprise, Sister Erma continued. *"The elders do not prohibit marriage, but there is a year of separation once a couple has permission to wed—to make certain they are strong in their love and commitment."*

If Fred and I had tested our commitment in such a manner, I doubt he would have taken his vows. Instead, he would have headed off for Baltimore without me. The thought gave me pause. The man I thought I was marrying seemed to vanish when he started drinking in Baltimore only a few months into our marriage. If we hadn't married, I wouldn't have suffered his abuse, but I wouldn't have Lukas, either. And I would have suffered most anything for my child. Still, to wait and be sure there was a strong commitment before taking marriage vows held a great deal of merit.

When I returned to the kitchen, I drew near to Sister Erma. "I saw Brother Bosch enter the dining hall. It is a surprise he is here for the evening meal, isn't it? What do you think his early return means?"

Sister Erma scraped the last of the potatoes into a bowl and then swiped her hands down the front of her apron. "I cannot say for sure. It could mean the elders had few matters to discuss. Or it could mean they came to a quick resolution to all of the problems facing them." She shrugged her shoulders and handed me the bowl. "Take this to the men's table, and then we will eat our dinner."

While placing the bowl on the table, I kept my gaze fastened upon Brother Bosch. I had hoped he would give me some sign of how things had gone, but he didn't look in my direction. I would have to wait until later to hear how the elders had responded to my questions.

As soon as the meal was over, we all stood and the same elder offered an after-meal prayer before the men and women began to depart. Although I still needed to clear the tables, I rushed out the women's door and waited until Brother Bosch descended the steps leading from the men's door. Several men surrounded him, so I waited at a distance until they finished talking to the elder and left.

I called to him as he turned to walk away. He glanced over his shoulder and waited until I drew near. "I was hoping to speak with you about the meeting with the Grossebruderrat today. Were you able to present my concerns to them?"

"Ja, I did. The elders are sympathetic to your situation, Sister Andrea, but they cannot undo what has already occurred. Your Vater signed a contract and received full payment for his land, the house, and other buildings located on the property. We are in possession of both the contract and the receipt signed by your Vater that shows he received payment. The elders are willing for you to review the documents, if you wish." He removed a pipe from his jacket pocket and filled it with tobacco. "As for the money paid to your Vater, they have no way of knowing what subsequent arrangements he made. They suggest you inquire at his bank or with any other relatives. He may have confided in one of them. Unfortunately for you, there was no additional money due to your father. He was paid in full."

My spirits plummeted. I had hoped to hear the full sum had not yet been paid. Though I knew it was unlikely, I had hoped for some pittance to help Lukas and me begin our life anew. "There are no other relatives, Brother Bosch, and my father didn't trust banks."

"Still, you should make certain. Having received such a large sum of money at one time, he may have changed his mind. I'll see about having one of the men take you to Marengo in the next few weeks so you can check."

"The next few weeks? I hadn't planned to remain in the colonies that long."

He arched his brows. "You have someplace else you can go?"

His question dropped around my neck like a heavy weight. "No. I have no place, Brother Bosch."

His lips tightened around the stem of his pipe, then curved in a smile. "The elders said you are welcome to remain in West until you decide upon your future. There is no time limit to their invitation. We are in agreement that your situation is different from that of most outsiders who come to the village seeking seasonal work." His steady gaze radiated warmth. "While you remain with us, you will be treated as one of us."

While I understood this was a meaningful gift from the elders, I wondered what would be expected in return. "Exactly what does that mean, Brother Bosch?"

He removed the pipe from his lips. "It means you may freely interact with members of the society and that you and your son will have the same privileges as our members. If you decide you would like to attend church services, you will be permitted; if you wish to attend quilt gatherings with the other sisters, you may do so." He pointed the stem of his pipe at my clothing. "You already dress much like the rest of us. After a time, you may decide you wish to permanently make a home with us."

"That is most kind." I added my thanks for his time and hurried off before he could see the tears beginning to form in my eyes. Deep inside I had hoped that even if the elders had paid my father all that was due, they would see fit to give me some additional money so that I could be on my way—an act of Christian charity. But the charity they offered was in a different and unexpected form.

I would never earn a wage while living in the colonies. Granted, there would be a stipend at the general store for my necessities, but going to another town without money for room and board would be out of the question. Besides, who would hire me? I might find work waiting tables or cleaning rooms in a hotel, but how much money would that pay? Certainly not enough to support my son and me. Like Werner, I had no skills that would earn me a livable wage.

I returned inside and trudged toward the kitchen with a sagging spirit and an ungrateful heart. Somehow, I needed to develop a plan for my future, but how could I do anything without money?

If only my father had kept me informed about the sale of the farm and what he'd done with the funds he received. But fathers didn't share such details with their daughters. That sort of thing was meant to be discussed with sons—and there was no son with whom my father could share information.

Sister Erma looked up when I entered the kitchen. "From your downcast face, I am guessing Brother Bosch did not have gut news for you."

I hiked one shoulder. "He told me what I'd already heard. The contract was signed, the money was paid, no one knows what my father did with the money, and there is nothing that can be done to help me."

Sister Erma gasped. "You mean they are going to make you and Lukas leave?"

"Nein. Their offer was quite generous. We have permission to remain as long as I want to stay, and the elders even agreed that Lukas and I should not be treated as outsiders. Still, I don't know how I will ever be able to leave if I can't earn any money." I dropped onto a chair near the worktable.

"Who can say what the Lord has planned for you, Sister Andrea. You should pray and seek His guidance. In gut time, He will reveal what you need to know. For now, be thankful for warm food and a safe place for you and your son."

"I'm sorry. I know I sound ungrateful for all you and the others have done for us. I truly appreciate your kindness, but—"

"No apologies are necessary. I am pleased to have you and Lukas in my home, but I hope you will take my advice and ask God to guide your future."

Unlike Sister Erma, I didn't think God cared about my future. After all, I'd done my share of praying while we lived in Baltimore, and God hadn't protected or guided me back then. Instead, I'd been left to fend for myself. God had more important things to occupy His time, and I no longer put much stock in prayer. It didn't seem to change anything—at least not for me.

The following week, Brother Bosch stopped at the Küche while we were cleaning up after breakfast. "I have arranged for Brother Dirk to take you to Marengo so that you may inquire about your Vater's money at the bank. I was going to take you, but my rheumatism is causing my body to ache. You should be ready to go with him in a few minutes. Take the boy with you. Is not gut for only the two of you to go alone in the wagon." He looked at Sister Erma. "I hope this does not cause you any problems in the kitchen, Sister Erma."

The older woman continued hanging the clean pots on the hooks above the worktable. "She is a gut worker, for sure, but we will make do until Sister Andrea returns."

Sister Greta, one of the kitchen helpers who appeared to be a year or two younger than I, frowned. "With Sister Ursula already released from her duties because of her baby, it will mean even more work for the rest of us."

"Is not for you to decide, Sister Greta. I did not ask for your opinion." Sister Erma motioned for Sister Greta to continue washing dishes, and though she did as she was told, her sullen look remained.

I wasn't sure why she was angry. I'd had nothing to do with Brother Bosch's decision. The elder's announcement had come as a complete surprise to me. Since arriving, I hadn't given much thought to his suggestion that I make inquiries at the surrounding banks. Probably because I was sure my father hadn't placed the money in a bank. However, if Brother Bosch wanted to provide me with a wagon and driver, I wouldn't argue. It would be good to spend a few hours away from the kitchen.

Brother Bosch held one hand against his aching back as he walked to the door. "If you do not locate your Vater's money, Sister Andrea, you should for sure think about putting your son into the *Lehrschule*. He needs to be learning with the other children. Brother Dirk says the boy is bright and already understands much of what is said to him in German."

I appreciated the older man's concern regarding Lukas's education, but I hadn't yet committed to remaining in the colonies. I told myself it was better if Lukas didn't become integrated into the community until I was certain about our future. And I'd been doing my best to help keep him current in his studies. Brother Bosch was correct, but I simply wasn't prepared to make my decision—not yet.

Sister Erma followed me to the dining room, where Lukas was sitting at one of the tables practicing his handwriting. I stopped and touched her arm. "Why is Sister Greta angry? Have I offended her in some way?"

"Nein. You have done nothing." Sister Erma tapped her finger alongside her eye and lowered her voice. "Sister Greta has an eye for Brother Dirk. I think she is jealous that you will have his attention this afternoon. You should not let her comments bother you."

"Maybe I should tell her that I am not looking for a husband. Do you think that would help?"

Sister Erma chuckled. "Nein. I think she would deny her interest in him. I have heard her whispering with the other women. She thinks he would make her a gut husband, but I do not think Brother Dirk has an eye for her."

I didn't want Sister Greta to be angry with me, but I had no choice in this matter. Brother Bosch had instructed me to be ready when Brother Dirk arrived. I motioned to my son. "Come along, Lukas. We are going to go to Marengo with Brother Dirk."

The boy hopped up from the table and scurried across the room. "The town where we got off the train?"

I ruffled his hair and smiled down at him. "Yes. You have a good memory. You were so tired when we arrived, I didn't think you would remember the name of the town."

He beamed and straightened his shoulders. "Brother Dirk says I have a good memory, too. I have learned the names of all the machines and most of the tools in his shop. When he asks for something, I know what he wants and can fetch it for him so he can keep working. He says I've been a big help to him."

Though I doubted Lukas could provide a great deal of help in the tinsmith shop, it was good to know that Brother Dirk provided encouragement to him. After having received nothing but disparaging remarks from his father, Lukas needed affirmation, especially from a man.

"I'm very proud to hear you've been helpful."

"Danke."

Spoken in German, his simple thank-you was a reminder that whether I liked it or not, my son was becoming accustomed to life in the colonies. No matter that I hadn't yet placed him in school with the other children, he was like a sponge soaking up the customs and language in which I'd immersed him.

"You're welcome," I replied. "We don't have to say everything in German, Lukas. We're still allowed to speak English."

"But Brother Dirk says I'll learn faster if I speak in German all the time."

Before I could reply, the kitchen door opened and Brother Dirk stepped inside. "Guten Morgen, Brother Dirk," Lukas called as he rushed toward the tinsmith. I was surprised when the boy wrapped his arms around Brother Dirk's waist and asked the tinsmith a question using perfect German.

The tinsmith chuckled. "Danke. *Ich bin . . .*" He glanced at me and switched to English. "I am happy to be here, Lukas."

Sister Greta stood at the other side of the kitchen, her gaze fastened upon the unfolding scene. Her frown had been replaced by a tight smile. "*Guten Tag*, Brother Dirk." She stepped around the worktable and flashed him a winsome look. "We have a few utensils that could use repair. I would be glad to bring them to your shop later today."

"*Ach!* There is no need for you to make a trip to the shop. I can take them now. I'll leave them with Werner on our way out of town."

Sister Greta's drawn smile vanished as quickly as it had appeared. "I would be happy to—"

Before she could complete her reply, Brother Dirk shook his head and stepped forward. "Which ones need my attention?"

Left with no choice, Sister Greta gathered the utensils and handed them to him. He traced his hand over the handles and the bowls of the large spoons and ladle. "Ja, these are in need of repair. I'll bring them back to the Küche in a few days."

With a look of defeat, Sister Greta retreated to the other side of the kitchen. I wanted to say something that would reassure her but decided to heed Sister Erma's advice. Besides, with Brother Dirk present, anything I might say would cause her embarrassment.

Brother Dirk tucked the utensils under his arm. "You and your Mutter are ready for our trip to Marengo?"

Lukas bobbed his head. "Ja!"

"Yes!"

I'd enunciated the word with such force that Sister Erma turned to look at me. "Something is wrong?"

I swallowed hard and softened my tone. "No, nothing is wrong, I'm just doubtful I'll meet with any success."

"Who can say what is success, Sister Andrea? You must trust the Lord that He will see to your needs. He has taken care of you and Lukas so far, and I know He will continue to provide." She patted my shoulder. "You need to put your trust in God, not in a bank, ja?"

I didn't want to contradict her in front of Lukas and Brother Dirk, so I gave her a quick smile and followed my son and the tinsmith out the door. To my way of thinking, it wasn't God who had taken care of us but the colonists. They were the ones who had seen to our needs. Maybe Sister Erma considered it the same thing, but I didn't.

Once we'd settled in the wagon and begun our journey, Brother Dirk pushed his hat further back on his head and looked in my direction. "Sister Erma has some gut advice, ja?"

"You mean about trusting God?" Not wanting to meet his intense stare, I tightened my hold on the side of the wagon and focused on the wild flowers blooming alongside the dirt road.

"Ja. He is a gut provider, don't you think?" He lightly slapped the reins and the horses picked up their pace.

"He didn't provide for us when we lived in Baltimore—it was Mrs. Adler, a woman who lived in our building, who supplied us with enough food to keep body and soul together. And it has been Sister Erma and the elders who have provided for Lukas and me since we arrived in the colonies, not God."

Brother Dirk chuckled and shook his head. "Have you not realized that God uses people to help other people? I do not think there has been any food dropping from heaven since the Lord fed the Israelites. God places a burden on the hearts of His people to help others. What you have received has been from God. He has been at work in your life helping you and Lukas survive."

I didn't want to disagree with Brother Dirk, but in this idealistic place he'd not dealt with the harsh realities I had experienced. Where had God been when my husband hit me? Where had He been when I held my crying son because he was hungry? Brother Dirk might be correct, but I didn't want to give credit to God for food or anything else that had helped me. If God had been hard at work to help us, surely He would have provided more than Mrs. Adler's bread and jam. Surely He would have protected us from Fred's abuse. I tamped down the thought that I had been the one who'd chosen to marry Fred and leave home. Brother Dirk's argument was persuasive, but I found it much easier to blame God.

When I didn't offer a response, Brother Dirk quietly talked with Lukas about handling the horses and then offered the reins to the boy. "You try to see if they will obey."

Lukas squared his shoulders and grasped the reins. After only a moment, he looked up at Brother Dirk. "How am I doing?"

"You are doing gut. The horses are staying on the road, and that's what we want, ja?" Brother Dirk leaned back in the seat and glanced at me. "You are unhappy the boy is learning to speak German, Sister Andrea?"

This man certainly didn't hesitate to ask questions. "I'm not sure where we will be living, so I don't want him to become too accustomed to speaking German all the time."

"The boy will not forget his English so soon. I think it is gut to know how to speak more than one language. It has helped you, has it not?"

He was right. While living in Baltimore, it had been of occasional help to speak German, and now that we were living in the colonies, I was pleased I could understand what was being said—at least most of the time.

"I just don't want Lukas to think this is his permanent home when I have no idea where the future will take us."

"I think that means you don't want him to like it too much, because if you want to leave, you fear he will protest. Am I right?" He shot a grin in my direction. "You can be truthful with me, Sister Andrea. I will think no less of you if you say you do not want to remain here."

"I'm not sure what I want—and that's the truth. When I left Baltimore, I wanted to return to my father's home and provide stability for my son. Now I don't know where I belong or what I want." I hesitated a moment. "Except, I do know I want to provide my son with a happy home."

Lukas glanced at me. "I'm happy right now, Mama."

"You see? The boy is content with God's provision. I hope you will soon find the same peace in your heart, Sister Andrea."

What was it that made this man and his arguments so compelling? Was it the tenderness of his voice, or perhaps his masculine build? Or was it his strong jaw and his sparkling blue eyes? Perhaps it was the kindness he exhibited toward Lukas and me. Or maybe it was a combination of all those appealing characteristics that warmed my heart.

CHAPTER 7

The trip to Marengo had been for naught. My father didn't have any money deposited in the bank, and as far as Mr. Fellows, the current bank president, could determine, my father had never conducted any business at the Marengo bank. A lanky man with a quick smile, Mr. Fellows had done his best to help me. While we talked, he suggested that Papa might have sent the money to another relative. When I advised there were no other living relatives, he suggested Papa might have invested the money in some other venture, such as mining. I immediately disregarded that possibility.

Although some thought farming a bigger risk than wagering money at the gaming tables, my father had disagreed. He considered himself a wise steward of his money and his farm a wise investment. In truth, he didn't believe in get-rich-quick schemes or understand people who did.

As we parted company, Mr. Fellows offered to make inquiries at other banks in the area on my behalf. I thanked him and gave my permission, though I didn't believe he'd find anything. I was now certain the money had gone up in flames when the house caught fire. Then again, perhaps Father had found a safe place to hide it somewhere on the property.

Once on our way, I glanced over at Dirk. "Do you think my father might have hidden the money in the barn?"

He arched his brows and shrugged. "I do not know, but if you want to look, we can go over to the farm before we return to the village."

I nodded. "Perhaps it will set my mind at ease to know for sure."

By the time we arrived at the barn, Lukas was fast asleep in the bed of the wagon. Dirk turned and smiled at the boy before he alighted and helped me down from the wagon. "Let him rest. This will not take us long."

Together we walked into the cavernous barn. When we'd first arrived, Lukas had explored most of the main floor and discovered only a few old farm implements, but another look wouldn't hurt.

Dirk motioned toward the loft. "I will go up there and look while you see if you can find anything down here. Unless you would prefer climbing the ladder?"

His wide grin told me he was teasing. "I think I will leave that for you. I am not fond of ladders." As he strode across the barn, I began my search in the areas that Lukas might have missed.

A short time later, Dirk returned down the ladder. "There is nothing up there except some old tools. Anything down here?"

I shook my head. "No, I'm afraid not."

"Did you look in all of the feed bins?"

"There was nothing in any of them. I'm sorry to have taken your time." I was certain making this journey would put him far behind schedule with his own work.

"Do not apologize. Is best to look and then you can set your mind at ease. Better you know for sure the money is not here."

I was thankful for Dirk's kind attitude. Unfortunately, the events of this day had furthered awakened memories of the discord that had existed between my father and me. Had I been the son my father always wanted, he would likely have kept me informed of his business dealings. Then again, if I'd been his son rather than his daughter, I would have remained and worked the farm, and it would never have been sold. Throughout my early years, I'd longed for a closer relationship with my father, but as I grew older and he continued to withhold his attention, I'd given up trying to make him love me.

I had hoped Lukas would fulfill Papa's desire for a son. Deep inside, I thought he might finally love me for giving him the gift of a grandson. But that was not to be. Perhaps it was best that I'd tamped down my love for him years ago. Though his death had made my circumstances more difficult, I hadn't suffered the grief I'd experienced when Mama died. She had loved me with every fiber of her being. But Papa? He'd wanted a boy so much he'd never even said he loved me.

When I left home with Fred, Papa was incensed. He wanted Fred to remain and farm the land, and he counted it against me when we departed for Baltimore. His harsh words remain emblazoned on my heart. *You want to escape the farm. If you'd really tried, you could have convinced your husband to remain in Iowa.*

Over and over, I told him Fred was the one determined to leave. Yet my father didn't believe me. Instead, he chose to place the blame at my feet. If only Papa had understood. If only we'd resolved our differences before he died. If only I had refused to marry Fred. If only . . .

Lukas was still sleeping when we got back in the wagon and didn't wake until we neared the kitchen house. Once we rumbled to a stop in front of the kitchen and Dirk set the brake, he jumped down and helped Lukas from the wagon.

The moment the boy's feet hit the ground, he looked up at me. His blue eyes glimmered with excitement. "Since Grandpa's money wasn't at the bank, does that mean we get to stay, Mama?"

While Lukas was delighted by the prospect of remaining in the colonies, I viewed our future less enthusiastically. "We'll remain for the time being, Lukas—until I can sort everything out." In truth, there was nothing else to sort out, but I wasn't prepared to admit I had no option but to remain here. For all of our married years, Fred had made the decisions about our future. After our first year of marriage, I had longed to return to the farm, but Fred wouldn't hear of it. Now that I had the power to decide where Lukas and I would live, I didn't have the resources. A wave of sadness rushed over me as I realized the irony of my current situation. It all seemed so unfair.

I startled when Lukas clapped his hands. "Does that mean I can go to school? You said you would let me go if we stayed here." When I didn't immediately answer, he grasped Brother Dirk's large hand and tugged. "Tell her to let me go, Brother Dirk."

Brother Dirk shook his head. "Nein. It is up to your Mutter to decide what is best for you. Maybe she needs a little more time to seek the Lord's guidance about the future."

Undeterred, Lukas released Brother Dirk's hand and turned to me. "Then we should go to prayer meetings. If we go there, everyone can pray for us."

Brother Dirk chuckled. "One thing at a time, Lukas, or you will test your Mutter's patience. Give her a little time before you ask so many questions."

I was thankful Brother Dirk didn't press me to give Lukas an immediate answer. Both Sister Erma and Brother Bosch agreed with Brother Dirk: They all thought Lukas should be attending school.

Lukas danced from foot to foot, unable to contain his excitement. "Will you decide about school before Monday? Please, Mama?"

"You should listen to Brother Dirk and give me time to think, Lukas."

"Brother Dirk didn't say you should think. He said you should pray." Lukas tipped his head and looked up at the tinsmith. "Isn't that right, Brother Dirk?"

"Ja, that is true, Lukas, but your mother must then think about what the Lord reveals to her." He shot a smile in my direction. "Ja, Sister Andrea?"

"If the Lord reveals anything to me, you can be sure I will think about it, Brother Dirk."

"Aw, that's gonna take too long. I don't have anything to do while the other kids are at school." Lukas stuck out his lower lip and folded his spindly arms across his chest.

"Since you want an answer right now, Lukas, I think we should wait and see if we are still here when school reopens in the fall. The school will soon close for the summer, and it makes more sense to wait."

Dirk shook his head. "School does not close for the summer in the colonies, Sister Andrea. The children are dismissed from classes to help with the onion and grape harvests, but there are classes all year."

"All year?" The air slowly escaped my lungs. "Then you will have to wait a while longer for my answer, Lukas. I'm not yet ready for you to begin school."

When Lukas grumbled, Dirk touched his shoulder. "You should not argue with your Mutter, Lukas. You need to accept and trust her decisions. She wants what is best for you." Although Lukas didn't appear pleased, he didn't offer any further complaint. Dirk stooped down in front of the boy. "If your Mutter agrees, maybe the three of us could go fishing tomorrow afternoon. On Sunday afternoons, there is time for a few hours at the pond." He glanced up at me. "What do you think, Sister Andrea? Would you like to spend an afternoon outdoors?"

Lukas opened his mouth, but Dirk sent him a warning glance. "Let your Mutter decide, Lukas. If she doesn't want to come along, maybe she will agree to let us go alone."

I wasn't certain who appeared more hopeful: Dirk or Lukas.

"If Sister Erma does not need my help tomorrow afternoon, then we can go." I wasn't eager to fish, but the outing would be good for Lukas, and I hoped it would take his mind off of attending school—at least until Monday morning.

Instead of waiting for me, Lukas ran inside. I was thanking Dirk for escorting us to Marengo when Lukas came flying out the kitchen door. "Sister Erma says you can go fishing with us tomorrow." He beamed at me. "Isn't that good news?"

I turned and met Dirk's warm smile. "It seems we will be going fishing with you tomorrow afternoon."

"Gut." He stepped to the wagon. "I better return the horse and wagon to the barn. I told Brother William I would be back before supper. I don't want him to worry."

When I entered the house, Sister Greta was alone in the kitchen. She greeted me with an icy stare that sent a shiver racing down my neck. No doubt she'd been in the kitchen when Lukas talked to Sister Erma about the fishing expedition. I silently chastised myself. Why hadn't I thought of her before accepting Brother Dirk's invitation?

Pushing aside Sister Erma's earlier advice, I stepped to Greta's side. "Have I done something to offend you?"

Her frown deepened as she studied me for a long moment. "Why do you encourage him?"

"Encourage him? You mean Brother Dirk?"

"Ja, of course that is who I mean. Is there some other man you are encouraging, as well?"

"I'm not encouraging Brother Dirk or any other man. Listen, Greta, I have no interest in a marriage. I don't even know how long I will remain in the colonies, so you should know I'm not going to encourage the affections of any man who lives here."

Greta removed a kettle from an overhead hook and banged it onto the worktable. "If what you say is true, why are you going fishing with Brother Dirk tomorrow afternoon?"

While she emptied jars of green beans into the kettle and seasoned them with bacon, I stepped closer. "Because he offered to take Lukas. I think he is trying to help my son adjust to the loss of his father and these new surroundings."

"I don't see why you need to go along. If it is Lukas he is trying to help, then why has he included you in the invitation?"

"Maybe he hopes to help me, as well, Sister Greta. My son and I have both lost a great deal in the last months, and our lives have been in a state of turmoil."

I thought I detected a momentary look of shame in her eyes. "You may be right. Maybe his only thought is to help your son, but I think it is more than that. If you are not careful, you will cause others to suffer."

Her words gave me pause. I wasn't sure if she thought I was going to hurt Dirk or her. Or did she think I would hurt both of them? I wanted to reassure her, but I doubted anything I said would ease her concerns. And in some respects, I understood her apprehension. Dirk was a handsome man with attributes any woman would desire in a husband and father. And, truth be told, I hadn't failed to notice that he possessed the many good qualities Fred had lacked.

Perhaps Greta's unease had been aroused because I'd displayed little sorrow since my arrival. After all, I'd lost both my father and my husband. Unlike most women who would be grieving the recent losses, I'd exhibited none of the deep anguish she'd likely expected to see.

She had no way of knowing that my love for Fred had been destroyed years ago—that as I'd suffered his abusive words and deeds, I had slowly grieved the loss of the man I thought I'd married. Though I was loath to admit it to others, word of Fred's death had filled me with relief rather than sorrow, but that didn't mean I was looking for a replacement. Likewise, she had no way of knowing my father and I had been estranged for many years.

"I could use your help in the dining room, Sister Andrea." Sister Erma stood in the doorway and motioned me forward. "Be sure to season the green beans, Sister Greta," the older woman instructed before disappearing into the other room.

I followed after Sister Erma. Any further discussion with Sister Greta would have to wait until another time.

After the noonday meal on Sunday, Sister Erma bustled into the kitchen. "No need for you to stay here, Sister Greta. The dishes are washed and dried, and I won't need your help until time to prepare for the evening meal."

Greta didn't budge. "I told my Mutter I would be here all afternoon. She agreed that with Sister Ursula away, I should stay and help." Greta lifted her nose in the air and pinned me with a disapproving look. No doubt she thought my absences from the kitchen were unfair, but Sister Erma was the one who made decisions regarding who would work and who could be gone.

Shortly after we'd arrived, I'd learned that Sister Ursula wouldn't return for at least another year. She'd had a baby a year and a half ago and, like all new mothers in the colonies, was allowed to remain at home with the child for three years. Since there were junior girls who helped after school hours, I doubted my occasional absences would have any impact upon the fine meals served in Sister Erma's Küche.

Sister Erma shrugged her shoulders. "You can stay if you'd like, Sister Greta, but I'm not sure what you're going to do." On Sunday afternoons, Sister Erma rested in the upstairs parlor and read her Bible. "I suppose you can join me upstairs." When Sister Greta made no move to follow the older woman, Sister Erma stopped and turned. "Unless you want to remain in the kitchen so that you will see Brother Dirk."

A tinge of pink colored Greta's cheeks as she rushed across the room. "If you are sure you do not need my help, then I will go home." She yanked open the door and disappeared without another word.

Sister Erma raised her brows and shrugged. "I am going upstairs. You and Lukas have a gut time fishing."

I sent Lukas outside to watch for Brother Dirk. While I sat at the table and waited, I wondered if working alongside Sister Greta in the future would prove uncomfortable. If we were going to work in harmony, I needed to find some way to ease the discomfort. Perhaps I could discover whether Brother Dirk had any feelings for Greta. Who could say—maybe he'd never considered her as a possible mate.

As I continued to give the matter some thought, I became pleased with the idea of arranging a match between them. If Brother Dirk wanted a wife and Greta wanted a husband, what could be better? I sat back in my chair and closed my eyes, savoring the idea of Greta showering me with her thanks.

"Mama!" Lukas ran inside and tugged at my hand. "I've been calling you."

I'd sent Lukas outside to watch for Brother Dirk and had become so engrossed in my imaginary matchmaking, I hadn't heard him. "I'm coming." I jumped up and followed him outside.

Brother Dirk stood on the porch holding fishing poles in one hand and a pail in the other. He handed the pail to Lukas. "You can carry this and I'll carry the poles."

Lukas peered inside the bucket and removed a tin can as we headed off toward the pond. "How come you brought this empty can?"

"The first thing we need to do is find some worms. I didn't have time to dig for them this morning before going to meeting. Once we locate some, you can put them in the can for safekeeping."

"I'm not afraid to pick up worms, are you, Mama?" Lukas marched between us, his thin body rippling with excitement. "How far is it to the pond, Brother Dirk? Do you think we'll catch lots of fish? Will we take them back to the house and cook them?"

Brother Dirk laughed as he shifted the fishing poles to his other hand. "You have asked so many questions, I am not sure which ones we should answer."

Lukas skipped a short distance ahead of us and then turned

around. His eyes sparkled with anticipation. "You should answer all of them."

Brother Dirk glanced at me. "I suppose I will go first. We will be at the pond in about ten more minutes. I'm not sure how many fish we will catch. It will depend on how hungry they are and if they like the worms we offer them." His brows dropped low on his forehead and he hesitated a moment. "What was the other question for me?"

"Will we take our fish back to the house and cook them?"

"You have a gut memory, Lukas." Brother Dirk grinned. "If we catch the fish, I think we will toss them back in the water to live another day. To feed all the people who eat in our Küche, we would need many more fish than we can catch this afternoon."

"Maybe not. Mrs. Adler read me a story from the Bible about how Jesus told the fishermen where to put their nets and they caught more fish than ever before. Do you think if we asked Jesus to help us, we could do that?"

Brother Dirk nodded. "Maybe. The Bible does say that with God all things are possible. Of course, He expects us to do our part, too, so you need to begin digging for worms."

My son's remarks surprised me. He'd never told me that Louise read him Bible stories, but it did make sense. Louise wasn't one to hide her faith under a bushel basket. Since Lukas hadn't been hearing much about the Lord from anyone else, she'd apparently decided she would teach him. During my time in Baltimore, I'd admired Louise's commitment to the Lord. Even though my own faith had diminished, I'd been impressed by Louise's dedication and faithfulness.

A soft breeze whispered through the sandbar willows and a stand of cottonwoods growing near the pond's edge. With each gust of wind, the cottonwood branches bent low and dipped their coarsely toothed leaves into the shallow water. Nesting birds twittered overhead as if to protest our noisy arrival.

Brother Dirk spread a blanket beneath a tree close to the water. "I didn't think you would want to help us dig for worms, but you can watch us from here."

Lukas had already removed a garden trowel from the bucket and set to work. I smiled as Brother Dirk suggested moving to a damper area of ground and looking beneath some stones.

Moments later, Lukas squealed with delight and lifted a fat worm high in the air. "Look at this one, Mama! He's going to catch us a big fish for sure."

"I believe you're right, Lukas. Maybe you should ask Brother Dirk to put the worm on your hook and into the water right away."

"Nein." Brother Dirk shook his head and laughed. "Lukas is going to learn how to put the worm on himself."

He stooped down beside Lukas, and I watched the two of them with their heads close together, Lukas giggling as he attempted to gain control of the wiggling worm.

Once they'd thrown their lines into the water, Brother Dirk strode back toward where I was sitting. "Would you like to move closer to the water to be near enough to see when Lukas catches a fish?"

"Yes, thank you." I wasn't quite so sure there would be any fish caught, but I didn't want to take a chance.

An unexpected shiver raced up my arm when Brother Dirk grasped my hand and helped me to my feet. Our gazes locked, but I forced myself to look away as a gentle rush of warmth spread through my body. What was happening to me? I pulled my hand from his grip and hurried toward the water as though I'd been hit by a round of buckshot.

I had intended to make a match between Brother Dirk and

Greta. Now I wasn't certain I wanted to see them together. Confusion gripped me as I stared at my rippling reflection in the pond. Greta was right. I needed to be careful or I would cause others to suffer—and if I didn't exercise caution, my son and I might very well be included among those who would be hurt.

CHAPTER 8

Throughout the night I wrestled with the unexpected feelings I'd experienced with Dirk during the day. The laughter we'd shared when Lukas caught a fish, a look we'd exchanged over a cup of water, the warmth of his smile as we'd enjoyed bread and cheese. All of these things had stirred emotions that I'd long since thought dead. I didn't want emotions to rule my future. That's what I'd done with Fred. Too late, I'd learned that making decisions based upon emotions could prove unreliable. Choices needed thought. *And prayer.*

Surprised by the notion that I should think about praying, I sat up in bed. Why had I been struck by the idea that I needed to pray about my choices? Almost as quickly as I wondered why I'd had the thought, I remembered the many people who had expressed the need for prayer before making choices—beginning with my mother. When I'd been determined to marry Fred, one of her first questions was, *"Have you been seeking God's will to know if Fred is the man you should marry?"* And when we prepared to depart for Baltimore, she'd asked, *"Have the two of you prayed about where you should live? Do you truly believe God is leading you to Baltimore?"*

Though neither of us had given the matter any prayer, we'd both nodded our heads. The result of that choice hadn't been good—for either of us. Since then, Mrs. Adler had professed her need to pray before making decisions. So had Sister Erma and Dirk. Maybe that's why I felt this quickening in my spirit. Or maybe this urge to seek Him actually came from God. The thought daunted me. Could such a thing happen to someone like me? Someone who had never before thought to pray before making choices? I wasn't sure, but I closed my eyes and asked God to direct my path.

"Please show me what I should do about Sister Greta. How to make things better between us. I don't know what to ask about Brother Dirk, but I'm uncertain about my future. I don't want to hurt him, and I don't want to hurt my son, either. Show me what I should do, and I'll do my very best. Amen."

It wasn't a prayer full of beautiful words; it wasn't even a prayer that expressed all the turmoil running through my mind. But Mrs. Adler had said that God knew our every thought. If so, He was aware that I needed help. He understood I didn't want to hurt the people who had extended charity when I'd had nowhere else to turn.

I inhaled a deep breath and leaned against my pillow. Come morning, I hoped my prayer would result in clear direction, for I didn't want any further tension between Sister Greta and me.

When the early-morning bell tolled a few hours later, I forced myself out of bed. I doubted I'd slept for more than an hour, but working in the kitchen meant rising early. There were some kitchen houses where workers came early to start the fires and begin breakfast preparations, but Sister Erma would have none of that. She liked the predawn ritual of starting the fires, grinding the coffee beans, and fetching the water.

Since my arrival, pumping water had become my chore. Though I didn't mind the task on these early spring mornings, with the onset of winter, my enthusiasm would no doubt diminish. The thought gave me pause. Would I be here come winter?

The aroma of fresh coffee was already drifting through the kitchen when Sister Greta arrived. "Guten Morgen." Her lips curved in a cheery smile. "Is going to be another beautiful morning, ja?"

I nodded my head, surprised by Greta's bright smile and friendly greeting. "I think you're right."

The darkened sky hadn't completely given over to a new day, so only a narrow slice of reddish-yellow sunlight shimmered on the eastern horizon. Yet it was enough to announce another spectacular day. A day that would be quite similar to the one Lukas and I had enjoyed with Dirk.

I cautiously eyed Sister Greta, wondering what to expect. Her cheerful attitude had caught me by surprise, and now I waited, pleased yet suspicious of her friendly behavior. While I pared the potatoes that Sister Erma would fry for breakfast, Sister Greta donned her apron and set to work slicing several loaves of bread that had been delivered by the bakery wagon only minutes before she'd arrived.

"So how did Lukas enjoy fishing yesterday?" Instead of looking up, she continued to methodically slice the bread.

"He was a little disappointed with his catch, but he had a good time."

She stopped slicing the bread. "He did not catch any fish?"

"Oh yes. He caught three, but he said a prayer before he began fishing and then expected the Lord to provide enough fish to feed the entire village."

Sister Greta laughed—not a mere chuckle, but a genuine laugh. "He should be thanking God for those three fish. I must remember to tell him that most people consider themselves blessed if they catch even one fish. Some of the boys say there are no fish left in that pond."

"There are at least three, since Lukas and Brother Dirk threw all of them back." Being careful not to cut myself, I sliced the potatoes into thin pieces that would cook rapidly in the hot grease. "Even though he was disappointed in the number of fish they caught, Lukas had a good time."

"And you? Did you have a gut time, too?"

I didn't want to lie, but I feared that being truthful might spoil the tentative camaraderie we'd now established. And then I felt that same nudge I'd received last night—the one that had caused me to pray. Only this time, it prodded me to tell the truth.

After exhaling a slow breath, I nodded. "Yes, I had a very nice time. Thank you for asking."

We were standing side by side at the worktable where no one else could overhear our conversation, so I decided it was time to clear the muddy waters between us. I'd need to choose my words wisely. Yesterday I could have easily told her I had no feelings for Dirk—today, that answer wouldn't be completely truthful. At the moment, I wasn't sure what I thought about Brother Dirk or my future in the colonies, but I needed to know if Sister Greta hoped to win his heart.

"Are you hopeful that you and Brother Dirk will one day have a future together as husband and wife?" My voice faltered as I asked.

"As husband and wife?" She shook her head. "Nein. Is that what you thought when I said you should be careful?"

"Wasn't it?" I arched my brows and met her intense stare.

"Nein. I have no interest in marrying Brother Dirk, although my Vater would be pleased if that happened. He has always thought we should marry, but I have feelings for another man." She retrieved platters for the bread and then returned to my side. "My feelings for Brother Dirk are those of an abiding friendship. He is more like an older brother to me, so I would not like to see him hurt. That is why I said you should be careful."

"I see." The tension in my shoulders eased. "Does your young man live here in West?"

She nodded. "Ja. His name is Benjamin Lutz. He works at the flour mill. He lives in another part of the village, so he doesn't eat at our Küche. We have been friends since we were in *Kinderschule*, and our affection for each other has increased through the years, but my Vater is not very fond of Benjamin."

"Why is that?"

"My Vater says Benjamin still acts too much like a child, but that is not true. Benjamin likes to laugh and have fun, but he works hard and he would be a gut husband for me." A rosy blush colored her cheeks. "And we love each other very much."

I smiled at her. "That's the most important thing."

"Ja, that's what I told my Vater, but he says he does not think Benjamin will ever be serious enough to be a gut husband."

Tears clouded her eyes and tugged at my heart. "We should pray that your father will see Benjamin as the fine young man you say he is." Where had that idea come from? The words were out of my mouth before I'd even given them consideration.

"Danke, Sister Andrea. To know you would pray for me means a great deal." She touched her hand to her heart. "I think if we both pray, maybe God will work a miracle for me, and my Vater will change his mind."

I wasn't so sure my prayers were worthy of a miracle, but perhaps God would answer Sister Greta's petitions.

After stacking the slices of bread on heavy china platters, Sister Greta stepped to the other side of the table and began forming sausage patties. "Sister Erma told me your husband died before your return to Iowa, but she did not say how long you had been a widow." Greta hesitated and glanced up, likely wanting to see if I found her comment painful or offensive. Still, she'd likely find it odd that a woman who hadn't been widowed for even six months would find pleasure in fishing with another man.

"My husband died at sea, and I was notified shortly before I returned to Iowa, so I don't know his actual date of death."

She looked away. "I am sure it has been difficult for you and Lukas."

I wasn't certain how much I should tell her, but decided that she might better understand my circumstances if she knew about the past. While we continued to work, I told her a little of what had transpired between Fred and me—not the ugly details, for I didn't think she needed to hear those—but the fact that our marriage had not been happy.

"So you do not feel the same grief many wives might feel at such a loss?"

I shook my head. "No, but I hope you will not think ill of me. I never wished for Fred to die, but in some ways his death has made life easier for Lukas and me."

"I cannot imagine what it would be like to fear being harmed by the man who has promised to love and protect you. And then you come home and discover your Vater has died. Such difficult times you have had." She wrung her hands together. "I am pleased we talked. Now I think I better understand."

Before I could ask Sister Greta exactly what she better understood,

Sister Erma bustled into the kitchen and eyed the pile of potatoes. "Those potatoes will never be fried in time for breakfast if we don't get them in the skillets." Soon lard was sizzling in several large skillets. The grease crackled and popped as the older sister heaped potatoes into the pans. "Is gut you cut them thin, Sister Andrea." The large metal lids settled with successive clangs as she placed them atop the skillets. After a quick glance at the worktable, she shook her head and pointed at the sausage patties. "Ach! The sausages are not cooked, either? What have you two been doing out here all this time? Even the applesauce is not in the bowls."

I offered an apologetic smile. "It's my fault, Sister Erma. We were talking and lost track of the time."

"I am glad you two are becoming friends, but our work comes first." She pointed to the empty bowls. "Hurry and get those filled, Sister Andrea. And Sister Greta, you need to fry the sausages."

We bobbed our heads in unison and scurried to complete our tasks before the breakfast bell rang. My heart soared at the thought of having a friend. Sister Erma had extended every kindness to me and to Lukas, but Sister Greta was closer to my own age. Asking her questions wouldn't be as difficult.

"Guess what, Mama!" Lukas rushed into the kitchen that afternoon. I stooped down and pulled him into my arms for a hug. He wriggled backward and looked into my eyes. "You need to guess. It's something exciting."

I remained in my crouched position. "Let me see—something exciting. You got to pet one of the horses."

His light brown curls flew into disarray as he shook his head. "That's not it. Guess again."

I scrunched my forehead into tight wrinkles and pretended

to be contemplating my next response. "You made a new friend today?" He shook his head and waited. "Brother Dirk is going to take you fishing again?"

He bit back a smile. "Not fishing, but Brother Dirk said he would take us somewhere on Sunday afternoon."

Sister Erma leaned across the worktable. "Can I play this game?" When Lukas bobbed his head, she smiled and pointed her finger to the east. "He told you about the lambs over in East Amana, ja?"

Lukas jumped from foot to foot, his enthusiasm contagious. "Can we go, Mama? Can we? Brother Dirk said it is the very best thing to see in the springtime. Even Werner told me almost everyone goes to see the lambs. Can we go, too, Mama? Please?"

I chuckled and lightly grasped his shoulders. "You need to take a breath, or I'll never have a chance to answer." His eyes flashed with excitement. "I'll talk to Brother Dirk, and if I can be away from the Küche on Sunday afternoon, then we can probably go."

He lunged forward and locked his thin arms around my waist. "Oh, thank you, Mama, thank you!"

"I said *probably*, Lukas. You need to remember that nothing is certain just yet." I leaned back and looked into his eyes. "Understand?"

"Yes, but I know we'll go."

I arched my brows. "And just how do you know that?"

"Because when you are with Brother Dirk, you're happy."

Sister Erma tipped her head to one side and stared at my son. "He has a gut understanding of people, ja? Strange since he is so young."

"Yes." I nodded my head but didn't elaborate.

There was no need to dredge up the past and speak ill of the dead. No need to tell Sister Erma that the boy had feared his own father. No need for her to know that a crooked smile or cocked eyebrow could create as much fear as a pounding fist. When Fred had been in the house, Lukas had remained alert and watchful for any changes in his father's disposition. Such behavior caused the boy to seem older than his years. Because of his father's erratic actions, Lukas had also learned to assess the conduct of others. And most of the time his instincts proved correct.

Lukas wasn't interested in Sister Erma's comments. Instead he squeezed my hand. "I told Brother Dirk I would return before supper and tell him what time he should come for us on Sunday."

I perched my hands on my hips. "Oh, you did, did you? Even before I say we will go, you're asking what time he should come for us?" I did my best to look stern, but I didn't fool Lukas.

He giggled. "I knew you would want to see the lambs as much as me. You do, don't you?"

I ruffled his hair. "Yes, I want to see the lambs, but first we must see what Sister Erma has to say about our outing." I glanced over my shoulder at the older woman.

"I think I would like to go along, too. I have not been to East to see the lambs for two years now."

Lukas clapped his hands. "So we can all go?"

Sister Erma nodded. "Ja, but you should tell Brother Dirk we will first need to do dishes after the noonday meal. I think we can be ready by one thirty."

Moving quietly along the rear worktable, Sister Greta scooped up the rows of dried noodles and placed them in a kettle of boiling chicken stock. When she turned in our direction, her face glistened with a sheen of perspiration. "I would be happy to take charge of cleanup after the noonday meal on Sunday. The two junior girls will be here to help."

"Ach! You know they don't want to do much on Sundays. They are eager to go and play games. The minute I leave, they will convince you to let them run off and enjoy themselves. Sister Margaret is on the schedule for Sunday. She will see that they complete their work."

"For sure, she will keep them busy." Sister Greta picked up a large wooden spoon and stirred the boiling noodles. "The three of you should leave as soon as you finish eating. That way you will have plenty of time. My Vater was there last week. He stopped to visit with Brother Richter, the head shepherd in East. It seems there have been lots of twins born this year, and some triplets, too."

After hearing of the multiple births, Lukas squealed with delight. "Please, Mama. Let's go right after we eat. I want to be there all afternoon and see as many lambs as I can."

Sister Erma turned toward Lukas. "You can go and see a few lambs over at the main barn here in West. Did you know we have some Shropshire sheep in our village, too? Not so many like in East, but we have a small flock, and Brother Josef might even let you feed one of his lambs. I don't think they would let you do such a thing in East. They are much more protective of their sheep."

Sister Erma's remark served as a reminder that the residents in each of the villages thought their own village was the best one in which to live. Although a strong bond existed among the seven villages, each one maintained its own unique character and sense of pride. For Lukas to think any other village more inviting could be considered an insult to those who lived in West.

Lukas's smile disappeared. "But I thought you wanted to go over to East, Sister Erma."

"Ja, I do. But you should remember we have some things in West they do not have in East. Our village has one of only two flour mills, and we have a general store that is larger and better than most. Maybe not so grand as the one in Main Amana, but very gut. You should not forget we have gut ponds for fishing, too. And here in West, we have one of only three tinsmiths in all of the villages." She folded her arms across her waist. "And I am sure our tinsmith is better than the other two."

Sister Greta cleared her throat. "Of course, we don't want to sound boastful. Such pride would be frowned upon by the elders. Isn't that right, Sister Erma?"

"Ja, you are right. Is not proper to boast. But to speak well of the place where you live is a gut thing." Her smile slipped a notch when she saw Sister Greta frown. Sister Erma inhaled a deep breath. "East has better flocks than we have in West." After choking out the compliment, she met Sister Greta's steely gaze with one of her own. "There! Does that make it better?"

Sister Greta covered her mouth but couldn't stifle a giggle. Soon Sister Erma and I joined in and filled the room with rollicking laughter. Lukas stared at us as though we'd all three lost our senses. Sister Erma was the first to regain her composure. With the corner of her apron, she wiped a tear from her cheek and waved toward the door. "You can tell Brother Dirk we will go with him to East as soon as we have eaten the noonday meal on Sunday."

I smiled as Lukas grabbed his straw hat and bolted for the door before anyone could stop him. Though I hadn't expected such a strong reaction, my heart soared at the thought of spending some time with Dirk.

CHAPTER 9

After Sister Erma and Lukas departed for Sunday meeting, the two girls assigned to help during meeting set to work washing the breakfast dishes while I worked with Sister Margaret preparing the noonday meal. There were always fewer workers on Sunday mornings, and Sister Erma rotated the schedule. She wanted each woman to have an opportunity to attend Sunday meeting as often as possible. Since I hadn't yet decided to attend church services, my presence in the kitchen allowed the others more frequent church attendance. I liked the rotating schedule, for it gave me an opportunity to become better acquainted with each of the sisters.

This would be my second time to work with Sister Margaret on a Sunday morning, and I had been pleased when Sister Erma told me she was scheduled to work. Sister Margaret was close to Sister Erma's age and had been working in the Küche since she'd turned fourteen years old. Her abilities far surpassed my own, and I was pleased to have her take charge.

She ran her finger down the posted menu and shook her head. "There will be some unhappy children today."

I peeked over her shoulder. "Liver dumplings?"

"Ja. The little ones complain when we serve them, but we cannot waste." She shrugged her shoulders. "When the butcher brings us liver, we prepare and serve liver. You want to learn how to make them?"

If I ever left the colonies, I doubted liver dumplings would be a dish I'd prepare. On the other hand, as long as I was living here, I might as well learn. "I'll be glad to follow your instructions."

She gave a firm nod. "Gut. I like that you are willing to learn something new. First we must grind the liver and pork."

While I tightened the metal meat grinder on the edge of the worktable, Sister Margaret put both of the other girls to work peeling potatoes. "Once they are pared and in cold water, you need to grate radishes for the radish salad." She started toward me but stopped and turned back to the girls. "Before you start the potatoes, go to the cellar and bring up eight quarts of applesauce. Be careful not to drop them."

One of the girls lifted a lantern from the hook as they walked outside. Inside the kitchen the loud creak of the cellar doors caused me to shiver. I'd made only one trip into the clammy storage rooms beneath the kitchen, and that had been with Sister Erma by my side. I wondered if the girls were as frightened as I'd been when I descended the wooden steps into those dank, shadowy rooms. I would much prefer grinding meat.

I'd finished grinding only half of the liver when I stopped for a moment and rubbed my upper arm. Sister Margaret stepped closer. "Your arm is hurting, ja?" She nudged me aside. "I will take a turn. You help the girls. They cut off half the potatoes when they try to peel them." She *tsk*ed and turned away.

The two girls grinned at me. They'd made little progress and Sister Margaret was correct in her assessment. If they continued cutting so deep into the potatoes, there wouldn't be much left to cook. After observing for a few moments, I stopped them and picked up a knife.

I could see they were both fearful of cutting themselves, and they weren't properly grasping or turning the potatoes. "You need to hold it like this and control the movement with your thumb as you slowly turn the potato." I finished mine and then handed the knife to one of the girls. "Now you do it." I had to correct her only one time, but soon she had gained confidence, so I turned to the other one. Though it took her a little longer, they soon were doing a good job.

Once the pork and liver had been ground and the potatoes set to boil, Sister Margaret sent the two young helpers to the dining room. "Make sure the silverware, napkins, and plates are in place, the pitchers filled with water, and the small bowls filled with jam. Open the jars of applesauce and pour the contents into the two large crocks."

"Which ones?" the girls asked in unison.

Sister Margaret sighed and pointed to a shelf. "Those two. Now hurry along, and when you've finished, come and see if I need you to do anything else." She'd barely had time to take a breath before she waved me forward.

"Come over here, Sister Andrea. We need to mix the dumplings."

The ground liver and pork, along with bread crumbs, eggs, flour, minced onions, and seasonings, were placed in a large bowl. While I began to combine the mixture, Sister Margaret soaked chunks of dry bread in water and then pressed out the excess water.

Once completed, she poured the dampened bread into the liver concoction. I continued the mixing process while she prepared the dressing for the radish salad.

Instead of forming the liver mixture into balls, I dropped the mixture by teaspoonfuls into the boiling salted water. Sister Margaret said it was faster, and I think she was right. However, some of my dumplings were much larger than others, and I hoped they wouldn't be raw inside. If that happened, I was sure there would be complaints.

A short time later, the bells rang and soon Sister Erma bustled into the kitchen and donned her apron. I glanced up from my dumpling duties. "Meeting was good?"

Sister Erma nodded and then looked in the boiling pot of water. I was thankful she didn't mention the fact that the dumplings weren't uniform in size. She arched her brows. "The extra bread crumbs to top the dumplings?"

"They're browning in the oven," Sister Margaret said. "We'll put them on the dumplings right before we serve. I didn't want them to get cold."

"Gut. I knew I could count on you, Sister Margaret."

Moments later, the meal was complete. The browned bread crumbs were sprinkled over the liver dumplings. Fresh parsley dotted the buttered boiled potatoes, and the sliced radishes were mixed with creamy dressing. Nutmeg was grated over the applesauce, and heaping plates of bread and bowls of jam were in place on the tables.

What had taken all morning to prepare was devoured in fifteen minutes. And those fifteen minutes had been far too long for Lukas. I barely had time to remove my apron before he appeared in the kitchen and announced Brother Dirk would return with the wagon in fifteen minutes.

Dirk

Sister Erma, Sister Andrea, and Lukas were waiting on the wooden sidewalk in front of the kitchen house when I arrived with the wagon. Lukas bounced from foot to foot while I helped his mother and Sister Erma into the wagon.

I reached out and gently squeezed the boy's shoulder. "Would you like to sit up front between your Mutter and me?"

"Ja!" He bobbed his head with boyish enthusiasm.

I hoisted Lukas onto the seat, and after I climbed aboard, the boy glanced over his shoulder. "Will you be lonely sitting by yourself, Sister Erma?"

The older woman chuckled. "Nein. I think I will be fine sitting by myself for a short time. Besides, with no one on either side of me, I'll have a clear view of all the scenery along the way." She pointed in the distance. "Did you see the woodpecker over there, Lukas?"

He twisted in his seat and looked back and forth. "Where? I don't see anything."

Sister Erma folded her hands in her lap and grinned. "I told you I have a much better view."

We'd gone only a short distance when Lukas tugged on his mother's sleeve. "I didn't like those liver balls we had for lunch, Mama. They didn't taste good. Let's don't have them anymore."

I gave the reins a light slap and chuckled as I recalled feeling the same way as a young boy. "There are foods that each of us likes better than others, Lukas, but there is one rule that is very important, so I want you to listen closely."

The boy gave him a wide-eyed stare. "What?"

"Never tell the cooks you don't like their food. If you insult the cooks, they might decide they don't want to cook anymore, and then what would we do?" Using my free hand, I patted my stomach. "We would all become very hungry, and that would not be gut." I leaned a little closer to the boy. "Maybe the next time we have liver dumplings, you should fill up your plate with more potatoes and salad and take only one small dumpling, ja?"

Instead of trying to convince Lukas the liver would make him grow big and strong, I'd used a technique my father had used with me: Provide a solution rather than a lecture.

Lukas nodded. "Maybe I won't take any dumplings at all. That would be even better."

"Now that you know you do not like them, you could do that. But you should always try new foods before you make a decision. Sometimes we can be fooled by the way things look."

Lukas pinched his nose between his thumb and forefinger. "And the way they smell. Cabbage stinks when it is cooking."

I glanced over his head at Sister Andrea to gauge her reaction. She shrugged her shoulders and nodded. "He's right. I'm glad it tastes better than it smells."

"And our Amana cabbages are the best for making sauerkraut, too," Sister Erma put in.

I patted Lukas's leg before he could comment on the sauerkraut. Sister Erma might not be offended if someone didn't like liver dumplings, but she would be slow to forgive any criticism of her sauerkraut.

I decided a change of topic might be in order. "Did you tell your Mutter what we've been making at the shop?"

Lukas straightened his shoulders. "Werner drew some new patterns and we're going to make them."

"Patterns for what?" Sister Erma asked.

"Some kettles that are shaped different than the old ones, some new cookie cutters, and some other stuff—I don't remember everything." The boy twisted around to face the older woman. "You can come and see at the tin shop. Can't she, Brother Dirk?"

"Ja. I am sure Werner would be glad to hear any of your ideas or suggestions for new kitchen tools, Sister Erma. His new designs have been well received by some of the outsiders who do business at our shop. I have seen his confidence begin to grow since he's been helping with new designs."

"I do not know that I could suggest anything new, but I will come by and see his latest designs. Anything that makes our work easier in the Küche is a gut thing. Maybe he should figure out a tool to help shape our liver dumplings. What do you think about that, Lukas?"

Lukas wrinkled his nose at the suggestion. "I think cookie cutters would be better."

Sister Erma chuckled and then pointed to the fields we were passing on our journey. "All of this land belongs to our people, Lukas. More than twenty thousand acres."

"How many sheep?" The boy wiggled around to look at her.

Sister Erma chuckled. "Sheep. That is all you want to think about. I am sure the head shepherd in East can tell you, but I have heard the men say there are more than three thousand sheep. Not so many cows or hogs, and a lot less horses, don't you think, Brother Dirk?"

I nodded. "Ja, less than three hundred horses. So we are very fortunate that Brother Herman gave permission for us to have a wagon and horses today."

Lukas frowned. "I think three hundred is a lot. How many did my grandpa have on his farm, Mama?"

"I'm not sure, Lukas. Probably fewer than ten."

A gust of wind whipped through the trees, and Lukas clapped

his hand atop his straw hat. "How come you need so many in West, Brother Dirk?"

"The land and animals are located in all seven villages, not just in West. There are more people, so we need more of everything." I cocked an eyebrow. "Understand?"

"I think so."

As the wagon rumbled along the dirt road, the warmth of the sun lulled Lukas, and he rested his head against his mother's shoulder. Once the boy went through a growing spurt, he'd soon be taller than Andrea. Her features were delicate, yet she possessed strength of spirit and protection that many women lacked. There was no doubt her love ran deep for the little boy sitting beside her. And though his hair was several shades lighter than hers, they both possessed the same curly locks—his untamed, hers pulled into a tight knot near the nape of her neck. Only occasionally did a wispy curl pull loose and frame her pale complexion. I forced myself to turn away when she glanced in my direction.

As we neared Lily Pond, she squeezed the boy's arm. "Look, Lukas."

Lukas stared in wonderment at the lily pads that floated atop the water and gave the appearance of a hovering green carpet. He strained forward for a better look. "Are there fish in there?"

I nodded my head. "Ja, there are fish. The lily pads cover the water and help to keep it cool for the fish in the summer."

Lukas stared at the pond for a moment longer. "But it would be hard to fish in there. I think my line would get tangled in the lily pads."

I winked at him. "Then it is gut you don't have to fish here."

Andrea pulled him close and he returned his head to her shoulder. How wonderful it would be if this could last. Since his arrival, I had become more and more attached to Lukas. More and more often, I had to remind myself that he was not my son. Yet the thought of living the rest of my life with this boy and his mother was never far from my mind. I could envision sharing my love with them, helping Lukas become a strong and upright young man while also enjoying Sister Andrea's endearing qualities.

Andrea's devotion to her son had first won my admiration, but I now found other things that kept drawing me closer to her. I had noticed the way she treated Sister Erma with much respect and love, and I'd watched the way her faith seemed to be blossoming here in the colonies. Most of all, I'd noticed she did not speak ill of her deceased husband, although I was certain she had cause to do so. Never had I met a woman so full of grace and inner strength.

I'd done my best to squelch thoughts of Andrea, but I'd been unsuccessful. No doubt she would eventually leave, but even that thought hadn't been enough to curtail my imagination. I had forced myself to remain mindful she was still in mourning, and I pushed aside the idea that the elders would likely find her an unsuitable match for me. After all, she'd not yet decided to become one of us.

Thus far, those thoughts hadn't impacted my prayers. In truth, I'd decided that if faith the size of a mustard seed could move a mountain, I had enough faith to keep Andrea and Lukas in West Amana. God knew the desire of my heart. God knew the depth of my faith.

Lukas roused to attention as we neared the sheep barn in East. "Hurry, Brother Dirk. Make the horses go faster."

I laughed at Lukas's enthusiasm. At his age, I'd felt much the same way when my mother and father had brought me to see the sheep. In fact, I still enjoyed the sight. I pulled back on the reins, set the brake on the wagon, and alighted. I held my arms out to Lukas and set him on the ground before helping Sister Erma down. My hands lingered on Sister Andrea's waist a moment longer than necessary as I lifted her down from the wagon, and the pink in her cheeks told me she'd noticed.

A crowd was gathered near the far end of the barn. While we were walking, I pointed in that direction. "There's a door down there where the sheep can move in and out. Sometimes when the lambs are very young, the shepherds keep them close to the barn. But some of the ones that are a little older will be running around."

Lukas grasped Sister Erma's hand. "Come on, Sister Erma. Let's see if we can count more lambs than Mama and Brother Dirk."

"I think we've received a challenge. Shall we hurry to catch up with them?" Sister Andrea nodded toward Lukas and Sister Erma, who had picked up the pace.

Dirk shook his head. "I think we will have plenty of time. If not, we'll have to count some of them twice." Sister Andrea's mouth dropped open, and I laughed. "Don't worry. I was only joking."

Wild flowers bloomed along the path, and the scent of hay carried on the breeze as we continued toward the barn.

Andrea grinned in response to my words. "I want you to know how much I appreciate the time you take with Lukas. He admires you very much, and you've had a wonderful influence upon him. He tells me he is going to be a tinsmith when he grows up."

Her words pleased me, but it was her charming smile that warmed my heart. "Having him at the shop has been gut for both of us. He makes my days brighter. And so do you." She stopped midstep and stared at me. I wanted to bite back the words, but that would be impossible. "I'm sorry. I should not have said that."

"Perhaps not, but it is nice to know that Lukas and I brighten your days."

I hoped she would say that I brightened hers, as well, but given her time of mourning, that was too much to ask. For now I would be content and continue to pray.

CHAPTER 10

Summer 1890
Andrea

As the months passed and summer arrived, I continued to pray about the future. Although I hadn't received an answer, I'd become more accustomed to the idea of remaining in West. In truth, my options were limited. Still, there were women just like me who somehow managed to survive in the outside world, women who were mothers and didn't have a husband to provide financial support. On a couple of occasions, I'd given thought to striking out on my own. Whether real or imaginary, my fears and the fact that Dirk would no longer be a part of my life stopped me.

Besides, where would I go? I didn't want to leave Iowa, for silly as it seemed, I still hoped to find the money my father had received for his farm. An inheritance wasn't of importance to anyone who lived in the village. No one here worried about money. Their daily needs were met. And so were mine.

Some days, the thought of leaving never crossed my mind. I

enjoyed the daily routine of working with the other sisters in the kitchen, and the provision of food and shelter had truly saved us. Lukas and I were happier in the colonies than ever before. Perhaps my contentment was a sign that I was supposed to stay here.

I had finally agreed that Lukas should further his education, so he had begun school last month. My decision pleased Lukas as well as Brother Bosch, Sister Erma, and Brother Dirk. We all agreed that continuing to deprive him of education or the friendship of other children was unfair.

At Lukas's urging, we'd been attending evening prayer meetings for the past six weeks. Being among people who lived their faith had stirred my desire to learn more about their beliefs. I decided prayer meetings would be a good place to begin that process. As I listened to the heartfelt prayers and concerns of the various members, a desire rose within me to read my Bible and pray more regularly. Though I was certain my faith didn't match that of the members, I'd drawn closer to the Lord in recent days, and perhaps Lukas had, too.

However, I soon realized it was time spent with Brother Dirk rather than the prayer meetings themselves that had motivated Lukas's attendance at the meetings. Each evening he would sit beside Brother Dirk and imitate his every movement. While I was delighted to see the two of them enjoy their time together, I worried Lukas was becoming too attached to the tinsmith. And so was I.

Each evening after prayer meeting, Dirk would join us at the Küche for a cup of coffee and a piece of leftover cake or pie while Sister Erma would tat and tell stories of life in the colonies when she'd been a young girl. No matter how many times he'd heard the accounts, Lukas would beg for the ones that made him laugh—tales of schoolboys hiding frogs in a girl's desk or chasing a skunk under the schoolhouse.

"Those boys always wanted the skunk to make a smell so the teacher would dismiss us from class, but one day he saw what they were doing." Sister Erma clucked her tongue and shook her head.

"And then what happened?" Lukas always asked that same question.

She winked at him and leaned close. "He told them if the skunk fouled our schoolhouse, he would send everyone home. Everyone but those ornery boys." She laughed until tears ran down her cheeks. "Those boys, they never did that trick again."

As Lukas's boyish features radiated with delight, memories of joyful times with my own parents flooded back—memories of a happy childhood. A childhood filled with love and warmth. This life in the colonies was giving my son a peek into a world he should have enjoyed since birth, one he'd never before experienced. Instead of criticism, anger, and a desire for personal possessions, he could see the true evidence of a good home and family: love. Perhaps my contentment and my son's happiness should be answer enough for me.

After I sent Lukas upstairs to get ready for bed, I grabbed my shawl and walked Dirk out. I wanted to thank him for helping my son adjust and helping him find his smile again. But before I could speak, he turned and said, "What was it like?"

I cocked my head to the side. "What was what like?"

"Your childhood." He smiled beneath the light of the full moon. "I saw your wistful expression, and I began to wonder what it was like for you. We were practically neighbors back then, and I wonder if our lives were similar or different."

His sincere desire to hear my answer caught me by surprise. Fred had never acted interested in what I was thinking or feeling, but Dirk genuinely seemed to want to know.

I pulled my shawl tighter. "I enjoyed a childhood that was like most, I imagine. There were chores, but there were many days of fun, too. We went sledding in the winter, and wading in the summer. I remember picnics with watermelon and making apple pie with my mother."

"So it was a happy time for you?"

"Yes. Very." I swallowed hard. "I was loved and I knew it."

"Why is there sadness in your voice now?"

I didn't answer right away, but Dirk didn't press. After several long moments, he trailed his hand down my arm. "Sister Andrea, your Lukas knows he is loved." His voice was so gentle, my heart squeezed. "No matter what has happened before, he is happy now. It is all over his face. You are a gut mother—a very gut mother." He squeezed my hand for a second before pulling away. "Gut night."

"Good night." My voice cracked when I spoke. "And thank you, Brother Dirk, for everything you've done—for us."

Lukas had plunged pell-mell into this new life, and soon after he began attending school, he begged to attend children's church on Sunday mornings. I'd given him permission, but I still wasn't ready to make that leap. The short and informal evening prayer meetings were one thing, but attending Sunday morning meeting might send a signal that I'd decided to make a permanent home in the colonies. A message I wasn't yet prepared to deliver.

On more than one occasion, Dirk had encouraged me to attend Sunday meetings, but I'd declined. I used my kitchen work as an excuse. Though he appeared disappointed, I'd gone on to explain that most evenings after Lukas went to bed, Sister Erma and I would sit side by side on the horsehair-stuffed sofa. By the light of the flickering kerosene lamp, we would take turns reading the Bible aloud. When I had questions regarding a particular

Scripture, she never failed to stop and explain. I hastened to add that for now, I preferred learning about God and His ways in the privacy of Sister Erma's parlor rather than in the church. Although I'd braced myself for the type of angry response Fred would have given, Dirk had merely smiled and agreed to respect my wishes. He'd even agreed that meeting alone with Sister Erma might be best for me right now. I still marveled at his kind ways. Perhaps one day such kindness would erase memories of Fred's ruthless behavior.

Sister Greta lifted another large handful of green beans onto her tray. "You are deep in thought, Sister Andrea. Something is bothering you?"

I shook my head. "No, I'm fine."

How long had I been silently sitting beside her cleaning green beans? Along with two of the other sisters, we'd come out to the back porch to prepare the beans for canning. The breeze provided a respite from the kitchen's daunting heat.

She nudged me and leaned close to my ear. "You are maybe thinking about Brother Dirk?"

I tightened my features into a mock frown. "You should not say such things where others can hear," I whispered.

Her eyes danced with mischief. "I think everyone can see how you two feel about each other. They don't need me to tell them."

Sister Erma cleared her throat. "Is not polite to whisper, Sisters. If you have something private to say, wait until the rest of us are not sitting nearby." The reprimand was gentle, yet clear and candid.

Sister Greta leaned forward on her chair and peeked around me. "Please forgive me, Sisters. I did not intend to be rude."

Sister Erma lifted the wooden tray from her lap and dumped the cleaned green beans into a large kettle sitting beside Sister Greta. "Intended or not, you need to be mindful of others in the future, Sister. Your apology is accepted. When you have finished, bring the kettle inside and we will blanch the beans."

The thought of returning inside to sterilize jars and blanch beans made me long to remain outdoors. With the woodstove burning hot enough to boil the large kettles of water, the temperature in the house would be more stifling than the July heat outside.

Once we were alone on the porch, Sister Greta continued her earlier conversation. "I think you should begin attending Sunday meetings. When Brother Dirk requests permission to court you, I am sure the elders will refuse unless you are considering becoming a member of the society."

I sighed. "There is plenty of time before I must decide whether I will become a member. As for Brother Dirk courting me—you seem to forget that my period of mourning hasn't yet ended."

"Ja, but the marriage was not gut. You told me he was cruel to you and Lukas. The elders might not require you to wait for your entire mourning period. Who can say? Brother Dirk could ask."

"No. It isn't proper, and if Brother Dirk and I are meant to have a future together, it will happen without asking to break the rules."

In her excitement, the tray of beans nearly slipped from her lap. "So you do think you will marry him? I knew it! The two of you are perfect for each other."

"Stop! You are drawing too many conclusions. We have never spoken of marriage, and whether we are perfect for each other remains to be seen. He is a wonderful man and Lukas is most fond of him."

Greta giggled. "And so are you—I can tell. I don't know why you insist upon waiting. Has anyone told you that here there is a year of separation after a couple is pledged to marry? Think about how much time you are wasting with all the waiting around. And I am sure Lukas would like to claim Brother Dirk as his Vater."

Although I remained doubtful about my future, Sister Greta didn't share my misgivings. She had already determined that I would marry Dirk and remain in the colonies. I wondered if she had spoken as candidly to him about our future. I decided it would be better not to know. I didn't want to be embarrassed the next time I was with him.

"We'd better hurry with these beans or they are going to fall behind in the kitchen. Sister Erma wanted to finish at least fifteen quarts before we start supper preparations."

"Ja, well, I do not think we have enough beans for fifteen quarts today. She always sets lofty goals." Sister Greta lifted the tray from her lap and stood. "Of course lofty goals are better than none at all, ja?" She dumped the tray of beans into the kettle. "You are coming with us to the pond after prayer meeting?"

I nodded. As the summer days grew warmer, several of us would walk to the pond after prayer meeting. Lukas and one of the other young boys would skip rocks while the rest of us sat beneath the trees and enjoyed the cool evening breeze. I had grown to enjoy this time together and had formed friendships with several of those among the group. The latest addition to our number was Benjamin Lutz.

I wasn't sure why Benjamin hadn't joined us until recently but guessed that Greta worried someone might tell her father. Perhaps she'd now gained enough trust in the group and believed her secret was safe with us. Right or wrong, Greta continued to fool most of the sisters who worked and ate in our kitchen house. They continued to think she hoped to marry Dirk.

No doubt her father believed the same thing, for each evening after prayer meeting, he cheerfully granted her permission to join the group. Should he discover that it was Benjamin Lutz who kissed her cheek and held her hand, I don't think he would have been so cheerful. While I worried her father might learn of the indiscretion and ban Greta from future outings, she didn't think beyond her next meeting with Benjamin.

I couldn't fault her desire to spend time with the young man—he was everything she'd told me: good-looking and kind as well as fun-loving. His antics made all of us laugh, especially Lukas and his young friend, Peter.

After I had finished cleaning my remaining tray of beans, I dumped them into the kettle and carried it inside. Sister Erma strode toward me and looked in the kettle. "That's all of the beans?"

I didn't miss her frown. She'd obviously expected more. "Yes."

"I told you we didn't pick enough for fifteen quarts." Sister Greta stood beside the stove, her face damp with perspiration.

"This will have to do for today. We'll do twelve quarts and the rest we will cook and serve for supper. Tomorrow we will pick more." She motioned to Sister Greta. "Take those beans out of the hot water. You can begin to fill the jars." She waved me forward. "Blanch those beans in the hot water."

Positioning herself at a nearby worktable, Sister Greta placed a wide-mouthed funnel in the first jar and carefully filled it with the blanched beans. Once she'd filled the jars, she poured some of the cooking water into each jar.

Sister Erma marched around the room like a commander leading a military unit. "Be careful you leave head space in those jars, Sister Greta. And use the wooden spoon handle to make sure you release any air before you put the lids on." She waved at Sister Margaret, who had been enlisted to help with the canning. "Make sure the water is boiling in the canner. Sister Andrea, those beans have been washed enough—get them into the hot water to blanch or we will be here all night."

By the time we'd completed packing and canning the green

beans, I didn't think any of us would have enough energy to cook supper. The jars sat in neat rows, a testament to our hard work and a declaration of what lay ahead—a hot summer of canning and preserving the garden's bounty.

"What about supper, Sister Erma? Do we need to begin preparations?" Using the corner of her apron, Sister Margaret wiped the perspiration from her forehead.

"Ja." Sister Erma bobbed her head. "Slice off some ham, and I'll scramble eggs. There's applesauce. And we'll cream some potatoes. It won't take long."

I turned toward the back door. "I'll go outside and peel the potatoes."

"I'll get the eggs and milk." Sister Greta followed close on my heels.

Sister Erma perched her hands on her ample hips. "And I will stay in here with Sister Margaret and clean up the kitchen."

Both of us rushed outside before she could change her mind.

That evening several of us walked to the pond. Lukas ran ahead with Peter while the adults followed behind.

Dirk stepped to my side as we moved along the narrow path toward the water's edge. "I am pleased you made it through your first day of canning vegetables in Sister Erma's Küche."

Together, we spread a quilt on the soft grass beneath the branches of a leafy red oak. "There were times this afternoon when I wasn't sure I would." I sat down on the blanket and waited until he dropped beside me. "To be honest, I'm not looking forward to tomorrow. Sister Erma thinks we can do even more tomorrow. I'm not so sure." I glanced toward the water. "Lukas! Not so close to the edge."

"The water level is down in the pond," Dirk said. "I don't think you need to worry too much." He scooted closer and grinned. "I have a better view of him if I sit a little closer."

"What do you think the elders would say if they saw you sitting so close to me?"

"I cannot say for sure, but they would probably be worried that you will convince me to leave the colonies." Keeping his gaze fixed on me, he leaned against the trunk of the tree.

"And would you? Ever leave the colonies?" I arched my brows and waited for his answer.

"Nein. I do not think I would ever leave here. I am not so gut with change." He yanked a piece of grass from the ground and threaded it through his fingers. "Does it make you sad or angry to hear me say I don't want to live elsewhere?"

"No, but I think if you truly wanted to live somewhere else, you would adapt to the necessary changes. I never thought I could live in a tenement house in Baltimore, but I did. And I honestly wasn't certain I could become accustomed to living here, but I have."

He laced his fingers through mine and a shiver raced up my arm.

"It pleases me to hear you say you have become accustomed to living here. More than anything, it is my hope that you and Lukas will want to stay and that one day we might become a family. I know I should not be speaking of these things, but I can no longer hold them inside. I hope I have not offended you."

My heart quickened. "You have not offended me." I swallowed hard, wondering if I should tell him that my feelings for him had intensified throughout the past months. To say such things would be unseemly and yet . . .

"Sister Andrea! Sister Andrea!"

Dirk jumped up and trotted toward the path. "Someone is coming from the village."

Moments later, a teenage boy I recognized as one who ate in our Küche appeared on the path. "Brother Bosch says you need to come to the doctor's office, Sister Andrea. He said you should come right now." The boy turned to leave.

"Wait! Why do I need to go to the doctor's office?"

The boy stopped and glanced over his shoulder. "I do not know, but I think you should hurry."

Fear gripped my heart. What could be so urgent? Lukas was right here with me, and I could see that he was fine. Why would the doctor need to see me? I swallowed hard. Had Sister Erma suffered an accident? Dirk placed his arm around my shoulder to steady me before he called Lukas.

As the boy hurried toward us, Dirk squeezed my shoulder. "We'll go together. Everything will be fine."

CHAPTER 11

Never before had the distance between the pond and the village seemed so far. I attempted to hasten my step, but my feet had a will of their own. And Lukas, upset by our early departure, cooperated even less than my feet.

When I tugged on his hand, he pulled away and stopped. "I want to stay with Peter. I can come back with Sister Greta and the others."

"Stop arguing, Lukas. I'm not leaving you behind. I've explained that we need to hurry. Now please come along." My frustration mounted when he didn't heed my command. He crossed his arms over his chest, glared at me, and jutted out his lower lip.

Dirk placed his hand on the boy's shoulder. "Lukas, it is important you do what your Mutter asks. Growing into a gut man means that you must sometimes put aside your own wishes and do as others ask. It also means that you do what you are told by your elders."

Lukas's shoulders slumped and his head hung forward until his dimpled chin touched his chest.

Dirk stooped down so that they were eye to eye. "There will be other times when you can play. Your Mutter has told you it is important for her to go back to the village, so you should not detain her. Such behavior only makes it more difficult for her." Dirk stood and extended his hand. "We will go now, ja?"

Lukas looked up and bobbed his head. "Yes." He trotted to my side. "I'm sorry, Mama."

"Your apology is accepted, Lukas. Now let's hurry."

As we rushed on, the dry grass and twigs crunched beneath our feet, and I inhaled the perfumed scents of summer. By the time we arrived at the edge of town, the lower half of a carrot-colored sun had descended in the western sky.

Lukas remained close on our heels as we stepped onto the wooden sidewalk and continued toward Dr. Karr's office. Perspiration trickled down my neck, and my stomach tightened when we arrived at the office door. I inhaled a deep breath before pushing down on the heavy metal latch. My nerves were frayed, and I startled when the bell overtop the door jangled to announce our presence.

The doctor appeared in the doorway between his office and the small waiting room and flashed a quick glance among the three of us. He crossed the room and stopped in front of Dirk.

"I think it would be best if you left, Brother Dirk." The doctor had lowered his voice to a whisper.

Dirk looked at me, and I didn't miss the concern in his eyes. "I told Sister Andrea I would stay with her. Has something happened to Sister Erma?"

The doctor ran his fingers through his untamed thatch of gray hair. "Nein. A relative of Sister Andrea has arrived. He is ill and wishes to see her."

Excitement bubbled deep within and I gasped. "My father? He's alive?" I rushed past the doctor, but before I stepped into the room, I stopped short.

"Hello, Andrea."

Dread and alarm replaced my excitement. I swayed, unable to believe my eyes. "Fred? Is that really you?" Worried I might faint, I leaned heavily against the thick doorframe and stared at the figure lying on the cot.

"A course it's me. Who'd ya think you was comin' to find?" His jaw was covered in thick whiskers, and his cheeks sunk inward like hollow bowls. Dark circles rimmed his eyes and his dark hair was matted and unkempt. "You ain't lookin' too happy to see me, but I 'spect that's cause you're surprised. Come closer."

When I didn't move, he gestured me forward. His once muscular body had wasted away. All that remained was an emaciated frame and his sunken, angry eyes. I moved a few steps, but not close enough that he could grab me.

"Mr. Brighton told me you were dead. I questioned him at length, and he assured me there was no chance you were alive." I had hoped to sound strong, but my voice quivered.

He'd sensed my fear and his lips curled in a cunning smile—the one he had always flashed at me when I hadn't obeyed him. The one that always preceded a blow to the cheek or arm. He enjoyed seeing my fear. "Come on over to the bed, Andrea. You can see I ain't strong enough to get up."

I couldn't deny he looked weak. Truth be told, he looked like he was knocking at death's door. But I'd lived with Fred for too many years, and I'd endured too many of his tricks and mean ways to trust him or anything he said. "If you're so weak, how did you make the trip from Baltimore to Iowa?"

"Ya haven't changed a bit, have ya, woman? Still haven't learned to respect yer husband." Before I could answer, his eyes darted to the doorway. "Is that my son hidin' over there behind his mama's skirts?" Fred scooted a bit higher on the bed and lifted his gaze. "And who are you?" His eyes glistened with suspicion.

I turned to see Dirk standing beside Lukas. He nodded at Fred. "I am Dirk Knefler, the tinsmith here in West Amana, and a friend of Sister Andrea and Lukas."

"*Sister* Andrea!" A hacking cough followed Fred's harsh laughter. When he finally regained his breath, he glared at Dirk. "She ain't nobody's sister. This here's my wife and that's my boy hangin' on to yer hand." He crooked his index finger. "C'mere, Lukas, boy."

Terror shone in the boy's eyes and he took a backward step. I nodded toward the waiting room. "You go in there with Brother Dirk. I want to talk to your father alone."

"Don't you be tellin' him to go in there when I already told him to come here." Fred's harsh reprimand was followed by another coughing spell. Ignoring him, I escorted Lukas and Dirk to the other room.

I glanced over my shoulder before stepping close to Dirk's side. "Would you take Lukas back to Sister Erma at the kitchen house? Tell her what has happened and ask if she will look after Lukas until I return home. Fred and I need to talk. It will be better this way."

Deep lines furrowed Dirk's brow. "Do you feel safe to be alone with him?"

"I think he is too weak to move out of the bed. Besides, I know to keep my distance, and Dr. Karr will be in his rooms. I'll call for him if I feel threatened in any way."

Dirk nodded. "I have so many questions to ask, but I know this is not the time." Sadness filled his eyes, but he smiled at Lukas. "Let's go back to the Küche and see if Sister Erma has any more of that gut coffee cake we had for dessert."

Lukas started for the door, then hesitated and gestured to me. "Why did he come back, Mama? He's going to spoil everything. I thought you said he was dead. Why did you lie to me?" He'd been careful to keep his voice low, and I was thankful Fred hadn't heard him.

I stooped down to face him, my heart breaking. Most children would be thrilled to have their father suddenly reappear. So would most wives. But that wasn't true for Lukas, and it wasn't true for me. My son was right. Fred was going to ruin everything. I shivered at the thought.

"I didn't lie, Lukas. That's what Mr. Brighton told me. After I talk to your father, I'll know more about what happened. You go on now." I leaned forward and kissed his cheek. "Everything is going to be fine. I promise."

I wasn't positive everything would be fine, but I would do everything in my power to protect my son from Fred's temper. I waited until Dirk and Lukas departed before I returned to the other room. I carried a straight-backed chair and placed it across from the bed—far enough that Fred couldn't reach me, but close enough that I could see his eyes. Mama had always said the eye was the window to the soul, and I'd learned to watch Fred's eyes during our years of marriage.

Fred looked toward the door. "Where's the boy?"

"I sent him back to the house where we live. He needs his sleep. He has school tomorrow."

"School? You're lyin' to me. It's the middle of summer. There ain't no school this time of year. You ain't foolin' me, Andrea. I know your tricks. You think you're gonna keep him away from me."

"I'm not lying. The school remains open all year here in the colonies. If you don't believe me, you can ask the doctor." I stood, but he waved me back to my chair.

"There's time enough to find out about school, but I ain't happy about ya disobeyin' me. I said I wanted to see the boy."

I sat down in the chair and inhaled a cleansing breath. "I think the two of us need to talk in private before you visit with Lukas. I have a lot of questions."

"Yeah? Well, I have a lot of my own questions, like where's the money Mr. Brighton gave you?" He fell back against the pillows. "And don't lie to me. I know he gave you that money from the widows' fund."

Disgust and anger welled up inside me until I thought it would boil over. Instead of concern over how we'd managed to survive during the many months since he'd disappeared, Fred was only worried about the money I'd received from the widows' fund.

"How do you think I paid for train fare and food to travel from Baltimore, Fred? When I arrived in Iowa, I didn't even have enough money to pay for a hotel room. Had it not been for the kindness of the colonists, we would have been sleeping in a barn." I inhaled a breath and leaned forward. "You said I haven't changed, but I have. You're the one who hasn't changed, Fred. You still think only of yourself."

"You're feelin' mighty brave while you got these folks to protect ya and I'm not able to get out of this here bed, but that's all gonna change soon as I get well." Perspiration dripped from his forehead, yet he yanked a blanket tight to his neck and shivered.

No matter how ill he might be, Fred hadn't forgotten how to intimidate and threaten.

He waved toward the door. "That doctor told me your father's place was burned out and he died in the fire. That true?"

"Yes. Now that I answered one of your questions, I'd like to know how you found me. How did you get here when you're so sick?"

"I traveled by train and wagon, same as anyone else coming from the East. 'Course I had to depend on good-hearted strangers to lend me a hand. Lots of folks took pity on me. All ya gotta do is give 'em a sob story, and they can't do enough to help ya." He shifted his head on the pillow. "On the other hand, them train conductors expect ya to give 'em something extra for their help. I wasn't about to give any of them the little money I had left. Once I got to Marengo I hired a wagon and driver, but when we were almost to the farm, I was in such pain I was out of my head, and the driver brought me to the doc's office here in West." His lips curved in a cruel grin. "Now wasn't that a stroke of luck?"

I opened my mouth to comment, but he narrowed his eyes and gave me a warning look. From past experience, I knew I best not interrupt. Even in his weakened condition, I feared him.

"'Sides, I knew you'd come back to your pa's farm. Where else would ya go? I was determined to find ya, 'cause I'm gonna need to be cared for. You're my wife, Andrea. You got an obligation to me. I come down with malaria while I was away." He pointed to his legs, which were covered by a crisp white sheet. "My leg got broke and ain't healed right, and I have a gash in my side that has some sort of infection. If ya don't believe me, you can ask the doctor."

His story didn't explain the fact that another sailor saw him washed overboard, but I knew he would grow angry if I peppered him with questions. Nevertheless, if he expected to gain my sympathy, a list of his ailments wouldn't be enough. "If you've come back thinking I can support you, you're wrong."

"You can sell the farm. Don't matter if the house burned. The land is worth a lot of money, and I ain't ever gonna be able to farm again."

135

There was no end to his self-serving behavior. "My father sold the land years ago, Fred. There's no land and no money. You came back here for nothing."

He clenched his jaw and pinned me with a hard glare. "I don't believe you."

I shrugged. "It doesn't matter what you believe. It's the truth." Though I didn't relish the thought of explaining all that happened since leaving Baltimore, I decided it would be easier simply to detail our experience rather than submit to Fred's interrogation.

When I finished, he rubbed his palm against his whiskered jaw. "So ya been living here with these fanatics ever since ya left Baltimore?"

"They aren't fanatics. They are good Christian people who saved us when all was lost. Their help and encouragement provided the shining light Lukas and I needed—and continue to need."

"Shining light? Well, I'm here now, so you can ferget about any shining light coming yer way." He sneered at me. "Yer my wife and we're gonna find out more about the farm. I think there's something fishy about them owning your father's land. We can probably prove your father never signed the deed. I bet they forged it. He wouldn't have sold it to these people. I won't believe it."

"It doesn't matter what you believe, Fred. He sold the land, and it's legally a part of the land holdings of the Amana Society. I told you the money is gone."

He shook his head. "I'm not willin' to accept that. Soon as I'm well enough, we're gonna find that money and then head west." He motioned to his leg. "Ain't never gonna be able to return to sea, so headin' west and gettin' a fresh start makes good sense. I hear there's lots of money to be made out there."

I stared at him, unable to believe my ears. He must have been delusional. Did he truly believe what he was saying? Maybe I should let him believe he'd find the money and I'd leave with him. Right now I didn't have the energy to argue. I felt like I was spinning in a whirlwind. I had a husband once again. I'd made vows to honor this man, but how could I? I needed time to think. I needed time to pray. I needed God's help.

"I'm going to go and speak to the doctor about your care, and then I'm going to go back to the kitchen house where Lukas and I are living. I work all day, so I won't be back until after prayer service tomorrow evening."

Sister Erma would doubtless give me permission to leave the Küche and visit with Fred after we cleaned up after meals, but I wouldn't ask. I would need every free minute to seek advice from Brother Bosch, Dr. Karr, Dirk, and Sister Erma. Visiting Fred tomorrow evening would be soon enough. In fact, it would be far too soon.

"Here ya are with yer husband who's been brought back from the dead, and all ya want to do is run off. You and that Dirk fella got somethin' going on?"

"You were never dead!"

"Maybe not, but ya thought I was, so it's the same thing."

"It is *not* the same thing." I gritted my teeth and pushed up from the chair. "I'll see you tomorrow evening."

"A kiss for yer husband?"

I shook my head and spoke with more strength than I felt. "No, Fred, there will be no kiss. Things have to be different here. I have to see you've changed. Good night." I hurried back to the parlor and calmed my ragged breathing before I tapped on the door leading to Dr. Karr's rooms.

The door opened and Dr. Karr motioned me forward. "Come in, Sister Andrea. We should talk."

His wife sat across the room with her mending. "Sit down over here." She patted the chair beside her.

Once I'd settled, Dr. Karr leaned forward. "Did your husband tell you he contracted malaria while he was at sea?"

I nodded. "Yes. How was it possible for him to travel across the country with all his problems?"

The doctor shrugged. "Where there is a will, there is a way. He must have been eager for a reunion with you and his son. He said he was in better condition before his departure, but he has been unwilling to explain how he came by his injuries."

I sighed. Fred hadn't been eager for a reunion with me—he'd had no place else to go. Like me, he'd expected to return to my family's farm, and like me, his plans had gone awry.

"In order to treat him, it will be best if he remains here until I can determine whether the Warburg's tincture will once again control his malaria. He tells me he quit taking the medicine before he left Baltimore. He also suffers from a terrible infection in his side." The doctor folded his hands together. "I cannot tell you what success I will have with his treatment. He is very sick, but I will do my best."

A huge dose of relief mixed with a small amount of guilt and fear washed over me. I shouldn't be thankful my husband's condition would prohibit him from coming near me, but I was grateful.

"Thank you, Dr. Karr. Is there anything I should do to help with his care?" I silently prayed he would reject my offer.

"Nein. My wife and I are accustomed to caring for those who need extra attention. You have your work at the Küche, and we have our work here." His eyes shone with kindness.

Only time would tell if Fred would heal—or if the doctor could withstand my husband's offensive behavior. As for me, God had provided the time I needed to think and pray, and I intended to make good use of every minute.

Fred Wilson

I rested against my pillow and watched Andrea walk out of the doctor's office. Durin' our separation she'd changed—and not in a good way as far as I was concerned.

Dealin' with physical pain was one thing, but it looked like Andrea and Lukas were set on causin' me a whole different kind of pain. Not the physical kind, of course, but the worrisome pain that comes when you lose control of people and circumstances. I didn't like that idea, not one bit. Andrea and the boy would once again need to learn the lessons I'd already taught 'em. Lukas wouldn't be too hard to manage, but with the protection of all these religious fanatics, Andrea might rebel when I tried to bring her down a notch or two. 'Course once I could get them out of this place, they'd both learn to toe the mark again. A well-placed slap could work wonders.

While in Martinique, I didn't have to worry about forcin' a woman to do my bidding. I closed my eyes and let images of my Caribbean beauty, Neyssa, dance through my mind. She hadn't needed to be taught how to please a man. I'd met her the first time our ship sailed from Baltimore to Martinique, and she was a genuine wonder. On the voyage home, I'd thought about nothin' but her. Neyssa had everythin' I wanted in a woman. She was beautiful, happy, and willin' to do my biddin'. When we set sail, she cried and said she'd be waitin' for me to return—and she was.

She'd picked up a list of arrivals from the shippin' office, and when we docked in Martinique months later, she was waitin' for me. That same bright smile and those same open arms that I'd lusted for ever since I'd left her. Those long days in the warm sun while we were in port were even better than I'd imagined. Neyssa's charms lured me and it didn't take long before she'd convinced me to remain in Martinique. But stayin' behind caused a whole set of new problems.

Over a few days and a lot of liquor, Neyssa, my shipmate John Calvert, and I developed an idea—a plan that was foolproof as long as John did his part. I never was sure if he decided to help because of our friendship or due to his drunken stupor, but it wasn't important. Once he agreed, I refused to let him go back on his word.

The two of us boarded the ship at dusk and signed in, but findin' a way to disembark after boardin' the ship and signin' the crew's list wasn't easy. If it wasn't for some good luck and craftiness, I wouldn't have made it back to Neyssa. Necessary repairs to a damaged dinghy provided the opportunity. Night fell and I lay hidden beneath a canvas as John and another buddy lowered the dinghy to the men waitin' below. Lucky for me, they placed the dinghy alongside several others in dry dock. I remained in the dinghy until I was sure the men had gone.

Under cover of darkness, I made my escape. I wasn't far from Neyssa's shack when my foot lodged beneath an aboveground tree root. As I dropped to the ground, my leg twisted and I heard an undeniable snap. A village healin' man did his best to pull the leg back into alignment, but it didn't work. The leg mended at an ungainly angle that rendered a permanent limp and left me in constant pain.

Durin' my convalescence, Neyssa was patient, but her open arms and sweet disposition didn't last. Once I was able to get around, she revealed her true nature. I discovered it wasn't me she liked so much as her own desire to leave the island and see other parts of the world—in particular, America. She'd heard sailors talk about the money that could be made in America, and she now wanted a new and better life. One where she believed she could find a rich husband who would buy her jewels and fancy dresses.

At first, I thought she was jokin' with me, but after weeks of her yammerin', I knew she didn't care about me. Did she really think I would take her to America so she could look for a rich husband? Stupid woman! I shoulda known better, but she'd tricked me with her feminine wiles. Yet I had the last laugh and tricked her in return. I had her fetch a list of arrivin' ships and told her I'd return once I figured out how we could board a ship that was due in port the next day.

Instead, I told the ship's captain that I could handle the work same as any other hand. At first he wasn't convinced, but I played on his sympathies and told 'im my injury had occurred at sea. That fact was enough to gain his pity and get me on the ship back to Baltimore and leave Neyssa to find herself some other sailor. Time would tell if she'd ever convince anyone to smuggle her aboard. I doubted she would, but I also doubted the wench would ever quit tryin'.

In the end, she'd proved to be just like Andrea—unwillin' to do my bidding.

"How is the pain, Mr. Wilson? You are feeling some better?"

I'd been lost in my thoughts and hadn't heard the doctor enter the room. "A little, but I'd be happy to have a little more of that laudanum."

The doctor removed his pocket watch and shook his head. "It's too early for more laudanum. You should try to sleep. Sleep is sometimes the best medicine." He shifted his leather bag to his right hand. "I must leave for a time to call on some of my patients. My wife is not here. Is there anything you need before I depart?"

"Naw, I can manage."

"Gut, then I will see you before too long."

I leaned back and once again let my thoughts wander. Strange for a man like me to be livin' among these do-gooders. I didn't like their religious zeal, but if it wasn't for the doc, I'd prob'ly be dead. I didn't like his questions. He'd done his best to find out about the gash in my side. I finally told him it was an accident, but nothin' more.

It had been an accident, but I could hardly tell the doc that after I'd attempted to commit a robbery and had killed a man back in Baltimore, I had the bad luck of trippin' on a loose cobblestone and falling on my own knife. With my bad leg and that gaping wound causin' me no end of pain, I still marveled that I was able to stay hidden until after all the commotion died down. Only then did I make my way to John Calvert's room in one of the tenements along the docks. He went down to the wharf and found a sailor who said he could sew me up. The pain was terrible, but the stitchin' was good enough to let me get out of Baltimore.

When I left town, I considered John a friend I could count on, but only time would tell if he was a real friend—a man I could trust.

CHAPTER 12

Dirk

Lukas grabbed my hand and held tight as we departed the doctor's office. The boy needed somehow to make sense of what had just happened, but I wasn't sure whether I could say anything that would help. There had been no opportunity to gain information from Andrea, but it was obvious Fred Wilson's return had created fear rather than joy in this young boy.

Sister Andrea had told me only little of her marriage to Fred—enough to reveal the years had been endured rather than enjoyed. But Lukas's unmistakable fear of his father indicated an even darker side.

We hadn't gone far when he squeezed my hand and looked up at me. "Do you think my father will make us leave and go with him?" His voice trembled. "I don't want to go. Can I live with you if he makes my mother move away?"

I needed to be careful with my answers. I didn't want him to think I would ever reject him, but I could not control his future. Only his mother and father could make those decisions.

"Already you are worrying about things that may never happen. Until we know more about your Vater's illness and why he has arrived, it does no gut to worry. There are more important ways to spend our time, ja? The Bible tells us we are to worry about nothing, but to make our requests known to God. This is what we must do."

Lukas didn't appear convinced. "I'll tell God, but if my father tries to make us move, will you let me live with you? Please?"

My heart ached. He didn't need to beg. I would be pleased beyond measure to have him live with me, to call him my son. But the choice was not mine to make. "This is my promise to you, Lukas. If your Mutter and Vater decide to leave the colonies, and if they agree to let you stay behind, I would be happy to have you live with me."

He released my hand and jumped up and down, clapping his hands together.

"Lukas! You must remember that I said 'if.' *If* is a very little word, but it is the most important part of what I told you. Unless your parents agree, there is nothing I can do. You understand?"

The boy remained undeterred. "I know you can make them agree. My Mutter will listen to what you say. She knows that you would take good care of me, and I would be safe with you."

His words were enough to tell me that Lukas had heard only what he wanted to hear: No matter what his parents decided, he planned to remain in the colonies. "It is true that I would do my best to give you gut care and for sure you would be safe with me, but your Mutter and Vater can do the same. Maybe they will not be here, but wherever they go, they will provide for you."

Now that I'd observed Lukas's reaction to his father, I recalled some of the boy's unusual behavior when he'd first arrived. Unlike most young children, Lukas had been fearful and wary when he initially visited the shop. He would flinch when Werner or I made a quick movement in the workshop, and he would jump aside when one of us moved past him. It had taken time to win the boy's trust. Now I was beginning to understand the significance of his timid conduct, and the understanding angered me.

How could a man, blessed with a gentle and lovely wife and a wonderful son, be anything but grateful? Did he not value the gifts God had bestowed upon him? If I didn't tamp down the fire that ignited in my belly, I would explode. Everything in me wanted to march over to the doctor's office and show Andrea's husband what it felt like to be on the receiving end of such treatment. However, the last thing Lukas needed was another angry man in his life. I took a deep breath to calm myself. I must remain composed and behave in a normal manner.

I pulled open the screen door and followed Lukas into the kitchen. The door banged behind us, and moments later Sister Erma appeared. "So finally you come home. I thought I would have to eat the leftover cake by myself." She lifted the tin cover off the plate and then glanced toward the door. "Where is your Mutter, Lukas? Did you feed her to the fishes?" She chuckled at her joke, but neither of us laughed.

I met her gaze. "She's at Dr. Karr's office."

The tin cover clattered atop the worktable. "Nein! What happened? She hurt herself at the pond? Has she taken ill?" She pinned me with a commanding stare. "Tell me!"

"She isn't hurt or ill. Her husband—Lukas's father—has arrived, and he is the one who is both hurt and ill."

Her lips screwed into a tight knot and her brows dipped low. "That is not possible. Andrea told me he is dead." She looked at the boy. "Your Vater, he is dead. Isn't that right, Lukas?"

Lukas started to bob his head, but then shook it instead. "He was dead. I mean, we thought he was dead, but now he's alive and he's at the doctor's office."

His lips trembled and I frowned at Sister Erma and shook my head. "This has taken Lukas and Sister Andrea both by surprise. Lukas is distressed and hasn't been able to sort it all out yet. None of us has. We can talk later." I pointed to the cake. "I think a piece of cake and some milk would help right now."

Sister Erma took my hint and didn't ask any further questions. Instead she busied herself cutting and serving the cake while silence hovered like a funeral pall. When I could bear it no longer, I cleared my throat. "The new wedding cake pan you ordered will be ready by the end of the week. Werner and Lukas have both helped me with it." I patted Lukas on the shoulder. "Didn't you?"

He nodded. "I got to cut a few strips of tin, but Brother Dirk did most of the work."

Sister Erma smiled. "Many hands make light work. If you had not done your part, it would have taken Brother Dirk longer to finish. I am pleased to know your hands helped to make the new pan. Wedding cakes are very special here. Did Brother Dirk tell you that?"

Lukas nodded his head. "Brother Dirk said it takes lots of cake batter to fill the pan, and the star shape is special for weddings. Maybe someone will get married and I can see one of the cakes."

Sister Erma chuckled. "To see a wedding cake is gut, but to eat a piece is even better. One day you will get to try some, and since you live in the kitchen house, you will always know when we are preparing for a wedding."

"I might not be living in the Küche. I might go and live with Brother Dirk."

Sister Erma's eyes opened wide, and her gaze traveled back and forth between Lukas and me. "What?"

Lukas had finished his cake, and I moved the plate from in front of him. "I think you need to go upstairs and get to bed. You have school tomorrow. If you're not in bed before your Mutter comes home, I'll be in trouble."

"I'll hurry, 'cause I don't want you to get in any trouble." He slid off the stool and bid us both good-night. Moments later, his shoes clattered on the stairs leading to the upstairs rooms.

Sister Erma folded her hands across her chest. "Now tell me what is this nonsense about Lukas's father. Start at the beginning and don't leave anything out, because I am confused."

I wanted to tell her she was no more confused than I, but that wasn't true. Much as I hated to admit the man existed, I had seen Fred and I knew he was alive. "I wish I could tell you it is only nonsense, but it is true. While we were at the pond, Dr. Karr sent one of the boys to fetch Sister Andrea. We didn't know why until we arrived at his office."

Sister Erma placed her palm across her mouth. "Ach! This is terrible."

"Ja, you are right. I saw her husband for only a moment to introduce myself. He looks very ill, but he also appeared angry."

"Illness and pain can sometimes cause people to behave in strange ways, but Sister Andrea has mentioned to me that her marriage was not happy. She once said her husband wasn't gut to her and the boy. When I questioned her, she said she did not want to speak ill of the dead, so we ended our discussion."

Sister Erma's comments were enough to confirm my greatest fears. This man would again make life unbearable for Andrea and Lukas. My muscles quivered at the thought that he might abuse them.

Sister Erma gathered the plates and carried them to the sink and then put a kettle of water on the stove to boil. "What is this about Lukas living with you? Where did he get such an idea?"

I recounted my earlier conversation with Lukas and then added, "The boy fears his father will force them to leave, so he was trying to plan the future for himself."

"Ja, but your idea is impossible. Sister Andrea would never leave her son, and I do not think the boy's Vater would agree, either. You should not have made such a promise, Brother Dirk." She walked to the stove, and using a thick towel to protect her hand, she lifted the kettle of hot water and carried it to the sink.

I stepped close to the sink as she poured the boiling water atop a few inches of cold water in the basin. "I did not promise he could come and live with me. I was very clear and told him that if his father decided to leave and if his parents agreed, then he could live with me. I explained that the possibility they would agree to such an arrangement was not favorable, but he heard only what he wanted to hear."

She dipped her hands into the dishwater and washed one of the plates. "Then you should have made sure he understood." She lifted the clean plate from the sudsy water and dipped it into the basin of rinse water. "It is clear Lukas thinks he can remain in the colonies and live with you."

"What's this about Lukas?"

I didn't hear the door and turned so quickly I nearly toppled into Sister Erma. "Sister Andrea! I didn't hear you come in." I detected a hint of suspicion in her eyes. "Sister Erma and I were discussing your husband's arrival—"

"And also discussing living arrangements for my son?" The anger in her tone caught me by surprise.

"Give me a moment and I'll explain." Doubt clouded her eyes as I detailed my conversation with Lukas. "I was only trying to help ease Lukas's fears, and I would never want him to think he was unwelcome in my home."

I breathed a bit easier when her shoulders began to relax. "I'm sorry. This has been a difficult evening. I know I can trust both of you." She glanced around me to include Sister Erma. "I keep hoping this is a bad dream and I'll wake up and discover there's no need to worry." She inhaled a deep breath and slowly exhaled. "Never did I imagine Fred would be the one I would see in the doctor's office. He has not changed. Even though his physical condition is poor, he still is the same harsh and angry man who went to sea." She dropped to a chair near the sink. "He believes I am lying to him about the farm and my inheritance."

"He should understand that if you still owned the farm or if you had received money from your inheritance, you would not be living here in the colonies." Why would Fred doubt Andrea's word?

"Somewhere deep inside, he probably understands it's the truth. But he doesn't want to believe I am penniless because that means he, too, is destitute." She leaned back in the chair. "I am uncertain what to think about the things Fred has told me. Mr. Brighton, the owner of the shipping line, told me Fred washed overboard in a storm and there was no chance he was alive, yet Fred has related a different story. I don't know what to believe."

"All of this is bound to leave you confused." Sister Erma dried her soapy hands on the front of her apron. "What does Dr. Karr say about his condition? Does he think he'll soon be up and about?"

Andrea shook her head. "No. He contracted malaria, but then for some reason, he quit taking the tincture prescribed for it, so his condition worsened during the journey here. The doctor needs to try to get that under control. In addition, he broke his leg and it hasn't healed properly. He tells me the leg causes him great pain and causes him to walk with a terrible limp. And on top of that, he has a serious infection in his side."

She massaged her forehead. "I don't know what Lukas and I

will do." She directed her gaze at Sister Erma. "I don't think I could ever live with him again, but he is my husband."

"This is not the time to think such worrisome thoughts. We will pray the good Lord will reveal His plan to us. Who can say what miracle the Lord might work in Fred's life. I have seen such things happen. We will all pray, ja?"

I nodded and so did Andrea, but I didn't know if my prayer would be the same as Sister Erma's. I would never pray for Fred's death, but I was not sure I could pray for him to be reunited with Andrea and Lukas. Selfish thoughts had taken me captive. I wanted Andrea and Lukas to become my family, and I ached to take Andrea in my arms and comfort her.

Surely God knew the two of them deserved better than what they had received from Fred Wilson.

Could I not provide them with a better life? What was I to do with the feelings I had developed for both of them? To deny I cared deeply for them would be an outright lie. But now that Fred had returned, I had no right to love them. Yet I could not disavow my love. It would be impossible.

With God, all things are possible.

The thought pierced my mind. I knew the truth of God's Word. Had Sarah not conceived a child in her old age? Had Moses not led the Israelites across the Red Sea? Had Jesus not been born of a virgin? Had He not risen from the dead? I knew all things were possible with God. Through His power, I could set aside my love for Andrea and Lukas and move on with my life.

But what if removing them from my life wasn't what I wanted?

CHAPTER 13

Andrea

The following morning, I assured Lukas nothing had changed. He would continue to attend school each day, and I would continue to work in the kitchen. I wasn't sure I'd totally eased his concerns, but at least he gave me a tentative smile.

"Can I still go to see Brother Dirk after school?" When I agreed, he sighed. "And I don't have to go to see my . . . my father?" His voice trembled as he uttered the final words.

"You don't have to go today. I am sure he will want to see you sometime soon, but it can wait for a few days. Try not to worry. I won't let him hurt you again, Lukas." I flashed what I hoped was a reassuring smile before pulling him into my arms for a brief hug. "We are going to be fine, Lukas." I looked into his eyes. "You believe me, don't you?"

"I want to, Mama, but if he wants us to leave, we'll have to do what he says, won't we?"

I straightened the corner of his shirt collar. "I think it will be a long time before your father is able to go anywhere, so let's not borrow trouble."

His eyes scrunched together. "What's that mean?"

I chuckled and traced my fingers through his brown curls. "It means if the problem isn't already on your doorstep, don't go looking for it."

His frown deepened. "But he is on our doorstep."

"Not quite, Lukas. Your father is in the colonies, but he's not able to do anything except follow the doctor's orders." I hugged him. "We're going to be fine. Now, I need to go downstairs and help Sister Erma and Sister Greta with breakfast preparations. You finish getting dressed and come down when you hear the breakfast bell."

I hurried down the stairs and grabbed my apron off the hook as I entered the kitchen. "Good morning, Sisters. I'm sorry to be late. Lukas was full of questions."

"Guten Morgen," they replied in unison.

I looked at Sister Erma. "Do you want me to slice the bread?"

Sister Greta was peeling and slicing potatoes. On Monday, Wednesday, and Friday, fried potatoes, bread, butter, syrup, and coffee were the usual morning fare.

Sister Erma continued to pour syrup into the pitchers that would be placed on each of the dining tables. "Ja, that would be gut."

Each morning the bakery wagon arrived at the kitchen and delivered fresh loaves to each of the kitchens in the village. On Saturdays, the delivery also included coffee cakes, which were sliced and then served on Sunday mornings. The coffee cake had quickly become one of Lukas's favorites and another reason he looked forward to Sundays.

Before I'd completed slicing the loaves we would serve at breakfast, Brother Bosch appeared at the back door and crooked his finger. "Would you join me on the back porch, Sister Andrea?"

I looked at Sister Erma for direction. She nodded. "You go ahead. We can manage."

There wasn't time to worry about what Brother Bosch might want to discuss, but I was sure it had something to do with Fred. Maybe he was going to tell me all three of us needed to leave the village. My stomach tightened into a knot as the older man turned to face me.

"You should know that the elders will meet this afternoon to discuss the arrival of your husband." He gazed out into the garden. "I understand he is without funds to pay for his medical care." He turned to look at me. "This is true?"

"As far as I know, it is true, Brother Bosch." Sadness gripped me and an unbidden tear slipped down my cheek. "He came here believing my father would provide for him. He doesn't believe that I don't have the money my father received for the farm."

"So this is why he is angry. When I stopped at Dr. Karr's office this morning, I could not understand why your husband was so quarrelsome. He said he did not want to talk to me." Brother Bosch reached into his pocket and removed his pipe. He held the bowl in his palm and rubbed the shiny wood with his thumb. "I am sure that he will soon understand and accept the truth, but I wanted to tell you the elders will make some decisions this afternoon."

"About Fred's care or about all of us?" I folded my hands together and squeezed tight to stop my fingers from shaking. All night I had lain awake and wrestled with my worries. I'd tried to pray, but soon my prayers spiraled into troubling thoughts of what would happen if we were forced to leave the village.

In truth, there was no reason for the members of the society to bear the burden of three strangers in their midst. Especially since only one of us was contributing anything toward our expenses. And my work in the kitchen didn't equal the cost of our food, shelter, and Lukas's education, not to mention the other necessities that had been supplied since our arrival.

Now, with Fred and the cost of his keep and medical expenses, would they believe our family too great a drain of their resources? I couldn't fault them if they did, yet my prayers had all begun with an appeal for understanding and mercy and continued with a plea for Fred to comprehend the depth of our need and develop a spirit of thankfulness. Once I prayed for Fred's change of heart, my thoughts became muddled and my prayers turned into meandering worries. Unlike Sister Erma, I hadn't yet learned how to surrender my troubles to God. I tried, but I wasn't convinced God could be trusted to handle my problems. After all, He hadn't handled them to my liking in the past—how could I believe He would do so now?

Brother Bosch cleared his throat. When I looked up, his eyes shone with compassion. He tapped a finger to the side of his head. "I think you were lost in your own thoughts and did not hear my answer, ja?"

"I'm sorry." I offered a weak smile. "What did you say?"

"I said the elders and I will discuss your husband's medical treatment as well as the welfare of you and your son. We want to do what is best for all three of you while remaining attentive to the needs of our people, as well."

My voice caught and I touched my fingers to my throat and swallowed hard. "Do you think we will be asked to leave?"

"There is no way I can speak for the rest of the elders, but it is my belief that we should continue to extend our hospitality to you and your family. I will do my best to influence the others, but I must bow to the majority in any decision that is made. You understand?"

I nodded. "Thank you, Brother Bosch. I will be grateful for

anything you can do to help us." He tucked his pipe back into his jacket. Though he'd twisted the pipe in his left hand throughout our conversation, he'd never stopped to light it. "You never smoked your pipe."

He grinned and patted his pocket. "A nervous habit, I am told."

Now aware that this conversation had been as difficult for Brother Bosch as it had for me, I admired him all the more. This was a man seasoned with grace and mercy, and I counted it a privilege to have him on my side. Even if the other elders decided we should leave the village, I was thankful for Brother Bosch. Win or lose, he would champion our cause with unbridled zeal.

"One thing I would ask, Sister Andrea." He hesitated a moment, his bushy brows dipping low over his serious brown eyes. "You could maybe tell your husband it would be gut if he would show some appreciation to Dr. Karr. Even though the office provides space for very ill patients, he should remember he is a guest in Dr. Karr's home. Your husband, he tends to criticize. And I do not think he shows the doctor proper respect."

I was sure there had been a discussion between Dr. Karr and Brother Bosch. No doubt the doctor had detailed Fred's grumbling complaints and insulting remarks. I didn't tell Brother Bosch that I'd spoken to Fred about his rude behavior the previous evening. To reveal I'd already attempted to correct the situation might cause Brother Bosch to rethink his position.

"I'll speak with Fred once I've completed my work in the kitchen after breakfast. If you think it would help the doctor, I could assist with Fred's care after the noonday meals and each evening."

Perhaps my presence would calm Fred's horrid manners. If not, he could direct his anger at me rather than at Dr. Karr or his wife. I shuddered to think what Fred had said or done since I'd left the doctor's office last night.

"I will report your willingness to the elders and to Dr. Karr. Although only God can know the condition of each soul, your husband behaves like a man who does not know God." He arched his brows.

"He has never acknowledged a belief in God to me." I didn't add that Fred had always mocked those who professed such faith. Right now, the less the elders knew about Fred's traits, the better it would be.

The bell rang and Brother Bosch glanced at the door. "I will explain his lack of faith to the elders. It may help them understand why he shows no gratitude. We will all need to be in prayer for him, ja?"

"That's what Sister Erma said, too."

I knew the Bible instructed us to pray for those who spitefully used and persecuted us. Fred certainly fit that description, but praying for him was so difficult. Prayers for Lukas or Sister Erma came easily to my lips. But Fred? My mind argued against repaying his cruelty with prayers to heal both his body and soul. It would take all of my strength to pray for him, but I would try.

"Sister Erma is a smart woman." He tapped a finger to his head and smiled. "I think we should go inside before she comes looking for us. Nothing displeases her more than a disruption in her schedule."

"Thank you for taking the time to speak with me, Brother Bosch. I hope you will seek me out after the meeting so that I will know the outcome as soon as possible." My hand remained fixed on the handle of the screen door.

"For sure, I will do that, but remember the Lord is in charge. You should cast your cares upon His shoulders."

I nodded, opened the door, and walked inside. Although I

wanted to believe the truth of Brother Bosch's comment, I felt as if the elders and Fred were the ones in charge of my future, not the Lord.

How did these people so easily place their trust in God? During our evening Bible readings and conversations in the upstairs parlor, Sister Erma had assured me I was making great progress, yet I wondered if I could ever attain such indisputable conviction. Right now, there wasn't time to ponder the question.

Sister Erma waved me forward. "Fill the bowls with potatoes and carry them in to the tables. It is almost time for the prayer."

I didn't miss her harried tone. While I'd been visiting with Brother Bosch, she and Greta had likely been scurrying around the kitchen like mice on a sinking ship. I filled the bowls, placed them on a large tray, and carried the tray into the dining room as Brother Bosch began the before-meal prayer. There was no choice but to come to a halt while still holding the heavy tray. My arms were shaking by the time the prayer ended, and I feared I might drop the entire tray of potatoes.

Sister Greta reached for the tray. "Let me take that."

I didn't argue. Instead, I followed alongside her and deposited a bowl at each of the tables. When we'd finished, I followed her back to the kitchen. "Thank you."

She glanced over her shoulder and grinned. "You would do the same for me. Besides, if you dropped that whole tray, we would have to start all over peeling and frying more potatoes. Everyone in the dining room would be unhappy with us."

"And we'd have to clean up the mess, too."

She hung the tray from a hook on the far wall and then returned to my side. "You had a gut talk with Brother Bosch?"

I knew this was her way of asking what we'd discussed—not that I minded. Ever since we'd discussed the nature of her relationship with Dirk, Sister Greta and I had become fast friends. "You know my husband has returned?"

Although news usually traveled quickly throughout the village, I didn't know how much she had learned last evening. If she'd not heard last night, I was sure Sister Erma had given her a few of the details this morning.

"Ja. Sister Erma told me he is at the doctor's office and he has malaria."

I picked up a slice of bread and slathered it with butter and jam. "And a bad infection in his side. And an injured leg." After taking a bite of the bread and jam, I explained what all had happened since last evening.

"Ach! I am so sad for you." She stepped closer, out of Sister Erma's earshot. "And Dirk—I am sure he is heartbroken. I know he hoped the two of you might have a future together. Of course, he was not certain you would decide to stay in the colonies, but I am sure he prayed you would. This changes everything."

Sister Greta's words sent a fresh prick to my heart. I, too, had thought about and prayed for those things concerning Dirk. Knowing the pain I'd caused him doubled the ache I felt. I swallowed the potato-sized lump in my throat. "Brother Bosch and Sister Erma say we need to pray for Fred—that he will have a change of heart and realize he needs to take a different path with his life."

"And you? What do you want, Andrea?"

I shook my head. "I don't think I have any choice in what happens, so it matters little what I want." Trying to keep my emotions in check, I inhaled a deep breath. "I am most concerned about Lukas. His fear of Fred runs deep, and he is very unhappy that his father has returned. In some ways, I think he blames me."

"You? Why should he blame you?"

"Because I told him his father was dead and now Fred has reappeared. In some ways, I understand. He trusted what I told him." I shrugged. "Of course, I trusted what Mr. Brighton, the owner of the shipping line, told me. I should be delighted my husband is alive, and yet—"

"It is hard to welcome his return when you lived with such unhappiness." She squeezed my hand. "I will pray that God will grant you joy and happiness now. I am not sure if that will be with Fred, but that is my fervent wish for you, and I do not believe anyone could find fault with such a prayer."

I choked back my tears. "Thank you, Greta."

Benches scraped across the wood floors in the dining room, announcing the end of the morning meal. We strode into the other room, and as we gathered the dirty dishes onto trays, Greta nudged my arm. "You will tell me what happens at the elders' meeting, ja?"

I nodded. "As soon as we've finished, I must go over to the doctor's office and speak with Fred. I'll come back as soon as I can."

I inhaled a deep breath and tried to calm my fears as I headed off to see Fred. I took comfort in the sound of my shoes clacking along the wooden sidewalk that lined the long trailing street. There was a peacefulness in this tidy village that I had grown to appreciate soon after we arrived. Though Sister Erma said I would find the same orderly design in all seven villages, I had my doubts. She'd laughed at my skepticism and gone on to tell me all of the villages had been modeled to resemble German *Dorfs*, with extended main streets and many intermittent offshoots. The barns and sheds were situated at one end of the village, the workshops and factories at the other. Although there was no calico or woolen mill in West Amana, the village did boast a large flour mill.

The houses, whether constructed of sandstone, brick, or wood, all displayed grapevine-covered trellises that helped keep the houses cool during the heat of summer and produced some of the grapes used to make jams and jellies. I strode past the Schaefer Küche, a reminder that I had left the kitchen work to Sisters Erma and Greta. However, if given a choice, I'd rather help in the Küche than visit Fred.

I took a bit of solace in knowing the midday lunches did not require a great deal of preparation. The midmorning and mid-afternoon meals had seemed odd to me when I'd first begun my work in the Küche. It had taken only a few days to learn that hard labor required full stomachs, and there was a great deal of hard labor in the village.

While the midmorning lunch, as Sister Erma referred to it, didn't usually require a great deal of preparation, it did interrupt our days. Midmorning lunch was served two and a half hours after breakfast, while the midafternoon lunch was served three hours after the noonday meal. Three and a half hours elapsed between the midafternoon lunch and supper.

Today they would serve brick cheese, apple butter, bread, and coffee for the midmorning lunch. Before departing, I had sliced the cheese and spooned apple butter into bowls. It hadn't been much, but Sister Erma said every little bit helped. I hoped my little bit would help them today.

I hesitated outside the doctor's office to gather my courage. I didn't want to argue with Fred. After a quick prayer that our talk would go well, I pushed down the heavy metal latch and opened the door. The bell jangled overhead, and Dr. Karr stepped into the waiting room.

"Sister Andrea! It is gut to see you." He traced his fingers through his thatch of gray hair.

Instead of entering the sick room, I stepped to the doctor's side. "I have spoken with Brother Bosch. He tells me that my husband has been a difficult patient and that he has been rude to you and your wife. Please accept my apologies."

"Ach! You do not need to apologize for the offenses of others, Sister."

"But he is my husband and you have provided care as well as your hospitality. I am going to speak with him about his attitude." I went on to offer my assistance caring for Fred during my breaks, but the doctor shook his head.

"We will wait to see how he progresses. The laudanum has helped him sleep, and the tincture may help the effects of his malaria. If his condition deteriorates, we may be required to transport him to the hospital in Cedar Rapids. For sure, such a journey would be difficult, but he is a determined man. In the meantime, we will be praying that his spirit will heal along with his body." He patted my arm. "You go and visit with him, but you have your duties in the Küche. Do not worry about his medical care. As long as the elders permit him to remain here, I will do my best to help him." He gestured toward the other room. "Now, you go on and see your husband."

I whispered my thanks and crossed the room. Inhaling a deep breath, I stopped a short distance from the door and whispered, "Please open his eyes and soften his heart." I had hoped to include much more in my prayer but was stopped by Fred's harsh voice.

"What are ya standing around for? Get in here, Andrea!"

A knot settled deep in my stomach as I entered the room.

CHAPTER 14

This conversation would be difficult. Seldom had I attempted to tell Fred what he should do or how he should act. My few endeavors had always been met with scorn and laughter. I wasn't certain if the laudanum would help his temperament, but after hearing his angry tone, I had my doubts.

Forcing a smile, I entered the room. "Good morning, Fred. You look a little more rested this morning. Did you sleep well last night?"

"You can quit puttin' on. You don't care how much sleep I got last night. Fact is, you were probably hopin' you'd find me dead this mornin'."

Careful to place the chair where he couldn't reach me, I sat down. My husband might be as weak as a kitten, but years of conditioning had taught me to keep my distance. Besides, his angry response signaled the laudanum hadn't quelled his temper.

"Believe what you will, Fred. I didn't come here to argue, so I won't attempt to change your mind."

"Why did ya come? Them do-gooders tryin' to get rid of me?"

My already flagging spirits declined another notch. Couldn't this man show a little appreciation and civility? "No one is trying to get rid of you, Fred. At least not yet."

"What's that supposed to mean? I got until tomorrow before they toss me out?"

"From what I understand, that will depend upon you." I folded my shaking hands and placed them in my lap.

He shifted his weight and grimaced. "Infernal leg! Pain in my side ain't as bad, but now my leg's achin'. Why don't that doc do somethin' to help my pain?"

"I believe he has given you laudanum for the pain, and he's cleaned the wound in your side. What did you want him to do? Remove your leg?"

Anger flickered in his eyes. "Is that s'posed to be funny? You'd like to see me gimpin' around with only one leg. That'd make ya happy, wouldn't it?"

"No, it would not make me happy," I snapped. If I didn't quickly change the course of this conversation, nothing I'd set out to accomplish would be achieved. I took a breath and calmed myself. "No, it would not make me happy," I repeated, this time keeping an even tone.

He narrowed his eyes, glared at me, and exhaled a guttural sound that proclaimed he didn't believe me.

Squeezing my folded hands until they ached, I organized my thoughts. I wanted to be clear and concise without provoking him. Changing Fred's mood would be no small task, but I needed to try.

"Due to our circumstances, we need to do everything in our power to make this situation work. Neither of us has money to pay for our daily needs or your medical care. The colonists have been very nice to Lukas and me, and they have extended that same consideration to you." I leaned forward and lowered my voice. "We need to treat them with the same respect and kindness, don't you think?"

"I ain't too worried. If they're the religious folks they profess to be, they should turn the other cheek—ain't that right? I think there's somethin' else about doing good to them that persecute you."

Strange how Fred could use passages from the Bible to his advantage. His defiant attitude hadn't changed a bit. "That's true, but there's also a passage that says to love your neighbor as yourself. You're not acting like you love anyone as much as you love yourself." Noticing his fierce look, I hastened to add, "I know it's difficult to be agreeable when suffering such immense pain, but if you could try a little harder, I know it would help our situation."

"What would help our *situation*, as you put it, would be some money so we could get outta this place. I'm still wonderin' if you're hidin' the money from me."

I sighed and shrugged my shoulders. How did one convince such a stubborn man? "I'm sorry you doubt me, but I think you know that I would not have remained in the colonies if I had found any money. Why would I take advantage of these people if I had money to provide a home for Lukas and me?"

He worked his jaw as if mulling over the idea. "If I find out you been lyin', I'll make your life miserable. You know that, don't ya?"

"Yes, Fred. I know that." I wanted to add that he'd made my life miserable for many years, but such a retort would only stir more animosity. I tamped down my irritation and continued to keep my voice low. "At the moment, we need help, and I don't know anyone who is going to assist us except the people in this village. Could you muster an occasional thank-you and perhaps be more patient? The doctor and his wife are doing everything possible to tend to your needs. You aren't the only person in the village who needs medical attention."

Instead of immediately answering, he stared at a small crack in the ceiling above his head. Finally he turned his head and looked at me. "I guess I can try, but they best not expect too much. I ain't never been one for thankin' folks at every whipstitch."

"You had a softer side years ago—before you went to work on the docks. I haven't forgotten the wild flowers you picked for me when you courted me—or the sweet words you said." I'd had to dig deep to force those words from my lips. Not because they were lies. They weren't. Fred had been a different man when he'd courted me, but soon after our marriage his behavior had changed. I hadn't seen evidence of that courting man for so long that I'd almost forgotten he ever existed. It was much easier to recall the man he'd become in Baltimore. The man who had treated me with anger and disdain over and over again.

He massaged his forehead as if attempting to force memories of those bygone days to the forefront of his mind. "Don't seem like I'll have much choice but to try." His features relaxed ever so slightly. "But don't expect too much."

I covered my mouth as a tiny gasp escaped. His sudden change of attitude astonished me. Though uncertain I could trust him, at least I could report a somewhat positive result to Brother Bosch.

"Thank you for your willingness to try, Fred. Any positive changes will benefit all three of us."

"Speaking of three—when you gonna bring Lukas back over here to see me? He didn't appear none too happy to see his pa among the livin'."

I didn't understand the sudden interest in Lukas. In the past, he'd always wanted the boy to remain quiet and out of sight. "Your arrival was a shock. To have you reappear after believing you'd died at sea isn't something that happens every day, now is it? He's young and it's difficult for him to comprehend what's happened."

"Stayin' away won't make it any easier to understand. Bring him over here after school."

Fear crawled down my spine. After striking a tentative agreement, I didn't want to anger Fred, but what about Lukas? I wasn't sure he could bear coming for a visit so soon. "He helps at the tinsmith's shop after school each day. All of the children help with various tasks throughout the village." I didn't add that Lukas went by choice—that he was too young to be apprenticed to any of the craftsmen in the village. "What if I brought him over in the morning before he goes to school?" I held my breath and waited, hoping he would agree.

"How 'bout you bring him over after supper?"

My ploy hadn't worked. I'd hoped to bring Lukas in the morning when he wouldn't have to stay long—when there would be a valid excuse for him to leave. I hesitated only a moment. "Once I finish my duties in the kitchen, I'll bring him over." I didn't mention the fact that we'd need to leave after a few minutes and attend prayer meeting. Better to wait until the time arrived. I wasn't sure what I would do if he objected, but I'd cross that bridge when I came to it. "Right now, I need to return to the kitchen. I've already been gone far too long."

"They know you got a sick husband that just come back from the dead, don't they?" He chuckled as if he thought his remark humorous.

"Yes, they know you're ill, but that doesn't mean that I'm excused from all of my duties. Besides, they're already shorthanded. If I'm gone, it leaves too much work for the others. They've already had to prepare the midmorning lunch without me. I need to get back and help with the noonday meal." I stood before he could offer any further objection. "Lukas and I will return this evening."

"I got nothin' to do but lay in this bed all day. You could stop over this afternoon, couldn't ya?"

"I'm needed to help in the garden this afternoon. The doctor says rest is the best thing to help you heal." I took a step toward the doorway. "Is there anything special I can bring this evening when we come to visit?"

Only books and magazines of a religious or agricultural nature were available in the colonies, but I didn't expect Fred would request reading material. He could read as well as most men who'd attended school through the eighth grade, but he'd never been interested in reading, not even the local newspaper.

"Maybe a pen and paper—and some envelopes."

His request surprised me. "I'm not sure how you'll be able to write a letter while lying in bed, but maybe I can bring a board of some sort." I looked around the room. "When I return, we'll figure out something that will work."

"That would be good."

It wasn't a thank-you, but at least he hadn't snarled at me. I bid him good-bye and hurried out of the doctor's office before he could suggest a good-bye kiss. I'd gone only a short distance when I spotted Dr. Karr waving to me from the other side of the street. I waited until a wagon filled with bags of grain passed and then joined him.

"Your visit went well?" The doctor arched his bushy brows.

"As well as I could expect. I think my husband will be a little less demanding in the future, but if his temperament doesn't change for the better, please let me know."

The doctor smiled. "That is gut to hear, but we must continue to pray for him."

I nodded my agreement while hoping I could count on Fred to keep his word.

There hadn't been time to speak with Brother Bosch prior to the noonday meal, but once the after-meal prayer had been recited, I looked in his direction. I sighed when he walked out the men's door at the end of the dining room.

Tray in hand, Sister Erma bustled into the room and began to clear one of the tables. "You spoke with Brother Heinrich?"

"Nein." I tried to hide my disappointment. "Maybe the elders didn't have time to complete all of their business before the noonday meal."

"Even so, he could have stopped long enough to tell you what they decided about your future." She gave a dismissive wave. "Men! Sometimes they do not think about how women worry."

Only moments after the words had escaped her mouth, Brother Bosch appeared in the doorway between the kitchen and dining room. His broad shoulders almost filled the narrow space.

"You can stop your work for a few minutes, Sister Andrea?" His brown eyes twinkled. "I do not wish to worry you or Sister Erma any longer."

Sister Erma snapped to attention. "For sure, she can come and speak with you. It is gut to know you do not wish to worry us any longer, Brother Heinrich." Apparently she hadn't been embarrassed to have her remark overheard. She motioned for me to join the elder. "Take as much time as you need. The schoolgirls are here to help."

I joined Brother Bosch on the back porch. Each of us sat down in one of the straight-backed chairs used by the sisters when we sat outdoors to clean vegetables.

"You went to visit your husband this morning?"

As a warm breezed drifted across the backyard, I told him of Fred's agreement. "I am hopeful he will keep his word and be more pleasant during the remainder of his convalescence."

Brother Bosch leaned back in the chair. "That is a gut report. I am encouraged to hear your husband has agreed to treat others with greater kindness."

"And what of your meeting? Was a decision made regarding our future?"

He smiled and nodded. "Ja. The elders are in agreement that we should continue to extend charity to your family. It has been decided that you and your son will remain in the kitchen house with Sister Erma and your husband will remain at Dr. Karr's office." He removed his pipe and filled the bowl with tobacco. "The doctor tells us his future health is uncertain. For now, all of you are welcome to remain."

I exhaled a relieved sigh. "Thank you. Your decision makes me very happy."

He lit the pipe and puffed until the tobacco glowed red. "Gut." He pushed up from the chair and blew a smoke ring into the air. "Still, we must remember to pray for him."

I wasn't sure how many times I'd heard that admonition. With so many people praying that Fred would change, surely God would look upon the request with favor. And yet, I couldn't help but wonder what the future would hold for Lukas and me. Even if Fred changed, I wasn't sure I could forget the past. Perhaps I could forgive what he'd done to me, but I could never forget the way he'd treated Lukas.

Throughout the remainder of the afternoon, I dwelled on what lay ahead. Not in six months or a year, but this very evening. After supper, I'd have to break my promise to Lukas. I'd tried always to keep my word to him, but this evening I'd have to keep my word to Fred instead of Lukas. Our future depended upon it. If I didn't appear with Lukas, I doubted whether Fred would keep his anger in check.

Once we completed washing and drying the supper dishes, I walked to the back porch and called to Lukas. He was playing near the chicken coop and came running toward me, his hair flying in the breeze.

"Is it time for prayer meeting?"

"Not yet." I stooped down in front of him and grasped his small hands. "We need to have a talk."

Once he learned we were going to visit his father, Lukas's smile vanished. "But you promised I didn't have to go today."

"I know. And I shouldn't have made that promise. Your father is ill and we need to be kind to him, Lukas. It's very important."

His eyes widened. "Why?"

"Because if we're nice to him, he'll be nice, and we'll be able to stay in the village while he gets well."

His mouth gaped open. "If Papa isn't nice to Dr. Karr will we have to leave?"

I struggled to find the proper answer. "I'm not sure, Lukas, but we need to do what we can to make sure your father doesn't become angry. One way we can do that is to visit him each day. I went to visit him earlier today, and he said he wanted to see you."

"You won't leave me alone with him, will you?"

"No, I promise. And we'll stay only until time for prayer meeting."

His lower lip quivered, but he nodded his agreement.

"Run upstairs and get several sheets of writing paper and a few envelopes and bring them down to me." As he raced toward the back door, I called after him, "They're in the top drawer of the chest."

I had only a small bottle of ink and one pen, so I hoped Dr. Karr would let Fred use one of his. Otherwise, I'd purchase a pencil at the general store. I didn't have the extra funds for a bottle of ink and another pen. Besides, I didn't know how many letters Fred would write. The fact that he planned to write any letters surprised me. I'd never known him to take up a pen—at least not during our marriage. Any letter writing had been my responsibility. Though I'd given it no thought when he'd made the request for writing supplies, I now wondered who had become so important to Fred.

"I found them, Mama." Lukas waved the paper and envelopes overhead, his face creased into a proud grin.

We hadn't gone far when I stopped short. "I need a piece of wood or something sturdy for your father to hold on his lap and use as a writing desk. He's not strong enough to get out of bed yet."

"Brother Dirk will have something. His shop is on the way." Lukas beamed at me, proud he'd thought of a solution to my problem. I agreed we would stop, though I wasn't fond of asking Dirk to fulfill one of Fred's requests. It didn't seem appropriate.

An overhead bell jangled as Lukas bounded into the tinsmith's shop. Moments later, Dirk appeared. A broad smile caused his eyes to crinkle boyishly, and I longed for what might have been.

He gestured toward the array of ladles, buckets, and pans that filled his worktables. "You are in need of a new spoon or bucket, Sister Andrea?"

I returned his smile. "No. We have a rather unusual request." I explained Fred's need for a writing desk he could hold on his lap while sitting up in bed. "I'm sorry to bother you, but Lukas thought you might be able to help." I glanced at my son, who was staring up at Dirk with adoring eyes.

"Ja, well, let me think for a moment." He rubbed his jaw and glanced toward the back room. "I know!" He stooped down in front of Lukas and described where he could find a particular piece of wood. "It is the shelf from the bookcase we removed last week. It will be nice and smooth. You remember?"

Lukas nodded. "I'll go get it." He rushed through the shop and into a back room.

As soon as Lukas disappeared, Dirk turned to me. "Tell me what has happened with Fred since last night."

I conveyed the decision the elders had made during their meeting, as well as my talk with Fred. "For now, we will remain in the village. Much depends upon Fred's health and his attitude."

By the time I'd related the day's events, Dirk's smile had vanished. "I cannot say I am pleased by what has happened, Andrea. On the other hand, I know that God has a plan and you are married to Fred. I wish to remain your friend, but we can no longer see each other as we have in the past. You understand?"

My heart felt as though it had stopped beating. Hearing him speak the words that ended what had only just begun for us felt like the declaration of a death sentence. I forced back the flood of tears that threatened. I couldn't give my emotions free rein—not now. My grieving would need to be done in private.

I swallowed hard and forced the lump from my throat. "Of course, but I hope that Lukas—"

"Lukas is always welcome here. I love your son and hope he will continue to come to the shop after school."

Before we could say anything more, Lukas returned with the piece of shelving. "I found it! This will work, won't it, Mama?"

I traced my fingers through Lukas's curls. "It will be perfect. Thank you."

We bid Dirk good-bye and continued toward the doctor's office while I silently prayed Fred would be kind to his son.

Much to my amazement, the visit went better than I could have anticipated. Fred thanked Lukas for seeking out the piece of wood to be used as his writing desk and complimented the boy when he exhibited his writing skills for his father. As the hour wore on, Lukas began to relax and Fred remained kind and encouraging. I wasn't sure what to make of my husband. Perhaps God was already answering our prayers.

Throughout the next two weeks, Fred continued to slowly woo Lukas. At first, the boy had been reluctant to even go near his father's bed. But as Fred encouraged his son in a quiet voice that he'd never before exhibited with him, Lukas's fears slowly dissipated. Granted, he remained close to my side during those initial visits, but soon he began to smile and answer his father's questions.

As the days passed, it was stories of Fred's life aboard ship that enticed Lukas. Once Fred noted the boy's interest, he'd seized the opportunity and each day he would regale Lukas with an exciting adventure or a funny story that intrigued him. Though I doubted that much of what Fred told the boy was the truth, I was pleased to see him make an effort.

I prayed his injuries were teaching him the importance of faith and family.

CHAPTER 15

The changes in Fred's demeanor continued to surprise me. Occasionally, I was reminded of the man I'd fallen in love with years ago. I expected his patience with Lukas to be short-lived, but as time marched on, he continued to win the boy's trust. He would never be as kind or gentle as Dirk—it wasn't fair to compare the two, yet I continued to do so. My attempts to push aside thoughts of a future with Dirk proved difficult. Without warning, my thoughts returned to him every night. Even though I prayed for God to snuff out my desire, the flame continued to burn in my heart.

I no longer visited Dirk's shop, and I tried not to look across at him in the dining hall and at prayer meeting. He no longer stopped at the Küche after prayer meeting, and although Lukas had protested at first, he'd finally accepted the decision. Maybe because he realized that his father's return had changed things.

Lukas now enjoyed the daily visits with his father. Both a checkerboard and Fred's unexpected patience while teaching the boy had seemingly sealed their relationship. At first, Lukas had been reluctant to try to play, but with Fred's encouragement, Lukas soon learned to enjoy the game as well as their time together. Now the two of them played checkers each evening before Lukas and I attended prayer meeting.

A schedule for our visits had been set—at least in Fred's mind. Each evening he anticipated a visit from Lukas and me, and each morning after breakfast, I was expected to be with him for at least an hour. Whenever my work didn't permit a visit, signs of Fred's former demeanor would resurface. Still, compared to the outbursts he'd exhibited during our final years in Baltimore, these occasional dour moods seemed negligible. And they were displayed only in my presence—never when Lukas or others were around.

This morning I arrived a half hour later than usual. When I stepped into his room, he looked up but didn't speak. He was writing a letter, and as I drew a bit closer, he folded the sheet of paper and moved it out of sight.

"I'm glad to see you're making use of the writing supplies. I wondered if you'd used any of the paper." I forced a smile. "I can bring more if you need it."

"I'll tell ya when I need somethin'."

His hair flopped down into his eyes. He needed a haircut, but today wasn't the day to suggest a trim.

"You're late. Figured you wasn't comin', like usual."

I winced at the biting comment but didn't take his bait. Attempting to defend myself would only increase his ire. I'd learned that lesson long ago, so I ignored his remark. We both knew I was seldom late. "The weather has been quite nice the last few days, don't you think?"

"How d'you expect me to know about the weather when I'm stuck in this bed?"

I considered mentioning the light summer breeze wafting through his open window but checked myself. He wasn't interested in hearing a positive response—or any response for that matter, at least not right now. My stomach muscles tightened around the oatmeal I'd eaten for breakfast, and I braced myself for a difficult visit.

"Your health has been improving each day. Perhaps it won't be long before Dr. Karr will permit you to sit in a wheelchair. If so, I could take you outside for a bit of fresh air." Had Fred been in a better mood, I would have suggested asking the doctor myself, but today I was certain he would rebuff my offer.

He arched one brow. "I ain't seen no wheelchairs around this place."

"I believe there's one in the examining room. I saw it when I was here with Lukas a few months ago."

The fact that Fred didn't inquire why Lukas had needed to visit the doctor didn't surprise me. Fred worried about only one person—himself. That characteristic hadn't changed at all.

"Guess I can ask the doc about the wheelchair. He says the medicine has my malaria under control, but the infection in my side ain't doing much better." He pulled back the sheet and lifted the edge of his bandage. "He says he don't want me moving too much—something about the infection spreading in my blood and traveling through my body. That don't seem possible, but since there ain't no other doctor close by, I guess I gotta believe him."

After the excellent care he'd received, Fred's criticism of Dr. Karr disturbed me. "He's a good doctor, Fred. I don't think you could find anyone better to care for you."

Fred hiked a shoulder. "Maybe. At least he ain't lookin' to be paid."

Along with his lack of thankfulness, his callous, selfish nature had reemerged in full force this morning.

I cleared my throat. "If you have any money, it would be gracious to offer payment, since the expense of your care is being borne by those who live in West Amana."

His nostrils flared. "You ain't foolin' me none, Andrea. You're fishin' to find out if I got any money hidden away. I already told you I'm broke, so you can quit your pokin' around. Money! That's all ya ever wanted from me."

I wanted to laugh aloud. He was the one who'd spent every cent on liquor and gambling. His ugly words had fouled the summer air that had smelled so sweet only minutes earlier. I pushed up from my chair. "I need to get back to the kitchen. Lukas and I will return before prayer meeting."

His jaw twitched. "You like the fact that you can up and run off whenever you want, don't ya? Jest you remember that once I can get out of this bed, I'll be the one tellin' you what you can and can't do."

His mood had gone from bad to worse, and memories of our life in Baltimore flooded back. I didn't want to believe that the changes I'd observed over these few past weeks had been a charade, but I decided this morning's behavior was a warning. I would need to be careful. I'd forgotten many of Fred's cunning ways.

I'd gone only a short distance when I looked up and saw Dr. Karr walking toward me carrying his medical bag. Using his free hand, he waved and motioned me forward. "Guten Morgen, Sister Andrea." He smiled and nodded toward his office. "You have been to see our patient?"

I returned his smile. "I have." For a brief moment, I considered asking about the wheelchair but quickly changed my mind. Fred had said he would ask, and I didn't want to be accused of interfering. Of course, if I didn't ask, he'd likely say I didn't care about his ability to go outdoors. I inhaled a deep breath and decided it would be best to wait and see whether Fred mentioned the wheelchair to Dr. Karr.

"We are seeing gut changes in him. I am surprised how much his attitude has improved." He grinned. "And most grateful, too. When he first arrived, I did not think I would be able to bear having him in my home." He shook his head and gazed into the distance, but soon his bright smile returned. "Now I could not ask for a better patient. There is pain when I probe his wound and change his bandage, but even with this he does not complain." The doctor's eyes glistened and he patted his hand against his chest. "I believe God is answering our prayers and your husband is having a change of heart."

"So he has not raised his voice or spoken in anger to you?" I didn't want to disagree with the doctor. I, too, had seen changes in Fred. But not as many as the doctor. And Fred's actions this morning, when there had been no one else around to hear, continued to make me wonder if he'd truly undergone any change at all.

"Nein. He continued to be somewhat gruff for the first few days, but since then, he has been calm, and it has been easy to manage his care. We must all continue to pray that these changes continue, ja?"

I wasn't certain there had been any genuine transformation, but time would tell. If Fred was treating the doctor with proper respect, I didn't want to say or do anything that might create undue alarm. Our being welcome to remain in the village depended heavily upon Fred's conduct, and I didn't want to say anything that might compromise our situation, so I agreed we should continue to pray. In truth, I knew God was the only one who could change Fred.

The doctor took his watch from his pocket and glanced at the time. "Your visit was shorter than usual today."

He hadn't framed the remark as a question, yet it was clear he expected an explanation. "We are short of workers in the kitchen." My answer wasn't an outright lie. We were short one worker. But Sister Ursula's absence wasn't why I was returning to the kitchen. After all, she'd been at home with her baby since before I'd arrived in West.

He nodded. "Then you must hurry on your way. You and Lukas will visit Fred tonight?"

"Yes, we'll be there at our usual time." I skirted past him and continued toward the kitchen house before he could ask any more questions. I didn't want to stretch the truth any further.

The morning lunch had ended only minutes earlier, and some of the men still lingered outside the dining room doors, talking and smoking their pipes. Sister Erma glanced at the clock when I entered the kitchen. "You left late, yet you are back early. Something is wrong?"

I shook my head. "There wasn't much to visit about, and I think Fred needed to rest. Lukas and I will go back this evening before prayer meeting. I thought you might need my help."

"For sure, I can always use your help. The rounds of *Handkäse* need to be scrubbed. Before the girls left for school this morning, I had them carry the crocks upstairs."

Without thinking, I wrinkled my nose. When I'd helped scrub the rounds of pungent cheese last week, I'd decided it was one job I hoped to never repeat. Still, scrubbing the rounds of hand cheese was preferable to arguing with Fred.

She gestured toward the backyard. "The boards you used for a table last week are leaning against the shed. Sister Greta will help you."

Greta frowned and sighed. She wasn't pleased with the assignment, either. Although most everyone liked eating hand cheese, none of the sisters enjoyed working with the smelly rounds. Upon inhaling my first whiff, I'd let out a shriek, pinched my nose, and backed up. Greta had laughed until tears ran down her cheeks.

I'd remained at a distance as she'd explained that the rounds were created by pressing milk curds through a sieve, adding salt, and kneading the mixture until Sister Erma declared that it had reached the proper consistency.

The cheese was then shaped into rounds that were flattened and set to dry before being stored in crocks that were placed in the cellar. Once the first mold formed on the rounds, it was scraped off before the rounds were again returned to the crocks. When the second batch of mold appeared, it was time to begin the washing process.

Each of the rounds had to be scrubbed with a stiff brush, a time-consuming and malodorous process that had to be repeated until the cheese rind attained the proper golden color.

I grabbed my apron from the hook and tied it around my waist as Greta crossed the kitchen. "Are you sorry you didn't stay and visit with Fred awhile longer?"

I shook my head as we walked out the door. "There are worse things than smelling Handkäse." Without elaborating any further, I pointed to the washtub. "If you want to pump the water, I think I can carry the boards and sawhorses by myself."

"Nein. Those boards are too heavy. We'll set up the tables, and I can fill the washtub while you move the crocks."

I didn't argue. The sawhorses and boards were heavy, and we worked in silence until we began to scrub the mold off the rinds. Greta dipped her brush into the washtub we had balanced at one end of the table. The heavy crocks balanced the boards at the other end. She shook the excess water from her brush and picked up a round of the cheese.

"What did you mean when you said there are worse things than scrubbing this stinking cheese?" Scrubbing with a vengeance, she attacked the mold on the cheese round.

Should I tell her my thoughts about Fred? Greta had become my confidante and knew of Fred's abuse while we lived in Baltimore, but I didn't know if I should keep these new suspicions to myself.

She nudged my arm. "What has Fred done?"

"I didn't say he had done anything."

"You are not so gut at hiding your emotions, Andrea. Do you no longer believe your secrets are safe with me?"

Her wounded look was enough to unseal my lips. "I am not sure Fred has changed at all. I think his good behavior may be merely an act to impress the doctor and Brother Bosch."

Her cheese round dropped on the table with a loud thud and her eyes opened wide. "What has he done to make you think this?"

I quickly assured her he hadn't harmed me before I detailed what had occurred at Dr. Karr's office before I returned to the Küche.

"You need to tell Brother Bosch. Each night at prayer meeting, he tells us how God is answering our prayers, and how much change he has observed in Fred."

I nodded. She didn't need to tell me: I had been present at those same prayer meetings and listened to those same comments. "I think I need to be sure before I do anything. This might have been a bad day for him. Old habits are difficult to change."

She leaned forward and narrowed her eyes. "You are making excuses for him. This should not continue. You are giving him permission to make fools of all of us."

"No!" Her words stung and I took a backward step. I couldn't believe she would say such a thing. "I love the people in this village, but I don't think it's fair to judge him after one episode. The future of our entire family depends on Fred."

Greta's shoulders sagged. "I forgot that you and Lukas would have to go with him if the elders decide he should leave the village." She picked up the cheese and continued scrubbing. "You are right. You should wait until you are sure." She wet her brush and then looked at me. "What will you do if you must leave with him, Andrea?"

I swallowed hard. "I don't know. If the elders believe he remains a cruel and callous man, it is my hope they will permit us to remain here—if Fred doesn't object. But if Fred wants us with him, he will cause far too many problems for the entire village. It would prove impossible."

Never before had I allowed myself to picture the full conse-quences of what would happen to Lukas and me. Now that I'd put it into words, the realization of what the future could hold rested heavily on my shoulders. I shuddered at the possibility of returning to my former life.

"I don't think Dirk would let that happen. He cares too much for you and Lukas."

I lifted another disc from one of the crocks and continued the scrubbing ritual. "Dirk could do nothing. The decision of the elders is what counts, and they must choose what is best for the entire village, not an outsider and her son."

Greta peeked at me from beneath her long lashes. "I think he would leave the colonies in order to protect you and Lukas."

I stopped scrubbing and gaped at her. "I would never want him to do that. His life is here. He would never be happy living outside the colonies."

She shrugged. "Do not be so sure. He has a gut trade and could find work in almost any town. I think change is not so hard when you have a reason."

"But I would still have a husband. Unless I misjudged Fred's behavior today, none of this will be easily resolved." I rested my arm along the edge of the washtub. "And as much as Dirk might want to help us, that cannot happen. We must forget each other."

She moved closer to my side as several robins took refuge in a nearby tree and warbled a cheerful song. "I am not sure he can forget you."

"He can. He must. One day he will find an Amana woman, one who can love him in return."

A pain shot through my heart as I spoke the words. Deep down, I wanted him never to love another woman. But such a thought was self-indulgent and foolish. He deserved a wife who loved him. Even more, he deserved to be a father. Dirk should be happy.

CHAPTER 16

Over the next few days, I continued to pray that what I'd told Greta was true: Fred had simply hit a rough spot and only momentarily returned to his old habits on the day he'd displayed such anger toward me.

However, I remained vigilant and carefully watched for any signs that Fred might be losing patience with Lukas. To my great relief, the boy still remained eager to visit and play checkers with his father. This evening as we headed toward Dr. Karr's office, he skipped along the board sidewalk, his arms swinging to and fro as though he had not a care in the world. I was amazed at how quickly Lukas had seemingly set aside memories of his father's abusive treatment. I assumed it was a testament to the child's deep desire to win his father's love. I prayed Fred wouldn't do anything to destroy the boy's blossoming trust. When Lukas reached the tailor's shop, he turned around and waited for me to catch up.

"Papa said he was going to teach me the game of chess. Do you know how to play, Mama?"

"No, I don't." I grasped his hand. "I didn't know your father played, either."

He bobbed his head and several brown curls fell across his forehead. "He says he learned when he was on the ship, but he doesn't have all the pieces."

"I see. And do you think you'd like to learn?"

"Uh-huh. Papa says it's harder than checkers, but you play on the same board with pieces that move in different directions." His eyes shone with expectation. "I think Papa likes me now, don't you?"

"He always liked you, Lukas, but things were much harder when we were in Baltimore." Though I didn't want to condone Fred's earlier actions, neither did I want my son to think his father had ever disliked him. Maintaining a delicate balance between the before and after and the good and bad was going to be more difficult than I had anticipated.

Lukas pushed the hair off his forehead and smiled. "He says now that I'm older, I can help him with things."

I stopped short. "What sort of things?"

When he began to tug on my hand, we continued onward. "I take his letters to the general store to be mailed." His face creased in a proud grin.

Why was Fred having Lukas mail his letters? And to whom was he writing? The one day I'd seen him writing a letter, he'd hidden it from me. Was it because he didn't want me to know about his letters?

I forced a smile. "And what other tasks have you done for him?"

"I stop at the store after school, and when there's a letter for him, I take it to him before I go to help Brother Dirk."

My curiosity had reached new heights. "Does that happen very often? I mean, does your father receive many letters?"

"Only two. But Papa said his letters are a secret, so I don't think I should have told you."

"I promise I won't say a word. You don't need to worry about telling me." I squeezed his hand. "And, Lukas?"

He gazed up at me. "What, Mama?"

"We don't keep secrets from each other. Don't ever be afraid to tell me anything. Do you understand?"

After a quick nod, he pointed toward the doctor's office. "Look! Papa's sitting outside." He turned loose of my hand and raced toward Fred. "Papa! Papa!"

The excitement in his boyish voice carried on the early evening breeze, and a strand of jealousy encircled and squeezed my heart. I should have been pleased to hear the boy's excitement, pleased by the establishment of this new relationship, and pleased that Fred now desired to spend time with his son. Yet a part of me resented the fact that he'd so easily won the boy's affection.

These jealous feelings had never surfaced when Lukas wanted to spend time with Dirk, but with Fred it was different. Fred didn't deserve such adoration—not yet. It didn't seem fair that he hadn't had to work any harder to gain Lukas's trust and affection.

I disliked my harsh feelings, but hard as I tried, my jealousy refused to be tucked away. My gait slowed as I watched my son and his father laughing together. Isn't this what I had longed for during those years in Baltimore? Why couldn't I appreciate this wonderful gift I'd now received? Why did I feel anger and jealousy rather than thankfulness and joy? Did I want Fred to suffer the way he'd made Lukas and me suffer?

"How come you're so down in the mouth?"

Startled by Fred's abrupt question, I forced a slight smile and shrugged. "I'm not down in the mouth—just thinking."

"I took your advice and asked the doc 'bout the wheelchair. Thought you'd be pleased." He leaned forward a few inches and lowered his voice. "Don't think he liked the idea much, but I finally convinced him."

"Was he worried about the infection in your side or the malaria?"

Fred pointed to his side. "The infection. I told him he worries too much. If anything happens, it will be my fault, not his."

He motioned to Lukas to get behind the chair. "Come on and push me, son. Let's take a walk."

Moving quickly, I stepped to the rear of the chair. "I'll push you. The chair is probably too difficult for Lukas to manage."

"Get outta there and let him push, Andrea. He's not a baby anymore." He looked over his right shoulder. "It ain't too hard for ya, is it, boy?"

"Naw, I can do it, Papa."

Suddenly I felt like the fifth wheel on a wagon. Though I didn't touch the handles of the wheelchair, I remained by Lukas's side in case he needed help. Fred might think the boy could push him without difficulty, but I was sure the board sidewalks would prove difficult for maneuvering the wheelchair.

"Ya coddle him too much, Andrea. Lukas is a big boy who can do lots of things if you'd just let him. Ain't that right, son?"

Lukas hesitated, his wavering uncertainty clear. When he looked at me, I nodded my reassurance and he agreed with his father. "Mama lets me do lots of things, too. She lets me go all around the village by myself, and she lets me go and make things at the tinsmith shop with Brother Dirk, and I can even clean the chicken coop, can't I, Mama?"

"Yes, and you do a very good job." I winked at him.

The wheelchair suddenly angled and caught on one of the wooden slats. Fred grabbed at the arms of the wheelchair.

"I'm sorry, Papa. Did I hurt you?" Fear edged the boy's voice.

"You're doing fine. I can take a bump or two." He motioned down the street. "Let's see if the barber is in his shop. I think I'd like a free haircut."

"I can trim your hair, Fred." In the past, I'd always cut his hair. "I'll bring my scissors tomorrow."

"Why should you do it when I can get a real barber to cut it for free? Wouldn't want the poor fellow sittin' around with nothin' to do, now would we?"

His question bore a mocking tone, and I wondered if he was baiting me. Did he want me to disagree or come to the defense of the barber? And why did he assume he could avail himself of anything in the village for free?

"I doubt the barbershop is open at this time." Maybe it was time to detail more fully the arrangements regarding his care. "The elders agreed to furnish you with free medical treatment as well as your room and board until you've healed, but I don't think they expect to offer you free haircuts when your wife can perform the duty for you."

He chuckled. "Won't hurt none to ask. We'll see how Christian these folks really are."

Once again, I was hearing remnants of the old Fred resurfacing. In spite of the heat, the hairs on the nape of my neck stood on end. "What made you decide it was your duty to test the faith of these people, Fred?"

He twisted in the chair and scowled at me. "It ain't your place to question me, woman. I'll do whatever I want. You understand?"

I'd gone too far and now regretted my decision to question him. I could withstand his angry words, but one look at Lukas was enough to tell me that Fred had frightened the boy. All color had drained from his face, and he clutched the handles of the wheelchair with such ferocity, his knuckles turned white. Hoping to reassure Lukas, I squeezed his arm and signaled that we would talk later.

He nodded, but the fear in his eyes remained. When we arrived at the barbershop a short time later, the door was closed and a sign hung in the window.

I stepped to one side of the wheelchair. "It says he'll be open at eight o'clock tomorrow morning."

"Want me to come over after school tomorrow and bring you, Papa?"

I touched Lukas's hand. "You're supposed to go directly to Brother Dirk's shop and help, remember?"

"He don't have to go there if I need him. He spends too much time with that tinsmith."

This time I didn't argue and neither did Lukas. I expected him to say he enjoyed spending time with Dirk, but he only tightened his lips. It seemed the boy's wisdom sometimes exceeded my own. We continued down the sidewalk—all of us silent until we finally neared the general store, where I motioned for Lukas to turn the wheelchair.

"We better start back to the doctor's office, or we'll be late for prayer meeting."

Lukas turned the chair and the three of us once again fell into silence until we had arrived at Dr. Karr's office. "Want me to push you inside, Papa?"

Fred nodded. "Might as well. The doctor will need to help me into bed."

Once inside, I instructed Lukas to tell the doctor we'd returned while I took over and maneuvered through the doorways and then placed the chair alongside Fred's bed.

Lukas bounded into the room moments later. "Dr. Karr said he'll come help you in a few minutes."

I took Lukas's hand and started for the door.

"Come over after school tomorrow, Lukas. I need your help."

I turned toward Fred. "He is supposed to go to the tinsmith's shop and help there after school. I'll be here in the morning and can help you with anything you need done."

He shook his head and smiled at Lukas. "I want my boy to come and help me. We do just fine together. Ain't that right, Lukas?"

Lukas bobbed his head. "Yes, Papa."

Fred gave a firm nod. "Then I'll see ya after school tomorrow." His glance shifted from the boy and settled on me. With a hard stare, he made the challenge clear—he expected his son to appear after school tomorrow and me not to interfere. To do so would only increase Fred's anger. I would explain to Dirk. He would understand.

One thing was plain: Fred hadn't changed his ways. At least not toward me.

There wasn't time to worry about Fred or his needs during the following week. Soon after we first arrived, I learned that onions and onion sets were grown as a cash crop throughout the villages. Each year the farmers planted far more onions than could ever be used in the colonies, and once the onions were ready for harvest, help was expected from among the garden workers, farm workers, and kitchen workers.

Although Greta and I hadn't helped dig the onions, Sister Erma volunteered our help with the sorting process. We began yesterday and there was little doubt we'd be sorting for at least two or three more days. I'd never seen so many onions in all my life.

Except for short breaks when we hurried back to help in the kitchen, we cleaned dirt from the onions that had to be sorted by size.

Using the back of her hand, Greta swiped a strand of hair from her forehead. She'd been unusually quiet all day. I moved a step closer to her. "Are you not well today? You haven't said more than a few words all morning."

She hiked one shoulder. "I am not sick, but I think my heart is going to break." As a tear slipped down her cheek, she removed a handkerchief from her pocket.

I glanced toward the women working on the other side of the drying rack, but they hadn't noticed Greta's tears. "What has happened?"

"I'll tell you later—when we're alone."

We continued our work in silence, but a short time later several of the women began to sing, and soon the rest joined in. I didn't know the song, but I hummed along, glad for any diversion. I couldn't imagine what could be troubling Greta, but because of her usually happy nature, I feared it was something serious.

As soon as we were dismissed to go back and help in the kitchen, I reached for Greta's hand. "Tell me what is troubling you."

"It's Benjamin." She burst into tears as soon as she'd uttered his name.

"Has something happened to him?" Perhaps he'd been injured while working in the flour mill.

"Nein. It is my father." Once again her tears flowed and she hiccoughed.

"Your father has been injured?"

"Nein. He opposes Benjamin."

My confusion mounted. She'd told me some time ago that her father wasn't fond of Benjamin, but I was sure something more must have happened. If she didn't quit crying, I'd never find out. "Blow your nose and tell me exactly what has happened."

She did as I instructed and then giggled. "You sound like you're talking to Lukas."

I chuckled. "I'm glad it worked."

"Benjamin's family is moving to Main Amana." She exhaled a deep breath.

"But why?" Brother Lutz was second only to the farm *Baas* in West Amana, a position of great responsibility.

"There is a need for another farm Baas in Main, and the elders believe Brother Lutz is best qualified to fill the position. He is pleased that he will have more responsibilities and be of greater service to the colonies. That means Benjamin will move, as well. I am sure they will be glad to have another worker at their flour mill."

"But what if he asks to stay here in West? Would the elders let him?"

She shook her head. "Families stay together. He could never suggest such a thing. But that is not the worst of it."

I didn't know how it could be any worse for her. Benjamin would be going to another village, and seeing him would be nearly impossible. Granted, they might be able to visit on an occasional Sunday afternoon, but the villages were several miles apart, and he'd have to walk.

I arched my brows. "What else has happened?"

"Benjamin spoke to my father and asked if he could seek the elders' permission to marry me. He wanted to gain their permission so that when he moved to Main, we could begin our year of separation." Her lips drooped and another tear slipped down her cheek.

"Your father would not agree?"

193

She shook her head. "He said he would not agree to the marriage and Benjamin should not go to the elders. If he does, my father will object."

"I'm sorry, Greta. I know this is very difficult for both you and Benjamin." I wanted to offer my help, but there was nothing I could do. I now knew the pain of being separated from the man you loved, and my heart ached for Greta. Still, she could hang on to hope that her situation might change. I, however, could only pray that God would remove my feelings for Dirk. I grasped her hand as we continued on our way. "Maybe once your father has had an opportunity to see the pain this separation causes you, he will rethink his decision."

She shook her head. "My father is a stubborn man. I don't think I could ever change his mind."

"Then maybe God will do it for you. We must continue to pray that he will see Benjamin as a fine young man and have a change of heart."

CHAPTER 17

September 1890
Dirk

Lukas bounded into the shop, strands of brown curls matted to his forehead and a bit of perspiration shining on his nose. I looked up from my workbench, where I'd been working on new gutters for the general store, and greeted the boy.

"Looks like you've been running or the temperature has warmed considerably over the last hour." The temperature had been fluctuating throughout the day, and I hadn't been outdoors since walking home from the Küche.

Though I enjoyed these early fall days when asters edged the walkways and gardens in our village and a few of the trees were starting to display varying shades of crimson and gold, today I'd skipped the midday lunch and remained inside to finish the gutters.

Lukas grinned and wiped his shirtsleeve across his forehead. "It is much warmer than earlier, and I ran from the doctor's office. I didn't want to be late."

I chuckled and pointed to his pocket. "You should use your handkerchief instead of your sleeve, and I have told you that I will not worry unless you are more than a half hour late. I know you sometimes stop to see your Vater after school."

His upper lip quivered. "Not very often."

"There is no reason to be upset, Lukas." I forced a smile. "It is gut that you want to see your Vater. I am pleased he wants to spend time with you."

Even though I tried to hide my jealousy, the boy likely heard the resentment in my tone. Fred had gained the boy's affection with greater ease than I'd thought possible. Fred's ability to so easily win his son's trust troubled me. Each day, I prayed for the boy's protection.

Andrea had never shared all the details of her life with Fred, but I had heard enough to know the man had not been a good father to Lukas or a good husband to her. And though I understood it would be best for their family to reunite, my feelings for both the boy and his mother remained far too strong.

I had considered severing ties with Lukas—telling him we no longer needed him to help after school. I could sweep the shop and place my tools back in their proper places at the end of each day, but such dismissive behavior would only pain Lukas. Besides, I couldn't bear the thought of not seeing him each day.

"Want me to sweep the floor or take the trash to the barrel?" His voice bore a pleading sound that tore at my heart. He wanted to make everybody happy. A big job for such a little boy.

"Nein. I am tired of working on these gutters. Would you like to help me with a new cookie cutter pattern?"

The worried look I had detected in his eyes only moments earlier was immediately replaced with one of joy. "Is it a pattern Werner drew?"

"Ja, it is. It's a special star. He thought the sisters would like it for their Christmas baking." I strode to the worktable and held up the pattern. "What do you think?"

Werner sat at a table near the rear of the room, but he perked to attention at the mention of his new design. "Tell the truth, Lukas. If you do not like it, I want to know. I can change it before Brother Dirk begins to make them."

Lukas stepped forward and took the pattern from my hand. After moving it about and staring at it for several moments, he gave a firm nod. "I like it very much. I think the sisters will like it, too." He leaned around me and looked at Werner. "I wish I could draw as good as you, Werner."

Werner beamed at him. "God has given me this talent. Maybe He will give it to you, too."

I tousled Lukas's curls. "We are all different and God gives each of us special abilities. Some of us can draw, some can work with tin, some can make shoes, some can work with animals, but all of us can serve God. As you become older, you will discover your gift and you can serve Him, too."

Lukas settled on the high stool next to mine. "My father says there isn't any God."

A chill rushed over me and the hair on my neck bristled. "Did he? And why would he say such a thing?"

"He asked me what I was learning in school. When I told him we study the Bible and learn about God, he said there is no God and I shouldn't believe what Brother Urbinger tells me or what I hear in prayer meetings."

"And did you tell your Mutter what you have told me?"

He looked at me with solemn eyes. "Nein. I do not want to cause them to fight. My father might become angry with me if I tell her. He likes me to keep secrets."

The boy's admission heightened my concern. I did not want to come between Lukas and his father, yet a father asking his son to keep secrets was not good. Especially if he was being told to keep them from his mother. Beyond telling his son there was no God, I wondered what other secrets Fred might be telling the boy. Did he not realize the added anxiety such a request would place on his son? I didn't want to condone the act, but maybe I could relieve a bit of Lukas's concern.

"Sometimes we all keep secrets. If you make a Christmas gift for your Mutter, you will want to keep it a secret so she will be surprised when you give it to her, ja?"

He nodded. "But Papa's secrets are different." He leaned close and rested his head against my arm. "Today he told me that when he is strong enough, we will go to my grandfather's farm. He said it's a secret, but I know you won't tell."

I smiled. "Your secret is safe with me." After hesitating for a moment, I looked into his eyes. "You can trust your Mutter, too. I know she will always keep your secrets."

I was not yet so old that I had forgotten the difficulty of keeping a secret. There had been times in my younger years when I thought I would explode if I could not tell at least one person a secret that had been entrusted to me. Fortunately, age and wisdom had helped me overcome that need. I had soon learned that all of my friends felt that same need, and soon the secret that had been for my ears alone resonated in the school yard.

He bobbed his head. "I know. When I told her about Papa's secret letters, she said she would not say a word, but I didn't want to tell her about visiting the farm."

I wondered about the secret letters but did not ask. If Lukas wanted to tell me, he would. In truth, it would probably be better if I did not know what was going on within their small family.

After measuring and marking a piece of tin, I handed the tin snips to Lukas. "You can begin over here by cutting out the star."

He curled his tongue between his lips and slowly began cutting the tin. Not wanting to ruin his concentration, I remained silent while he worked his way around the points. When he looked up at me, I nodded and motioned for him to continue. "You are doing a gut job. For sure, this will be a fine cookie cutter."

Once he'd finished, he held up the piece of tin and carefully examined his work. "I went off the line. One point is uneven." His lip quivered.

"No two people are alike and no two cookie cutters are exactly the same, either. You did a fine job and you should not be discouraged. I could not have done so well at your age."

Lukas's eyes brightened. "You couldn't?"

"Nein. You should be very proud of your work. I do not know any boy your age who could cut tin with such fine precision."

He squared his shoulders and pointed to another piece of tin. "Will you make the edges of the star from that piece?"

"Nein. *You* will cut the edges and the handle, but I will solder them. The straight lines will be much easier than the angle. I will help you use the foot shear." I had already marked the piece that would form an edge for the cookie cutter. "There is enough time for you to cut it before we must clean the shop."

Lukas hesitated and then looked at me. "My papa says we're going to be rich someday. Do you think that's true?"

"I do not know what is in the future for any of us, Lukas, but I know for sure I will never have lots of money or own my own land, but I still feel rich. I have gut friends, a warm house, plenty of food, and work that I enjoy. That is enough to make me rich."

Lukas's thin eyebrows pinched together. "That's not the kind of rich my papa was talking about. He says we're going to have lots of money."

"Did he tell you where he was going to get all this money?"

The boy shook his head. "When I asked him, he said he would tell me when the time was right, but I don't know when that will be." Worry creased his youthful forehead.

I gestured toward the piece of tin. "Go ahead and cut the strips." I gently squeezed his shoulder. "Money is not something you need to worry about."

My thoughts wandered while Lukas cut the tin. Fred seemed to be making plans of some sort, yet I could not imagine what they would be. How he would become rich overnight was beyond my comprehension. When he arrived, he told Andrea he had no money, and he had done nothing to increase his wealth while recuperating at the doctor's office. In his zeal to win the boy's affection and by thinking money would impress Lukas, Fred had likely woven a tale of lies. If not, he was keeping things from his wife.

Telling Lukas a story about being rich did not bother me much. However, Fred's disbelief in God concerned me a great deal. I worried he would attempt to undermine the boy's budding faith. Though I longed to speak with Andrea about my suspicions, I would not break my word to the boy.

In truth, speaking with Andrea was not an option. To be alone with her would prove much too difficult. Each day I asked God to remove this longing for her from my heart, but my feelings still remained strong. I had hoped that as time passed, I would forget the sound of her laughter and the tenderness of her touch. Instead, one look at her in the Küche and every remembrance of our times together rushed back like a flooding stream. Rather than talking to Andrea, I would do my best to be a positive influence upon her son. In the meantime, I would talk to Brother Urbinger. The schoolteacher would immediately become aware of any changes in Lukas's outlook regarding his faith and God.

Once Lukas finished cutting the metal, he, Werner, and I joined forces to clean up the shop before the dinner bell rang to announce the evening meal. Lukas carried the last of the trash outdoors to the barrel as the bell tolled in the distance.

The three of us walked to the Küche together and waited near the men's door until Sister Erma flung open the doors. On cue, the men and women entered and walked to their tables. Once we had recited the before-dinner prayer, benches scraped on the wooden floors as we all sat down. Hoping for a glimpse of Sister Andrea, I glanced toward the doorway leading from the dining room into the Küche.

Instead of Andrea, Sister Greta stood framed between the two rooms. She met my gaze and gestured, but I was unsure what to make of her signal. She tipped her head as though she wanted to speak to me outdoors, but I could not leave the table, and she could not leave the Küche.

Uncertain what to do, I shrugged and hoped she would realize I had not understood what she wanted. Except for the clanging of silver on china, the only noises in the Küche were the sounds of banging pots and pans or the clatter of spoons scraping food into heavy bowls. Talking during mealtime was frowned upon, and since we were allotted only fifteen minutes to eat our meals, the elders seldom had to remind us to remain quiet. Besides, unless there was urgent work requiring our attention, we could visit for a short time after the meals.

When we were finished, all of us stood and recited the after-meal prayer. Lukas trotted toward the kitchen to visit with his mother, and I strode toward the men's door. I hadn't gone far when Lukas returned and tugged on my hand.

"Sister Greta would like to talk to you. She said she would meet you out near the chicken coop."

"Thank you, Lukas." He grinned and trotted back toward the kitchen while I exited out the men's door.

I had hoped to speak to Brother Urbinger, but it could wait until tomorrow. The schoolteacher enjoyed talking, and if I started a conversation with him, it could be a half hour or longer before I could break away. I didn't want to take a chance and leave Sister Greta waiting. She'd had enough disappointment to bear.

As I circled around, I caught sight of her. Instead of standing near the chicken coop, she'd moved to the edge of the garden and was pulling weeds from the flowering border of mums and asters.

"I did not know the Küche workers also had to weed the flower beds." I smiled as I approached.

She sat back on her heels. Her lips curved in a strained smile. "Thank you for coming, Dirk. I know you are busy."

I arched my brows. "Never am I too busy for a friend. You should know I am always pleased to visit with you, Greta." I leaned against the chicken coop. "How can I help you?"

She stood and closed the few steps between us. "My Vater remains steadfast in his dislike of Benjamin. I thought my Vater would change his opinion once he saw how much I love and miss Benjamin—that he would relent and agree to our marriage—but it has made no difference."

"Do you want me to speak with him? Do you think that would help? If so, I am willing to try."

"Nein. He believes that I should set my mind on another man, and then I will realize Benjamin is an unsuitable prospect."

I wasn't certain where this was going to lead, but the conversation had become uncomfortable. "Maybe that is a gut idea. If your love for Benjamin remains steadfast, your Vater may accept that he has been wrong. Then perhaps he will grant permission."

"That's what I have been thinking, too." She inhaled a deep breath. "I am glad you agree."

"What about August Murbach or Christoph Baum? They are both nice fellows. I think either one would please your Vater."

She shook her head. "Brother August wants to remain single. His Mutter told Sister Erma."

"Then what about Christoph? He is nice looking enough and a fine watchmaker, too."

She frowned. "He has already asked the elders for permission to marry Sister Anna. Did you not know?"

"I would not have suggested his name if I had known." I had seen Christoph only yesterday. "When will he leave for his year of separation?"

"Sister Anna said they have received permission to marry, but the elders haven't decided about their separation yet. There is a need for Christoph in West, so who can say—the elders may let him remain here, which would be very nice for both of them."

"Ja, for sure it would." I massaged my forehead and tried to think of some other prospect. "Maybe by tomorrow I can think of someone else."

She folded her arms against her waist and glared at me. "What about you, Dirk? You're the one I want to help me, not Christoph or August or anyone else."

"*Me*? But I—"

"But you are what? In love with Andrea?"

She didn't give me a chance to admit or deny her question.

"Well, I am in love with Benjamin, so that makes it ideal. My Vater will think it is perfect. He has always wanted us to be together."

"Ja, but what if your Vater discovers this is only a trick? I think he would be angry with both of us. There would be no defense for our behavior. Both of us would be demoted to children's church—or maybe forbidden to attend Sunday meetings."

The longer we talked, the more I disliked this idea. Unless a member remained home due to illness, being absent from Sunday meetings meant only one thing—the elders had deemed your misdeeds especially serious. Being relegated to children's church would be an embarrassment, but not as serious as being banned from meetings. And even more important, this idea of deceit went against all of our teachings—against God's Word.

"I do not think—"

Greta grasped my arm. "It is my only chance, Dirk. Please say you will pretend to care for me. You haven't been anywhere with the rest of us since Andrea's husband arrived. We will have fun, like the old days, but we should not tell anyone we are playacting. If my Vater found out, he would be furious." She tightened her hold. "Please help me."

Greta was my friend. I did not have the strength to refuse her. But what would Andrea think?

CHAPTER 18

On several occasions over the next two days, I considered telling Greta that our decision had been made in haste and we should consider a different solution. The names of other single men had come to mind, and any one of them would doubtless satisfy her father's wish for a mature, conscientious, godly husband for Greta. Perhaps she might actually fall in love with one of them—something that would never occur between the two of us.

I had not been surprised by her father's reluctance to give the couple his blessing. Benjamin was a godly young man, but his behavior often appeared immature and childlike. He enjoyed laughter, fun, and practical jokes more than most, and while Greta found him charming, her father considered Benjamin's carefree attitude unsuitable for a grown man. If Benjamin had behaved in a more restrained manner in the presence of the older men, I would not be in this predicament.

Though it didn't appear to deter Greta in the least, the thought of being banned from meetings continued to plague me, and after prayer meeting I hurried to her side. "We need to talk."

She smiled at me in such a beguiling manner that I took a backward step. "Vater is watching us. You should not back away from me." She tipped her head to one side and batted her eyelashes.

"Stop doing that, Greta." I glanced over my shoulder and caught sight of Andrea. She was watching us as closely as Greta's father was. My stomach clenched. "Did you speak to Andrea about this plan of yours?"

"Nein. For either of us to tell anyone would be a mistake. It is too easy to forget and let things slip. She might mention our plan to Sister Erma, and she would tell my Mutter, who would then tell my Vater, and then—"

"And then we would both be banned from meetings for weeks, maybe months." My muscles tightened at the thought.

"Ja, so you should keep your lips sealed." Greta's charming smile returned as her father and mother approached.

"Brother Dirk! Is a fine evening, ja?" Greta's father lightly slapped my shoulder. "You should walk back to the house with Greta. I am sure she would enjoy your company."

Unless I moved quickly, my opportunity would disappear. I needed to call a halt to this idea before it went any further. I came alongside her and then motioned for her to fall back a short distance. "I have decided this arrangement is not a gut plan. It goes against everything we believe."

Any sign of her earlier smile disappeared. "There is no reason to change things. The plan is perfect." Her angry words hissed on the evening breeze.

Startled by her animosity, I returned her frown. "It is a very bad idea. Now that I have had more time to think, I cannot agree to deceive your Vater. If you are determined to carry out this idea, you will need to find someone else."

She stopped midstep and glared at me. "You already agreed, Dirk. You cannot go back on your word. Besides, you know I have no interest in anyone other than Benjamin. And how could I tell another man what I have told you? They would never agree to spend time with me if they knew it was only a scheme so that I could eventually marry Benjamin."

I sighed. It would do no good to tell her she might find another man more appealing once Benjamin moved from the village. She had considered this plan for a far longer time and in much more detail than I had imagined. "Let me have some time to think about some other idea."

Her mother stopped and glanced over her shoulder. "Greta! You should continue walking."

She dismissed my suggestion with a shake of her head. "You are supposed to be my friend. Friends help each other, Dirk."

We were within hearing distance of her parents, so I lowered my voice and leaned closer as we walked. "It is unfair to deceive your Vater, and I do not think our heavenly Father would approve of such a decision, either. There must be some other way."

"There is not. Besides, I told my Vater you asked to take me on a picnic next Sunday afternoon." She smiled. "He was very pleased to give his approval."

I gasped. "But I did not invite you to go to a picnic next Sunday. I have not invited you to go anywhere."

"I know, but I wanted to move forward with the plan. You had already agreed, and I decided the sooner we began, the sooner I could tell my Vater that my feelings for Benjamin have not changed." Her eyes flashed with anger. "Don't make a fool of me, Dirk."

My stomach muscles tightened. "I will go to the picnic, but only as your friend, and you should not take this plan any further. Do not tell others we are courting, and understand that I will not ask for your father's permission to court you. If anyone asks, I will tell them we remain no more than friends." I met her fiery gaze. "I do not want you to tell others untruths that will later cause you embarrassment. You understand what I am telling you, ja?"

She clenched her lips together and marched off without an answer. There was no doubt I had angered her. If I had refused to help her when she first asked, I wouldn't be in the middle of this precarious situation. Though she hadn't agreed, I would have to trust that Greta would go no further with her scheme.

Andrea

Sister Erma bustled into the kitchen on Sunday wearing her black gauze cap with delicate black tatted edging and her sheer black wool shoulder shawl. Tucked in the crook of her arm, she carried her Bible and *Psalterspiel*, the large book that contained the psalms and hymns sung during Sunday meetings.

She stopped in front of the kitchen door. "Before long, the snow will fly and I will need to replace this lightweight shawl with my heavy one. Each year the seasons pass with greater speed. As you get older, you will notice." Her eyes clouded with a hint of sadness as she turned to face me. "You have any questions before Lukas and I depart for meeting?"

I shook my head. "Lukas is waiting for you on the porch." I had given him strict instructions to remain on the porch. The grass remained wet with early morning dew, and I didn't want him going to meeting with wet or dirty shoes.

"The two of you are going to visit Fred this afternoon?"

"If you do not need me to help in the kitchen." Greta normally helped prepare supper on Sundays, and I assumed she would do so today.

"Greta is going to attend a picnic, and I told her I could make do without her if she did not want to come back early." Sister Erma shifted the books to her other arm. "She has been sad since Benjamin moved to Main, and I thought the picnic would be gut for her."

I was surprised to learn that Greta would be attending a picnic this afternoon. In the past, she had always told me whenever she had special plans. "I can come back early. Fred will understand." I gestured toward her arm. "Have Lukas carry the Bible and *Psalterspiel* for you. It will make him feel important."

She chuckled as the bell tolled from the village tower. "And it will make the walk to meeting much easier, too. We better hurry or we will be late."

I rushed to the door as she stepped from the porch. "Should I prepare a picnic basket for Greta?"

Sister Erma turned. "If you have time, that would be nice. Otherwise, she can see to it after we return from meeting. Pack enough for two. Brother Dirk will be escorting her."

"Dirk?" I'd barely whispered his name, but Sister Erma heard me. She turned and gave a firm nod.

"Is gut, ja? I think Brother Dirk will cheer Sister Greta, and I think it will go the other way, too." She twisted her fingers back and forth to emphasize her point.

My stomach squeezed tighter than a pair of new leather shoes. I wanted to shout that it was not good, but I forced a smile and gave a slight nod before turning away. Had Greta avoided telling me because she knew the news would give rise to questions—and injured feelings? Did she believe it would be easier for me to discover the information from someone else? I caught my lower lip between my teeth. Those ideas weren't the reason.

Instead, I was certain she hadn't mentioned the outing because she knew I would question her for details. And if that was her supposition, she was correct. Although she had every right to go on a picnic with Dirk, her secretive behavior caused my thoughts to scatter.

While the two kitchen helpers peeled and sliced potatoes, I prepared the horseradish sauce to be served with the beef. My nose and eyes watered as I grated the pungent root. Usually the junior girls would have been assigned the task, but today I wanted an excuse for my tears. I had lost Dirk as a friend, and now it seemed I would lose Greta, as well.

While the girls went into the dining room to set the tables, I sliced bread and slathered it with butter before wrapping it in a cloth and placing it alongside a small packet of sliced beef in the wicker basket. I doubted they would want to take a jar of soup, but Dirk would likely want some of the fried potatoes and some of the horseradish sauce for his beef.

The dinner bell tolled as I placed the basket on a worktable at the far end of the kitchen. I hurried to check that the girls had completed preparations in the dining room and then returned to the kitchen. I wanted to be present when Greta arrived.

Sister Erma was the first to enter the kitchen. "I will be downstairs as soon as I change my dress and shawl."

"No need to rush. Everything is ready."

She glanced over her shoulder. "The food is not ready until I have tasted it. You learned this a long time ago, did you not, Sister Andrea?"

I smiled as she disappeared from the room without waiting for my answer. On my first day in the kitchen, I had been warned that nothing should be placed in the serving bowls until it had passed Sister Erma's taste test. "If you put food in the bowls and it needs more seasoning, then it wastes too much time," she'd explained.

Sister Erma usually decreed that the foods prepared by Greta or me needed more salt or pepper, or perhaps some additional dill or extra chives. At first, her critique of my food preparation had frustrated me, but it hadn't taken long for me to learn that her assessments were correct. I doubted she would find my horseradish sauce perfect. She considered sauces and gravies her specialties.

The hinges on the back door creaked, and I turned to see Greta entering the kitchen. I moved to the far end of the kitchen and stood beside the table, my hand resting on the wicker basket. "Is this what you've come for?"

Her smile lacked its usual warmth. "You did not need to prepare the basket. I told Sister Erma I could do it after meeting."

"Sister Erma tells me you are going on a picnic with Brother Dirk."

She crossed the room, but I continued to rest my hand on the handle of the basket. Her gaze settled on my hand. "Ja. Unless he decides on another spot, I think we are going to the pond."

"Why did you not tell me you and Dirk were going on a picnic this afternoon? When I asked you if you had any plans for today, you never mentioned your outing. Why is that, Greta?"

She frowned. "Because it slipped my mind. I do not understand why you are annoyed that I am going out for the afternoon. Sister Erma gave me permission."

"And is your father happy now?"

Greta perched her hands on her hips. "What do you mean by that question?"

I knew she understood what I meant, but since she asked, I

forged on. "He wants you to marry Dirk. You told me that when I first arrived. Now that Benjamin is gone, it appears that you have set your cap for Dirk."

"What does 'set your cap' mean?"

"That you intend to win his affection and marry him."

She reached for the basket, but her lips remained sealed.

"So it is true. When I first asked you about Dirk, you told me that you were friends and you thought of him as a brother, nothing more. It seems you've changed your mind."

She tugged on the basket. "You have a husband, Andrea. What happens between Dirk and me should not concern you. Not at all."

I released my hold and took a backward step. She was right. Shortly after Fred arrived, I had told myself that Dirk deserved to be happy, to marry and have children. But I hadn't meant it. Not unless it included me.

CHAPTER 19

"Sister Andrea!" Brother Bosch greeted me with a wide smile and sparkling eyes as he crossed the backyard. He sat down beside me on the porch, where I was cleaning beets. "I know you are busy since Sister Greta is helping with the potato harvest, but I wanted to talk to you about your husband."

Early this morning, Sister Greta had departed for the potato field in a horse-drawn wagon filled with other sisters. Although each kitchen house had its own garden, there was only one potato field for the entire village. As a result, each Küchebaas provided one worker during each week of harvest. Those of us who remained in the kitchen were expected to complete the duties of our sisters harvesting in the field.

Sister Greta had been pleased to receive the assignment. Since her outing with Dirk, our friendship had become strained. We communicated what was necessary to keep the kitchen operating smoothly but discussed little else. I knew she would enjoy visiting with the other sisters while working in the fields, and a part of me wished I had been assigned the task. Perhaps Sister Erma would send me next week.

I dropped my knife onto the wooden tray. Any mention of my husband's name was enough to gain my full attention. "There is a problem? Has he returned to his old ways with Dr. Karr?"

"Nein. The doctor reports your husband has remained respectful—most of the time." Brother Bosch pulled the familiar pipe from his jacket. "He is not a perfect patient, but no man is perfect—only our Lord. With God's help, your husband has changed some of his harsh ways, but old habits are slow to die." He filled the bowl of his pipe with tobacco before he continued. "You know the doctor has declared Fred well enough to take walks, ja?" He arched his brows and waited.

"Yes. On my recent visits, we have been taking walks. I have observed his strength increasing each day." I didn't add that I had become increasingly concerned about what was going to happen when the doctor declared Fred well enough to be discharged from his daily care.

Brother Bosch struck a match and held it to the bowl of his pipe. I waited while he puffed on the stem and the tobacco glowed red. He gave a satisfied nod as his smoke ring was carried off on the morning breeze. "This is gut, but now that he has been able to walk about the village, he believes he is ready to move from the doctor's office."

My heart thumped with such ferocity, I placed my hand on my chest. "And Dr. Karr? What does he think?"

Brother Bosch had leaned close and cupped his ear to hear my whispered questions. "He believes your husband could live elsewhere as long as he continues to return to the office each day to have his wound examined and his bandage changed. He is not positive the malaria is completely controlled, but that could be regulated during daily office visits."

I hadn't been oblivious to Fred's physical improvement. And though I wondered about our future once Dr. Karr discharged him, I hadn't expected to face the challenge this soon.

"So the doctor wants Fred to move from his house?" I squeezed my trembling hands together.

"Nein. It is Fred who wants to leave the doctor's house. He tells the doctor he wants to be reunited with you and his son." Brother Bosch permitted his gaze to wander across the backyard before turning back to me. "This presents us with an unforeseen problem, Sister Andrea."

"And what is that?"

"Here in the villages, we have hired outsiders to work for us when needed—men who could help in the fields during harvest and planting seasons, and single women to help in the kitchens from time to time. Never before have we had an outsider family live among us." He held the pipe bowl in his hand and pointed the stem in my direction. "We do not have proper accommodations for such a circumstance. There is a dormitory for the men, but we cannot place your family there, and the elders believe it is unsuitable for a family of nonmembers to live in a house with members." He hiked one shoulder. "I agree with this principle."

I understood that moving our family into a house occupied by colonists could present a multitude of problems, especially if Fred wasn't on his best behavior. To have a female outsider living in the kitchen house was not unusual, but the elders would never agree to move Fred into Sister Erma's apartment with Lukas and me. Had they decided we should leave the colonies? How would we live? And how would I find the strength to live with Fred?

"Have the elders arrived at a decision?" My voice trembled and I swallowed hard.

"Ja, and this is where I will need your help."

Not wanting to miss a word he would say, I leaned toward him. "Anything."

He smiled. "Do not answer so fast. You should wait until you hear what I will ask, Sister Andrea."

Although I nodded my agreement, there could be nothing he would ask that would meet with my disagreement. Brother Bosch would never ask me to do anything improper, so I eagerly waited to hear his request.

"Even though your husband could live in private quarters, the elders agree it would be in the best interest of everyone in our village if he remained at Dr. Karr's office."

My shoulders relaxed as he uttered the reprieve. "That decision is fine with me, Brother Bosch."

"Ja, but we doubt it will be fine with your husband. The elders would like you to go with me when I deliver the news. They fear your husband may direct his anger at Dr. Karr after I depart. If you are present, they believe you can help to soothe his anger and convince him this is a gut decision for his health and for your family."

"When will you tell him?"

"If you are willing to go with me, we could go before prayer meeting this evening."

I nodded. "I am willing. Should I meet you at the doctor's office?"

He reached forward, knocked his pipe against the porch railing, and watched the charred tobacco scatter across the bricks below. "Ja. I will wait outside until you arrive."

As Brother Bosch turned to leave, I picked up a beet and my knife and set to work while trying to prepare for any opposition

Fred might pose. I didn't relish tonight's meeting, but a confrontation with Fred would be easier than the alternative. If he didn't agree to reason, we would have to leave the village—and I had many arguments against that option.

Not long after Brother Bosch departed, Sister Erma appeared at the back door. She wiped her hands on her apron as she stepped outside. "I see Brother Heinrich was here to visit with you."

"He was." I continued cleaning the beets. "Are we going to can beets this afternoon?" The large basket held far too many for one meal, but I hadn't seen any canning jars in the kitchen this morning.

She sat down in the chair Brother Bosch had occupied a short time ago. "Ja, I was going to the cellar to bring up some jars." She picked up one of the beets and rolled it in her palm. "Did Brother Heinrich bring you some special news?"

She'd withheld her curiosity as long as possible. I nodded. "Yes. He's going to meet me at the doctor's office this evening before prayer service." I detailed the remainder of our conversation and answered her ensuing questions. Once satisfied that she'd been fully informed, she stood and gestured toward the cellar doors. "I need to get started washing and boiling jars, or there will not be enough time to can beets this afternoon."

I would have preferred to wait until tomorrow, but I didn't offer my opinion. In truth, it was probably better if I remained busy throughout the afternoon. I wouldn't have time to worry about what Fred might do or say when we met with him later that evening.

Hours later, Lukas hurtled into the kitchen. I turned on my heel and motioned for him to be careful. Jars of the recently canned beets now stood on the worktable, and I envisioned them crashing to the floor.

"Why are you running, Lukas?"

"Papa said he's going to move from Dr. Karr's office. Did you know?" Still panting, he leaned forward, rested his hands on his thighs, and gasped for air.

I hurried to his side. "What else did he tell you?"

"He needs a wagon to help move his trunk. Should I go and ask the farm Baas?"

I shook my head. "No. If anything is needed, I'll see to it."

"But Papa said I should tell you. I don't want him to be mad at me." His lower lip trembled, and I stooped down beside him.

"You don't need to be afraid, Lukas. I'll make sure your father knows you did what he asked. In fact, I don't want you to go with me when I visit this evening. Brother Bosch wants to talk with your father, so he is meeting me at Dr. Karr's office. You can stay here and walk to prayer meeting with Sister Erma." I stroked his arm. "Does that help lessen your fear?"

He straightened his shoulders. "I didn't say I was afraid. Papa says only babies are afraid."

"That's not true, Lukas. Sometimes fear is what keeps us safe."

He pushed damp curls from his forehead. "You mean like coming in the house when there's lightning or when it's dark outside?"

"That's right." I wasn't surprised by the examples Lukas had given me. He'd once seen lightning strike a ship at the Baltimore docks that resulted in a fire. Since then, he'd been fearful of lightning and would run inside whenever storms threatened. Just as Lukas had learned about lightning, he'd discovered that the streets around our tenement building changed from worrisome to terrifying at night and healthy fear required we remain indoors after sunset.

"You won't tell Papa I was afraid, will you?"

His pleading tone pained me. In spite of Fred's past neglect and anger, the boy still longed to win his approval. "No. I'll tell him you gave me his message. If he's angry, it will be with me—not you." He didn't appear completely convinced, but he wandered back outside to wait for the supper bell.

I said a quick prayer of protection for my son and then sighed. Fred would be angry with me, of that I was certain. He would not like being told what to do, and because I was joining Brother Bosch in the delivery of the news, I would be the target for his anger. It was a small price to pay for a few more weeks of peace in Amana.

Brother Bosch was waiting when I arrived at the doctor's office. "I'm sorry to keep you waiting."

"No apology is needed, Sister Andrea." He nodded toward the door. "You are ready?"

I inhaled a deep breath and nodded, but I didn't know if I would ever be ready to face Fred when I knew he was going to hear unwelcome news. I'd said a prayer on my way to the doctor's office and hoped Brother Bosch had done the same.

Brother Bosch held the door and I led the way toward Fred's room. Before Fred caught sight of me, he hollered from his room, "Did Lukas tell ya to bring a wagon to move my trunk, Andrea?" I stepped through the doorway, but Fred looked above me and settled his gaze on Brother Bosch. "I wasn't expecting any other company. Brother Bosch, ain't it?"

The older man nodded, crossed the room, and moved two straight-backed chairs close to Fred's bed. "I came with your wife because there is a matter we need to discuss."

With a wary look in his eyes, Fred pointed to himself and then to Brother Bosch. "You and me? What we got to talk about?"

Brother Bosch cleared his throat. "About your living arrangements."

"Oh, that. Ain't nothin' to discuss. The doc said I was good enough to move outta this place. I'm gonna borrow a wagon to move my things. My family should be livin' together."

The elder scooted forward on his chair. "So you are planning to leave the colonies and live elsewhere?"

"Not yet—ain't got the money I need to do that right now, but I want to live in a place where Andrea, me, and the boy can be together. Then, soon as I get things arranged, we'll be movin' on."

I wasn't certain what Fred had in mind or how he planned to arrange anything from a sickbed. He might be well enough to move from the doctor's office, but he wasn't well enough to work and earn money. And even if he was, saving enough to go anywhere would take a long period of time.

Brother Bosch rested his arms across his thighs. "Dr. Karr has told me what you want, Mr. Wilson, and our elders who make decisions for the village have met and discussed your living arrangements."

Fred's eyelids dropped to half-mast. "And?"

"You will need to remain here at Dr. Karr's office." Brother Bosch carefully explained the reasons for the decision and then sat back in his chair. When Fred remained silent, he said, "You understand why we have made this decision?"

"So you God-fearin' people don't think it's important for a family to live together?"

Brother Bosch shook his head. "That is not what I said. I have explained that we do not have the ability to provide you with what you desire."

Fred's jaw twitched and his fingers tightened around the sheet that covered most of his body. "I been walkin' up and down these here sidewalks, and there's all kinds of houses, but you're tellin' me there ain't no place in this whole village where we can live together?"

"That's correct. If you don't agree with our decision, you are always free to leave. Otherwise, the living arrangements must remain as they have been since you arrived." He waited a moment. "If you have no other questions, I'll leave you to visit with your wife."

The elder hadn't been gone for long when Fred suddenly stretched sideways and grasped my wrist. "You told 'em you didn't want to live with me, didn't ya?"

I wrested my arm from his grip and moved my chair to the other side of the room. I should have known better than to sit so close. "No. I didn't know the doctor had agreed you could move elsewhere until Brother Bosch came to tell me of the elders' decision."

Fury flashed in his eyes. "You expect me to believe that?"

"Whether you believe me or not makes no difference. The fact remains that we have no money and nowhere else to live. If we don't abide by their decisions, we will be without a place to lay our heads."

Fred rubbed his jaw. "Maybe we could make do in your father's barn. I could still return to see the doctor."

I gasped. "Winter is coming, Fred. How long do you think we could make do living in a barn? Besides, that barn does not belong to us. If you want to go and live in there, you go right ahead, but Lukas and I will remain where we are. I'm not going to let you put our son at risk—not anymore, Fred."

"Don't you be tellin' me what you will or won't do. You got you a lot of spunk since you come here to live. You think that old man is gonna protect you for the rest of your life? One day we'll be leavin' this place, and don't you think I'm gonna forget any of this."

The bell tolled in the distance and I stood. "I won't be back until tomorrow evening. It's potato harvest and we're short of help in the kitchen. In the meantime, I'm sure you'll maintain your good humor with Dr. Karr."

"Sarcasm ain't becomin', Andrea."

I turned and rubbed my wrist. "Neither is your rough treatment, Fred."

Eventually Fred would be well. What was I going to do then to protect Lukas—and myself?

CHAPTER 20

Once Greta and I had finished cleaning the kitchen on Sunday evening, Sister Erma casually mentioned that I was to work in the potato field beginning tomorrow morning. The prospect of working outdoors this week appealed to me, but a quick glance at Greta revealed her displeasure with the decision. We had been at odds since I'd quizzed her about picnicking with Dirk, and I didn't want to prolong the silence between us.

Both Dirk and Greta had every right to enjoy time together. And if I couldn't be with Dirk, Greta was a good choice for him.

I hung my dish towel to dry on a nearby rack. "If Greta would rather harvest potatoes, I'm willing to work in the kitchen, Sister Erma."

"Nein." She untied and removed her large apron. "The kitchen workers have always taken turns. Greta would not expect to go to the field every week." Turning her ample body toward Greta, she smiled. "This is right, is it not, Greta?"

"Ja, Sister Erma. We have always taken turns, but Sister Andrea did not grow up in the colonies, and she does not know how we harvest."

Sister Erma perched her hands on her hips and laughed. "She did not grow up cooking for fifty people, either, but she has learned how to do so in my Küche. Harvesting potatoes takes no special skill. Sister Andrea can pick up a row of potatoes as quickly as the next sister."

"Ja, but if she would rather be in the Küche—"

Sister Erma waved her to silence. "Last week you had the benefit of free time each evening, and I am sure Sister Andrea would enjoy the same privilege in the coming days."

Last week I had expected Greta to help clear dishes and clean the kitchen after supper, but Sister Erma explained that the kitchen workers who helped with harvest were released from all duties in the Küche—even helping clean the kitchen after supper.

Greta opened her mouth to protest, but Sister Erma shook her head. "It is settled. You will work in the Küche with me. Sister Andrea will go to the field and harvest potatoes."

"And next week?" Greta's tone bore a trace of determination.

Sister Erma arched her brows. "Maybe we will draw broom straws. Or maybe I will wait and see who has maintained the best attitude while working with me in the kitchen."

Greta clamped her lips together, yanked her apron from around her neck, and flung it on a hook near the door. "Guten Tag, Sisters." Her shoes pounded an angry beat as she crossed the wooden porch.

Never before had I seen Greta behave in such a manner. Though I wanted to help resolve this problem, I feared any further attempts to influence Sister Erma would only make matters worse. I would wait until after prayer meeting. By then, the older woman might be willing to discuss the problem in a little more detail. Until then, I'd go upstairs and see if Lukas needed help with any schoolwork.

Since the incident with Fred, I had deviated from my usual visiting schedule. While I hadn't discouraged Lukas's visits with his father, my visits had been less frequent. Lukas's desire to spend time with Fred remained firm, and when he returned home after his visits, he was quick to share stories of their time together. With Fred's increasing stamina, they'd been taking more walks, with Lukas acting as his father's guide through the village and surrounding area. Feeling he was both needed and appreciated by Fred had produced a steady increase in Lukas's self-confidence. While I was thrilled to see the changes taking place, I prayed Fred would do nothing to destroy the boy's trust.

I climbed the stairs to the second floor, weary from a long day in the kitchen. The moment I appeared in the doorway of the upstairs parlor, Lukas jumped up from an overstuffed rocking chair. "Are we going to see Papa now?" His face creased with undeniable excitement as he hop-skipped toward me.

"I thought we might work on your reading or arithmetic lessons before prayer meeting." I sat down, but when he didn't move from the doorway, I patted the cushion of the divan.

He glanced toward the hall. "I finished my schoolwork, and Papa will be waiting for us. He asked me why you haven't been coming as often." His eyes shone with concern.

"I told your father I had to work extra hours because of the potato harvest." I leaned back and closed my eyes.

"But you could come with me now. You're done working, aren't you?" Even his pleading tone wasn't enough to convince me.

"I am, but I'm very tired and want to sit here until time for prayer meeting. I promise we'll go and visit your father tomorrow evening."

A wave of guilt assaulted me. Not because I felt it necessary to meet Fred's expectations, but because I had disappointed my son. While I didn't want to misjudge Fred or cause Lukas to mistrust his father, I worried about the future. I longed to discuss Fred's behavior toward me with Brother Bosch or Dr. Karr, but they'd seen nothing except positive change. Would they think I possessed an unforgiving heart and refused to see the improvements Fred had made?

If I could talk to Dirk, I was sure he would understand and perhaps offer sound advice, but I couldn't go to him. To discuss my marital problems with an unmarried man, especially with a man who still held my heart, would be particularly inappropriate. And if Greta found out, it would escalate the problems between us. No, I couldn't talk to Dirk.

Thankfully, Lukas returned to the rocking chair without further argument. After only a few moments, I closed my eyes and recalled how peaceful and worry-free life had been before Fred appeared.

Early Monday morning, I stood on the wooden sidewalk in front of the Küche and waited for the wagon. Only the future would tell if my talk with Sister Erma last evening would produce the desired effect. After prayer meeting, I had explained and taken responsibility for the breach between Greta and me. Sister Erma had observed the change in our friendship and was wise enough to know it centered around Dirk, but she listened as though she'd seen or heard nothing. Once finished with my story, I asked her to assign Greta to the potato field next week, which would be the final week of the harvest.

She patted my hand and nodded, but there had been no firm agreement on her part. Instead, she said, "We will see. I am pleased to hear you speak of your responsibility for what happened. Still, Greta has some part in this, too. And neither of you have conducted yourselves in a way that would be pleasing to God."

I agreed with her assessment but hoped that my offer to forgo the opportunity to harvest next week proved my commitment to ease the mounting differences between us.

Dust curled from beneath the wagon as the horses plodded down the hard-packed dirt street. The driver had already made most of his stops, and the women waved and called out greetings as they approached. With the driver's assistance, I climbed aboard and joined the other women. Laughter and chattering abounded on the ride, and I soon joined into the easy conversation.

Sister Dorothea, one of the sisters I'd met at meeting, sat beside me in the wagon. She was a pleasant rosy-cheeked woman who immediately made me feel welcome. "This is your first potato harvest, ja?"

I nodded. I'd grown up on the adjoining farm, but my duties had consisted of preparing meals for farm workers rather than helping in the fields. The Amana women helped only with potato and onion harvests, but beyond helping in the garden, my knowledge of harvesting was nonexistent.

"Helping with harvest is gut fun, but it can be hard work, too." She pressed her palm to her lower back. "Too much bending hurts the back." She pointed her index finger in my direction. "Here is good tip for you. If your back begins to hurt, sit down in the dirt between turns of the plow. You should have time to rest a little unless there are lots of potatoes."

The women sitting close by agreed with the advice. "Is gut to have time to sit, but is also gut to have lots of potatoes so our stomachs are full," Sister Margaret said.

The chatter continued until one of the women began to sing.

Soon the others joined her and clapped their hands. The song was unfamiliar to me, but I clapped along and hummed the tune while taking pleasure in the simple performance.

Once the wagon rumbled to the edge of the field and the horses came to a halt, the driver set the brake and the women clambered down without assistance. Sister Dorothea motioned for me to follow her. "Come with me. We gather over here and the farm Baas assigns our rows." She pointed to an area at one corner of the vast field, where a large man wearing a floppy felt hat stood waiting. "Stay beside me and we will be assigned to work alongside each other. Then, if you need help, I'll be nearby."

I was grateful for her kindness but hoped I would be able to keep up without any help. Though it was prideful on my part, I wanted to prove myself as capable as the other women. The farm Baas motioned to the four sisters standing at the front of the group. "You four take the first four rows at the far end."

They scurried off, and he assigned the next four sisters to the rows adjoining the ones he'd just assigned. And so it went until all of the rows had been assigned. As Sister Dorothea had predicted, I was assigned to work a row beside her. The plow hadn't yet turned our row, and we knelt down at the end of the field while we waited.

"I expected to see Sister Greta waiting for the wagon. Did she work in the field last week?"

"She did, and you?" I wondered if any of the women were assigned to work two weeks in a row. Perhaps Sister Dorothea and Greta had discussed the possibility that they might work together this week.

"Nein, but I worked alongside Greta during onion harvest last year, and I enjoyed her company." Seeming to realize she might have hurt my feelings, she patted my arm. "But I am pleased to work with you, as well."

I offered my thanks and agreed with her assessment of Sister Greta. My words appeared to ease her earlier sense of embarrassment, and she soon told me about her work in Sister Fredericka's Küche. A short time later, the horses snorted and trotted toward us, pulling the wooden plow and unearthing the potatoes in our rows. As soon as we had filled our large woven baskets, Dorothea and I helped each other carry and dump them into one of the nearby wagons.

Our first rows had been particularly full, and by the time midmorning arrived, I needed to lift my apron often to wipe perspiration from my forehead. Row by row, our group progressed through the field, and I was thankful the crop had been less abundant on the later passes of the plow. We finished our next row and I sat down, not caring that the damp dirt would likely stain my dress.

Several of the younger women began tossing clumps of dirt, and soon a contest began to see who could throw the greatest distance. "Do you want to join them?" Sister Dorothea gestured toward the group.

I laughed and shook my head. "I would much rather rest."

"I am sure Sister Greta would be out there throwing dirt if she were here. She enjoys a gut time." When I didn't immediately respond, she took a drink of water from one of the nearby jars we had brought with us. "I am told by a couple of sisters that Greta hopes to marry Brother Dirk. Is this true?"

My stomach clenched. Greta and Dirk were already talking of marriage? I wanted to avoid Sister Dorothea's question, but she was looking at me with such intensity, I felt obligated to respond. "I am not sure. She has not confided in me."

Her eyebrows pulled together. "Since you work together, I am surprised you would not be aware of such plans. Perhaps there is no truth to what I've heard—or maybe I misunderstood. Let me ask Sister Hulda."

She shifted to her knees in an effort to stand, but I reached out and stilled her. "Greta and I haven't had much time alone over the past weeks, so what you have heard could very well be true. There's no need to ask Sister Hulda."

Confusion clouded her gray eyes, but she returned to a sitting position. "But Sister Hulda's the one who told me. If I misunderstood . . ."

I didn't give her an opportunity to complete her argument. "Rather than ask any of the other sisters, wouldn't it be best to ask Sister Greta? Then you can be sure you've received the proper answer." My insides churned. If word got back to Greta that several of the sisters had been discussing her relationship with Dirk, she'd likely think I'd been involved. Such talk would create greater difficulty between us.

"I suppose that would be best." Even though she agreed, Sister Dorothea didn't appear particularly pleased by my suggestion.

For the remainder of the day, we continued our work and I had to agree that, although my back ached a bit, working outdoors among the other women was enjoyable. There was laughter, singing, and a great deal of chattering as we loaded the wagons with potatoes. Sister Dorothea seemed to forget our earlier discussion and chatted at length. As we rode back into the village, I was pleased that I'd have several more days to work alongside these women.

Rather than going directly into the kitchen house, I decided to check on Lukas at Dirk's shop. If Dirk didn't need him, we could walk over to see Fred. If we went now before supper, it would be a short visit and Fred wouldn't expect us to return before prayer meeting. At least that was my hope.

The sound of a wooden mallet pounding on tin echoed as I walked into the tinsmith's shop. I glanced about, hoping to catch sight of Lukas, but from where I stood, I could see only Dirk's back as he hammered. At the far end of the room, Werner sat hunched over a worktable, drawing a design of some sort, but there was no sign of Lukas.

Werner glanced up and caught sight of me. "Guten Tag, Sister Andrea."

"Guten Tag," I replied.

Dirk dropped his hammer onto the worktable and whirled around. His eyes lit. "Andrea! For sure, this is a surprise. Sister Erma has sent something for repair?"

I shook my head, my mouth suddenly dry. The sight of his broad shoulders and square jaw sent a shiver coursing through my body. I had reasoned with myself that stopping for Lukas was a sound idea—that it would decrease my time with Fred. But in truth, I'd come here not because of Lukas or Fred, but because I wanted to see Dirk. And now I knew it was a mistake. Being so close to him made me long all the more for what could have been.

His face creased with worry. "Has something happened to Lukas?"

"What do you mean? Lukas isn't here with you?" I clutched my hands together and attempted to remain calm, yet panic seized me. "Where is he?"

"I do not know, but I doubt there is any reason to worry. He is probably with his Vater. I thought perhaps he had come to the Küche and you had given him permission to go for an early visit." His gaze settled on my dirt-caked hands. "But you have been harvesting potatoes today?"

"That's right. I haven't seen Lukas since breakfast." I took a backward step toward the door.

He stepped closer. "I am sorry. I should have checked to make sure."

I turned to leave.

"Wait, Andrea. I'll go with you."

"No. For Fred to see us together would not be good."

Taking long strides, he followed me to the door. "You will send word if Lukas is not with his Vater so I can help find him, ja?"

Glancing over my shoulder, I nodded in agreement. Each step of my pounding feet echoed in my ears. What if he wasn't with Fred? I needed to remain calm. Dirk was likely correct. While I continued to run, I silently prayed that my son would be sitting at his father's bedside.

The bell over the front door jangled as I entered the doctor's office, but no one appeared. Not even the doctor's wife. I rushed into the bedroom. Lukas wasn't there—and neither was Fred. Where were they?

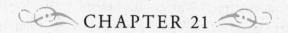

CHAPTER 21

Dirk

My chest constricted as Andrea raced down the street. I longed to run after her, but she was right. It would anger Fred to see me with her. Still, I couldn't go back and work without knowing whether Lukas was safe. What if something had happened to the boy? I should have gone and looked for him when he didn't appear after school. To simply assume he was with Fred was irresponsible. I couldn't follow Andrea to the doctor's office, but I could go and look at the Küchehaas. Maybe Lukas had gone to visit his father and then returned home to complete his schoolwork.

The late afternoon sun glowed golden orange and had lost much of its midday warmth. Surely the boy would not have gone far. I leaned inside the doorway of the shop. "Werner! If anyone needs me, I will be at Sister Erma's Küche. When you finish drawing the designs, sweep up the shop. I will return before time to close."

Without waiting for a response, I hurried off at a trot. I silently offered up a prayer for the boy's safety. As I rounded the back of the Küche and bounded up the steps of the porch, I panted for air. The run—or perhaps my fear—had taken more of a toll than I'd expected.

Sister Erma threw open the back door, and her eyes grew wide with surprise. "Brother Dirk! What a clatter you made. I thought a wild animal was preparing to attack." Her laughter ceased as she took stock of me. "What has happened?"

Before I could answer, Greta stepped onto the porch. "Dirk? What is it?" Her forehead creased with concern.

"Lukas. Is he here?"

"Nein." Greta shook her head and stepped closer. "Why do you ask?"

Still panting, I explained Andrea's unexpected appearance at the shop. "She has gone to see if he is with Fred." I inhaled a deep breath. "I thought maybe he came back here. She is troubled that I did not check on him earlier."

"Ach!" Sister Erma flapped a dismissive wave. "Lukas is a young boy. Children like to explore and forget the time. When the dinner bell rings, he will come running."

"You are probably right, but Andrea is very worried and I wanted to ease her concern. To see her so upse—"

"Sister Andrea has a husband." Sister Erma's frown deepened. "He is the one who should help to ease her concern, not you. Especially since the two of you have been courting." She gestured toward Greta.

"Could you give us a few minutes alone so we can talk, Sister Erma?" Greta directed a beseeching look at the kitchen Baas.

"Ja, but do not take too long. Soon it will be time for supper, and we still have much to do." After pinning me with one final sour look, Sister Erma returned inside.

Greta grasped my shirtsleeve and tugged. "Over by the side of the house where no one will hear us." She maintained a hold on my sleeve until we'd descended the porch steps and were out of earshot. Wheeling around, she touched her index finger to the side of her head. "You need to use your head, Dirk. Do you think any other man in this village would act as you have?"

Her bitter tone startled me. "Ja, I think they would. Are we not supposed to care and look after one another?"

"Ach! Do not try to make excuses for yourself. If Sister Andrea had gone to any other craftsman in the village, he would have sent his apprentice rather than leave his shop. If he thought the boy was in real danger, he would have rung the village bell."

Anger caused her voice to increase an octave, and I held a finger to my pursed lips. "I thought you were worried about being overheard. You do not need to talk so loud. I can hear you."

She frowned and moved closer. "You should be careful or word will travel to her husband that you are in love with Andrea. Do you think others do not see what I do?"

"There is nothing for anyone to see except my concern for Lukas." My words were punctuated with more irritation than I had intended.

"Your anger tells a different story, Dirk. I know you love Andrea, and so does Sister Erma." She sighed and glanced toward the kitchen. "Did you not hear what Sister Erma said to you? She does not appear convinced that you have set aside your feelings for Andrea."

"Right now, I care little about such nonsense. I am worried about Lukas." I didn't want to argue further, but my comment only served to further annoy Greta.

She inched closer and glared at me. "You are supposed to be my friend, Dirk. You said you would help me. You care more about a married outsider than you care about me and our years of friendship."

The sting of her words made me take a backward step. "I think I will leave before our friendship is completely destroyed."

She grasped my shirtsleeve. "You should honor your word to me, Dirk."

"I am sorry you think me dishonorable for changing my mind, but I cannot go any further with this plan. I am still willing to speak with your Vater and ask that he reconsider his decision. I went to the picnic with you, but I will not try to influence others to believe something that is untrue. I want us to remain friends, and I hope you do, too."

Her angry stance melted and she leaned close and grasped my arm as the kitchen door opened and Sister Erma appeared.

"Greta! I need you in the Küche." Sister Erma's voice bore a note of urgency.

Before she rushed off, Greta shot me a cunning grin and I realized she had been performing for Sister Erma. I might have changed my mind about her plan, but it was clear she had not. With or without my help, she was going to do everything possible to convince others that we had moved beyond friendship. She had ignored my decision, and her bold behavior angered me, but right now I was more concerned about Lukas.

I longed to go to the doctor's office and see if the boy had been found, but such a move would be foolish. I had to remember that Andrea was Fred's wife. To think of her as another man's wife seemed impossible, but I had to accept what I could not change.

I would never be able to extinguish my love for Andrea without God's help.

Andrea

I stepped inside Fred's bedroom at Dr. Karr's office, the sound of my footfalls muffled by the multicolored wool carpet. Perhaps

Lukas had wanted to play outdoors and Fred had agreed to sit in the yard with him. Resting my hands on the windowsill, I leaned forward, scanned the yard, and caught sight of Fred and Lukas walking along a path near the rear of the house. A whoosh of relief escaped my lips but was soon followed by a wellspring of anger. Both Lukas and Fred needed to know the worry they had caused me—and I was going to deliver a message they wouldn't soon forget.

As I turned to leave, my gaze fell upon some letters stacked on the small oak table near Fred's bed. Curious to know who had been writing to Fred, I stopped and glanced toward the window. They were still a distance away. Lukas had mentioned stopping at the general store to mail and pick up letters for Fred, and I'd once seen Fred writing a letter, but that was the extent of my knowledge regarding his correspondence.

I picked up one of the envelopes and removed the pages from inside. To read Fred's private mail wasn't proper, but the envelope was already open—and I was his wife. He shouldn't be keeping secrets from me, should he?

My heart pounded an increasingly erratic beat as I scanned the contents, shoved the pages back inside, and opened the next envelope. I had read only a portion of the second letter when I glanced outside to check on Fred's whereabouts. I gasped when I saw Lukas and Fred circling around the side of the house. My hands shook as I tucked the letter into the envelope and straightened the stack. I hoped I'd placed the pages in the proper order.

When I heard the bell jangle, I stepped across the threshold into the parlor. "Lukas! I have been worried sick about you. Where have you been?"

Fred brushed past me and into the bedroom. He motioned for Lukas to follow him, and I trailed behind the two of them. When

I entered the room, his gaze shifted from the stack of letters to my face. "How long you been in here, Andrea?"

"Not long. I have been worried sick. I came back from the potato field and went to the tinsmith shop to get Lukas. I thought we would come for an early visit, but Brother Dirk said he hadn't been there." I frowned at Lukas. "Do you know how frightened I've been not knowing where you'd gone?"

"Stop that nonsense, Andrea. You keep acting like Lukas is a baby. He'll soon be a man. Ain't that right, son?"

Lukas beamed. "Yes, Papa. Pretty soon I'll be as tall as you." He straightened to his full height and squared his shoulders.

I wanted to tell him it would be many years before he'd be a grown man, but I didn't want to start an argument with Fred. "That doesn't mean I won't worry when you're not where you're supposed to be. Why didn't you go to the tinsmith shop after school today?"

Lukas glanced at his father. "I was on my way there, but when I stopped to see if Papa had anything he needed, he said I should stay here. He gets lonely. Next time I'll tell Brother Dirk."

"You don't owe him no details 'bout where you go or don't go, son. Only person you need to answer to is me." Fred tightened his lips in a defiant angle.

My anger mounted, but I would not let Fred pull me into an argument in front of Lukas. I needed time alone to digest what I'd read—and to worry over what was in the letters I'd not reviewed. "The supper bell is going to ring very soon, Lukas." I reached for his hand. "We need to go home and wash up before supper."

"You go wait outside, boy. I want to talk to your mother alone for a few minutes."

"Yes, Papa."

I grimaced. *Yes, Papa. No, Papa. Whatever you say, Papa.* What had happened to my son? I feared Fred had won the boy's confidence and now had Lukas in the palm of his hand. Either that or he feared disobeying Fred. I couldn't be certain which was correct, and I doubted whether Lukas would tell me.

"I need to get back, Fred." I inched toward the door.

He scowled and shook his head. "Not till we're done talkin'." He grabbed the stack of letters and held them in his fist. "You read these, didn't ya?"

"Why do you find it necessary to accuse me of wrongdoing at every turn?" I didn't want to compound my misconduct with a lie, but I doubted I'd find any other way out of his interrogation.

"Because I saw the look on your face when I came in here. I can tell when someone is lyin' to me."

"Can you? Is that because you've had so much practice yourself?" I inched a few steps closer to the door. "Your letters don't interest me, Fred. And if you don't want people to read them, I suggest you put them away. Who knows? Dr. Karr or his wife may take an interest in your letters, and if they should contain anything unseemly, it could influence your ability to remain here."

"And yours, too, *dear wife*." He smirked. "Just remember, everyone else thinks I'm a changed man. You may have trouble convincin' them otherwise. Don't cause me no trouble, Andrea, or you'll rue the day."

I startled when the bell over the front door jangled. "Dr. Karr, how are you?" My voice caught and I struggled to gain control.

"I am gut, Sister Andrea. Will soon be time for supper, ja?"

I nodded. "I was just leaving." Before Fred could further detain me, I hurried from the room and out the door. "Come on, Lukas." I grabbed the boy's hand and hurried toward the kitchen house, unable to shake the fear chasing after me.

"What's wrong, Mama?"

I glanced down at Lukas and shook my head. "Nothing." I forced a smile. He didn't appear convinced, but it was the best I could do.

Sister Erma wheeled around when we entered the kitchen a short time later. "Ach! I am glad to see the lost boy has been found."

"Go upstairs and wash, Lukas. I'll be up in a minute." I turned to Sister Erma as he scurried through the kitchen. "How did you know I was worried about Lukas's whereabouts?"

"A short time ago, Brother Dirk came to see if he was here. He told us you had gone to see if the boy was with his father. For some reason, Brother Dirk believed it was his responsibility to help find the boy." She pinned me with an accusatory stare.

"I was concerned and too quickly cast blame on Brother Dirk. I will apologize as soon as possible—and thank him, as well. It was kind of him to search for Lukas."

Grasping a coffee server in each hand, Greta stepped around me on her way to the dining room. Once she was in the other room, Sister Erma drew near. "I think it would be best if you stayed away from Brother Dirk. I can tell him of your apology and offer your thanks. For Greta's sake, you should not encourage him."

I clasped a hand to my chest. "Encourage him? Is that what she thinks? I have done no such thing."

"You may not consider it encouragement, but it is obvious to Greta and to me that Dirk still cares for you. If she is to have a chance with him, you need to refrain from any contact with him." She arched her brows. "Ja?" I nodded and she glanced toward the doorway. "You should go upstairs and wash. Supper begins in five minutes."

My mind whirled with the day's events. What had been pleasant hours working in the potato field had evolved into a day I would never want to repeat. In such a short time, I had managed to offend Dirk, Greta, and Sister Erma; I had been torn with worry about my child; I had been verbally attacked by Fred. And then there were those letters.

Those letters! My knees threatened to buckle and I sank onto my bed. Those letters had opened the door to more trouble than I could even imagine.

CHAPTER 22

The following morning while I waited for the wagon that would once again carry me to the potato fields, I continued to worry about Fred's letters. The only sleep I'd had last night had been filled with bad dreams that resulted in little rest. I had tried to reach some conclusion about what I should do, but each idea I'd had resulted in a bad outcome. If only I had someone in whom I could confide, someone who could advise me.

I still didn't want to believe what I'd read, but given Fred's lies, how could I trust him to tell me the truth? Could Fred truly be responsible for the death of another person? Had my husband somehow staged his own death?

From what I'd gleaned in the letters, there had been an altercation after Fred had returned Stateside, one that had caused the wound in his side. The injury had been inflicted when he'd attempted to rob a gentleman who happened to be a wealthy banker—a banker Fred had killed. Pinkerton agents were on the case and had questioned Fred's former shipmate and author of the letters, John Calvert.

The letters had detailed that before his departure for Iowa, Fred had made promises to Mr. Calvert—promises to send him money in exchange for information regarding any progress in the investigation and for keeping Fred's whereabouts secret. It seemed Fred's former shipmate had a vast knowledge of what had occurred during the failed robbery and murder, but whether he'd been present during the incident wasn't clear. Perhaps the other letters he'd written bore additional information, but I doubted I'd ever have an opportunity to read them.

One thing was certain: Mr. Calvert was bringing pressure to bear. In the second letter, he threatened to tell the Pinkerton men where Fred was hiding if he didn't send at least two hundred dollars by the end of November and the remainder of the money by the first of next year. My breath had caught when I'd read Calvert's final sentence. *Get your wife's father to turn loose of his money or you'll soon be in prison.* Fred hadn't told Mr. Calvert of my father's death or the fact that we were penniless. Instead, he'd kept the man dangling. I doubted my father would have granted Fred's request, but the promise had seemingly been enough to satisfy Calvert. Where did Fred think he'd obtain such a large sum of money?

Anger swelled in my chest. Not only had he planned to take advantage of my father, but after receiving refuge in the colonies, he'd written and told Calvert his exact whereabouts. With a stroke of his pen, Fred had placed everyone who lived here in danger. What if the Pinkerton agents came here? While in Baltimore, I'd read newspaper accounts regarding the Pinkerton agents and their prowess in hunting down criminals. I'd also read of mishaps in which innocent people had been injured and died during some of the agents' crime-fighting forays. The worry that something similar could happen here was the cause of my fitful sleep last night.

"Guten Morgen, Sister Andrea." Several of the ladies called to me as the wagon rumbled to a halt.

"Guten Morgen, Sisters." I climbed into the wagon and sat down next to Sister Dorothea.

"You did not sleep well last night?" Sister Hulda tapped beneath one of her eyes. "Dark circles mean not much sleep."

I smiled and nodded. "Ja, I had trouble sleeping."

Sister Dorothea edged closer. "I heard that there was trouble with your little boy yesterday. No wonder you could not sleep last night."

For a moment, I was struck speechless. How had Sister Dorothea, who lived in a different part of the village, heard about Lukas? Did every morsel of information travel so quickly? If so, I could not imagine what method was being used to pass the messages.

"How did you know?"

She shrugged and grinned. "Sister Greta came to visit with me after prayer meeting last night. She said your little boy was lost or had gone off somewhere and you could not find him. I am glad he was not injured. He is able to attend school today?"

"Yes, of course. Lukas went for a walk with his father instead of going to the tinsmith's shop."

"To Brother Dirk's shop. Ja, I know. Sister Greta said that the boy goes there each day and spends time with Brother Dirk. She mentioned you went there after we came back from the field yesterday."

"That's true. I did go there. I had planned to take Lukas to see his father, since I didn't have to help prepare supper last evening."

I felt a strong need to defend my actions, yet I wasn't sure why.

Was it my own guilt because I'd relished the idea of seeing Dirk? Or was I angered because Greta and Dorothea had been discussing Lukas and me? Right now, I wasn't sure.

"Ja, is gut to have your evenings free so you can visit your husband. How is his health? Sister Greta says he has several injuries."

Yesterday I had suggested Dorothea ask Greta about any possible plans to marry Dirk, but it seemed their entire visit had revolved around me and my family. "Did Greta mention Benjamin or Dirk during your visit last night? I know she must miss Benjamin a great deal."

"For sure she is heartbroken that her Vater will not give his permission for them to wed, but that Greta—she is always thinking." Dorothea touched her index finger to the side of her bonnet. "She is a girl who comes up with some gut plans. Always she has been the same—thinking of a way to get what she wants."

"I am sorry her father was unwilling to accept Benjamin. He seemed like a nice young man."

"Oh ja, he is a good fellow—so full of fun. He makes everyone laugh with his joking. And a gut heart, too. Always, he is ready to help others. Benjamin and Greta would make a gut pair, but her Vater is thinking she should marry Brother Dirk."

"So she told you they are going to marry?"

"Nein. She told me her Vater wants her to marry Brother Dirk. That is not the same thing. I think Sister Hulda misspoke. Greta has not yet agreed to marry Brother Dirk."

Dorothea chuckled. "Besides, first he would have to ask her."

Relief washed over me like a spring freshet. I shouldn't have been so pleased. Both Greta and Dirk deserved happiness, but I was sure they would not find it with each other—at least that's what I wanted to believe. Right now, that thought made it easier for me to see them together.

Dirk

That afternoon I was pleased when Lukas bounded into the shop. I looked up from my work and motioned him forward. "I am glad to see you. Werner has traced some patterns for a new angel cookie cutter. You can cut them out for me." I extended a pair of tin snips, but he didn't step forward. "You are going to stay and work, ja?"

"Are you angry because I went to see my papa yesterday?"

Lukas took a tentative step forward when I smiled. "Nein, I am not angry that you went to see him, but do you remember what I told you not long after your Vater arrived?"

As he bobbed his head, a corkscrew of brown curls fell across his forehead. "You said I should always stop by the shop first so you would know where I had gone."

He moved close to my side and I turned on my work stool to face him. "Ja—so I would know where you were, but also so I would not worry about you." I reached out and placed my arm around his shoulder. "Yesterday, both your Mutter and I were very worried about you. She has already told you this, ja?"

"Papa says she treats me like a baby. He says there is no reason for anyone to worry about me. He says I'm a big boy and I can take care of myself."

"Is true you are a big boy, but even big boys do not want to worry others. They still want to please their Mutters. Werner is much older than you, but his Mutter would worry if he was not at work and she could not find him." I turned and looked at Werner. "Is that not right, Werner?"

"Oh ja. The whole village would be able to hear her shouting at me if I did such a thing. And I would not be allowed to go and have fun with my friends for many, many days—maybe two weeks," he said, holding up two fingers.

The boy gaped at Werner. "Two weeks?"

I grinned at his high-pitched squeak. "I do not think your Mutter plans to be as strict with you, but you should remember that the Bible teaches that children should obey their parents."

"Ja, but Papa said I didn't have to tell anyone but him what I was doing."

My anger swelled. Why would a father teach his child to disobey? Such reckless instruction could lead Lukas into a pattern of rebellious behavior and conflict. Was Fred so eager to win his son's affection that he would set aside all sense of right and wrong? Or was Fred using his son to hurt Andrea? Surely not. Yet the thought lingered.

Brother Bosch and Dr. Karr believed there had been great improvement in Fred's demeanor. While he might be displaying good behavior in their presence, I doubted those changes were genuine.

I didn't want to dispute the boy's father openly, but Lukas needed to understand that he could not defy the wishes of his mother, the rules of the village, or God's commandments.

"Since you now understand how much worry your disappearance caused your Mutter and me, I hope you will abide by the rules we have given you. Even if your Vater tells you it is not necessary, I do not think you want to see your Mutter so displeased and worried again, ja?"

I did not want to overstep my limits with the boy, but the elders had recently assigned him to help in the shop after school. If Lukas remained in the village, I would eventually judge the boy's ability as a future apprentice, but I was also his mentor. While

Lukas was under my supervision, I was expected to train him to behave in an honorable manner.

Lukas stepped around me and traced his index finger around the angel's form that Werner had drawn on the piece of tin. "I know she was worried, 'cause she cried and hugged me real tight, but then she scolded me." He looked up at me. "I would have stopped to tell you, but Papa said we were going to take a long walk so I should come straight to the doctor's office after school." His lips quivered. "Are you still mad at me?"

"Nein." I handed him the tin snips. "So, did you and your Vater go on a hike into the woods?"

He worried his lower lip between his teeth. "Papa said it was a secret."

Once again, the secrets. Was there no end to Fred's manipulation of his son? "If you do not want to talk about where you went, you do not have to, Lukas." I would not pressure the boy, although I wondered why a walk in the village should be kept secret.

He shot a smile in my direction. "I can tell you. You'll keep my secret." He drew close, cupped his hands around his mouth, and whispered in my ear. "We walked part of the way on an old path behind Dr. Karr's office and then along the dirt road."

Werner pushed away from the worktable and removed his leather apron. "I am going to go to the general store and pick up the mail."

"Danke, Werner."

Werner had already picked up the mail earlier in the day, but he had obviously sensed Lukas's discomfort and decided to give us some time alone. I didn't know if there was anything more that Lukas wanted to tell me, but I appreciated Werner's considerate behavior. He was becoming a fine apprentice, and his artistic talents continued to impress me, so I hoped to put his talents to use beyond my shop. Though I didn't know if the elders would agree, I thought Werner's artistry might be used to paint pictures and provide added income. When I'd discussed the possibility with him, he'd been agreeable, though he'd been quick to say he didn't want to leave my shop. A fact that had warmed my heart.

Werner was gone only a few minutes when Lukas laid down the tin snips. "Papa got tired while we were walking and had to rest, so we didn't get as far as he wanted."

"I am sorry to hear he got tired, but your Vater has made gut progress with his recovery. Very soon, I am sure he will be able to walk as far as he wants."

The path Fred had taken surprised me. Instead of walking through the village, or along the well-trodden trails through the woods, he'd taken an overgrown path where he wouldn't be seen.

Was Fred attempting to leave with Lukas? Had he hoped to flag a train? But he had no money for train fare, and he wasn't strong enough to jump on and off a train like many of the hobos who sometimes arrived in the colonies. And what of Lukas—the boy could not have managed such a feat. No, Fred's plan had not been to depart on a train. Then again, perhaps he'd hoped a passing wagon would transport him to Marengo—but then what? I silently chided myself for harboring such worrisome thoughts. After all, Fred and the boy had returned, safe and sound.

Lukas leaned close. "Know what else?"

I smiled and shook my head. "No, what else?"

"We're gonna walk to my grandpa's farm."

My stomach constricted and I stared at the boy. "You and your Vater? Is that where you were going yesterday?"

"Yes, but Papa said he was tired and his side hurt. I was glad 'cause I was tired, too. He says we'll go another day when he's stronger. But I hope he goes alone."

The distance to the farm that had been owned by Andrea's

father was not overly far. When they first arrived, Andrea and Lukas had walked from the farm with Brother Bosch. However, Fred had taken a path that wound them away from the farm before turning back in the right direction. They had likely walked two miles and still were a distance from the farm. Had Fred chosen that path because he didn't want anyone to know he was going to the farm? Trying to figure out this man made my head ache.

"Did your papa want to show you something at the farm?"

Lukas continued to snip around the angel's skirt. "Nein. He said we were going there to find something, but he didn't tell me what it was. I think it's a surprise. Maybe that's why he wanted it to be a secret."

"You may be right." I pointed to the line where he should cut and wondered if Fred thought he might find Mr. Neumann's money in the barn. If so, he'd be sorely disappointed. "Your secret is safe with me." I hesitated for a moment. "Did you tell your Mutter what you have told me?"

He shook his head. "Papa said we should not tell her because she would worry that he was walking too far. I told him there was a shorter way, but Papa said his way was better." Lukas wrinkled his nose. "I don't think his way was better, but I didn't tell him. Sometimes he gets mad when I don't agree with him."

The boy's comment heightened my concern and confirmed my thoughts that Fred had not changed as much as the doctor and Brother Bosch believed. Still, I could not betray the boy's trust. I would keep his secrets, but I would also do my best to keep a close watch on Fred and his whereabouts.

CHAPTER 23

Fred

I had to remain calm and make the boy comfortable with my plan. If I didn't, I'd fail. And I could not fail.

The tone of John Calvert's recent letter had been enough to set my teeth on edge. The man had become downright belligerent. Since I left, he'd forgotten how well I could wield a knife. If I was back in Baltimore instead of hidin' out in this village of zealots, I'd slit his throat when he tried somethin' like this. He'd probably decided my injuries offered him the protection he needed. And right now that was true. He had the upper hand, but that wouldn't last forever. Calvert needed to be reminded that I was a man with a long memory and a long reach. He was tryin' to scare me. Though I hated to admit it, even to myself, his threats did make me worry. But until I could get my hands on some money, there wasn't much I could do except return the favor and put a little fear in his heart. I needed to remind him that murdering two men instead of only one wouldn't change much of anything for me. I could only be hanged once.

Lukas wouldn't be here for at least a half hour, enough time for me to pen a few lines and tell Calvert his threats and demands better stop or he'd need to watch his back. I didn't know if my warnin' would be enough to buy me more time, but I didn't have many choices. To save myself, I'd turn on Calvert in a minute. He needed to remember that if I'd turned on that woman in the Caribbean and killed that banker, I could just as easily turn on him.

"I hurried like you said, Papa." I startled and the boy stopped short. Uncertainty shone in his eyes. "I'm sorry, Papa. I didn't mean to scare you."

Never in my life had I seen a kid with so many fears. Lukas's timid behavior angered me, but I tamped down my irritation. One day I'd knock some sense into him, but this wasn't the time or place. Right now I needed him to see me as a generous and loving father.

Forcing a smile, I motioned the boy forward. "I didn't hear you come in the door, but I'm glad you're here." I glanced at the clock. "You didn't tell no one 'bout our plans, did ya?"

"No, Papa, but maybe we should tell someone in case you get tired and we can't make it back in time for supper."

I clenched my jaw. "No, Lukas, that ain't the way we're doin' this. I told you it's a secret. We won't need no help. I'm much stronger now."

He hesitated but bobbed his head. Doubt shone in his eyes, but he was afraid to resist me. Likely 'cause he hoped to gain my love. Back when I'd been Lukas's age, I had hoped to win my father's affection, too. For years I'd tried, but then I'd learned I didn't need him or his love. Havin' feelings for other people only caused pain and slowed progress. One day I'd teach Lukas the lessons it had taken me years to learn, but he wasn't ready just yet.

"No time to waste. Come on, boy." I pointed to my walking stick. "Get that for me."

"It will be easier and lots faster if we go through town and not on that path behind the doctor's office." He handed me the walking stick. "No one will know where we're going."

I had planned on taking the back route, but the boy was right. It took too much time and the path was hard to tread. I'd need my strength once we got to the barn. "Yer right, Lukas. We'll take the shortest route."

He beamed at me, pleased I'd accepted his suggestion.

"How come you want to go to the barn so bad, Papa? Did you leave some of your stuff there when you and Mama moved to Baltimore?"

"Not exactly, but I'm hopin' to find somethin' I think someone else left there."

The boy skipped alongside me. I wanted to squeeze his shoulder and tell him to walk, but I figured I better let him be for now. Otherwise, he'd probably turn tail and run back to his mother, and I was gonna need him when we got there.

"What're you hoping to find? Is it something I'll like, too?"

"You gotta wait and see. I'm not sure we'll find it, and I don't want you to be disappointed if things end up going sour."

"Sour? Like milk?" Confusion clouded his eyes. "Sister Erma says sour milk makes good biscuits and pancakes."

I squeezed the walking stick until my hand ached. I didn't know how much longer I could put up with the boy's silly questions. But there was no one else I could trust, so I'd have to put up with his foolish remarks and keep smilin'. That was the hardest part. Actin' like I enjoyed being with him.

He tugged on my sleeve. "Is that what 'going sour' means, Papa?"

"Naw, it means when things don't go the way you hope they will."

"Ohh. Like when we didn't make it to the barn last time?"

I nodded. "Yep. You could say that plan went sour." Maybe the boy would shut up for a while if I gave him a reason. "We need to quit talkin' until we get to the barn, so I can think."

"What you gonna think about?"

I wanted to slap the back of his head and shut him up, but I held back. Instead, I placed my index finger against my lips and gave him a stern look. He shrank back and didn't say another word until we arrived.

"Are you done thinking, Papa?" His whisper echoed in the huge barn.

"I'm done, but that don't mean you need to jabber a whole lot. We got us some work to do."

"You feel good enough to work?"

I drew in a deep breath and tried to keep from looking mad. "I don't mean work like cleaning out the barn. I mean we got to start lookin' around."

Dust motes danced in the waning sunlight. "What are we looking for, Papa?"

"Look for anythin' that don't belong in a barn, like a suitcase or a canvas bag, or a box of some sort." I pointed my walking stick to the left side of the barn. "You look over there and I'll look on this side."

The boy appeared confused, but soon he hurried to the other side of the barn and began to search in earnest.

"Be sure to move any piles of straw and make sure there ain't nothin' underneath."

"I will, Papa, but so far there's nothing. And no piles of straw, either."

From time to time I glanced in the boy's direction and I could see he was doin' his best. He even emptied out an old corn crib to make sure there was nothing beneath the bit of rubbish that had accumulated inside. Between the two of us, we checked each of the stalls, but found nothin' but dust and dirt. I didn't know how much time had passed, but from the dwindlin' light comin' through the barn door, it wouldn't be too long before the bell rang to announce the end of the workday. Once that happened, there would be no time to spare. We would need to start back to the village. If Lukas hadn't returned by the time the supper bell rang, he'd be missed and there would be too many questions.

When I'd finished on my side of the barn, I called to the boy. "Looks like there ain't nothin' here."

The boy ran to my side. "Mama and I didn't find anything when we looked, either."

I inhaled a sharp breath. "Why didn't you tell me you and your mama already searched this place?"

At my sharp tone the boy took a backward step. "Y-you never asked me."

"Well, I'm askin' now. Tell me everything and don't leave nothin' out." The boy's lips trembled, and I gently patted his back. "I'm sorry, Lukas. I didn't mean to frighten ya. It's just that you shoulda told me before we spent all this time lookin'."

"Mama never said she was looking for a bag or box like you did. She just said we'd see if we could find anything special that Grandpa maybe left in the barn, but we never did."

"You sure she didn't find something and jest didn't tell you?"

He shook his head. "Not unless she looked some more after

I went to sleep, but I think she would have told me. She doesn't keep secrets."

Let the boy believe his mother was a saint—I knew different. I was sure the money had to be somewhere in this place. Whenever Andrea's father had any spare time, he could be found in this barn. It was his favorite spot, and what man wouldn't put his valuables in his favorite spot?

I glanced toward the loft. It was my last hope, and I'd saved looking there until last. I woulda hidden the money up in the loft, but I wasn't so sure about Andrea's father. He'd aged, and climbin' up there wouldn't have been real easy for him. Then again, maybe he'd decided there were lots of people who might come into the barn, but not many who would climb into the loft.

"Your mother go up in the loft to take a look?"

"She wanted to, but it was dark and she said her dress might get tangled on the ladder. I think she was going to go up there the next morning, but Brother Bosch came so we left with him."

"And she ain't never come back here and gone up there?"

He hiked his shoulders. "I don't think so."

"C'mere, boy." I waved for him to join me at the bottom of the wooden ladder leadin' to the loft. When he was beside me, I pointed to the ladder. "You climb on up there and take a good look around."

Lukas took several steps away from the ladder and looked up. "I-I-I don't like to go up high. It scares me."

"Hooey! You're a big boy—ain't that what I told you afore? Now, get on up there and take a looksee." It was takin' everythin' in my power to keep from yankin' the boy up out of his shoes and pushing him up that ladder. "C'mon now and give it a try. I know you can do it."

I reached back, grabbed his shoulder, and pushed him forward.

His complexion turned a pasty shade and tears rimmed his eyes, but there wasn't no time for tears. The boy needed to grow up and show he had some backbone. I nodded and forced an encouragin' smile when he put his leather boot on the first rung.

"What if I fall?" His lips trembled.

"You ain't gonna fall. Besides, I'm standin' right here and I'd catch ya. You trust your pa, don't ya?"

"Yes, but—"

"Ain't no time for excuses, boy. Get on up with ya."

He took two more steps, but then he froze. "I can't, Papa."

No matter what I said or did, he wouldn't move another step. My anger swelled until I thought my chest would explode. *Keep calm, keep calm.* Over and over, those two words banged around in my head like a pounding drum. I reached up, grabbed him around the waist, and yanked him off the ladder. His eyes grew wide when he landed on his backside.

"Sorry, boy. Thought I had a better hold on ya. Not hurt, are ya?"

He shook his head but twisted to one side and rubbed his hip. "I'm okay, Papa. I know you didn't mean to drop me."

Not only was the boy scared of his own shadow, he couldn't figure out when I was tellin' the truth or mockin' him. And that worked to my advantage. "'Course I didn't mean it, boy." I dropped my walking stick beside him. "Since you ain't grown-up enough to help your pa, I guess I'm gonna have to go up this ladder myself. I sure do hope this gash in my side don't tear open."

I rested my palm against my side and waited to see if he'd make a move, but he stood there—still as a stone. I thought maybe he'd want to prove himself grown-up and rush to take my place on the ladder. Instead, he shook his head and glanced toward the loft.

"I don't think you should go up there, Papa. We should go back to the village, and I can ask Brother Dirk if he'll come and help us. Brother Dirk is real brave and real strong. He could climb up there easy."

The mention of the tinsmith's name set my teeth on edge. Both Lukas and his mother thought that man was perfect. I closed the distance between Lukas and me and leaned down until we were almost nose-to-nose. "I don't need no stranger's help. That's why I brought my son, but if you ain't gonna help me, I'll go up there myself. Jest you remember that it's gonna rest on your shoulders if I tear open this gash in my side."

I stared hard at the boy, but he still didn't move. All the time I'd spent actin' like a lovin' father had been for times like this—when I needed help and could use him. But Lukas had too much of his mother in him. He'd never amount to anything. He'd never be anything like me.

I curled my lip in disgust. "Maybe while you're sittin' down here, you can say one of them prayers you and your mother are always chantin' with them other zealots."

A smile eased across his lips and he nodded. "For sure, I can do that, Papa."

There it was again—bein' too stupid to tell the truth from a lie or at the very least, a strong dose of scorn. I grappled up the ladder, unwillin' to let this chance pass by. When I reached the top rung, I leaned my upper body forward and rested for a moment. A severe pinchin' feelin' had gotten worse as I climbed the steps, and once I crawled into the loft, I lifted my shirt. A bit of blood had leaked onto the bandage, and I shouted a curse.

"What's wrong, Papa? Didn't you find anything up there?"

"Shut up, boy! I ain't had time to look. That gash in my side is beginnin' to open, and it's all your fault."

Maybe now he'd get up enough guts to come up here and help

me. I waited and listened, but instead of footsteps on the ladder, I heard him repeatin' another one of those idiotic prayers he'd learned since comin' here. I pulled down my shirt and clenched my jaw as I turned over and crawled toward the far end of the loft. The musty scent of hay filled my nostrils and I sneezed. Another pain ripped through my side, but I continued on. I wasn't going to fail. I couldn't. That money had to be here, and I was gonna find it.

When I finally made it to the far corner, I turned and sat. Leaning my back against the weathered wood, I looked around the entire loft. There wasn't much up here. Along with an old grain cradle, an ancient pitchfork rested in a small mound of hay. A small portion of an old ladder and a rusted sickle lay on the floor not far from me. Swallows roosted overhead amidst the countless cobwebs clinging to the rafters.

After pushing to my feet, I reached for the pitchfork. Thinking to use it as a substitute walking stick, I cursed when the handle broke and I fell to the floor. As I shifted to one side, my gaze settled on the rafters and I gasped. A waning shaft of sunlight glimmered overhead.

Keeping my eyes fixed on the rafters, I pushed to a stand and then stepped closer. My heart pounded an erratic beat as I caught sight of a metal box wedged into the corner of two rafter beams. That had to be the money. Now all I had to do was get it down from there.

I stepped close to the edge and looked down at the boy. "Lukas! I need you to come up here and help me. Ain't no cause to be afraid. Even with my bad leg and this gash in my side, I made it. You can, too. Show your pa that yer a brave fella."

"Maybe we should come back tomorrow, Papa. It's getting dark and soon it will be time for supper."

No use wasting any more time on the boy. He was useless. I

glanced over my shoulder. Maybe that piece of ladder would get me up high enough. Probably why it was up here. Johann had likely left it up here after he'd hidden the money. Determined to succeed, I anchored the ladder against the wall. I wasn't leaving without that box.

"You comin' down, Papa?"

The boy's whiny question set my teeth on edge. "You don't see me, do ya?"

"No, but I wish I did."

I wasn't gonna waste my time on useless conversation with the boy. Carrying the broken pitchfork handle, I gritted my teeth and slowly climbed the ladder. I worried one of the rungs might give out and send me sprawling, but I reached the second rung from the top without incident. Holding the top rung with one hand and the pitchfork handle with the other, I stretched to one side and poked at the metal box. As the box dislodged and fell to the floor, a sharp pain ripped through my side. I shouted a string of expletives that matched some of the worst I'd ever heard aboard a ship.

Slowly I descended the ladder. The box was enough to make me forget my pain. Using the metal prongs of the pitchfork, I forced open the lid. Moments later, my shouts of excitement echoed throughout the barn.

CHAPTER 24

Goin' back to the village was slowed by the pain in my side. If I hurried, I feared the wound would completely reopen. I leaned heavily on the walking stick, but with each step I could feel the dampness of the oozing wound. I'd hidden the box under some hay in a corner of the loft. It was the best I could do with my pain and bleeding. Lukas had seen the blood on my shirt when I descended the ladder. His complexion had turned as pale as bleached muslin. He peered at me as we neared the village. "Is your side still bleeding, Papa?"

I nodded. "The time to be worried 'bout me was back there in the barn when I asked you to climb that ladder, not when we're on the way home."

The boy turned silent and looked away. "I'm sorry, Papa. Maybe we shouldn't have gone till you were better."

"Ain't up to you to decide when we should do things. Besides,

I reckon it was worth the pain 'cause I found somethin' that's gonna make life a whole lot easier."

"What'd you find, Papa?"

"Don't you worry none 'bout what I found. I'll tell ya when I get good and ready. You was too scared to help me, so you don't get to know everythin'."

"I'll try harder next time, Papa. I really will."

I almost told him it was too late for apologies, but I had to pull back and do my best to treat him with a little kindness. I needed him to keep his trap shut about what we'd been up to. I patted his shoulder. "Sorry I been so hard on ya, boy. I jest want you to grow up and learn to do things on your own. Can't go through life scared of every little rabbit that jumps in your path. Ain't that right?"

His thin brows furrowed into a V between his eyes. "I'll try, Papa." He hesitated a moment and smiled at me. "But I'm not scared of rabbits. I like animals."

I blew out a long breath. If I didn't need to keep the kid from shootin' off his mouth, I'd let loose and let him have it. How could one kid be so aggravatin'? "Before we get back, I want you to repeat what I told ya about goin' with me today."

"'Papa and me went for a walk in the woods, and'—should I say you fell down and hurt your side?"

"Good! That's what we'll say. I stepped in a hole out in the woods, twisted my foot, and fell."

Lukas pointed to the left. "Then shouldn't we go that way so we'll be coming from the woods if anyone sees us?"

"Good thinkin', boy! You're gonna make your pa proud of you yet."

He squared his shoulders and grinned. I didn't point out that he'd be tellin' a lie. After all that Bible teachin' he was getting in this place, he'd probably change his mind if I mentioned anything about lyin'.

The supper bell tolled as we stepped off a path leading from the woods. We were equal distance from the doctor's office and the place where Andrea and the boy lived, and since the doctor's wife still carried meals back to my room, I turned him toward the kitchen house. "You go on so there's not a lot of questions. Remember, we was in the woods."

He smiled real big. "I remember, Papa."

"Run now, so you ain't late."

I held my side as he took off at a trot. The boy hadn't been much good at the barn, but in the end, I'd managed to make him feel important, which might prove even more helpful. He'd become an accomplice of sorts, and I could more easily manipulate him if needed.

Once the boy was well on his way, I turned and continued on, still holding my side. I had gone only a short distance when I saw the doctor and his wife on their way to the dining hall. There was no mistakin' when he first noticed me, 'cause he came runnin' at a gallop.

"What's happened, Mr. Wilson?"

I moved my hand from my side and waved toward the kitchen house. "I'll be fine. You go on with your wife and have supper."

One look at my blood-soaked shirt and the doc shook his head. "Absolutely not. We need to see to your wound."

His wife's eyes widened as she approached. "You go on and care for your patient, Wilhelm. I will carry supper back for both of you."

Instead of waiting for his answer, she continued down the sidewalk. The doctor cupped my elbow, but I shook him off. "Thanks, but I can do fine the rest of the way. The walkin' stick is all I need."

The doctor frowned. "Where have you been and what happened that you have reopened the wound?"

His look of exasperation grated on me. This had been the most important day of my life. I was a rich man. A little blood oozing from my side didn't matter one bit, but the doctor would never understand—not unless I told him my true whereabouts and what I'd discovered today. And that would never happen.

"I stepped in a hole and fell while walkin' in the woods with my son." I grimaced for effect.

His frown deepened. "I thought we agreed you would limit your walks to the sidewalks or level streets in the village."

"I shoulda taken your advice, Doc, but it's too late to change things now, ain't it?"

The doctor nodded to a small group of men who were passin' by on their way to supper. Except for height and weight, they all looked alike. Same felt hats, same dark pants, same suspenders, and same white shirts. After years of seein' men and women in all sorts of colors and styles, the sameness here disgusted me. People should think for themselves, but the folks who lived here were willing to let someone else make all their decisions. They didn't have to think about anythin'—not even what clothes they should wear. It seemed to me the only thing they gave much thought to was makin' it to them prayer meetin's every night. Never heard of such hogwash before comin' here. What sane man went to church every day?

The doc never did answer me, but I figured my question didn't really need an answer. We both knew what had happened today couldn't be undone. And I knew he'd do his best to get me mended. No doubt it was gonna take longer to be healed up enough to get outta here, but now with that money, my worries were over.

Andrea wouldn't know nothin' about the money till I was long gone—and that was as it should be. She could stay here with the boy. I sure wasn't gonna take 'em with me. Andrea would be trying to run off at ev'ry turn, and the boy would be a downright nuisance. Besides, goin' it alone meant more money for me.

Soon as we got to the waiting room, the doc motioned me toward the room where he examined his patients. "I want to take a good look at your wound and have my medical supplies close by."

I didn't argue. When he told me to lie down on the table, I did, but not without a groan escapin' my lips. Maybe I'd done more damage than I thought.

The doctor shook his head. "You are a foolish man, Mr. Wilson. We were so close to having you well, and now we must start over. You have ripped out the stitches, but maybe it is for the best."

I lifted up on one elbow to look at him. "What's that mean?"

"Looks like there was some infection in there, and it wasn't ever going to heal quite right. Did you notice how red the edges were becoming? I'll need to clean it out. It will hurt, but it must be done."

He was right about the pain. I gritted my teeth and even yelled at one point, but he kept on working. When he finally gave a nod and stepped away from the table, I opened my eyes. "You done?"

"Ja, for now."

"For now? What else you gotta do?"

"I have cleaned the wound and packed it. Once I am certain the infection is completely gone, I will stitch it up again and hope that you will heal quickly. I am surprised the infection had not caused your temperature to rise."

I hadn't put together my not feelin' good with that gash in my side. Didn't figure one had anythin' to do with the other, but it appeared I was wrong. Since I was mending, the doctor didn't check out all that stuff every day, but even if I'd known, it wouldn't have mattered. Nothin' would have stopped me from going over to that barn today.

The doctor helped me up from the table and back to my room. Even using my cane and his help, it was no small feat. The pain made me feel weak, and a couple times I thought I was gonna pass out. His wife returned with supper while he was helpin' me into bed.

She fluttered around the room carryin' a metal basket on her arm. "I have supper. Would you like to sit in your chair, Mr. Wilson?"

The doctor shook his head. "He cannot sit in the chair right now."

"Truth is, after having the doc work on me, I think I need to rest awhile afore I try to eat anything." I forced a smile. "But thank ya for your efforts."

"You rest, Mr. Wilson. I'll put your food on top of the heating stove to keep it warm. You can ring that bell when you feel you're ready to eat."

The thought of trying to push myself into a position so I could fork down a few bites of food was enough to ruin my appetite. I'd wait until mornin'. Maybe I'd be able to get myself into an upright position by then.

I asked the doctor about giving me some laudanum, but he decided it wasn't necessary. 'Course, he wasn't the one feeling the pain. I considered usin' a few curse words to let him know what I thought of his decision but held off. Until I was well enough to get the money from the hayloft and leave town, I'd have to be careful what I said.

When the morning bell rang, I groaned and covered my ears. I felt like I'd gotten to sleep only a few minutes before they started that incessant clangin'. I longed to get back to sleep, but moments later Dr. Karr stepped into the room.

"Guten Morgen, Mr. Wilson. How did you sleep?"

"I didn't. You shoulda given me some laudanum."

He ignored my comment and drew closer. "Let me have a look at your side." After pullin' down the sheet, he lifted the bandage and poked around on my side.

I let out a yelp and glared at him. "That hurts!" I wanted to add a few expletives but figured I'd get in big trouble if I didn't watch my tongue.

"Ja, I am sure it does, but I am not the one who went walking in the woods against my doctor's orders. When you disobey, you must suffer the consequences." He secured the bandage and pulled up the sheet. "I will bring your breakfast when I return. Until then, you should rest." He turned and strode toward the door without comment.

"How's it look, Doc?" I pointed to my side. "You think it's gonna heal soon?"

"If you do not do as you are told, it will never heal, Mr. Wilson. I am hopeful the wound is clear of infection and we will be able to stitch it back up in a few days. Only time will provide that answer. Until then, I suggest you do as you are told."

"Don't you worry, Doc. I'll be right here in this bed when you get back." He continued out the door without sayin' anything else. I needed to get back in the doctor's good graces.

If I could get a letter written to John before Lukas stopped to see me, I'd send him to the general store. With any luck, the mail would go out on a late afternoon train. Even though I couldn't send him the money, I wanted to let John know it would be comin' his way soon. 'Course, he might not believe me, since I'd been stallin' for time ever since I left Baltimore.

I woke up a short time later when the bell over the front door jangled. I expected to see Dr. Karr or his wife return with my breakfast. Instead, Andrea walked into the room, carryin' the familiar metal basket used to deliver my meals. She glanced around, and looked at the larger table on the other side of the room.

"Dr. Karr was called to see a patient, and his wife was joining some other sisters to quilt. I said I would bring your breakfast." She lifted the metal lid and reached inside the basket.

"Wait. I'm not sure I can make it over there to eat, and the doc said I shouldn't get out of bed without his help. Did he tell you I could get up?"

"He was in a hurry and we didn't discuss where you should eat. Probably better if you stay in bed." She gestured to the board balanced against the wall. "I'll put your food on that board Lukas brought for you to use for writing letters when you were still bed-fast." She balanced the board across my lap and then placed the food, a cloth napkin, and silverware in front of me.

"Ain't ya gonna tuck the napkin around my neck?"

She stiffened at my question. "No, and I'm not going to feed you, either. Exactly what were you and Lukas doing yesterday?"

"Why? What did he tell ya?" I did my best to stay calm. If Lukas had told her about what I'd been up to, I'd wring his neck.

"It isn't so much what he said, but the way he acted."

"Well, how did he act? I don't know what you're talkin' about, Andrea. You ain't makin' sense." I spread the napkin across my chest. "And don't be givin' me those provoked looks."

She sat down in the chair and folded her hands in her lap. "He acted like he was trying to avoid me—like he didn't want to tell me what happened. Did you have him do something he shouldn't have?"

"Why you accusin' me of wrongdoin', Andrea? The boy probably didn't want to tell you because he knew I wasn't supposed to go walkin' out in the woods." I spread butter on the buckwheat pancakes before dousin' them with maple syrup. "Wish they'd serve pancakes every day instead of those fried taters."

"You should be thankful you get any food at all. Beggars can't be choosers, Fred."

"Always got a smart remark, ain't ya."

She ignored me and looked away. Except for the sound of silverware clanking on china, the room remained silent till I finished breakfast. As soon as I pulled the napkin off my chest, she jumped to her feet and took the wooden board from my lap. After placin' the dirty dishes in the metal container, she closed the lid. Holdin' the wooden board in one hand, she started across the room.

"I want that over here," I said.

She turned and looked first at me and then the board. "This? What for?"

"I wanna write a letter." I pointed at the table. "And bring me that writin' paper and an envelope from over there."

After puttin' the board across my lap, she returned for the paper and envelope. "I suppose you would like a pen and ink, as well?" She didn't wait for an answer before gathering the items and placing them on the board. Instead of preparing to depart, she returned to the chair and sat down. "I'm in no hurry. I'll wait and take your letter to be mailed."

"You go on. Ain't no need to wait. It's gonna take me a while to figure out what all I wanna say. Lukas can mail it after school."

Instead of gettin' up, she smiled real big. "I'd be happy to help you with the letter."

"I don't need no help, just time alone to think. You best get on back to your kitchen work."

271

She paused a minute after she stood up and looked at me like she had somethin' she wanted to say but wasn't sure she should. Finally, she picked up the basket and stared at me real hard.

"I've been diligently praying to see some changes in you, Fred."

I tipped my head back and laughed. "Well, you can quit your prayin', Andrea, 'cause I ain't plannin' to change no time soon."

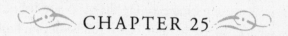

CHAPTER 25

Andrea

A week had passed since Lukas came home and announced that the doctor had stitched up his father's wound again. Lukas was pleased by his father's progress, but I'd noticed that ever since the accident in the woods, Lukas appeared anxious. Several times I asked him questions, but he'd been less than forthcoming. And though I wanted to probe further, I feared he would withdraw from me. And Fred wouldn't provide any answers—he was even more evasive than Lukas.

With Fred on bed rest, there had been no opportunity to read any more of his letters, and he'd now placed them out of sight. While I believed the letters would reveal more of what had happened during Fred's absence, I feared the contents would make it impossible for me to feel safe living with him again. And then what would I do?

Knowing that Lukas longed to win his father's approval increased my concerns even more. I worried that his recent anxiety was connected to Fred, and he was somehow manipulating the boy. I needed a confidant, but my choices were limited. If I discussed my concerns with the elders, they might decide Fred's presence could cause unwanted disruption to life in the colonies. If they asked him to leave, Lukas and I would be expected to go with him. I shuddered at the thought.

Once we had completed cleaning the breakfast dishes, Sister Erma waved me toward the door. "Go on and visit your husband, but try to return before we begin the noonday preparations. Greta and I will take care of the morning lunch."

I removed my apron and hung it near the back door. "Danke." A twinge of guilt assailed me as I opened the door. Once the potato harvest had ended, I had returned to my usual schedule and hurried off each morning to visit Fred. Truth be told, I would have preferred to remain in the Küche, but I couldn't say such a thing without causing raised eyebrows. "I'll be back in plenty of time. I promise."

The door banged shut behind me, and I inhaled a whiff of sweet autumn air. Rays of bright sunshine shone on trees full of colorful leaves. Though I had left the kitchen with every intention of visiting Fred, when I should have turned left, I continued straight—on toward the tinsmith's shop, where I would find Dirk.

Perhaps Lukas had confided in him. If so, maybe Dirk could answer some of my concerns regarding the boy's recent unease. These were the things I told myself before I entered the shop. As I stepped across the threshold, I ignored the nagging feeling that I should turn away. I should be going to visit my husband instead of confiding in another man.

"Guten Morgen, Sister Andrea. It is gut to see you." Dirk's broad smile drew me toward him like a ray of sunshine on a cold winter day. "What brings you to my shop this morning?"

I glanced around, hoping he would be alone. He grinned and glanced over his shoulder. "Werner has gone outdoors to draw some sketches. He is now painting pictures as well as helping here in the shop. Did Lukas tell you?" When I shook my head, Dirk pointed to some paintings sitting on a shelf across the room. "The boy has great talent, so I spoke to the elders. They agreed with my suggestion that he continue his artwork. The paintings will be displayed for sale in the general store. Already two outsiders have purchased artistic pictures."

"That's wonderful. You've been so good to help Werner."

"He is the one with the talent. And the elders have even agreed that he will get extra credit on his store account for each sale, which makes his Mutter and Vater very happy." He hesitated a moment. "So that is why I am alone this morning."

"I am glad." The moment I'd uttered the remark, I could feel the heat rise in my cheeks. "I mean, I am glad to have the opportunity to visit with you privately. I wanted to speak with you about Lukas." I feared my hurried explanation only made me sound more foolish.

"Why don't we sit down." He carried a couple of the stools to the area at the front of the shop. For us to be alone in the back would be inappropriate. And even though we were sitting where we could be seen, I wondered what Brother Bosch might think if he walked into the shop right now. No doubt he would not approve. But that didn't stop me. I accepted Dirk's offer and sat down opposite him.

"I have been worried about Lukas and wondered if you have noticed any changes in his behavior." I looked up and was met by his quizzical gaze.

"Lukas has not been coming to the shop after school. A couple days before Fred reinjured himself, Lukas came by and told me that he would be going to see his father each day after school and would not be able to come to the shop. I thought you knew."

I couldn't believe my ears. "So Lukas has not been here at all?"

"Nein. He said his Vater wanted more time with him." Dirk massaged his forehead. "I should have spoken with you to make sure, but I did not think Lukas would agree to such an arrangement without first talking to you."

"Before Fred arrived, that would have been true, but it seems that he is having quite an influence upon Lukas—and I fear it is not for the better. At home he is distant with me, and when I ask him questions, he tries to avoid direct answers." I wrung my hands together. "He has not been the same boy since Fred arrived."

"If you would like, I can speak to him and see if he will confide in me. I could draw him aside after prayer meeting and tell him how much I miss him at the shop." He cleared his throat. "I do miss Lukas."

"And I'm sure he misses you, as well. Perhaps that's why he has been so quiet. He didn't want to tell me he wasn't coming to the shop. I'm sure Fred warned him against telling me." My anger bubbled like a kettle of boiling water. How dare Fred teach Lukas to be dishonest!

I wanted to march over to the doctor's office and confront him this very moment, yet that would only make matters worse. There would be time to deal with Fred later. Right now I needed to remain focused upon Lukas and how to help him. I wasn't sure why Fred wanted to keep the boy so close, but I doubted it was for any reason that would benefit Lukas.

"Why don't you talk to Lukas after prayer meeting? I don't know if you can discover what's bothering him, but it won't hurt to try." I hesitated a moment. "How is everything going between you and Sister Greta?" I waved my hand. "Never mind. I should not have asked—it is none of my business."

He chuckled. "You do not need to apologize. I am guessing she told you that I do not wish to participate in her strategy to win her Vater's approval to marry Benjamin."

Learning his interest in Greta had been no more than a ruse caused a sense of relief to wash over me. "She has not said anything to me, but I wondered if something was wrong. She has been a little sour lately."

After he had explained the plan, he said, "I am not proud that I agreed to play any part in this. I should have refused from the outset. I knew it was wrong, but Greta has been my friend for years and I wanted to help her. She had already arranged the picnic, so I agreed to escort her, but I told her I would do nothing further to help with her plan."

I heard the shame in his voice and wanted to comfort him, but I remained silent and let him continue.

"She is unhappy with me. I do not want to destroy our friendship, but I couldn't agree to deceive her Vater."

No wonder Greta had been so sullen. I thought I had done something to anger her. Now her actions made more sense to me.

"What if— No, never mind." I shook my head.

Dirk reached for my hand then quickly pulled back. "Tell me, Andrea. What were you going to say?"

"What if you gained Greta's permission to speak with her father and tell him what she had planned? Maybe if he knew the lengths she was willing to go to in order to gain his approval, her father would understand how much she loves Benjamin. Her father admires you, Dirk. If you spoke to him, I think he would listen."

He arched his brows. "I do not know if he would be convinced, but it would not hurt to try. For sure, I would be willing to speak to him."

"But first you must ask Greta. If she thinks it is a bad idea—"

"You do not need to worry. I will first gain her approval. But I think this is a gut idea. Danke, Andrea."

I nodded and glanced toward the door. "I should be on my way. I promised Sister Erma I would return in time to help with noonday preparations. And I need to stop by and see Fred for a few minutes, or he'll tell Lukas I didn't stop by to see him."

"And does it bother Lukas when you don't visit Fred?" Dirk asked while he followed me to the door.

"If I don't make a visit to his father, Lukas will ask why. I think it's another way Fred manipulates both of us into doing what he wants." I smiled and shrugged. "And of course, his tactics usually work. Thank you for your offer to help, Dirk."

"Ja, of course. It is gut we could both help each other."

Though I shouldn't have been pleased by what Dirk had told me, it delighted me to hear him say he did not wish to marry Greta. However, the warm glow evaporated like a morning mist when I considered my selfish spirit. Would I ever be truly free of my feelings for Dirk?

As I walked to the doctor's office, I thought about the vows I'd made when I married Fred. Deep within, I knew I must set aside my feelings for Dirk, honor my marriage vows, and trust God to change Fred into the man he should be—a man who would love and protect his wife and son.

Two days later, Greta and I began the weekly chore of cleaning lamp chimneys and trimming the wicks of the kerosene lamps that hung on the walls in the dining hall. A large pan of soapy water sat alongside the rinse water on one of the long tables. She washed one of the chimneys and dipped it into the rinse water before handing it to me to dry. "Thank you for trying to help. Brother Dirk spoke to me about your suggestion."

I continued to work the soft cloth around the interior of the lamp chimney. "Do you think it would help to have Brother Dirk speak to your father?"

She nodded. "I told him he could try. I did not think my Vater would listen. I expected him to be very angry about my attempt to deceive him."

I arched my brows. "So Brother Dirk has already spoken to him?"

"Oh ja. We went together after prayer service last night. I did not think it was fair for Brother Dirk to speak with Vater alone. Since I was the one who came up with the plan, I thought I should be there to help explain. Besides, if Mutter or Vater had heard any of the comments I'd been making to the other sisters, Vater might be angry with Dirk. I needed to explain that Dirk only went to the picnic with me because I had already asked permission and he did not want to embarrass me." She turned away. "When Dirk said he would not be a part of my plan, I decided I could still make others think we were more than friends."

I now knew why Sister Dorothea had considered Greta and Dirk a couple who planned to marry. Greta had carefully dropped a comment here and there—just enough to convince the sisters and anyone else who might ask questions.

"Does Dirk know that you involved him more than he agreed?"

She bobbed her head. "I told him. He was not happy to hear what I had done, but he has forgiven me."

I was surprised Greta had taken her plan so far, but I was pleased she'd been honest with Dirk—and her parents. I was almost afraid to ask how her father had taken the news. Her facial expression didn't reflect whether the discussion had met with a good or bad reaction. "And did your father become angry?"

"Nein. At first, he appeared confused. But once Dirk fully explained what I had hoped to accomplish, he said he would reconsider his decision." She smiled and handed me another dripping glass chimney. "He asked me to leave and he talked with Dirk for a short time. Once Dirk left, my Vater called me back into the parlor and spoke to me. He was unhappy that I had tried to deceive him, but he was even more disappointed that I had involved Dirk and then deceived him, as well." She sighed and shook her head. "I know I was wrong and I am sorry for what I've done, but Vater has agreed to reconsider and seek the Lord's guidance about my future."

"I am pleased to know he is willing to reconsider his decision. I think your father cares very much for you. I am sure he wants to be certain you are happy."

She exhaled a long breath. "Ja. I tried to explain to him long ago how much I love Benjamin, but he did not listen."

I finished drying the remaining chimney and placed it on the table alongside the others. "I know, but fathers want to protect their daughters. As a mother, I know I would do most anything to protect Lukas. Try to remember that his actions are based in love for you—not to make you unhappy."

"I know you are right. Sometimes I forget that he wants only the best for me." She leaned forward and picked up the wick trimmer. "I'll trim the wicks. You can hand me the chimneys."

I carried several chimneys as we crossed the room. With careful precision, she reached up, cut straight across, and then made carefully angled cuts along each side of the wick.

I handed the chimney to her and she gently set it in place. "The room will shine tomorrow."

"Ja, the dining room is always brighter the day after we clean the chimneys and trim the wicks." When we finished, Greta surprised me with a quick hug. "Thank you for being a gut friend, Andrea. I know my mood has been disagreeable over the past weeks, and I am sure it has been difficult to be pleasant when I am around."

"We must continue to pray that your father will make a decision that will be best for you and Benjamin," I said as we carried the buckets of water and other cleaning supplies to the kitchen.

In addition to praying for Andrea's situation, I would be praying for my own circumstances. Lukas and Dirk had talked after meeting the night before last, but Lukas hadn't yet confided in me. Thus far, there had been no opportunity to speak with Dirk. In truth, I hoped I wouldn't have to go to him. I wanted my son to come to me with his problems and concerns. But I worried Fred had won his heart and his mind. How did a mother protect her son from his own father?

When Lukas returned a short time before supper, I greeted him on the back porch of the Küche. "Did you stop to see your father today?"

"For a while, but I went to work with Brother Dirk first." A sheepish look shadowed his blue eyes. "I quit going to the tinsmith shop after school. Papa said he needed my help more than Brother Dirk did."

I nodded but remained silent and waited for him to continue.

"Brother Dirk talked to me after prayer meeting the other day. He said he missed having me work at the shop." He looked up. "And he said he was disappointed that I hadn't kept my vow to help him, and that a man needs to keep his word." Tears glistened in his eyes. "I wanted to go to work at the shop, but Papa said that a good son did whatever his father told him. Even when I tried to explain that everyone in the village was expected to do what they could to help, he wouldn't change his mind."

My heart ached for Lukas. He'd been torn between his desire to win Fred's affection and breaking his word.

"Papa said family comes before anything else and that we are going to leave the colonies as soon as he's well." A tear trickled down his cheek. "I said you might not want to leave, but he said you have to do what he says."

"I don't think we need to worry just yet, son. Before we can leave, your father needs those stitches to heal. Besides, even if he wants to leave, he'll first need money." I pasted on a brave smile. "Once he's well enough to work, he'll need to go somewhere and earn enough wages to send for us." My response didn't seem to calm Lukas, and I pulled him into a hug.

"But what if he had enough money? Would we go with him?"

I released my hold and looked into his eyes. "You are worrying needlessly, Lukas. Your father has no money."

I glanced up and caught sight of Brother Bosch. He waved and called a greeting. "I need to have a word with Sister Erma. Is she inside?"

"She is. And I'd better get back to my duties before the supper bell rings." I leaned close to Lukas's ear. "We can talk more later, but I'm glad that you decided to keep your commitment at the tinsmith shop."

Brother Bosch followed in my footsteps as I returned to the kitchen. He lifted his nose in the air as he stepped inside. "The smells in this Küche are like a little piece of heaven, Sister Erma."

She waved her hand at him. "Just because you give me the compliments, do not expect a bigger bowl of filled noodles on your table."

The elder laughed. Soon after I started working in the Küche,

I learned that Brother Bosch had a fondness for filled noodles. No doubt he was pleased to see they were on this evening's menu.

"I expect only my fair share, Sister, but there will be an extra outsider eating with us today, if that is not an inconvenience for you."

She wagged her head. "Nein. One more is not a problem. A new field worker?"

He shook his head. "No. A visitor to our villages." He glanced in my direction. "One who is most unexpected."

CHAPTER 26

I paid little heed to Brother Bosch's comment, but after he departed, I wondered if the doctor had declared Fred well enough to eat in the dining hall. His appearance would certainly be unexpected, and even though he'd been here several months, he was considered a visitor. Is that why Brother Bosch had looked in my direction?

A knot tightened in my stomach. What if Fred exhibited rude behavior during the meal? He enjoyed making others feel uncomfortable, and he would find the fact that we did not speak during meals an unnecessary rule. Would he care so little about Lukas and me that he would jeopardize our welfare here? I wanted to believe he wouldn't, but my mind told me otherwise. If he would teach his son to disobey me, he would care little about offending the residents of the village—or me, for that matter.

"Sister Andrea!" Sister Erma nudged me. "You are lost in your daydreams. We have work to do."

She gestured toward the empty china serving bowls and soup tureens sitting on the worktable. I nodded and began to fill the tureens with pea soup. Fred would turn up his nose at the soup—he disliked pea soup. My hands trembled as I wiped the edges of the tureens and placed a lid on each one.

"Shall I take these to the dining room?" I turned to face Sister Erma.

She looked at me as though I'd lost my mental faculties. "Ja. They cannot eat the soup if it is out here, can they?" With a quick flit of her hand, she motioned for me to take the tureens into the other room. "You are acting as though this is your first day in the Küche."

I offered a feeble smile and hurried to do her bidding. There wasn't time for an explanation. Sister Erma wanted action, not excuses. Complaints regarding her Küche were far and few between, and she expected it to remain that way.

When the final bell rang and the doors of the dining hall opened, I focused on the men's door and looked for Fred to enter and take his seat with the other outsiders. Instead, a neat-appearing man wearing a brown wool suit sat down at the outsiders' table. I blew a sigh of relief. Since there was no sign of Fred, I'd likely misinterpreted Brother Bosch's expression when he had mentioned the visitor. Still, I wondered who the stranger might be and what had brought him to West Amana.

Because of the train stations in Main, Homestead, and South, those villages were frequently visited by salesmen or buyers from the large cities. Visitors to West were mostly farmers and their wives from the surrounding area, locals in need of repairs to their household wares or farm equipment—visitors who didn't eat their meals in our kitchen houses.

From all appearances, I wasn't the only one interested in the stranger. It seemed everyone in the dining hall had taken a turn looking in his direction. My earlier apprehension eased, and I moved back and forth filling bowls and platters at my usual pace. The stranger wasn't shy about taking in his surroundings. While he ate, he appeared to study the room and each of us, as well.

Once the after-meal prayer had been recited, I was surprised to see Lukas rush out the men's door of the dining hall. Usually he stopped to tell me good-bye before heading off to visit Fred before prayer meeting.

As I stacked the dirty plates and placed them on a large tray, a shadow fell across the table and I looked up. Brother Bosch and the stranger stood on the other side, both of them staring at me.

A tingling sensation swept over me as I looked into the visitor's dark eyes. His hard stare caused me to flinch, and dread made my dinner sit heavily in my stomach. I turned away, gathered a handful of dirty silverware, and hoped he would leave, but I knew he wouldn't. He was here about Fred. I was sure of it.

Brother Bosch tipped his head toward the visitor. "Sister Andrea, this is Mr. Shaw. He would like to speak with you." He gestured toward the back porch. "I think there would be more privacy outdoors."

I glanced back and forth between the two men and nodded. After placing the fistful of dirty silverware on the tray, I scooted it from the table and carried the tray to the kitchen. Sister Erma frowned when she caught sight of the stranger following me.

She pointed a wooden spoon in his direction. "Only workers are allowed in the kitchen." When Brother Bosch appeared, she dropped the spoon to her side. "Is against the rules for him to be in here, Brother Bosch."

"Ja, ja. We are going outside." He motioned toward the back door. "It is easier this way."

Her frown remained intact, but she didn't argue. I shrugged and hoped she would understand that I hadn't directed them through the kitchen. "I will be back to help in a few minutes."

Mr. Shaw stopped at the door and glanced over his shoulder. "It may take longer than a few minutes."

In spite of the kitchen's warmth, I shivered. What could possibly take more than a few minutes? If this man was here about Fred, wouldn't it be easier for him to go and speak to Fred? With my insides tossing about like cream in a butter churn, I stepped outside.

"I will wait over here by the tree so that Mr. Shaw may speak to you in private, Sister Andrea."

Before he could move, I shook my head. "No, please stay. I have nothing to hide, and I am sure Mr. Shaw won't object if you are present during our conversation." I folded my arms across my waist and returned his stare. "Will you, Mr. Shaw?"

The man walked down the porch steps and halted. "If you don't mind others knowing your business, I don't mind." There was a callous tone to his voice—one that signaled that he was accustomed to getting his way.

A man like Fred.

Yet Mr. Shaw didn't appear to be of the same ilk—he seemed better educated, and certainly better dressed. Brother Bosch stepped to my side while Mr. Shaw stood across from us. To any onlookers, we would look like three people engaged in a pleasant conversation, but from the moment I'd met Mr. Shaw, I knew this talk would not be pleasant.

"I'm not a man who beats about the bush, Mrs. Wilson, so I'll get right to the point. I'm here regarding your husband, Fred Wilson. He *is* your husband, isn't he?"

I nodded. "I am sure Brother Bosch has already told you I am married to Fred Wilson."

He shrugged. "He did, but a man in Baltimore said he thought Mr. Wilson might have married some gal down in Martinique, name of Neyssa. Wanted to be sure I got things straight."

My stomach roiled. Who was Neyssa? Had Fred been involved with another woman while he was gone? Is that why he hadn't returned from the Caribbean? "Who was this man in Baltimore who told you about another woman, Mr. Shaw?"

He shook his head. "Sorry, but I promised I wouldn't say. I can tell you the information came from a reliable source, a man who sailed to Martinique on the same ship as your husband."

While I did my best to digest the unexpected news, Mr. Shaw removed a small notepad from his pocket. "Has your husband ever spoken to you about a robbery or murder in Baltimore?"

I reeled and took a backward step. So the letters were true. Fred had been involved in a terrible crime. Brother Bosch reached around my waist and walked me to the porch. "You should sit down, Sister Andrea."

My gaze remained fixed on Mr. Shaw as I sat on the porch step. Should I mention the letters I'd read? I couldn't chance Fred knowing I'd read his mail. Fear gripped me, and I swallowed hard. "No, he has said nothing about such things."

"I see. Well, Mr. Bosch tells me that your husband has been treated by the doctor ever since he arrived in Iowa. Did he tell you how he happened to injure himself?"

"Not in any detail. The malaria is common among sailors who travel to the Caribbean. As for the other injuries, I assumed they happened in Martinique or on his return voyage." One look at Mr. Shaw's eyes and I could see he didn't believe me, but I didn't want to tell this stranger that I spent as little time as possible with my husband. Though I was ashamed to admit it, I hadn't asked for details—partly because Fred became angry when I peppered him with questions, and partly because I feared him. Now, however, Mr. Shaw was quite interested.

"My husband could more easily answer your questions, Mr. Shaw. You'll find him at Dr. Karr's office." I hesitated a moment. "Are you an officer of the law, Mr. Shaw?"

He cleared his throat. "I am a Pinkerton agent charged with apprehending the man who shot and killed a banker in Baltimore." He tugged on his necktie. "I have every reason to believe that man is your husband, Mrs. Wilson."

I gasped. "You believe my husband is responsible for a murder? I know Fred has many faults, but I do not want to believe he would kill anyone. Who told you he is the one who shot him?"

"A sailor has given us many details that have been very helpful, but I am mainly relying upon the investigation that has been conducted by our agency. Please understand that I do want to talk to your husband, and I will carefully weigh his answers. However, I thought it best to speak to you beforehand."

I surmised the detective wanted to see if Fred's story would align with mine. "Fred hasn't told me anything about the incident. If you like, I can accompany you to the doctor's office. Otherwise, I'll go inside and finish my work." Though my voice remained strangely calm, my insides quivered like Sister Erma's rhubarb jelly.

"I believe I'd like you to come with me, Mrs. Wilson. If your husband becomes upset, having you present may help calm him." He turned toward Brother Bosch. "Would you please explain to Mrs. Wilson's supervisor, sir?"

Brother Bosch gave a slight nod. "I think it would be wise for you to go with Mr. Shaw, Sister Andrea. Your husband is quick to anger, and I know the detective would like to avoid difficulty with him."

"I am not certain my presence will prove helpful, but I'll go along." I would have been more comfortable if Brother Bosch had come with us, but he returned to the Küche.

While we walked to Dr. Karr's office, my conversation with Mr. Shaw quickly became one-sided. I attempted to discover how much he knew about Fred and if he had any genuine evidence that would prove Fred had committed such a shocking crime. However, Mr. Shaw was more accustomed to asking rather than answering questions, and I soon found myself being quizzed about my childhood, my marriage to Fred, our life in Baltimore, and my subsequent adjustment to living in the colonies.

"So you have only one child?"

"Yes. Lukas left after supper to come and visit his father, so I would ask that before you talk to Fred, you permit me to send him back to the kitchen house."

"Of course. Though my questions and appearance might suggest otherwise, I am not heartless. I am certain of your husband's guilt, but what you will eventually tell the boy is your choice. If at all possible, we will leave without trouble."

I stopped short. "Do I understand that you intend to take Fred with you in the immediate future?"

He nodded. "That is my plan."

"So he has no opportunity to prove his innocence or guilt? He must simply do as you tell him?" I still didn't want to believe Fred was capable of murder, and it didn't seem right that this stranger could appear and haul him off to . . . to where? I had no idea where he planned to take Fred.

He took my elbow and propelled me onward. "He will have a trial in Baltimore. That's where the crime was committed, Mrs. Wilson. That's the way the law operates." He looked at me as if those few words should explain everything.

"But you're from the Pinkerton Agency. You're not a policeman or a sheriff. Surely something more is required before you forcibly detain someone."

"I have paper work that permits me to return your husband to Baltimore, Mrs. Wilson." He reached inside his pocket, withdrew several papers, and then handed them to me.

I stopped, and in the waning light, looked at a sketch of my husband. In bold block letters below his likeness were the words *Wanted, Dead or Alive, $500 Reward.* My mouth turned dry and I clutched a hand to my chest as Mr. Shaw grasped my elbow.

"Please don't faint on me, Mrs. Wilson." I didn't miss the concern in his eyes when he looked down at me. "I realize this is a shock to you, but you are better off without your husband." He hesitated. "I wish there were some kind way to have said that, but there isn't. Fred Wilson is a ruthless murderer who deserves to be punished. Even though he is wanted dead or alive, it is my intention to take him back to Baltimore for trial."

"But if he would attempt to escape—?"

"I'd have no choice."

I shivered and offered a silent prayer. A prayer that Fred would see the error of his ways and repent, that he would realize the only way to true forgiveness was through his heavenly Father, and that he would open his heart to receive God's forgiveness. But if Fred had not turned to the Lord when he'd been surrounded by believers and blessed by their mercies, would he turn to the Lord now?

"The doctor's office is right over here." After opening the door, I gathered my skirt and stepped inside.

The jangling of the overhead bell was followed by an eerie silence. Usually Lukas would call out and greet me, or I would hear him talking to Fred when I entered the office. I gestured for Mr. Shaw to follow me, but I came to a halt when I looked into Fred's room.

I clutched my throat. "They're gone." Panic seized me. Turning on my heel, I collided with Mr. Shaw. I attempted to push him from my path, but he didn't budge. The man was as solid as a brick wall. "Move! I need to find my son."

"And I need to find your husband." His voice bore a sharp edge. "Where are they?"

My mouth gaped open. What was wrong with him? Why would he think I knew where they were? Wasn't my fear evident? "I don't know, but I'm going to go and look. Get out of my way."

He grasped my shoulders and held firm. "You'll do no good if you take off in a panic. You need to settle yourself and think where the boy and his father might have gone."

I shook my head and tried to wrench free from his grasp. "We need to ring the village bell and sound an alarm. Everyone will come running to help us find Lukas."

He continued to hold tight. "No! That's the last thing we are going to do, Mrs. Wilson. Ringing that bell will place your son in more danger. I have a feeling your husband knows something is amiss and he's attempting to get out of town."

I ceased my attempts to get free of his hold. "Why would Lukas be in more danger? How would Fred know he's in any danger?"

"Your son saw me in the dining hall. I have a strong suspicion he told Fred of my presence. I should have stopped him before he left the room."

Who did this man think he was? Under different circumstances, I would have taken him to task. However, the only thing I cared about at the moment was finding Lukas.

"If your husband is attempting to flee and has the boy with him, the bell will signal the discovery of their disappearance. Criminals take more chances if they believe their captor is closing in. Given your husband's medical problems, he will depend heavily upon the boy to help him. We don't want your husband to become frantic and subject the boy to further danger, do we? What if he decided to use your son as a shield to protect himself?" He took a backward step and made a sweeping gesture toward the waiting room chairs. "Shall we sit down and discuss our plan of action?"

I nodded and sat down in the chair facing the window. I wanted to have a clear view if Lukas should appear.

Mr. Shaw seemed to care little about watching out the window. No doubt, he was certain neither Lukas nor Fred would reappear in the near future. "I want you to think about any place your husband and son might have gone. Anywhere they've mentioned that might be a good place to hide."

The question had barely passed the detective's lips when Dirk appeared outside the doctor's office. Mr. Shaw's face crinkled into a disapproving frown when I stood and gestured for Dirk to come inside.

Dirk nodded to Mr. Shaw and sat down beside me. Concern filled his eyes. The detective attempted to interrupt me while I explained he was a Pinkerton agent who had been sent to apprehend Fred, but I was undeterred by his endeavor.

I nodded toward Fred's room. "Both Fred and Lukas are missing. Mr. Shaw asked if I know anywhere they might be hiding. I can't think of any place they might have gone." Before Dirk could suggest ringing the village bell, I explained why the detective advised against it.

"Ja, well that sounds like wise thinking." Dirk rubbed his jaw. "Has the doctor released Fred to go outdoors?"

No doubt Dirk was remembering that Fred and Lukas had gone on walks before he injured himself in the woods. "Only far enough to sit outside the office, so they wouldn't have gone for a walk." I glanced outside. "Has Lukas ever mentioned—"

"The barn!" Dirk jumped to his feet. "Come on."

Dirk waved for us to follow, but Mr. Shaw remained in his chair. "What barn? There are a lot of barns in this village." He gestured for Dirk to slow down. "Don't go running off half-cocked. We need to think things through and move carefully so the boy doesn't get hurt."

Dirk stopped, but his hand remained poised on the metal door latch. "The barn on the Neumann farmstead. The land that belonged to Sister Andrea's parents. Lukas told me that he and Fred tried to walk there one time."

Lukas had never told me of such an incident. I wanted to quiz Dirk, but there wasn't time. We needed to go and look before nightfall was fully upon us. "I think Brother Dirk is right. We should look there first."

He stood and looked at Dirk. "You got a weapon you can bring with you?"

My breath caught and I shook my head. "Please, no weapons. My son is with him."

"We do not believe in taking up arms against our fellowman, Mr. Shaw. You will locate no weapons in the village."

Mr. Shaw patted his side. "There's at least one weapon in this village, and if I know Fred Wilson, there's more than the one that's holstered to my side."

Terror seized me. If Fred had a gun, Lukas was in grave danger. Fred wouldn't hesitate to use Lukas as a shield. I had to protect my son.

CHAPTER 27

Dirk took the lead, with Mr. Shaw close on his heels. I followed behind, my shorter legs and long skirt proving a hindrance. "Slow down!" My lungs screamed for air as I hollered at the men.

Mr. Shaw slowed his pace and glanced over his shoulder. "Maybe you shouldn't go any further, Mrs. Wilson."

When I shouted my objection to the suggestion, both men came to a halt. "It is my son we are looking for, Mr. Shaw. You will not keep me away."

"Actually, it's your husband that I'm after. The boy may not even be with him. Perhaps he went off to play with some of his friends. If there's violence, it would be better if you weren't there." He wiped the perspiration from his forehead. "Besides, you're slowing us down."

Dirk grasped Mr. Shaw's arm. "We should slow our pace. I know Sister Andrea will not be left behind."

Mr. Shaw sighed. "Come along, then. I suppose we'll have to move slower. If she arrives after us and makes a great deal of noise, she'll alert Fred if he's in there."

"*She* can hear every word you're saying, Mr. Shaw. I'm not some absent third party." The man's ability to annoy me momentarily overshadowed my concern for Lukas. "I suggest we move on. The barn is ahead and to the left."

After Mr. Shaw had advised Dirk and me that we should keep talk to a minimum, the three of us tramped through the high grass and overgrown weeds until we were near the rear of the barn.

Mr. Shaw motioned for us to gather close. "Dirk and I will go around to the front of the barn and try to sneak in and see if anyone is there. You stay out here. With Fred's injuries, he shouldn't be able to run very fast. If the boy is in there, I'll send him out to you as soon as I can."

"But I . . ."

Dirk grasped my hand. "Listen to what he says, Andrea. You must remain out here and pray for the safety of all of us." He looked deep into my eyes. "If Lukas is inside, I will protect him with my own life. You know that, ja?"

My voice caught. "I know."

"Come, Dirk." Mr. Shaw bent low and disappeared around the corner of the barn.

I squeezed Dirk's hand. "I will be praying—for all of you." I leaned against the rough barn boards and bowed my head. I prayed the Lord would protect all who might be injured during any possible encounter—but most of all I prayed the barn would be empty.

As darkening skies cast eerie shadows, birds fluttered through the trees to nest for the night. Barren tree limbs swayed in the chilly evening breeze, and I let out a muffled yelp when dead weeds brushed against the hem of my skirt. Hopefully, no one had heard me.

I swallowed hard and wiped my perspiring palms down the front of my dress as I continued to pray silently. Would this waiting never end? Surely they had reached the front of the barn by now. What was taking so long? Maybe I should at least move to the side of the barn.

I'd taken only a few steps when I heard Lukas shout. "Papa! Papa! Someone's coming in the barn." A brief silence followed. "Did you hear me, Pa? I think someone came in."

"Hush up, boy!" Even from a distance, Fred's command seethed with anger.

"Lukas! Come to me." Immediately I recognized Dirk's voice, but Lukas didn't reply.

Mr. Shaw had been adamant that I remain outside the barn, but I couldn't bear not knowing what was happening inside. Maybe Lukas would come to me if I called. I edged around the corner and moved toward the front of the barn. The door stood ajar and I picked my way closer, hoping to catch a glimpse of Lukas.

"I know you're in here, Wilson! Come on out and there won't be any trouble. You don't want that boy of yours to be hurt, do you?" Mr. Shaw's voice boomed through the yawning expanse. "Send him out the door so we can settle all this trouble like grown men." In the distance I heard a whimper. I tensed and peered around the edge of the door. Lukas must have been hiding in one of the stalls. "C'mon, Fred, your boy is scared. Be a man and do the right thing."

"Who are you?"

At the sound of Fred's voice, I looked up toward the loft. He and Lukas weren't together, yet Lukas hadn't run to Dirk. He could easily make it from the stall to the space where Dirk and Mr. Shaw had positioned themselves.

"Edward Shaw. I'm a Pinkerton agent sent here to take you back to Baltimore. We both know you can't stay up in that loft forever. I'd like to make this easy for all of us, so why don't you come down and turn yourself in."

"Ha! You'd like that, wouldn't ya? What'd ya pay John Calvert to give me up? That dirty scumbag."

"Every man has his price, and Calvert was tired of waiting on you. Truth is, he figured you were playing him for a fool. He thought you were lying about sending him money."

"Well, you can go on back to Baltimore and tell him he's the fool." A shot rang out, and when Dirk and Mr. Shaw dropped to the floor, I followed their lead and fell to the ground.

A mixture of fear and anger welled in my chest, and I cupped my hands to my mouth. "Tell Lukas to come out of the barn before he's caught in your gunfire, Fred."

"I shoulda known you'd be out there somewhere, Andrea. You can't wait to be rid of me, can ya? Well, Lukas and me, we're a team now. If you wanna see the boy alive, you best tell Shaw and your friend Dirk to get outta the barn. I got my gun trained on Lukas, and if they don't clear out by the time I count to five, I'll shoot the boy."

I gasped and clutched my throat. "Let him leave, Fred, and I'll come in there and take his place. Please!"

"The boy ain't leavin'. You know me well enough to believe I'll hurt him, so you best tell them two to get outta the barn. And Lukas—you stay put in that stall. I can see you from up here."

Bile rose in my throat as I screamed for Dirk and Mr. Shaw to come outside. Dirk scooted backward on his stomach, but Mr. Shaw remained in position. I hissed for him to retreat. Instead, he appeared to take aim with his gun.

"Fred, you don't want to do anything you'll regret. The boy's done nothing. What kind of man would threaten harm to his son in order to save his own hide?"

Another bullet whizzed overhead. "The next one will be aimed at the kid. Now get outta the barn."

Lukas's whimpers had risen to tearful sobbing, and I longed to run into the barn and comfort him. Dirk backed out of the barn and drew close to my side. "I'm sorry. I should have gone after him, but Mr. Shaw held me back."

"Mr. Shaw is the one with a gun. He should have gone after Lukas, not you. It appears the only thing that interests him is getting Fred turned in for his reward." Dirk pulled me back when I attempted to gain another peek inside. "I don't think Fred would shoot me if I went in there. I'll call out and tell him I just want to comfort Lukas."

"I think you should stay here. Fred may tell you to come inside, but I do not believe you can trust him. Come with me; I have an idea." Dirk took my hand and led me to the opposite side of the barn.

When we had rounded the far corner, he gestured to a door beneath the dilapidated overhang that had been used to protect the animals from bad weather. I tugged on his hand. "I think my father nailed that door shut years ago. We won't be able to get it open without making a great deal of noise."

"We freed the door weeks ago when the elders talked about wintering some animals over here. If all goes well, we should be able to get inside without Fred hearing us. You can wait by the door, and I will sneak around the stalls and get Lukas."

He reached for the door, but I grasped his arm. "Wait! What if Mr. Shaw thinks you are Fred and shoots? We should have told him what we were going to do."

"If he thinks I am Fred, he is not a very gut Pinkerton agent.

He can see the ladder Fred must use to come down from the loft." He waved toward the front of the barn. "If you want, you can go back and tell Mr. Shaw, but we are losing daylight and I am going in. The darkness will give Fred more protection and advantage."

"And Lukas is going to become more and more frightened." Even if I went to tell Mr. Shaw, Dirk would be inside before I could tell him the plan. "I'll follow you inside."

Dirk held a warning finger in the air. "You stay here. Otherwise neither of us will go in. I want your promise that you will not follow me, Andrea."

My heart thumped in my chest. I didn't want to promise. I wanted to go to my son. Yet I trusted Dirk and understood there was more chance of being detected if we both entered. "I promise."

Without warning, he leaned forward and kissed my forehead. "I have no right to kiss you, and kissing you on the forehead is not at all the kind of kiss I'd like to give you. But if something should happen to me, I need you to know I love you. I thank God every day that you and Lukas came into my life."

He didn't give me a chance to respond before entering the barn. My insides quivered in a mixture of fear and delight. I held my breath and waited, my fear mounting by the minute. Surely the quiet meant no one had spotted Dirk.

"Please, Lord, keep Lukas and Dirk safe." Over and over, I repeated that same prayer. I couldn't bring myself to pray for Fred or Mr. Shaw. They had created this dangerous situation and neither seemed to care that they had placed Lukas in harm's way. If they desired the Lord's help, they would need to pray for themselves.

My breathing eased a bit. By now, Dirk must have been with Lukas. I kept my gaze fixed on the door, certain Lukas would soon appear. Only moments later, I heard the tromping of feet and another shot rang out. I covered my mouth to squelch the scream that threatened. No matter what, I must remain quiet. If Fred discovered I was along the side of the barn, he'd turn his attention back to Lukas.

"Looks like you took a bullet, Mr. Shaw." Fred's shout was followed by vile laughter. "You better try and get outta here 'fore ya bleed to death."

A knot settled in my stomach as the minutes ticked by. Except for hooting owls and chirping locusts, silence reigned. I didn't know how much time elapsed, but I started when Fred shouted to Lukas.

"Get over and see if he's dead, boy. Don't be a coward. Do what yer pa says. He won't shoot ya. If he's alive, he knows I'm sendin' you over to check on him."

I waited, holding my breath.

"Lukas! Get over there and see 'bout that Pinkerton agent or I'll aim this gun at your skinny little backside. Go on!"

I leaned close to the door and strained to listen. "I-I-I'm going, Pa. Don't shoot me." Lukas's voice trembled with fear, and I wanted to thrash Fred. How dare he treat his son with such hateful disregard! A muffled sound of footsteps soon followed. "I-I-I think he's dead, Pa. He won't answer me."

"Hold your hand near his nose and mouth and see if he's breathing," Fred shouted.

"He's not breathing, Pa."

"That tinsmith didn't come back in the barn, did he?"

"No, Pa. It's just you and me—and Mr. Shaw. I'm going back over to the stall. I don't want to stay beside a dead man."

"You need to come up here and help me, Lukas. I don't want to hear no cryin' 'bout you're scared to climb the ladder. I'll be waitin' right up here and help you. See? I'm goin' over there right now to—"

A shot rang out and a strangled cry was followed by a loud thump. Lukas screamed. Dirk called to the boy as Mr. Shaw yelled for them to keep calm. I leaned against the barn, my heart pounding and palms perspiring.

I could keep quiet no longer. "Someone tell me what's going on!"

The door burst open and Lukas rushed into my arms. His body shuddered and I held him tight.

"I think Papa's dead." His voice caught and he thrust his face against my shoulder as sobs racked his frame.

"You were very brave, Lukas." Dirk appeared and stooped down beside the boy. "I know this is very hard for you, but you did the right thing."

Lukas lifted his head from my shoulder. "Mr. Shaw said he wouldn't kill Pa, but he did."

"Nein. Your Vater died because he fell from the loft and hit his head on the floor," Dirk explained. "Mr. Shaw's bullet was not what caused his death. If your Vater would have come down like Mr. Shaw asked, he would still be alive. For sure, it is sad that he has died, but he made that choice—not you, or me, or Mr. Shaw." Tears continued to stream down the boy's cheeks, and Dirk wiped them away with his handkerchief.

"Did you hear my pa say he was going to shoot at me?" Lukas's voice warbled into high pitch before he finished the question. He sniffed and looked at me. "Do you think he was really going to? I tried to do what he said, but he still didn't like me, did he?"

I cupped his cheeks between my palms. "You are a sweet and wonderful little boy, Lukas. And, no, I don't think your father would have shot at you. He thought that if he scared you, you would do what he said."

"But I had to do what Mr. Shaw said 'cause he was right there beside me." His eyes grew wide. "And he had a gun, too."

Dirk leaned forward and took Lukas's hand. "But Mr. Shaw never said he would shoot at you, did he?"

"Nooo." Brown curls fell across his forehead as he shook his head. "Mr. Shaw said Pa would quit shooting if I said he was dead. So that's what I did, but that was a lie."

Dirk smiled. "This one time I think it is gut that you told the lie. Mr. Shaw wanted to keep all of us safe."

Confusion flickered in Lukas's eyes. "But if Mr. Shaw would have gone away, Papa would still be alive."

"Your father was involved in some very bad things back in Baltimore." I inhaled a shallow breath, uncertain how much to tell the boy right now. "Mr. Shaw couldn't go away. It was his job to take your father back there."

"I think you and your Mutter should go back to the village and ask one of the men to bring a wagon to the barn. Mr. Shaw and I will stay here." Dirk stood and placed his hand on Lukas's shoulder. "Do you think you could do that for me?"

Lukas nodded and squared his shoulders. He was trying so hard to be brave, yet I wondered how all of this would affect him in the days and weeks to come. I had prayed for his safety and God had provided. Now I would pray that God would erase these terrible memories from my son's mind.

CHAPTER 28

The following days proved difficult. Mr. Shaw took care of arrangements regarding Fred's body. When I said I didn't think he should be buried in the village cemetery, Mr. Shaw agreed. He needed proof of Fred's death, and since photographs were seldom taken in the colonies, there was no photographer. Besides, I thought the idea of photographing a dead man repugnant.

The village carpenter constructed a wooden coffin for Fred. Two days later, the coffin was loaded into the baggage car of the train Mr. Shaw boarded for Baltimore.

"It's better this way," he'd said. "I'll see that he's buried in Baltimore. I can write and give you the name of the cemetery, if you'd like." I told him it wasn't necessary. I had no intention of ever visiting Baltimore again.

Though I had little remorse over Fred's death, I did find myself thinking of those early days when he'd been a different man. He'd never been overly kind, but when I married him, I believed him to have many redeeming qualities. Trying to understand how a man could change so much plagued me. Had I done something to cause those dreadful changes? Was it being married and having a child? Had he wanted to escape to a carefree life? How had he justified resorting to robbery and murder?

I would never have the answers. Truth be told, I couldn't answer the questions Lukas had posed since his father's death. After the incident in the barn, he became fearful and timid, startled by every loud noise or unexpected circumstance. At night, I heard him whimpering in his sleep, and it tore at my heart. What damage Fred had done in such a short time. The boy had longed to win his father's love, but Fred had loved no one but himself.

My days seemed strangely distorted now that Fred was gone. I'd become accustomed to rushing to the doctor's office in between my duties at the Küche. It seemed odd returning to the former routine, both for me and for Lukas. His schedule had been interrupted when Fred arrived, and his current readjustment was a daily reminder of his father's violent death.

Dirk was doing his best to rally around Lukas and me, and his attention proved valuable to both of us. Together we talked through much of what had happened, but Lukas withdrew at times, and I wondered if there were secrets he was protecting. Dirk cautioned me not to push him too fast. "He will tell all when he is ready. Give him time."

Days later, I was preparing to go to the cellar for milk when Lukas returned from the tinsmith shop with Dirk. A gust of cold wind swept across the floor as they stepped into the kitchen.

Dirk quickly pulled the door closed behind him and shivered. "It is getting colder out there."

"But not too cold," Lukas added.

Dirk nodded and motioned me toward the dining room while Lukas remained in the kitchen with Sister Erma. "Lukas wants us to go to the barn with him."

I arched my brows. "The barn? You mean where his father . . ." I left the question unfinished and stared at him.

"Ja, he says he has something to show us."

My thoughts raced. What could he possibly show us in that empty barn? "I don't think it's a good idea. He will relive what happened, and his bad dreams will begin anew."

"I did my best to talk him out of the idea, but he says it is important. I think we must trust his word on this, Andrea." He tipped his head to the side. "You are the one who said he has been holding back. Maybe this is what he needs to do in order to free himself from what happened there."

I didn't believe returning to the barn would be helpful, but Dirk was right: I had encouraged Lukas to confide in us. To discourage him now would be wrong. I glanced toward the kitchen. "I need to speak with Sister Erma."

Dirk nodded and called Lukas into the dining room while I went and spoke to Sister Erma. She nodded her agreement. "Ja, I think we can manage without you for a while if you can first get the milk from the cellar."

Before we departed, Dirk and Lukas went to the cellar for the milk while I went upstairs and retrieved my cape and a warmer coat for Lukas. When they returned to the kitchen, I held out the coat to Lukas. "You need to change coats. It is getting colder outside. By the time we return, the sun will be setting."

Lukas ran ahead as Dirk and I quickened our steps to help ward off the chill in the air. Dirk moved closer to my side and touched his finger to my forehead. "These lines tell me you are worrying too much. I do not think this will be as terrible as you imagine. Lukas wanted to go to the barn. Neither of us ever mentioned he should return. Please try to set your worries aside."

"I know you are probably right, but I wasn't even in the barn when all the shooting happened, and I don't want to go back there."

His lips parted in a smile. "But I admire that you are willing to go for your son's sake." Somehow Dirk always knew exactly what to say.

As we approached the barn, Lukas slowed his pace and waited for us to join him. I was glad he hadn't rushed ahead. I clasped his hand and he squeezed mine in return, each of us gathering strength from the other. "Do you want to talk before we go inside, Lukas?"

"No, I'll tell you in there."

The heavy barn door creaked a loud protest as Dirk pulled it open. The three of us walked inside as the late afternoon shadows fell across the straw-strewn floor. Everything seemed so much the same as the last time we'd been there that I shivered at the remembrance.

Lukas gestured toward the ladder leading to the loft. "The first time I came here with Papa, he got real mad 'cause I wouldn't climb up there. I told him I was scared of going up high, but he said I should be a man."

I squeezed his shoulder. "But you're not a man. You're a boy, and going up that ladder is a scary thing. When I was a little girl, I wouldn't go up there, either."

Lukas's eyes brightened a bit. "Did you ever go up there?"

"Not until I was fifteen years old, and even then, I was frightened. I tripped on the hem of my skirt and almost fell, so that was the last time I was up there."

"You only ever went up there one time?"

I nodded my head. "Yes. Your grandpa didn't think girls should work in the barn, so there really was no reason for me to be up there."

"But boys are supposed to help, and Pa wanted me to go up there 'cause of his side was hurting so bad. He said we were looking for something."

"What? Is that why you came here?"

"I came 'cause Pa said he needed my help. He wanted to find something someone else left up there. And he found it, too."

I shook my head. "You need to tell me everything, Lukas."

His lip quivered. "You can go up there and see. Pa said he found something, but I never went up the ladder to look. When we came back the last time, he wanted me to go up and help him bring down a metal box, but I was still afraid."

My mind reeled. A metal box? Could my father's money be hidden in the barn loft? Would he have done such a thing?

Dirk stooped down in front of the boy. "And now what do you want to do? Did you want to go up there and see if your Vater was telling the truth?"

Lukas shook his head. "I don't want to climb the ladder, but you or Mama can go up and see."

"Since your Mutter does not like climbing that ladder, either, I will go and see what I can find." Taking long steps, Dirk strode toward the ladder and in no time was into the loft.

I waited, not sure if I wanted Dirk to find the box. If it was there, and if it did contain my father's money, it would mean Lukas and I could leave the colonies and start a new life somewhere else. Of late, I'd given no thought to ever leaving. I'd become accustomed to the routine of my daily chores and enjoyed visiting with the other women. I had slowly embraced the faith of these people and found my place among them. They had given me hope and been a shining light during the darkest hours of my life.

Since Fred's death, I'd permitted myself once again to consider a future here—a future that included Dirk. Late at night as I lay in bed, I dreamed of him as my husband, but the money would change all of that. Just as Fred had appeared and ruined everything, the money could do the same now.

Lukas pranced from foot to foot. "Do you see it up there? I think it was over in a corner. That's where Papa was when he hollered down to me that he found something."

"Nothing yet, but I'll check the other side. He may have moved it." Streaks of waning light shone through the loft door and cast Dirk's shadow in front of us.

"I don't think there's anything up there. We should probably leave. Sister Erma will soon need my help in the kitchen."

"Not yet, Mama. Let Brother Dirk look. I don't think Papa was lying about the box."

"We can wait a little longer, but then I need to go back to the Küche." Even though I didn't want Dirk to find the money, I couldn't deny the boy's pleading request. He wanted to believe at least one thing his father had told him was true.

"I found a metal box shoved under a pile of hay!" Dirk's shout echoed in the cavernous barn.

"That's it. That's it! I'm sure that's the box Papa found. Open it up, Brother Dirk." Lukas rushed to the foot of the ladder, his voice ringing with excitement.

"Ja, there is money inside. I am going to bring it down."

I felt as though my heart had dropped into the pit of my stomach. I clasped my arms around my waist, unable to believe Fred had actually found my father's money—and unable to believe that, even in death, Fred could again disrupt my life.

Dirk's shoes clapped on the wooden ladder as he carefully descended while holding the metal box beneath his arm. After he had stepped off the last rung, he extended the box to me. I shook my head, not wanting to touch it—wanting it to disappear so that I would not have to make hard choices. "Lukas can carry it."

The boy eagerly reached for the box and held it under his arm. "One time, Papa told me money makes you rich. Are we rich, Mama?"

I locked gazes with Dirk. "We were already rich, Lukas. Money is not what makes a person rich."

"It isn't?" His voice was filled with wonder, and I smiled at the curiosity in his eyes. "But it's lots of money and we can go and live anywhere. That's what Papa said."

"It probably is lots of money, and having money means you can buy many things, travel different places, and live wherever you want. But having money and being rich are two different things. Being rich means we have peace and love and friends who help when we're in need. We were rich before we found the money because we had already received friendship, love, and security right here in the colonies. Your pa didn't understand God's truth about money and being rich."

"But Papa said—"

"He was wrong. We don't need to talk about this anymore, Lukas." I gestured for him to move along, and soon he was several steps ahead and out of earshot.

"Why are you angry? I think you have confused Lukas. He expected you to be pleased. When you returned to Iowa and learned your Vater's farm had been sold, the boy became aware you needed money. Now you tell him money is not important. He does not understand why that has changed."

"I didn't say money wasn't important. I said it didn't make us rich. There is a difference."

"Ja, I agree there is a difference, but that difference is not what makes you angry, is it?"

I shook my head. He was right—I would have been thrilled if we had found the money when we first arrived. But we hadn't. Our lives had changed. When Fred arrived, I knew I would eventually be forced to leave the colonies, but since his death, I had again readjusted my thinking. There was no decision needed. Lukas and I would remain here. The money changed everything. Instead of circumstances dictating my life, now I had choices.

The thought of making those choices warred within me. When I was a child, my father had made decisions for me; when I was an adult, Fred had made them. Circumstances in Baltimore had forced our return to Iowa, but I'd had no other choice. There'd been nowhere else to go. But now—now I had a choice.

With my father's money from the sale of the farm, I could purchase a house and send Lukas to a fine school. One day he might even decide to attend college and become a physician or pharmacist. I might meet a man and . . . and what? Fall in love? I was already in love. I gave Dirk a sidelong glance.

He'd stated his love to me before rushing into the barn, but his life had been in danger back then. Since that time, we'd been together a great deal, and though I believed he cared for me, he hadn't again professed his love. Perhaps because he thought it improper to speak of love or marriage when I'd been a widow for less than a year. Yet how could that be? He'd been affectionate before Fred's return and I'd been a widow for only a short time—at least I'd thought I was a widow back then. Had he experienced a change of heart since Fred's death? I wasn't sure, and it would be improper to ask. Besides, I didn't have the courage. I might receive an answer that would break my heart.

He continued to stare at me as we walked toward the Küche,

still waiting to hear why I was angry. But how could I say all these things to him?

"The money complicates things for me."

"Ach! Now I understand. Having the money gives you the ability to leave the colonies and make a new life. Without the money, you did not have to make a decision about your future. The decision was made for you because of circumstances. Am I right?"

"Yes, you're right." He knew me so well. My brief answer had said it all. He understood my dilemma.

"But this is not a reason to be angry with Lukas. You are angry because you are faced with a difficult decision." A stiff breeze tugged at his coat, and he pulled the collar high around his neck. "If you would like to talk about the future, I would be pleased to come over to the Küche after prayer meeting and we can visit."

His offer soothed my anger and I nodded. "I would like that very much."

He shoved his hands into his jacket pockets as we stopped outside the kitchen house. "Then we will talk." He hesitated a moment. "But remember, Andrea, the answer you seek should come from God. We will visit this evening, but you should pray and seek God's guidance. I will do the same."

Dirk's final comment that he would also seek God's guidance caused me to wonder even more if he'd set aside any ideas of a future with me. Had he received some sort of revelation from God, or had the elders advised him against marriage to me? Could he alter his feelings so quickly?

Myriad ideas hopscotched through my mind during meal preparations, and as we cleaned the kitchen, I continued to wander about, lost in my own thoughts. Sister Erma expressed frustration when she was required to repeat her questions several times. Even though I apologized, I immediately returned to my private thoughts of Dirk and wondering if we would have a future as a family.

During the evening prayer meeting, my supplications weren't for others in need. Instead, I begged God to reveal what He would have me do about my future and to give me a sign whether He wanted me to remain in the colonies or leave. Heaviness settled on my heart when I thought of leaving, but I needed something more tangible—especially if Dirk had changed his mind about me. Was he the only reason I wanted to remain in the village, or was it truly because this was the place where I wanted to make a new life with my son? And would Dirk ever consider leaving the colonies?

I had my doubts about that, but I asked God to give both of us clear answers about the future and whether we were meant to be together or apart. Adding those last two words had been difficult, but if I was going to ask God to reveal His will to me, I had to be prepared to accept His answer.

After meeting, Dirk and I returned to the Küche. Once Sister Erma and Lukas had gone upstairs, we settled in the kitchen. He leaned across the worktable, and my heart fluttered with more vigor than the bubbling kettle of water atop the stove.

His lips curved in a gentle smile. "I have been praying a great deal since we parted earlier today. I want you to know that my feelings for you have never changed—even when Fred arrived, my love for you remained steadfast. But because I believed there would never be an opportunity for us to be husband and wife, I did try to extinguish all feelings for you."

I swallowed hard. "And were you successful?"

"Nein. I think you know I was not. I considered asking the elders to send me to another village because seeing you was too difficult."

"Did they turn down your request, or did you change your mind about asking them?"

"I never asked. Not being able to see Lukas was the deciding reason. Even though he had been spending more time with Fred, I wanted to be here to support him. He is a fine boy, but I recognized his need for the encouragement of a man."

I poured coffee into two cups and handed one to Dirk. He stared into the brown liquid for a moment. "My father died when I was very young. As a boy, I felt the same longing for approval that I recognized in Lukas."

His words warmed my heart, but he'd still spoken only about our past—not our future. I lifted my cup and took a sip of coffee. "And what about our future, Dirk?"

He placed his spoon on the saucer and looked into my eyes. "Our future will depend upon what you decide—where God leads you. As long as you remain in the village, it is my hope that I may continue to see you and Lukas. But until you have made a final decision, our future remains unsettled."

"You told me before that you wouldn't leave the colonies. Do you still feel the same?"

Dirk rubbed his jaw. "I feared you would ask me that question again. I would never let you support me with your money. And though my skills would permit me to earn a living, I believe my skill as a tinsmith belongs to the colonies. It is here that I received my training, and it is here that I should use those abilities." He leaned forward and grasped my hand. "This is the place where my faith was born, and as much as I love you, I cannot leave."

I nodded. "You've given me the answer I expected."

"Please do not make your decision because of anything I have said, Andrea. This decision must be between you and God."

I looked down at the metal box in my hands. After all we'd gone through, did this box hold God's answer?

CHAPTER 29

"Sister Erma has agreed to bake the wedding cake." Greta clapped her hands together like a schoolgirl.

"Ja, I have agreed, but that does not mean the two of you should be standing here talking instead of peeling the potatoes. We have little time to prepare dinner and many months before your marriage to Benjamin, Sister Greta. It is a long time until next November."

"October! Don't make it longer than a year, Sister Erma." Greta chuckled and picked up a paring knife. "Ja, but gut planning means a wonderful reception, and I want the very best food at my celebration." Reaching for a potato, she nudged my side. "Everyone wants to attend the wedding receptions at Sister Erma's Küche. They know she serves the very best food."

In spite of again urging us to hurry with the noonday preparations, Sister Erma grinned at the compliment. "Years of practice make for gut food, and you should continue practicing right now,

Sister Greta. One day you may have a Küche of your own to supervise, and you will want people to speak well of the food you serve."

At the moment, the only thing that Greta wanted to talk about was the recent approval of her marriage. Her father had finally given his blessing to the couple, and the elders had granted permission, as well. Even better, the elders decided that the year of separation had already begun when Benjamin and his family moved to Main Amana.

I was delighted for Greta and Benjamin but longed to have that same clarity in my life. If only God would reveal what I should do. I was scheduled to meet with the elders tomorrow. While they knew the money had been found, I had not discussed any form of payment for the many services they had provided for Fred. The society deserved to be paid now that I had my father's money. Strange how it seemed things had started to come full circle. Money the society had paid for my father's land might one day be returned to them. Of course, that would depend upon my final decision regarding the future.

Though I continued to pray and seek a sign from God, nothing had been forthcoming. At least nothing that I'd seen or heard. If the money would simply disappear, I'd know it was a sign from God. For now, it remained at the bottom of the trunk in my bedroom. What I wanted wasn't so much—God had performed much greater miracles. He had raised Lazarus from the dead and made a path through the Red Sea. Causing money to vanish wouldn't be difficult for God.

I'd said as much to Sister Erma, but she had *tsk*ed and shaken her head. "You should not think of God in such a way. He is not a performer who does our bidding, but a heavenly Father who knows what is best and provides what we should have at the right time. His ways are not always ours to understand."

I knew Sister Erma was right. I couldn't put time constraints on God, nor could I dictate how or what He would reveal about my future. But I wanted to be sure my decision aligned with His, and I wasn't certain how I was supposed to know.

Dirk's kindness and patience exceeded my expectations, and with each passing day, my love for him grew stronger. Yet I withheld a small piece of my heart, fearful I couldn't endure the pain if the Lord should direct me to leave the colonies. Since Fred's death, Lukas and I had continued our daily routines, and I wondered how he would react if I suggested a move.

He'd made no further mention of the money or of being rich, nor had he talked about buying a house somewhere else. In fact, he'd not even spoken of Fred, other than asking if I thought his father had gone to heaven. I wanted to avoid responding, but he insisted upon some sort of answer, so I told him the truth. I said I didn't know for sure. "No one can speak with certainty about whether another person will go to heaven. We may think we know, but that's a matter between God and each of us. If a person believes what the Bible teaches and has accepted Jesus as Savior, then he will go to heaven, but I don't know if your father ever invited Jesus into his heart."

The boy had slowly nodded and then walked away. My answer may not have pleased him, but he seemed to understand that I'd given him the only answer I could.

Lukas continued to help Dirk after school and made friends with boys from school. As our time in the colonies passed, his command of German grew and so did his friendships. For that I was grateful. His life here more closely resembled the childhood I had planned for him—a time of freedom and joy where he could play with friends and eventually grow into an upstanding man. Though I had never envisioned him living in the Amana

Colonies, his life here in Iowa held much more promise than it ever had in Baltimore.

But was it enough? Was I doing my son a disservice if we remained here? Life in the outside world would provide more material possessions and possibly more pleasure. But possessions and pleasure didn't necessarily mean happiness. And Fred's life and death were evidence of pain and tragedy, all wrought by the love of money.

While we continued to prepare the noon meal, my thoughts skittered about, thinking first of what I wanted—marriage and a life with Dirk—and then of what God might want. I tried to think of something I could do in the outside world that might provide a benefit to others and serve the Lord in a better way than I could by living here in the colonies. But I could think of nothing.

I carried one of the bowls of sliced raw potatoes to a large cast-iron skillet sitting atop the stove. Bacon grease sizzled and popped in readiness for the potatoes, but before I could empty the bowl into the pan, a loud blast sounded in the distance, and the kitchen floor quaked beneath my feet.

I quickly turned to Sister Erma. "What was that? It feels as though the ground is trembling. Is it an earthquake?" I'd heard tell of such catastrophic events but never believed I would experience one myself.

The village bell began pealing the dreaded toll that signified a disaster, the alarm that alerted all men from the fields and other designated workplaces—a sound that none of the villagers ever wanted to hear.

Both Greta and I followed Sister Erma as she hurried to the back porch. "Was not an earthquake. There was an explosion— did you not hear it?"

Greta and I nodded in unison. Sister Erma stepped from the

porch, cupped her hand to her forehead, and slowly surveyed the surrounding area. "Over there!" She pointed in the distance. "The flour mill has exploded! That is the noise we heard."

Greta gasped and touched her fingers to her lips. "If Benjamin hadn't been sent to live in Main, he would be there right now."

Sister Erma continued a few steps farther into the yard. "The first bell had already rung. The men should have been out of there."

She was right. Since it took time for the men to come from the fields and surrounding workplaces, an early bell sounded before the actual time for meals to begin, and that first bell had already sounded. If the workers had immediately left the flour mill, their injuries might not be extensive. On the other hand, if they hadn't gotten far enough away, the blast and tremors seemed severe enough to cause injuries. No doubt the flour mill had been destroyed.

We stood helpless as the bell continued to clang and men and horse-drawn wagons raced toward the west edge of town. I had been to the mill only once. Together with a group of others, we'd taken a picnic lunch and gathered near the small creek that meandered nearby. Dirk and the others called it the mill ditch, but I thought "mill creek" a more charming name for the shallow waterway.

Dirk had laughed at my aversion to the name. "When the mill was constructed, it was hoped the creek would supply power, but there was never enough water," he'd explained. "Soon, the creek became known as the mill ditch, and a steam boiler was procured and used to power the mill instead."

The huge wooden mill sat atop a thick limestone foundation and boasted a tall brick chimney. The building dwarfed the shallow creek that meandered below. Little wonder it hadn't been able to provide sufficient power to operate the machinery.

Dirk had motioned toward the rocky creek bed and flowering

shrubs near the water's edge. "Even though it runs dry much of the year, it is still a nice spot for a picnic. If you dislike that we speak of it as a ditch, then you can call it a creek or whatever name suits you. We will still know you mean the mill ditch." His comment had made me laugh.

A sense of foreboding hovered as I wondered how many men might be injured and what the loss would mean to the village. Farmers from surrounding areas brought their grain to be milled and paid with a portion of their flour—flour that supplemented what we used in the bakeries and in our kitchen houses.

Sister Erma motioned us back to the kitchen. "We need to prepare food to take to the men. For sure, they are already hungry, but they need to remain at the mill to help." Instead of frying the potatoes, we filled metal containers with loaves of rye bread, brick and hand cheese, cottage cheese, barley soup, applesauce, and bread pudding that we had already prepared for the noonday meal. While Greta and I were completing the task, Sister Erma went out to flag down one of the wagons.

When she returned to the kitchen a short time later, her cheeks were rosy from the chill. "The wagon is waiting out there. You and Greta go and help serve. I'll stay behind. If more food is needed, send word back with one of the young boys and I'll prepare more."

The driver loaded the food into the freight wagon and then helped Greta and me on board. After only a short distance, he gestured toward the rolling terrain. "Hold on. I am going to go off the road. It is shorter this way."

The wagon lurched about like a ship on stormy seas, and I wondered if there would be any soup left in the large metal pot by the time we arrived. When we topped a small hillock, the remnants of the mill came into view. I gasped at the painful sight. Only the limestone foundation remained.

The driver pulled back on the reins and called to the horses. After setting the brake, he jumped down and helped Greta and me to the ground, then removed the heavy wooden staves and dropped the sides of the wagon. "Better to stay a little distance from where they are working. There are many boards and much wreckage. You could get hurt. As they get tired, the men will take turns coming for food. When the supply runs low, send that boy there for more." He pointed to a young boy sitting nearby, transfixed by the nearby disaster. "His name is Luther. He is my son. He knows where Sister Erma's Küche is located."

Greta and I set to work arranging the food in the wagon, and soon several men trudged toward us. When I saw Dirk among them, I stepped to the side of the wagon and greeted him. His clothing and hands were covered in dirt, and I didn't miss the pain in his eyes. "How bad is it? Are there many who have been injured?"

He shook his head and wiped his face with a handkerchief. "Never have we had such a thing happen in our village. To lose the mill is tragic, but we can be thankful there was only one death, an outsider. Dr. Karr says the injured will all recover."

"What happened? Does anyone know?"

"The boiler exploded. It crashed through the roof and fell seventy-five yards from its fastenings. If most of the men had not already left for the noonday meal, they would have been scalded by the escaping steam and boiling water during the explosion." He leaned against the wagon and inhaled a deep breath before he continued. "The remainder of the roof caved in, and there is nothing left but the foundation. Wood and bricks are scattered all over. A few men were hit by flying debris as they headed back toward the kitchen houses."

"Do they know what caused the explosion?"

Dirk hiked one shoulder. "So far we have been told that the mill manager was off sick today, and one of the outsiders who claimed to have experience was running the engine. It seems the man must have lied about his abilities, because he allowed the water to become depleted in the boiler. After the rest of the men left for the noonday meal, he turned a supply of fresh water into the red-hot boiler, which caused the explosion."

One by one, exhausted men came to the wagon for food and water, all of them uttering their disbelief. I continued to offer food, coffee, and water as I listened to them discuss the effect this loss would have upon the village. The cost to rebuild the mill and replace the machinery would be enormous.

We'd been at the site for several hours when Brother Bosch approached the wagon. "There is no need to remain any longer. The men will stay and continue with their work throughout the afternoon but will come to the kitchen houses for their evening meal. I am sure Sister Erma will need your help. I will drive you back to the Küche." There was a sound of defeat in his voice that I'd never before heard.

"I can see you are tired, Brother Bosch. Perhaps you should rest at the Küche for a while before you return."

His lips tilted in a weary smile. "Nein. I will go back. I want to be sure there are no signs of smoldering fire in the wreckage."

"You look far too weary. If you must return, couldn't you rest first? I am sure Sister Erma would not mind if you went upstairs to the parlor."

"We will see; we will see," he softly replied as he flicked the reins.

Once we arrived at the Küche, the aged elder climbed down from the wagon and helped us carry the leftovers and dirty containers into the kitchen. Sister Erma greeted him with a warm smile. "Ach! You are exhausted, Brother. Sit down and let me pour you some hot coffee. It is gut and strong and will help to keep you awake." Without waiting for an answer, she filled a cup and pushed it in front of him. "I am eager to hear a report of the damage."

"There is a little gut news and much bad news." Brother Bosch related the death and injuries and then moved on to describe the total destruction of the mill.

"You said there was gut news and bad news. I am waiting for the gut news."

He arched his thick brows. "I have already told you there was only one death and few injuries."

She gazed heavenward. "Ach! That is the gut news?"

"It is gut news when you consider how many men work in that mill and could have been killed or suffered terrible burns." He bent his head and stared into the coffee. "I do not know how we will manage to replace the mill. There is not enough money to begin such a big project right now. And who can say how soon we will have the necessary funds." He lifted his cup and took a swallow of the steaming brew. "We must pray and believe that God will provide."

Sister Erma nodded. "He has always provided for us, and He will take care of this need in His own time and in His own way."

As I stood in the doorway to the dining room and listened to their conversation, I was overcome by a powerful feeling deep inside. I had enough money to rebuild the mill. Here was the sign I had been praying for ever since Fred's death. There was a need for the contents of that metal box, a need much greater than an elegant house or fancy clothes for Lukas and me. These were the people who had helped my son and me when we had been without food or shelter, and they now deserved my help. This village had been a shining light during my time of darkness. To help them would give me great joy. God had provided my answer—He had given me a sign. A sign I would not ignore.

When Brother Bosch prepared to depart, I drew close to his side. "I know there is much for the elders to decide in the coming days, but you will recall I am supposed to meet with them tomorrow. Do you think they will still meet with me?"

"We will need to meet and discuss what has happened today and what plans should be made about the future of the mill. We will speak with you before we begin that difficult conversation."

I prayed in earnest before and during prayer meeting and knew I was not mistaken about my decision. Though weary from digging through rubble for most of the afternoon, Dirk agreed to come to the Küche after prayer meeting. "I promise I won't keep you very long, but there is something important I want to tell you."

We sat opposite each other at one of the worktables in the kitchen. "Ja, what is that?"

"I have received my answer. I am going to remain in the colonies."

"Tell me what God has revealed to you."

My stomach clenched. His response was more solemn than I'd anticipated.

Being careful to leave nothing out, I explained how I had come to know I had received an answer to my many prayers. A glimmer of excitement flashed in his clear blue eyes, and his familiar smile slowly spread across his face. "You're absolutely certain you want to stay?"

I giggled. "Without any doubt, I know this is where I want to be." I stood to refill his cup with coffee.

"And you want to marry me?" The spark in his eyes ignited with a passion that made my knees go weak.

My mouth suddenly went as dry as a wad of cotton batting. I bobbed my head and swallowed hard. "Very much."

He stood, came around the worktable, and gathered me into his arms. "I am the happiest man alive." He lowered his head and gently kissed my lips.

"Ach! What is this we have going on in my kitchen, Brother Dirk?" We both turned to see Sister Erma pointing her finger in our direction. "This is not gut. You two should know better than this."

"You will not gain any apology from me, Sister Erma. I love Andrea and it is my plan to ask the elders for her hand in marriage. I do not think a little kiss is such a bad thing when a man is prepared to ask for a woman's hand, do you?"

She tilted her head and grinned. "As long as the man does not wait too long. When is it you will speak to the elders?"

Dirk laughed. "You are as pushy as an eager Vater, but since you have asked, I will tell you. Tomorrow I will go with Sister Andrea to the elders' meeting."

Sister Erma dropped her hand to her side and smiled. "Then I agree that a kiss between you is not such a bad thing. In fact, it is a gut thing. A very gut thing."

CHAPTER 30

The following morning, Dirk patiently waited while I walked upstairs with Lukas.

"Make sure you wear your heavy coat to school. It is cold today."

"I wish I could go with you so I would know right away what the elders say." His eyes shone with excitement. "Did you put the cookie cutter in your pocket?"

"Not yet, but I am going to get it right now." Last night he'd asked me to take it along so that I would be thinking of him during the meeting. After I'd listened to his nighttime prayers, he confided that he would be very sad if we had to leave the colonies. I reassured him that I would tell the elders of his desire to live in West Amana.

I donned my coat, placed the angel cookie cutter in my pocket, and retrieved the metal box from inside my small trunk. This morning I hoped the elders would agree that we could remain here.

Membership in the society required a forfeiture of all worldly goods, other than personal belongings and family keepsakes. Though some found such an idea hard to accept, I thought it freeing. For me, the concept of communal property was a reminder of the early church, when believers cared for one another as they shared not only their belief in Christ but also their worldly belongings.

To be able to help those who had assisted Lukas and me would bring immeasurable joy. My only worry was whether the elders would agree that I should permanently join them. I knew they would not be swayed by money. Their questions would deal with my faith and my reasons for making such an appeal.

After bidding Sister Greta and Sister Erma good-bye, I handed the metal box to Dirk. He secured it under his arm, and I hurried ahead toward the meetinghouse. I didn't want to be late.

Taking long strides, Dirk came to my side. "We do not need to run. We will be there on time if we walk." He grinned down at me.

Though his calm words were soothing, I continued my rapid pace. Only when he stopped did I slow and glance over my shoulder. "What are you doing? Come on."

Slowly he stepped toward me and gently grasped my elbow. "Why are you so worried? The elders are kind men who are going to ask you some simple questions. There is nothing to fear."

He continued his leisurely pace. I'd have to slow my stride or leave him behind. "That is easy for you to say, but you can't be sure. You've never had to ask to become a member." I arched my brows. "Have you?"

"Nein, but during my first *Unterredung*, I was so nervous I could not speak when I stood before the elders. Of course, I was a young boy with much to confess."

"What is Unterredung?" I'd never heard anyone mention the word before.

"It is an annual service of confession and spiritual examination in which we stand before the elders and church members and admit our wrongdoings during the past year."

I gulped. "Out loud? In front of everyone?" The thought left me weak-kneed.

"After the first time it is not so bad, but as a child it was a fearsome thing for me. Besides, you will have little to confess. You are a gut woman."

Dirk's disclosure of his fear during the Unterredung was meant to ease my fear. Instead, it increased my worries. Neither Sister Erma nor Sister Greta had ever mentioned such an event, nor had I attended any meeting where I'd observed such an occurrence. I gave Dirk a sideways glance, hoping to discover he had been joking with me, but his serious countenance remained.

"When will this happen—the Unterredung?"

He stopped short. "I have caused you more worry. I am sorry. I hoped to lighten your concern with a story from my childhood. Have I ever lied to you?" I shook my head and he smiled. "Then please believe me when I tell you there is nothing to fear today or during an Unterredung. Always, I will be by your side to help you."

"Danke, Dirk." I tried to slow my breathing as we neared the meetinghouse.

He shifted the metal box and held it out to me. "You should present this to the elders after you have finished speaking to them."

Taking the box from his hands, I smiled. "We shall see if they will be pleased to welcome me."

"Ach! You need to stop all this gloomy thinking." He touched his fingers to my lips and gently pushed them into a smile. "Walk into the meeting room with a smile and joy in your heart. The elders are going to enjoy their visit with you."

I glanced toward the women's door. "Where will you be?"

"I'll wait in the foyer just inside the men's door. Once they have given you their decision, tell the elders that I am waiting and we wish to speak to them together. One of the elders will likely be waiting to lead you into the meeting."

After a quick nod, I headed toward the door but stopped and turned after only a few steps. "But what if—"

He placed his finger against his lips and shook his head. "No gloomy thoughts. Remember?"

My heart thumped a loud and rapid beat, and fear pinched a tight band around my chest as I climbed the steps and entered the women's door. Dirk was right. Brother Bosch was waiting for me. Upon seeing his smile and twinkling eyes, my heart quieted and the invisible strap loosened its hold.

"Come, Sister Andrea. The elders are waiting to hear what you have to say." He led me into the room. "You may be seated in the chair across from us."

While he walked around the table and sat down, I placed the metal box on the floor and took my chair before the group. Though they didn't appear completely formidable, their countenances didn't offer the reassurance I had hoped for. I was thankful for the presence of Brother Bosch—and the fact that he would lead the meeting.

He nodded at me. "You may begin, Sister."

The six elders carefully listened as I cleared my throat and expressed my desire to make a permanent home for Lukas and me in West Amana.

When I hesitated, Brother Bosch smiled at me. "There is no need to go into your background or how you came to be living among us. We all have knowledge of those circumstances, but we will need to ask you some questions regarding your faith."

The questions weren't difficult or unexpected. I was asked to affirm my belief in Jesus as my Savior and my willingness to abide by God's precepts and the rules of the society. After giving the elders a positive response to their questions, I folded my hands in front of me. "It is my hope that you will permit us to remain here and become members of the Amana Society."

I held my breath and waited. Would they give me an immediate decision, or would I be required to wait hours, days, or weeks for them to decide? Dirk believed they would make an immediate decision, but Sister Erma said when matters were not clear to them, the elders would wait upon God for an answer. Having waited a very long time for my own answer from God, I prayed this decision would be immediately clear to the men sitting in front of me.

The men leaned close together, their murmurs muffled and indistinguishable. A short time later, the elders returned to their upright positions. Brother Bosch was the only one who looked at me. I thought my heart might explode as I waited for him to speak. "We want to explain that when a suitable candidate requests membership in the society, there is usually a period of probation where the candidate is asked to sign an obligation to labor faithfully, abide by the regulations of the community, and demand no wages." One of the men drummed his fingertips on the table, but after a stern look from Brother Bosch, the drumming ceased. "This probationary period is at the discretion of the Bruderrat, and since we believe you have already revealed you are willing to meet these obligations and have stated your accord with the religious doctrines of the society, we will waive the probationary period."

I was so relieved, I wanted to shout. Instead, I quietly thanked the men and added, "I will do my best to honor your decision."

Brother Bosch inhaled a deep breath. "I am sure you will, Sister Andrea. We will want you to sign a Covenant, and after Brother Frederick reads the Constitution, you will be asked to sign it, as well. Once you have done so, you will be admitted to full membership with all the rights and privileges given to all of our members."

Signing the Covenant took only a moment, but reading the Constitution proved a lengthy affair. I did my best to carefully listen to each of the Constitutional articles, though I noticed two of the elders closing their eyes. After Brother Frederick completed the reading, Brother Bosch looked up.

"If you agree with our Constitution and still wish to become a member, you should sign here." Brother Bosch pointed to an empty space. I stepped forward and, using my best penmanship, signed my name.

"We are in agreement that you are now one of us, Sister Andrea." He leaned forward and glanced at the other elders.

In one unified moment, they offered their assent. I gasped and clutched my hand around the angel tucked in my pocket. We'd been accepted! We had a home where we would forever be safe and secure.

"Danke, Brothers. I am humbled by your acceptance of me." I leaned down and picked up the box. "When I first came here, I had nothing to offer in payment for all your kindness and the medical treatment given to my now-deceased husband, but this box was recently recovered from my father's barn. Inside is the money the society paid him for his property. It is my hope that there is enough to rebuild the mill as well as to purchase a new boiler and the other equipment needed so that West will once again have a fine flour mill." I stood and placed the metal box on the table in front of them.

From the pleasure that spread across their faces, I knew they were quite pleased. "We gratefully accept the gift of your possessions, Sister Andrea. There is great need among us, and God has answered."

I waited a moment and glanced toward the men's door. "Brother Dirk has asked if he may join us. There is something he wishes to ask that affects both of us."

"Ja, of course we will speak with him." Brother Bosch sent one of the elders to fetch Dirk. When they returned, Dirk stepped to my side.

"I have come before you to ask permission to marry Sister Andrea. I understand that it has not been long since her husband's death, but because of the special circumstances and since a year of waiting is required before marriage, it is my hope that you will agree to our marriage."

Once again, the men gathered together and spoke in hushed voices. I glanced away from the elders and looked at Dirk, who graced me with a smile that warmed my heart. Though I remained uncertain whether the elders would agree to the arrangement he had proposed, he appeared confident.

His lips formed the word *smile*, and I immediately did his bidding. He was right: Smiling seemed to make things better, especially waiting. Moments later, the elders sat back in their chairs and Brother Bosch gave a firm nod. "We have agreed that you may begin your waiting period immediately, Brother Dirk. Permission is granted for you and Sister Andrea to marry after one year has passed."

Dirk took a step forward. "And the separation? Is it your wish that I move to another village?"

"In most cases, you know we would do so. However, you are needed here in West. We discussed sending Sister Andrea and her son to another village, but since the boy has already been required to deal with many difficulties in his young life, we think such a move would not be wise. It is agreed that Sister Andrea and her son will remain with Sister Erma, and you will remain at your shop. The boy may continue to work with you. We believe it will help him and strengthen your bond before you marry his mother."

My heart soared as I listened to the decision. I wanted to leap across the table and hug Brother Bosch, but I remained as still as a statue while I rubbed my thumb against the angel in my coat pocket. Lukas and I would soon have a permanent home, and my son would have a father who truly loved him.

CHAPTER 31

November 1891

In some ways it seemed as though I had waited all of my life for this year to pass, yet in other ways, it seemed only yesterday that Dirk and I stood in front of the elders and received permission to wed. Now that our wedding day had arrived, it was difficult to think Lukas and I would leave the Küche and make our home with Dirk in the rooms above the tinsmith shop.

As I glanced around the bedroom, a twinge of pain pricked my heart. I would miss living here. Of course, I would continue my work downstairs in the Küche, but it would be different. And I'd seen the sadness begin to set in with Sister Erma, as well. She'd become accustomed to having us around in the evenings. Now she would have to adjust to being alone again. Of late, I'd been praying there would be someone who would fill the void our departure would create.

For now I pushed aside any sad thoughts. This was a day to celebrate and enjoy.

"Let me see your dress." Sister Erma stood in the doorway of the bedroom and gave a firm nod. "Ja, it looks gut." When she circled her finger in the air, I obediently turned around. "Stop there." She stepped forward and tucked the corner of my shawl into my waistband. "I brought you this lace cap to wear. It is the one I wore for my wedding."

I stared at the beautiful black lace with slender silk ribbons. "I couldn't—"

"Of course you can." She lifted it and placed it atop my head. "It is perfect for you, just as it was perfect for me."

"Danke, Sister Erma. You are most kind." I traced my fingers along the silk ties. Wearing black to be married still seemed strange to me, but I had learned to accept sitting separately at meals and church meetings. And though it had taken a while, I had learned to accept this custom, as well.

"When you return from the meetinghouse, all will be ready." My reception would be different from Sister Greta's. After her wedding, the wedding guests had returned to the kitchen house for coffee, cocoa, and coffee cake. Later, they had gone to Greta's home for her reception. Although the food had been prepared in the Küche, it was customary to hold the reception at the home of the bride. I was pleased that my entire reception would be held in the Küche, where there was more room and the food would not have to be transported to another house.

I nodded, thankful she'd been so willing to assist me. Helping prepare for Sister Greta's wedding had proven good practice, as well. "I know my reception will be as grand as Greta's."

"For sure, I think your reception will be even better. Every bride should believe her reception is the finest." She winked at me. "You should hurry, or Brother Dirk will think you have changed your mind. He and Lukas are waiting downstairs. Lukas is eager to get back and have a piece of the special wedding cake."

The cake, three layers deep and each one a different flavor, had been baked in the special star-shaped cake pans made by Dirk and used only for weddings.

Dirk and Lukas stood at the bottom of the stairs, both of them in their best dark suits, and both of them wearing smiles as bright as a summer day. Dirk extended his hand. "I was beginning to think you would never come down those steps, but I would have waited forever for this moment."

The sweetness of his words washed over me, and I grasped his hand. "When Fred returned, I did not believe you and I would ever be together. Thank you for waiting for me even then."

Lukas wrinkled his nose. "I'm going to wait in the kitchen. Maybe Sister Greta will give me a cookie."

Dirk chuckled, but when I started to follow Lukas, Dirk gently pulled me close. "I wish I could wipe away all those years you and Lukas suffered, but I know I cannot. What I can do is promise you this, Andrea. You never need to live in fear again. We will fill our home with joy, and soon those bad memories will fade for both you and Lukas. From seeing you and me, our son will learn what true love is."

A tear trickled down my cheek, and Dirk thumbed it away with such tenderness my heart threatened to break. Then he covered my lips with his own and sealed his vow to me with a breathtaking kiss full of hope and promise.

NOTE TO READERS . . .

While there were occasional fires and explosions at the various mills in the Amana Colonies, the flour mill in West Amana did not explode as depicted in this story. However, it was demolished around 1938. When you visit the colonies now, you'll no longer see the old flour mill in West Amana.

-Judy

SPECIAL THANKS TO . . .

Special thanks to William (Bill) Metz of Middle Amana, for his valuable assistance. Not only did he answer my many questions about tinsmiths, he gave me a guided tour of his basement workshop, where he maintains many of the original tinsmithy machines, patterns, and tools. He also demonstrated how he continues to use those tools to create many items from the old Amana patterns.

Special thanks also to Michele Maring Miller and David Miller of West Amana, for providing pictures of the old West Amana flour mill as well as answering questions, giving directions, and taking me on a tour of Michele's art studio.

Judith Miller is an award-winning author whose avid research and love for history are reflected in her bestselling novels. Judy makes her home in Topeka, Kansas.

More Stories in the
HOME TO AMANA Series

To learn more about Judith and her books, visit
judithmccoymiller.com.

In the quiet communities of the Amana Colonies,
Karlina Richter and Dovie Cates are searching for
answers. When they finally uncover the truth, can their
hearts survive its discovery?

A Hidden Truth

When unforeseen circumstances drive Jancey Rhoder
to follow her parents to the Amana Colonies, she'll
be forced to reconsider everything she wanted out of
life—and love.

A Simple Change

If you enjoyed *A Shining Light*, you may also like...

As the Mennonite town of Kingdom, Kansas, is plagued by strange incidents and attacks, three young women have their faith in God and their community tested to the limits. Will they all survive the dangerous road ahead?

ROAD TO KINGDOM by Nancy Mehl
Inescapable, Unbreakable, Unforeseeable
nancymehl.com

When their attempts to control their own destinies backfire, can Cate, Addie, and Molly learn to trust God with their lives—and with their future husbands?

THE COURTSHIPS OF LANCASTER COUNTY by Leslie Gould
Courting Cate, Adoring Addie, Minding Molly
lesliegould.com